LEGACY
SHATTERPOINT

LEGACY
SHATTERPOINT

BOLGER BOOKS

Cover Design: Vila Design
Developmental Editing: Jonathan Oliver
Copy Editing and Proofreading: Enchanted Ink Publishing
Book Design and Typesetting: Enchanted Ink Publishing

The text type was set in Minion Pro

ISBN: 9781069477101 (E-book)
ISBN: 9781068870798 (Paperback)
ISBN: 9781069477118 (Audiobook)

WWW.BRADLEYELLIOTT.CA

For the Reynolds Family

LEGACY

SHATTERPOINT

BRADLEY ELLIOTT

BOOK 4 OF THE LEGACY SERIES

PROLOGUE

7 YEARS AGO, GCH YEAR 16,496

A flash of light appeared against the blackness of space as a ship exited hyperspace deep within the decimated ruins of the Yanara System, disappearing an instant later.

"Helm, Engineering, status reports," the ship's captain, Marcus Gerhardt, commanded.

"We're in the Yanara System, sir. One hundred thousand kilometers from the jump point marker, as expected," Ensign Reesor reported from the helm, a hint of excitement and nervousness in his voice.

Lieutenant Clarkson's hands worked the engineering controls as he responded, "Cloak and temporal shields are both up, sir. All systems are nominal."

The captain nodded. "Ops, scan the system."

"Scans coming in now, sir," the operations officer, Lieutenant Hamilton, replied. "The system is littered with debris, Captain, and the astrometric data is way out of date. We're lucky we didn't jump right into something!"

"What's the status of the black hole?" the captain asked, knowing the risks of jumping in so close to the deadly phenomena.

"The singularity is where it should be, at least, approximately eight hundred and twenty-three million kilometers away, but the rest of the system is all over the place. It looks like the free fall into the black hole has accelerated since the last survey mission scanned the system, and the gravity from the gas giants has thrown hundreds of other large objects around."

"Acknowledged. Bring up the scans on the holo-display."

The scans appeared a moment later, showing the Yanara System, the star shedding a trail of fire as it formed an accretion disk around the black hole, highlighting the edges of the ravenous gravitational monster. Debris littered the system, the fallout of massive collisions between several of the rocky inner planets and moons at high speeds. The data continued pouring in, the display filling out with increasing detail, showing signs of devastating impacts on many of the system's moons and other celestial bodies. All of their orbits now skewed as they corkscrewed and toppled towards the black hole, its gravity slowly, inevitably drawing them in.

"Temporal readings?" the captain asked.

"There are *massive* traces of chronometric radiation and heavy concentrations of tachyons coming from the moon around the fifth planet, sir," the temporal officer, Lieutenant Winters, replied.

The captain paused for a moment, considering. "Are there any active temporal signatures?"

"Negative, sir, looks like whatever happened here, it's over now. I'm not detecting any active readings."

"Tactical," the captain said, turning across the bridge.

Lieutenant Commander Klassen, the ship's XO, looked up, swiping her hand from her console towards the holo-display where the data projected for the crew to see. "I'm detecting numerous ships in orbit around that moon, sir, at least twenty, but it's hard to say for certain at this range with all the interference."

The captain rose, motioning to the tactical and temporal officers to join him as he moved towards the holo-display, small red icons appearing near the fifth planet, where the unknown ships held their position. "What do you think?" he asked, turning to Winters. Her eyes were fixated on the scans of the unknown ships and the fading temporal readings.

"Something *big* happened here, sir," she said, her voice grave. "This was a planned temporal event. There's no way this was an accident," she added, her eyes meeting the captain's and first officer's.

"What makes you so certain?" the captain asked.

Winters looked back at the holo-projection. "First, those ships appear to be in a defensive formation, based on the distance from the moon and their deployment. They're not there to help with some accident. They're *guarding* the planet, sir."

"I agree with the lieutenant," Klassen commented.

Winters nodded, meeting the first officer's eyes for a moment, hoping she hadn't overstepped, then continued. "Second, the residual energy readings and the tachyon wave patterns indicate that whatever temporal event happened here, it was *significant*."

"How significant?" the captain asked.

"My best guess is a massive breach, sir… Based on these readings, I'd estimate a hundred years, maybe more," Winters said.

"There's no telling how bad the damage could be from a temporal jump that far back," Klassen said.

The captain nodded thoughtfully, taking a breath as he paused for a moment, again considering. "Anything else, Lieutenant?"

"I think they chose this system for a reason, sir. The singularity's gravity bends space-time. I suspect they used this to help initiate the temporal event, hoping that it would hide it from our sensors or possibly even enhance it."

The captain stroked his chin. "What do you think?" he asked, turning to his XO.

"I think we need to get down there quickly to investigate," Klassen replied. "But first, we're going to need some backup."

"Agreed," the captain said, letting out another breath, feeling the tightness in his chest as the gravity of the situation took hold. "Time to call in the Fleet."

Thirty minutes later, a barrage of flashes appeared as twenty-eight GCH ships exited hyperspace at the jump point. The vessels quickly formed up, setting a course for the fifth planet. The commander of the small fleet stood on the bridge of the battlecruiser, *Exeter*, her hard eyes fixated on the holo-display before her and the enemy targets ahead.

"*Exeter* to *Switchback*, this is Admiral Janus. Do you copy?"

The image of Captain Gerhardt appeared on the screen. "Yes, Admiral," he replied crisply.

"Status report."

"The enemy ships are holding in a defensive position around the moon of the fifth planet, ma'am. We scouted ahead and were able to scan them without being detected. We believe they're Ularan, Admiral."

"Ularan?" Admiral Janus said, her brow furrowing. "What the hell are they doing way out here?"

"That's a good question. Whatever it is, it's not good. Our scans indicate two battleships, six cruisers, and a mix of destroyers and frigates in support. We're sending our reconnaissance data over now."

"They're protecting something..." the admiral mused.

"That's our theory as well, ma'am. We can't be sure what they did – if they sent someone or something back or instead pulled something forward – but my temporal operations officer believes that they initiated a massive breach. The most significant ever recorded."

"So, they're not going to give up whatever it is they got without a fight."

"Yes, ma'am, we believe so."

"Very well, Captain, we'll give them a chance to surrender, and if they refuse, we'll engage. I want you and your ship to hang back. We'll clear a path, and when I give the signal, I want you to find the source of the temporal event and investigate."

"Understood. We're prepped and ready."

"Good work, Captain. I'll go see if they want to talk, but be prepared to move quickly. We have the edge in numbers on them now, but they may have reinforcements nearby, so you may need to pull out on short notice if things go sideways."

"Yes, ma'am."

"Good luck, Captain. *Exeter* out," the admiral said, closing the channel, then turning to her tactical officer and ordering the battle group to increase speed, moving forward in an offensive formation.

The battle raged on the other side of the moon as the *Switchback* moved silently under cloak around the far side of the planet, awaiting the admiral's signal.

Navigating through the system had been extremely treacherous. Debris from planetary collisions, along with innumerable micro-meteorites and asteroids, all caught between the gravity of the remaining worlds and that of the black hole, had forced them to change course and react several times to avoid collisions and detection. As they moved past the outer planets, the gravitational pull adjusted the trajectories of the asteroids and debris, causing them to veer off wildly before the grip of the black hole wrapped its invisible claws around them once more, pulling them back on a course towards oblivion.

Finally, after a tense journey, they were in position, monitoring the engagement while attempting to locate the source of the temporal readings on the moon below.

"Status?" the captain asked softly, standing next to the first officer's station, not wanting the rest of the crew to overhear while they focused on their work.

"It's bad, sir. The Fleet is winning so far, but we're taking heavy losses. The *Crimson Horizon* and the *Venture* are both gone. Three more ships have taken heavy damage and are falling back, but the rest are still in the fight," she replied, her voice heavy.

"The Ularans?"

"They're in much worse shape. Half their ships have been destroyed, and the rest are taking a pounding. They won't last much longer if they don't pull out or surrender. Either way, whatever it is they're protecting, they're willing to fight to the death for it!"

"Acknowledged," the captain said somberly. "We'll hold till—"

"Sir," Hamilton interjected, "Admiral Janus just sent an encoded transmission. She's ordering us to proceed to the surface now and report back as soon as we have something."

"Understood," he said, moving back to his chair and activating his harness. "Helm, take us in. All hands, battle stations!"

The *Switchback* began its descent seconds later. The crew bathed in the red lights of the bridge, uncertain what awaited them below, the ship shaking around them as it passed through the dense atmosphere.

"Sir, I have something," Winters called out, turning to face the captain.

"Let's have it, Lieutenant."

"I'm detecting a large structure near the equator. The tachyon wave patterns all emanate from there, and I'm detecting lethal traces of chronometric radiation."

"Helm, take us in for a wide approach. All stations, passive scans only. I don't want to alert them to our presence."

"Aye, sir," the crew responded.

Minutes passed as they made their way closer to the source of the temporal disturbance.

"We're approaching the structure, sir," Reesor reported from the helm, taking them around in a wide, slow pass.

"Looks like multiple buildings connected in sequence to a massive domed structure," Lieutenant Hamilton reported from Ops, bringing up a visual on the main screen.

The image appeared, the line of the buildings reminding the captain of a scepter, the structures forming the shaft, with the dome at the top.

"Captain, I'm detecting multiple weapons platforms along the sides and some more on top," Klassen added. "But strangely, no shield generators."

"Tactical analysis," he replied, staring at the sensor data that appeared in the holo-display before him.

"The complex is heavily defended, at least six fixed missile launchers and two heavy repulsor cannons."

"Can you take them out?"

"I think so. We might take a few hits, but if we come in low and fast under cloak, I think I can get them all before they lock on."

"Strange that they wouldn't have shields…" the captain mused, concerned there could be something else at play.

"It's likely the electromagnetic effects from the shield modulators," Winters interjected, the XO and the captain turning to face her as she continued. "Ularan shield tech uses a series of polarized quantum relays to power their modulators. These would disrupt the temporal scans needed to lock on to a target. Even if the generators weren't on, they could still affect a chronoton field's stability. They couldn't risk installing them anywhere near the complex, or the quantum reaction could have collapsed their temporal field."

"Nice work, Lieutenant," the captain said. "Very well. Helm, plot a course based on the XO's attack run."

"Attack course plotted, sir," Reesor replied.

"Execute!"

The *Switchback* accelerated rapidly, diving towards the planet's surface, then leveling out as it set a course straight for the ominous gray complex looming ahead. The ship de-cloaked as they closed the distance, pulling up to allow for optimal targeting.

Klassen fired seconds later. Half a dozen particle beams streaked out from the *Switchback* along with a barrage of missiles, targeting the repulsors, while the beams hit each of the facility's missile launchers, destroying them in quick succession.

The *Switchback* shook suddenly, plasma fire striking the underside just as it completed the attack run, two objects appearing on the holo-display seconds later behind it and closing fast.

"Report!" Captain Gerhardt called out.

"The base had several recessed plasma cannons that our scans didn't detect!" Klassen replied. "We're taking heavy fire, and two missiles launched before our strike could take out the final launcher!"

"Helm, evasive pattern delta. Engineering, reengage the cloaking system!"

The ship banked hard to port, twisting as it attempted to evade the enemy plasma fire. Reesor dropped them down close to the deck, pouring on speed. A second later, the cloak activated, the enemy fire ceasing shortly thereafter.

"The missiles are holding their last course; they've lost their lock!" Klassen reported, turning to the captain while Reesor maneuvered the ship in a wide arc out of their path.

"Damage report," the captain said.

"Minor damage to systems, but our ventral armor took a bit of a pounding, sir," Lieutenant Clarkson reported from the Engineering station.

"Tactical, can you get a lock on those plasma cannons?"

"Yes, sir, my AI's triangulated their locations. I think I can take them all out if we swing by for another pass. I recommend raising standard shields though. If we take too many hits before we take them out, we could be in trouble."

"Agreed. Helm, lay in another attack run and keep us low to avoid their fire till we're within ten klicks of the base," the captain said. "Ops, prepare to de-cloak when we hit the three-K mark, then run full active scans. Let's make sure there's no other surprises waiting for us."

"Aye, sir," both officers replied.

"Targets locked in," Klassen said, her voice hard. "Helm, take us right along the starboard side of the complex and invert the ship as we pass overhead. I'm going to make sure we take them all out in one pass."

"Yes, ma'am," Reesor replied, already working his hands feverishly at the controls.

"Take us in," the captain said, Reesor increasing their speed, the image of the enemy complex appearing in the distance once more on the main viewscreen, growing larger by the second.

Reesor banked the ship, inverting it as they passed overhead, their cloak dropping and shields activating as Klassen fired at the hidden plasma cannons, raining down a barrage from above as she let loose with the *Switchback*'s formidable weapons array.

The ship banked to port, circling, waiting to see if any enemy fire followed, Klassen's fingers ready to target any remaining weapon systems if they revealed themselves. Seconds passed with no sign of a counterattack. Scans filled the holo-display, showing multiple fires and cascading explosions, the fallout of Klassen's deadly strike.

"No sign of active enemy weapons, sir," she reported, a hint of satisfaction in her voice.

"Ops, report," the captain said.

"Scans complete, sir. I've got a general layout of the complex and have located a possible entry point in one of the smaller buildings, at the opposite end from the dome. I'm not detecting any life signs, but with all the radiation, it could be affecting the sensors," Hamilton reported.

"Winters, what have you got?"

"I've located the epicenter of the temporal event, sir. It's in the heart of the dome and heavily shielded, but there's no doubt that's where whatever took place here occurred."

"Very well. Helm, take us to Hamilton's infiltration point and land the ship. The rest of you, gear up. Full combat suits and radiation protocols. Hamilton, Reesor, the structure looks big enough for heavy armor. I want you both suited up as soon as we land."

The *Switchback* set down moments later, the ramp near the back of the ship opening and four heavily armed and armored figures appearing, stepping down into the darkness of the rocky, windswept alien landscape. They moved forward, rifles up as two portals on the bottom of the ship opened to either side, illuminating them in a soft blue light. Seconds later, large, powerful suits of armor, Chronomancers, emerged, touching down with an audible thud.

The armor stood nearly four meters tall, dwarfing the officers who moved in formation between the two heavily armed guardians. "All right team, stay frosty. We don't know what's waiting for us, but we have to assume we're in for a fight," Captain Gerhardt said, passing through the protective bubble of the *Switchback*'s temporal shields, their own personal shields their only protection if another temporal event occurred.

The captain led his team towards the towering outer walls of the nearest building, sweeping the area ahead for signs of ambush as they approached, grateful to make it across the open area without opposition.

"Clarkson, override the door," the captain commanded, the squad moving into position. "Hamilton, take the left flank. Reesor, take right. Winters and Klassen, hold a defensive perimeter."

"Roger that," the squad replied, executing the orders with the speed and precision of a well-trained and experienced combat unit.

Clarkson held his right arm close to the outer door panel, his suit morphing to form three nano-projections, reaching out and connecting with the interface. A few seconds later, the lights on the panel turned blue, and the doors opened with a soft hiss as the pressurized air inside escaped.

"Hamilton, take point. Reesor, cover his flank. Clarkson, on me. Winters and Klassen, watch our backs."

The squad entered the structure, sweeping the area as they went. Large banks of flashing lights lined the walls as they moved down the central corridor. Conduits filled with optical cables connected the computing cores that filled the warehouse-sized building, enough to run a small city.

"Captain, we appear to be within the perimeter of the structure's temporal shielding. I recommend we switch ours to minimum and engage full combat shields," Winters suggested.

"Acknowledged. Squad, reduce power to temporal shields and switch to combat shields. Keep a tight formation. There's bound to be resistance at some point, so—" The Captain paused, his comms uplink to the ship activating. A second later, Admiral Janus's voice filled his helmet.

"Captain Gerhardt, do you read?"

"I read you, Admiral," he replied, raising his arm with his fist closed, his squad acknowledging the command as they moved into a defensive formation.

"The Ularans are in full retreat, but one ship jumped away several minutes ahead of the rest, and we suspect they may be calling in reinforcements."

"Understood, Admiral. We're inside a complex on the surface now, making our way towards the source of the temporal event."

"Any enemy contacts yet?" the admiral asked.

"Nothing so far, ma'am. The chronoton radiation levels down here are critical in most sections and appear to be deadly in the core of the complex. It could be that they only have minimal personnel defending the nexus point. Even with our armor and shields, we've only got an hour, maybe two at most, down here."

"Understood, Captain. Stay on high alert, but try to hurry. We gave better than we got, but they put up a hell of a fight, and if they return in force with fresh ships, we may be forced to retreat."

"Acknowledged, Admiral. We'll work as fast as we can. Gerhardt out." The captain turned to his team. "Let's move. We may not have a lot of time, and every minute counts."

The squad pressed forward, sweeping through the structure as they went, weapons ready while their scanners continued gathering data.

"Winters," the captain said, his HUD displaying a map of their current location, now deep within the complex. "What do you think?" he asked, flipping their comms to a private channel.

Winters hesitated for a moment, then spoke, choosing her words carefully, trying to keep the fear she felt growing inside from creeping into her analysis. "The technology is advanced, sir, more so than anything the Ularans are known to have. I'd guess they've likely traded with or stole from half a dozen other species, including a bit of Confederation tech. And this facility is brand-new, clearly designed around a singular purpose."

"Opening a breach?"

"More than just a breach, sir. Based on the data my scanners are picking up and my AI's analysis, I'd say that they were attempting to achieve something highly...*targeted*."

"What makes you say that?"

"Well, all the temporal engines I've ever studied were designed to create a breach, typically large enough to get a ship or at least a landing party through."

"Agreed. Most breaches are meant to send a force back to disrupt the timeline or forward in an attempt to steal advanced tech. What makes this different?"

"It's hard to say. It's more the little things. The massive amount of computing power, the power generators we passed in the last section, the way this entire structure appears to be laid out." Winters hesitated. "I think they weren't just trying to open a breach; I think they were targeting a very specific time and place with a *very* narrow window of focus."

The captain remained silent, considering for a moment. "What's your recommendation, Lieutenant? Should we return to the ship and jump back to before they executed the breach to try to stop it, or should we push forward?"

"I think..." Winters paused, considering the ramifications, then took a breath. "I think we need to press forward, sir. Find out exactly what we're dealing with, then we can make the call."

"Very well, but if we encounter heavy resistance, I'm pulling the team and we jump back a few days, call in the Fleet, and prevent whatever happened here from taking place, even if it means glassing the surface of the planet."

Winters swallowed, considering the risks if their temporal shields were breached, knowing their one chance to stop whatever took place here could be lost forever. "Yes, sir," she said, her heart pounding in her chest as they came to a large pressure door. "The dome should be just beyond these doors."

"Clarkson," the captain said, flipping his comms back to the squad channel and gesturing towards the door. "The rest of you, be ready. We don't know what's on the other side of this door, but we're likely in for one hell of a fight."

Clarkson went to work as the squad formed up into defensive positions, the Chronomancers' formidable weapons armed and ready. The door slid open a few seconds later, an audible hiss accompanying it as the two atmospheres met one another. The squad held their position, their fingers on the trigger, while they waited for the inevitable attack to come from the blackness ahead.

"Lights," the captain whispered.

Each of them activated the lights on their suits and rifles, the Chronomancers' beams dwarfing that of the rest of the crew.

Seconds passed, the beams cutting through the darkness as they revealed fractions of the massive open space. A drop of water echoed in the cavernous chamber, the only sound breaking the silence. Winters's light swept the giant dome-like roof overhead while the rest of the crew focused on the area ahead, the space nearly double the size of a large stadium.

"Anything?" the captain asked, his eyes sweeping the room.

"I've got nothing, sir. No enemy contacts," Klassen reported.

"Launch drones," he said, keeping his rifle up as he stared into the blackness, the beams from their lights the only thing providing a sense of depth to the huge open space.

Clarkson stepped forward, tossing a cluster of spheres into the air, each activating and racing into the abyss, sweeping the room. Detailed scans quickly came back as they mapped the area. "No life signs, sir."

"Very well. Reesor, Hamilton, watch our six. The rest of you, with me," the captain ordered. "Spread out and stay alert," he added, anticipating the trap he knew could spring any second but knowing that time was of the essence. "Looks like there's a structure of some kind in the middle."

Winters headed for the center of the room. "Sir, look at this!" she said, stopping near a deep gouge in the metal floor. "Looks like some kind of massive energy wave struck out. Highly volatile plasma from the looks of it, damaging the surrounding area."

"I've got another one over here!" Klassen chimed in from thirty meters away. "And another. Lots of burn marks too!"

"Me too," Clarkson added from the other flank, taking in the surrounding devastation.

Winters moved closer to the huge circular platform ahead, four towering arms reaching up as tall as a three-story building around it, scanning the area intently. She stopped for an instant, her foot splashing down into a wide pool of water surrounding the platform. "This is the focal point, sir, absolutely no question. Chronoton radiation is off the charts. We can't stay here long, even with our shields and the rad protection in our suits."

"Acknowledged," the captain replied. "What do you make of it?"

"The arms are highly sophisticated, filled with a variety of technologies from forcefield generators to gravity field modulators to sensors. There's a few other pieces of tech in there my scans and AI can't identify," she added, continuing to analyze the data.

"What about the platform?" Klassen asked, scouting ahead, stepping over another wide canyon of shredded metal that wound its way across the floor.

"It's some kind of metal alloy. Looks like a mix of daramite, titanium, and something else. Sensors are having trouble identifying it. There's a series of sensors all over the bottom of the platform and a large device of some kind in the center. I'm not sure what it is, but the chronoton radiation coming off of it suggests that it's a temporal-focusing device of some kind."

"I've got something!" Clarkson called out. "The drones just found this," he said, sweeping his light towards the wall ahead, a glint of light from his rifle reflecting in the distance.

"Looks like it may be a control station. Clarkson, Winters, go check it out," the captain ordered.

"Aye, sir," Winters replied, signaling to Clarkson as they disappeared into the blackness while Captain Gerhardt stood for a moment, studying the platform, his scans revealing evidence of stress and metal fatigue in the highly durable alloys, compounding his concerns as he switched to a closed comm with his XO.

"What do you think, Amala?" he asked, his voice betraying the deep sense of unease he'd kept hidden from the rest of his crew.

"I've never seen anything like this before," she admitted, studying sensor data coming into her HUD. "But I think Winters is right. This entire complex, the unprecedented scope and scale of it all, appears to be designed for precision temporal operations."

"Should we pull out now and jump back?"

"I..." She hesitated. "I think we need to find out what the damage is first. Admiral Janus is up there still, so whatever happened, at least it's not catastrophic to the GCH. We can still pull out if we need to, but I think we need to get to the bottom of this, Marc. I mean, where the hell is everyone? If they got what they wanted and abandoned this facility, then why didn't their ships just leave before we got here?"

The captain took a breath, resolving his will as he pushed his fears and doubts aside, knowing his XO was right. "All right, let's continue our swee—"

"Sir!" Winters called out. "We've found something."

"On our way," he replied, heading towards the control console, where Winters stood with Clarkson, Klassen meeting him halfway as he approached. "What have you got?"

Winters nodded to Clarkson, the engineer holding out his arm, pulling up a scan from one of the *Switchback*'s flyby passes on the holo-display before them. "I think Winters is right on the money, sir," he said, the scans zooming out, showing the entire system slowly free falling into the black hole. "This entire complex is designed to use the proximity of the black hole to not only bend space-time but to *significantly* amplify the effect. My AI was able to pull the logs from this console. They show that the central power core was fully charged at a capacity of nineteen thousand petawatts when they triggered the event. From what we can piece together, it appears that they routed the power into a highly focused temporal breach before depleting all of the core's energy in a matter of minutes. My AI can't crack their command-and-control system yet to decipher where or when they were targeting, but, well..." Clarkson hesitated, looking at Winters.

"It's bad, sir. *Really* bad," Winters said. "Like nothing on our records or ever even attempted before. I thought, from some of our initial scans, that it could be a significant breach, maybe a hundred years based on the readings, which is already unheard of! But..."

Clarkson jumped back in, picking up where Winters left off. "But based on that kind of power and the exponential effects from the proximity of the black hole to bend space-time..." he said, shaking his head as he let out a quick breath. "Sir, they could have reached out ten-to-fifteen thousand light-years, and forward or back, up to a millennium!"

"My God!" the captain said, quickly realizing why the Ularans had been willing to fight to the death to protect such a devastating weapon. He stood silently for a moment, absorbing the information while considering the implications, his mind racing. Most temporal events went forward or back a few years, maybe a decade or two, in the most extreme cases. The power and precision required for anything beyond that was simply too immense to comprehend.

Somehow, though, the Ularans had found a way. He turned to Klassen. "They could have done almost anything with that kind of reach."

"Where are they, though?" she replied. "Wouldn't their fleet have pulled out right away if they'd gotten what they wanted?"

"Maybe they left their ships behind to protect their weapon," Clarkson suggested.

"Maybe they—" Winters was cut off as data from the drone appeared suddenly, flashing on Clarkson's display, drawing their attention.

"Sir, one of the drones is detecting a hidden door!" he reported.

"Where?" the captain asked urgently.

"One hundred thirty meters from here, along that far wall. Looks like the walls there are heavily shielded, maybe to keep out the radiation from in here."

"All right, let's move. Hamilton, take point. Clarkson, get that door open. The rest of you, delta formation on me."

The squad sprinted into action, the noise from Chronomancers echoing with each step as the team took up positions around the area the scans indicated.

Clarkson quickly got to work, cycling scanning and visual modes to cut through the cloaking field, then initiating a particle-scattering field to take it down. He moved towards a console in the wall to the side, his suit reaching out to connect tendrils of nano-material while his AI overrode the controls. The door slid open a moment later, a narrow staircase coming into view.

"Reesor, Hamilton, stay out here and cover our six," the captain ordered, knowing the heavy suits of armor wouldn't fit down the stairs. "The rest of you, on me."

The crew moved stealthily down the long, dark flight, sonic dampeners to maximum, a faint white glow illuminating the corridor at the bottom. They hit the last step and pushed forward, keeping a tight formation, Klassen taking the lead and crouching over slightly while Winters took up a position behind her and kept an arm pressed to her XO's back, her rifle beside her, ready to provide supporting fire if needed.

The end of the corridor came into view seconds later, opening up to a brightly lit room. The team moved into position, flanking both sides of the door, stopping just before the threshold, taken aback by what they saw. "Looks like some kind of…medical bay," Klassen whispered.

The captain signaled the team forward, Klassen leading the way, sweeping with her rifle. The room was large, enclosed with clean white walls and medical equipment filling the space. Klassen moved around a cabinet full of medical supplies, then stopped suddenly. "Freeze!" she yelled. "Hands where I can see them, now!"

Winters instantly fell in beside her, weapons ready.

Two Ularans stood frozen a few meters ahead, standing beside what appeared to be a medical pod. They looked at one another, then slowly complied, raising their hands above their heads.

Winters and Klassen closed on the two aliens, taking up positions on either side, rifles trained.

The captain moved forward, stopping a meter from the two prisoners, then lowered his helmet, the rest of the team following suit. "I'm Captain Marcus Gerhardt, Galactic Confederation of Humanity, Temporal Enforcement Division," he said, his voice booming with authority and impatience. "You are in direct violation of the Treaty of Temporal Interference. Identify yourselves and explain your actions!"

The Ularan on the right spoke first. "I am Calnious, and this is my colleague, Havar. Please, we are scientists with the Ulara Imperiate working on a classified project."

"Your classified project is a temporal *weapon*," Klassen interjected, her tone venomous.

"What have you done?" the captain asked coldly, cutting to the heart of the matter, knowing that the Ularan fleet could jump back in at any time, and they could quickly go from captors to captives if Admiral Janus's forces were outnumbered.

"There is much that you must know and little time," Calnious said, a thin trickle of blood streaming from his nose.

"Are you all right?" the captain asked, suddenly aware of how pale both men looked, even for Ularans, noticing for the first time the boils on their hands and skin.

"Please, Captain," Havar said, moving slowly, running his hand through his stringy black hair, a large clump coming away from his head. He held it out, staring at it somberly. His pale-yellow eyes met the captain's. "We're dying," he said, his voice weak.

Winters quickly scanned them both. "I'm detecting heavy concentrations of chronoton radiation, sir. They've both received lethal doses."

"None of that matters!" Calnious said grimly. "We need to get him to our people. Please."

"Your ships are gone," the captain stated plainly. "Our fleet offered them a chance to surrender and explain, but they decided to fight instead. What little of your forces that survived have pulled out of the system."

The two scientists looked at one another, knowing now why their attempts to contact their ships had failed. "We will be dead soon, Captain, but our people will never stop looking for him. He is the key!" Havar said emphatically.

"Captain, there's a bio-sign in the medpod," Klassen interjected. "Scans show he's…humanoid."

"What is the meaning of this?" the captain said, towering over them as he stepped closer.

"Please, let me explain," Havar said. "Many millennia ago, a virus infected our people, twisting us into the form you see before you. This is why we are here. We believe that technology from the race you call the Ancients holds the key to the salvation of our people."

"How?"

"We have discovered, through extensive research using thousands of medical and historical databases, that extremely rare genetic anomalies appear in the genomes of different species from time to time. These anomalies, we believe, are recursive genes, allowing these unique individuals to interface with Ancient technology. These cases are immeasurably rare, nearly one in ninety trillion, based on our estimates. And none have occurred in any living lifeform registered today. During our historical research, we found three such cases. However, when we ran our simulations, we determined that we could not remove them from their own times without significant temporal repercussions," Havar said.

Calnious continued. "For years, we continued our search until we finally found a candidate who was viable. A humanoid male, from nine hundred years in the past, on a planet in the Terran System called Earth. The records indicate he'd registered with a program designed to match stem cell donors, and as part of this process, they collected a sample of his DNA."

"Where did you get these *records*?" Klassen asked suspiciously.

"One can purchase just about anything on the black market, for a price," Havar admitted candidly.

"What made this individual viable was the circumstances surrounding his death," Calnious added. "According to Terran records, he is suspected to have died from drowning and his body was never recovered."

"It was the perfect opportunity in that we could pull him from his time without risking a disruption to the space-time continuum," Havar finished.

"We only wish to restore our people to their former selves. We believe there is Ancient technology still out there that could cure our people!" Calnious pleaded, his body trembling, a drop of blood streaking down from the corner of his eye, leaving a trail down his cheek as more followed.

"There could also be Ancient *weapons* technology out there as well," Klassen commented.

"It is possible," Havar said. "There are factions amongst our people with different agendas. We represent a faction that only wishes to restore our people above all else. There are more…militant groups, however, who would go much farther. That is why we only had twenty ships in orbit. We've strived to keep knowledge of this facility, and our actions, known only to a few of our kind."

"Why didn't people from your ships come and get him already?" Winters asked.

"He needed immediate medical attention. First, to resuscitate him from drowning, then specialized treatments to repair the damage from the radiation and the temporal displacement," Havar replied, steadying himself on the medical pod, slumping over slightly while struggling to speak. "He wasn't…stable enough to be transported. The procedures, however, are nearly complete."

"Amy?" came a voice from inside the pod. "Amy?" it repeated, louder this time.

"Who is he?" Winters asked.

Calnious reached towards a small console, moving slowly, his hands trembling as he pressed a button, the medical pod tilting forward to reveal a man inside, his hair disheveled, beard ragged, and skin bearing the marks of fading radiation burns. The man's eyes went wild as he saw Winters. "Amy!" he shouted, pulling at his restraints.

Calnious pressed another button, gas filling the medpod. The man's eyes flickered, his body becoming limp, his struggles diminishing. He looked at Winters one last time, his eyes fighting to stay open as he said her name softly, then fell back into a sedated sleep.

"This," Calnious said, "is William Jackson of Earth. And he is here to save us all."

CHAPTER 1
PURSUIT

Jackson ran as fast as he could, pushing his body and the stealth suit to their limits, his lungs burning with every stride.

In the distance behind him, he could hear trees snapping like toothpicks as his pursuer tore through the jungle, gaining on him. A deafening roar echoed through the trees, scattering birds from the canopy, as the creature barreled ahead, sensing its prey was near.

Two explosions rang out, followed by a roar of fury, the sounds of destruction growing louder and closer still.

"I think we just pissed it off!" Jackson called out, looking over his shoulder.

"I believe that is an accurate assessment, William," Bits responded dryly. "Turn right here."

Jackson turned, rounding a tall, thick tree, reaching out with his right arm, the suit morphing into a tentacle-like tether as it grasped the trunk, allowing him to swing around in one fluid motion, maintaining every ounce of precious speed.

The thick jungle ahead blocked his view, a wall of overgrown vegetation spreading out before him. Bits switched visual modes in Jackson's heads-up display, allowing him to see through the dense foliage, spotting an open path beyond. As he leapt through a barrier of huge, palm-like leaves, the jungle ahead opened up, the sound of rushing water growing closer.

The extraction point.

The sounds of the jungle being trampled behind him grew louder, his pursuer gaining as he fought back a wave of exhaustion, his muscles screaming for a reprieve as he pushed himself to keep going, forcing his aching body onward.

He broke through the tree line, the ground ahead ending abruptly, his feet sliding on the loose dirt. Jackson reached out, grabbing hold of a vine, barely managing to stop himself just short of the precipice. He looked out from the edge of the towering escarpment. Huge waterfalls stretched out all along the edge for nearly a kilometer to his left, cascading and crashing violently into the raging river in the valley some two hundred meters below.

"Bits! Where's our ride?"

"Our signal is still being jammed; you're going to have to get out of range."

"Damn it. All right, let's do it!"

Jackson took several steps back, then sprinted towards the edge of the cliff, leaping into the air. As he jumped, he stretched out his arms, Bits reshaping the suit and forming wings spanning several meters across. He was nearly away from the cliff when he was suddenly violently pulled back.

Jackson looked back as a massive armored arachnid cleared the trees, a thick, sticky web streaming from its body. The creature wasted no time, pulling on the webbing with its powerful legs, reeling him in.

He twisted his body, using one of his wings to slice through the tether, freeing himself, as he dove into the wind stream, then spread his wings once more and curved up, out of its range. High above, the arachnid thrashed its legs, striking the edge of the cliff, launching boulders towards him, forcing him to weave around them as he swooped upward and out of their path.

"Whoo!" he called triumphantly. "That was way too close!" Suddenly, an alarm went off in his ear. "What now?"

"I'm detecting multiple incoming," Bits replied urgently.

Eight icons appeared on his sensor display. "Analysis."

"They appear to be a species resembling dragonflies. Highly agile and very fast."

"Yeah, and the size of a fucking fighter jet! Options?"

"We cannot outrun them out in the open, but the valley floor offers a number of potential options for cover," Bits suggested, bringing up a topographical analysis.

He stared at the map, the river raging at the bottom of the canyon, the culmination of the waterfalls high above meeting, then rushing towards the distant sea. Foam-capped aquamarine whitewater roared and twisted, flanked by a rocky shoreline on either side, running up for several meters before the jungle regained its grasp, the dense vegetation pouring over its edges. The river twisted and turned as it ran its violent and ancient course. Large rocky formations jutted out from the sides and along the banks, and islands rose up in the center of the river. Overhead, bridges of windswept stone crisscrossed the canyon, along with cliffs where the water had eroded the ground out from under them. The suit's sensors registered elevated wind speeds and identified several areas where dangerous crosswinds whipped through, compressed by the curvature of the canyon.

It'll have to do, Jackson thought. He dove for the river, closing the distance to the raging torrent of water below. "How long until we can contact the ship?"

"We're approaching the edge of the jamming signal's range. Fifteen seconds," Bits informed him as Jackson darted towards the shoreline, hugging the underside of a rocky outcropping for cover. Seconds ticked by, the flight of predators tracking him as they approached from above.

"Comms restored," Bits announced. "The *Phoenix* is en route. Intercept in one minute, forty seconds."

"How long until the dragonflies overtake us?"

"At our present speed, forty-five seconds."

"Shit! All right, let's see what we can do to keep these bastards off of us," Jackson said defiantly, the outcropping ending as he swooped down, just above the raging water, weaving back and forth.

A gust of wind caught him a moment later, sweeping him sideways. Bits reacted instantly, firing the thrusters, then reforming the suit from a glide configuration into a sleeker, more aerodynamic and acrobatic form, sharpening its edges and forming small ailerons on the wingtips and Jackson's feet to assist with maneuvers.

Jackson's body strained as he cut through another powerful crosswind, using all of his skill and concentration to keep from becoming a stain on the rocks, the valley narrowing ahead. Bits increased power to the suit's thrusters, adding more speed and giving Jackson more control. He looked up in his HUD, watching as his pursuers broke off, moving to a higher altitude where they could line up for a controlled attack vector.

Smart, he thought. *Why take a chance down here when you can wait for an opening to pick me off.*

"Bits, map out a course to provide the maximum amount of cover. They're going to come at us as soon as the valley opens up again," he said, watching as two of them broke formation, anticipating the attack to come.

Bits highlighted a route in Jackson's HUD and he followed the flight path, deftly weaving around the rocky formations jutting out from the banks and keeping below the thin canopy of tree branches which hung out over the river.

A spray of whitewater shot up ahead where the river slammed into a rocky island in the center, splitting into two. A waterfall dropped on each side of the island, creating clouds of mist. He pulled up, catching a glimpse of a large, four-winged shadow briefly visible on the mist as it overtook him from above.

He searched in his 360-degree view, watching as the closest dragonfly lined him up to strike. He banked sharply to the left around another rocky island, evading the creature as it dove, attempting to shred him with its jaws.

Jackson narrowly missed an outstretched tree, dodging back into the center of the river. The first attacker moved above once more while two more swooped down at him.

"Bits, prepare countermeasures," he said, looking ahead as the valley widened, the two dragonflies diving in unison, flanking him on either side, attempting to box him in while a third took a position above him, preparing to attack.

The wings of dragonflies on either side fluttered faster than his eyes could see, creating a powerful wind, making it more difficult to maintain control as they took turns darting in towards him, each attempting to drive him towards the other so that it could grab hold with its mandibles, only the razor-sharp tips of his wings keeping them at bay.

The predator above dropped sharply, attempting to engulf him as it swooped down towards his feet. A blaze of light erupted from the legs of his suit as a dozen small flares shot out, striking the dragonflies on both sides and forcing the one behind to pull up to avoid the deadly projectiles. The scorching magnesium ignited the wings of the ones on either side, burning through them in seconds, sending their bodies crashing into the river below at terminal velocities.

Jackson waited for a second, the predator above coming at him again. He pulled back, slowing his speed at the last second, the dragonfly overshooting him, committed to its dive. Jackson fired a particle beam from a weapons port on his shoulder, clipping the dragonfly's wings and sending it tumbling into the rocky shoreline like a bug splattering on a windshield.

The formation of dragonflies above adjusted their flight path to take the places of their fallen comrades, closing on him.

"Bits, how long till the *Phoenix* is here?"

"Twenty-six seconds."

Jackson scanned ahead, looking for cover, the river widening as it approached a series of rapids, then turning, the flow funneling into a rocky V-shaped gorge with towering cliff walls replacing the jungle on either side. "Bits, alter our course for that large outcropping. Right there, where that long, wide ledge hangs out almost all the way across. Take us directly beneath it."

"Acknowledged," Bits replied, calculating the optimal flight path as he anticipated Jackson's plan.

The massive dragonflies increased their speed, sensing the opportunity for the kill as Jackson raced for the cover of the ledge, the natural chokepoint denying him room to maneuver and evade their attack. The rapid buzzing of their wings filled his ears as he looked back in his display, the formation now just ten meters behind him and closing fast. "Their jaws twitched in anticipation as they jockeyed for position, each wanting to be the first to reach him.

He passed under the towering ledge, the dragonflies following close behind, the sound of their wings reverberating and echoing off the canyon walls.

"Now!" he shouted.

Bits fired several controlled particle beams, shattering the massive ledge and sending rocks ranging from small shrapnel to large boulders tumbling down upon the formation of dragonflies. The falling rock struck the predators, their wings torn and bodies crushed as they crashed into the raging rapids below, consumed by the avalanche of debris, their huge forms disappearing beneath the foamy waves.

Jackson pulled up out of the canyon and into the open, scanning for any other signs of pursuit.

"William, I'm detecting more inbound enemy targets. ETA, forty-three seconds."

"How long until the *Phoenix* is here?" he asked, the ship de-cloaking in the distance seconds later ahead of him. "Never mind," he said as he shot forward, Bits maneuvering the ship to line them up on a parallel course, then opening the cargo ramp and reducing speed.

Jackson stepped onto the ramp, his boots magnetizing as he touched down, while Bits retracted the wings. He rushed up the cargo ramp and forward through the ship to the bridge.

"Good work, buddy," he said, taking a seat at the helm.

"Now let's get the hell off this Insectoid-infested rock," he added, plotting an escape vector and accelerating upwards while Bits reengaged the cloak.

The ship gained altitude, turning away from the incoming wave. In the distance, Jackson could see a dense cloud of winged Insectoids approaching on sensors, pushing aside the thoughts of what would have happened had they caught him and focusing instead on their escape.

"I'm detecting seventeen enemy ships in orbit. They are generating massive amounts of charged particles in the upper atmosphere," Bits informed him.

"What the hell are they up to?" he asked, thinking out loud as he brought up the visual sensor feed on the main viewscreen, the image illuminating the bridge in the glow of dancing reds and greens. "Shit," he blurted out, suddenly realizing what they were attempting to do. "They're creating an artificial aurora effect!"

"Affirmative. The aurora is spread out across a wide area in the upper atmosphere, thousands of kilometers across."

"Will they be able to detect us if we pass though?"

"Yes. The charged particles will interact with our cloak, creating a silhouette of the ship."

"Can we go around?"

"They've launched fighters from the base on the surface, and even with our cloak, we still create a small signature from our sublight engines, along with air-pressure disturbances while in the atmosphere. If they get within ten kilometers, it is likely we will be detected."

"And those ships above can keep moving to cut us off," he said, realizing they were boxed in. "To hell with it, we're punching through!"

"William, I do not recommend that course of action."

"I know, but right now, we have the advantage. We know where they are, but they don't know where we are. So, they're covering a huge patch of sky and attempting to flush us out. We need to pick our spot," he said, studying the formation above. "If we go through here" – he pointed to a gap between the two largest ships – "we'll take some fire, but those battle cruisers are far too big and slow to come after us. They've spread their smaller, faster ships to the edges, casting their net as wide as they can and expecting us to make a run further out. So, we hit them were they least expect it, at their strongest point," Jackson explained emphatically, suddenly realizing how insane his plan sounded.

Captain Delgado would be proud, he thought, smiling to himself.

Bits remained silent for a moment, running hundreds of simulations through his processors. "Very well, but I must caution you that the margin for error is very slim. I calculate your od—"

"Ah, ah, ah! Han Solo rule, remember?"

"Never tell you the odds, I know," Bits replied, slightly deflated.

"Exactly. Now, let's do this!" he called, altering their course while Bits fed him to-the-second corrections, and they headed towards the space between the two hulking battle cruisers.

"Here we go!" Jackson said as they approached the thermosphere, the glowing aurora dancing vividly before them as the two cruisers loomed above. "Full power to engines! Raise the shields as soon as they detect us and prepare countermeasures!"

The *Phoenix* entered the aurora, suddenly lit up in the red-and-green light like a brilliant black dagger streaking through the sky. The battle cruisers grew closer in the display as the ship rocketed towards the gap between them.

"We've been detected. Raising shields," Bits said as the closest cruiser began turning, Jackson maneuvering the *Phoenix* in response, attempting to keep as close as possible to their stern, where their weapons were weakest, hoping to avoid the worst of it as they passed.

Fire from the second cruiser grazed their shields, its full broadside facing them, letting loose as they raced to close the gap of open space between them and the first cruiser.

Jackson pushed the engines past the red line, closing the gap and flying as close as he could to the hulking battleship, forcing the second cruiser to cease fire to avoid hitting their sister ship.

The *Phoenix* rocketed past the cruiser, both vessels opening fire as soon as it was clear, the ship rocking as the barrage of fire connected multiple times. Jackson ignored the hits, focusing on the controls, using their speed and agility to maneuver, twisting to avoid the worst of it as most of the fire missed or grazed their shields.

"Shields down to twenty-eight percent," Bits warned. "Sixteen percent," he corrected as the enemy fire continued, Jackson doing everything he could to maneuver the ship and keep their targeting sensors from locking on. "They're launching missiles. Thirty-two incoming detected! Preparing countermeasures."

"How long till we can jump?"

"Forty-four seconds."

He looked at the display, the missiles closing fast. "We're not going to make it!"

"We're clearing the aurora effect."

"Reengage cloak and activate the stealth drive!" Jackson called, maneuvering the ship hard to starboard, then again up and to port as it disappeared off the Insectoids' sensors, the cruisers firing at random as they attempted to predict its path.

Jackson flipped to the tactical display, the ship's sensors showing the other Insectoid vessels breaking orbit, attempting to cut off their escape vectors while they pulled farther away.

"We're clear of the planet's gravity!" he said. "Engaging hyperdrive!"

The XV-151 System disappeared behind them as they entered hyperspace seconds later, Jackson letting out a sigh of relief. "Bloody hell! That was way too close!" he said, taking a moment to let the adrenaline high taper off, his heart still pounding in his chest. "Bits, contact FoxBlind and tell them that we've accomplished our mission and are en route back to base."

"Acknowledged," Bits replied.

"You've got the conn, buddy," he said, standing and feeling the strain in his legs from the exertion in the jungle, along with an overwhelming sense of exhaustion suddenly catching up with him.

It had been nearly a day and a half since they'd infiltrated the XV-151 System, making their way to the fourth planet undetected and sneaking into the Imperium outpost there. Once inside, Jackson had made his way to the well-guarded data core, recovering several exabytes of critical intel. Bits also implanted a hidden communications protocol that would covertly retransmit any messages sent from the outpost to the GCH, at least until it was discovered, giving them some insight into any responses the enemy sent as a result of his incursion.

On the way out, however, he'd run into a sentry, a humanoid-like species of Insectoid he'd never encountered before but one able to see through his cloak. The creature hit him with several energy blasts from its rifle, his shields overwhelmed by the close-range impacts and his cloaking system fried from the powerful surge. Jackson fired back, hitting it with a plasma bolt from his wrist, while he targeted it with a flamethrower from his other arm, engulfing it seconds later. The weapons fire, however, had triggered an alarm, and he'd been on the run ever since.

As he stood stretching, he replayed the events in his mind, knowing how lucky he was to be alive. "I'm going to hit the shower," he said, walking slowly off the bridge, limping slightly, his right calf tender as he made his way gingerly into the operations room, where he stood on the platform and removed the suit.

He rubbed his stiff neck, stretching it from side to side, then made his way back to the living quarters and hit the shower. Five minutes later, he emerged, feeling refreshed and reenergized as he stood by his locker, staring at the contents. Several clean uniforms and flight suits hung from hooks, along with the rest of his clothing, folded neatly on three small shelves. His personal effects rested on a shelf at the top, where he had several photos he'd printed, each displayed in a small frame. One of his brother and his family. Another of his parents. A photo of the crew from before their mission to Vishnara, the first Ancient site they'd investigated; Henrik, Daria, Kelara, Verris, Admiral Valentyen, and him standing lined up and smiling brightly. He also had the picture of Amy and him that Bits had recovered, along with one of

Verris. He kissed his index finger, touching it to Amy's face, then did the same to the picture of Verris, a wave of guilt washing over him.

It had been some time since he'd checked in with the hospital on Archon, the war keeping him constantly occupied. Verris was still in a temporal stasis, that he knew for certain. The doctors had promised to let him know the moment she awoke in exchange for him being patient. Nearly a year and a half had passed since then, but they still hadn't developed a way to work inside the temporal field, the only thing keeping her alive. The toxic shock from the liquid isilium had nearly killed her, and if they couldn't remove it while she was still protected from the effects of time, she'd be dead in seconds once removed from the temporal suspension field. Doctor Stevenson had been in touch with him several times to provide updates, but so far, they didn't have a viable way to remove the isilium and repair the damaged tissue in her brain.

He hadn't seen her in all that time, the war and his responsibilities keeping him engaged far from the core systems. He thought of her less often, he found, his work consuming him. A wave of guilt hit him as he looked at her picture, remembering the good times they'd had and how much he missed her.

With Amy, at least, he'd had closure, but Verris still haunted him every time he saw her, a wound in his heart that wouldn't heal.

He finished dressing, then headed to the mess, picking out something to eat and grabbing a flask of water, then proceeded back to the bridge, where he sat in the command chair to eat his dinner.

"What's the news, buddy?"

"Now that we have crossed back into GCH space, I have multiple data streams available that may be of interest: galactic news, updates on the war, Terran sports scores, and more."

"Hmm, let's see what's happening in the playoffs."

"The Stanley Cup finals are set to begin in three Terran days. Montreal and Dublin will play, with Dublin gaining home-ice advantage."

"Montreal, eh? Amy would be happy. I figured this was Edinburgh's year, but I guess Dublin was too much for them. How is Man U doing?"

"They are in second place currently and not scheduled to play for five Terran days."

"Nice. Can you please let me know when the streams are ready for both games? I think that I need a distraction. Too many ops lately. Too many close calls. I can't remember the last time I kicked back with a beer and just watched a game."

"I will set an alarm for you when the games are ready."

"Thanks. Hey, is there any mail?"

"Yes, you have two new messages: one from Ensign Jones and one from Dr. Duratis."

"Bring up Daria's message."

The viewscreen came to life, an image of Dr. Daria Duratis appearing. "Hello, Will, I hope that things are well with you and you're staying safe. I was experimenting with that bio-sample that you sent me from the Tilesium System, and unfortunately it wasn't viable for cloning, but I did get some excellent genetic-profiling data. Thanks for thinking of me. That's exactly the kind of thing I'm always looking for, and I appreciate you going to the effort of keeping your eyes open and sending it my way. You know how I am about butterflies!" She paused, her face becoming serious. "I talked to Kelara the other day. She's...she's been better. She's putting on a brave face, but I could tell that she was pretty shaken up. Her unit was deployed to provide support to an Outlier colony, which was overrun last week. They were in the thick of it for several days while they tried to evacuate, but there were simply too many colonists and not enough ships. The Insectoids sent in wave after wave." The doctor paused, shaking her head. "She said it was a slaughter. Only seventy thousand or so colonists survived out of over a hundred thousand!"

Jackson shook his head slowly. Many of the Outliers had been hit hard, taking heavy losses. With the GCH Fleet battered, it was all they could do to protect critical strategic assets, and there were few ships to spare to protect the breakaway border colonies.

"Kelara said," Daria continued, "that she and her unit had some pretty heavy gear, including three Annihilators, but even that wasn't enough, and six members of her unit didn't make it out." She paused again, her brow furrowing. "She told me that there was this one little girl that she saw. She'd been dead for at least an hour before Kelara had arrived, but there was something about the look on her face that haunted her. After the six members of her unit went down, she just snapped, I think. She said that she was the last one off of that rock. Her armor was crawling with Insectoids when Helo finally overrode her commands and fired the thrusters to get them out of there. Honestly, Will...I think that ever since the *Viceroy*, she's had a death wish to die in battle like her father."

Jackson sat silently, absorbing the information, recalling the bloodlust that Kelara had let loose on the Reptilian battle station.

"She's supposed to rotate out of action in a few days, so I've pressed to her come here to Delconia for some shore leave. Hopefully she will. I think it will help her take her mind off of things. I can't imagine what it's been like for both of you, out there on the front lines.

"In other news, I've had some interesting developments here. The Imperium deployed a new species last month in the campaign on the Enphinius. A species of centipede which are highly toxic. They have a special mucus coating on them that we've never seen before. It makes them undetectable to our sensors. The centipedes managed to dig under the perimeter wall of the 2nd Battalion's forward operating base and caught them unaware. There were heavy casualties before a unit of mechs could engage them, but the centipedes were so toxic that even the mechs had to be decommissioned and disposed of after the engagement. I was fortunate to have a chance to study a mostly intact specimen that was sent to the Ministry of Exobiology. We had to put it in the Level Five Quarantine lab orbiting Delconia's moon. This is the 358th newly documented species that the Insectoids have used so far that I know of. They keep changing tactics, using different species in each engagement to exploit weaknesses in our defenses. I guess when you have a population of decillions and over fifteen million known species to choose from, it's easy to find new weapons of war."

The doctor paused for a moment, a look of sadness appearing on her face. "Sorry…I feel like that's all we ever talk about anymore. Everything, it seems, comes back to the war… How are *you* doing, Will? I really hope that you're keeping safe. Try to stop in at Delconia if you're near the core systems. It would be wonderful to see you. Johansen and I have been getting together at least once every week or two, and he'd love to see you as well. He keeps complaining that he doesn't have anyone to watch Earth movies with anymore, and he feels like he's betraying you somehow by watching them without you. He told me to tell you that he's saving something called *Star Wars* for you. I think that was what he called it. Anyway, you should really send him a comm if you have a chance. He misses you, but you know how he is. He doesn't want to bother you since we're safe here in the core and you're out there on the front lines. Just know that we all miss you and that we're thinking of you.

"I do have a bit of good news. I checked in with Dr. Stevenson on Archon the other day, and they have a promising experimental treatment that they're developing for Verris. They're still running simulations, but they're feeling optimistic. I'll keep you posted, and know that I'll be there for her when she wakes up if you can't be. I know how you can't control where you're sent these days."

Jackson smiled for what felt like the first time in months, glad to know that Daria would be there for Verris if he couldn't be and happy to hear that there was some potential progress on finding a way to treat her.

"Oh, I almost forgot. I ran into the admiral the other day. He was on Delconia and stopped in to take me out for lunch. He's still at GCH Intelligence doing tactical and strategic analysis, and he said that he might be recruiting you for something soon. Sorry, that's all that I know. Anyway, please take care of yourself out there. Tell Bits I say hello. Hopefully, this awful war will be over soon, and we'll all be back together again. I'll try to send you another comm soon. Take care."

Jackson sat silently for a few moments, thinking about his friends, especially worried about Kelara, having wished that he had said something to the admiral to get her help. At least she was going to see Daria, and maybe Henrik, soon. *That should help a bit*, he thought, wishing that he could be there but knowing that he wouldn't be back to the core systems anytime soon.

Admiral Scott, his new CO, was keeping him extremely busy these days. It was tough work, but he felt as though he was making a difference. In the past year and a half since the war began, he'd completed thirty-five solo covert ops against the enemy, along with participating in several joint operations with other units. He knew he was doing good, important work, but despite that, it pained him to know that no matter what he did, the GCH just couldn't seem to turn the tide of this war.

Daria's right, he thought. How do you fight an enemy that has millions of times your numbers and thousands more ships? Even with the GCH having a more powerful fleet with better weapons, combat armor, legions of mechs, and better technology, it simply wasn't enough. Even with the androids helping to coordinate battlefield engagements faster than a human mind could react, smart weapons, and drones, it wasn't enough to tip the scales in their favor against the sheer numbers and variety of troops that the Imperium could throw at them.

The part that really burned him was their time to replenish their numbers. A humanoid needed at least eighteen years to grow and develop before they could even be considered for military service, and even then, it took months to train them to the most basic level. Even with the GCH's incredible infrastructure and manufacturing capabilities, they still couldn't make mechs as fast as the enemy could smash them into scrap.

Meanwhile, the Insectoids could produce new broods of soldiers in anywhere from a matter of weeks to months, and most were combat ready within days or weeks of being born.

Command was beginning to get desperate as the Fleet's losses continued to mount. In all of the previous conflicts with the Insectoids, they had never adapted this well. Technology had always given the GCH the upper hand, and when they lost a battle, they damn sure won the next five. Somehow, though, the Insectoids were ready not with just numbers but with new tactics, technology, and vessels of their own. They'd adapted their combat tactics significantly, mining their entomological data and finding the species most adept at countering humanoid defenses, then used them with military precision to exploit the GCH's weaknesses.

In the year and a half that had passed, the GCH had lost thirty-one systems along the border, at least a dozen of which were inhabited. Five of them Outlier colonies and two Vicara class planets among them with populations that were somewhere between the stone and industrial ages. Tens of billions of humanoids had died or were now living under Imperium rule, and the Insectoids were only growing bolder. The last three systems they had conquered were all in a straight line, like the tip of a spear, taking them deeper into GCH territory and cutting off supply lines.

Normally, their tactic was to take a system along the border, then move up or down several thousand light-years and target another. This had always been their strategy, and it had worked reasonably well, as they forced the GCH Fleet to redeploy up and down the border to counter their actions, often exposing another weak point to attack in the process.

Up to this point, the GCH had been almost entirely on the defensive, with not a single attack aside from a few strikes in the first days of the war, having taken place in a system that the Insectoids had held before the war began. It was almost unimaginable.

"This damned war…" Jackson said out loud. "My God, Bits, did you ever think that it would come to this?"

"I'm afraid that this war is like nothing that has ever been seen before, William. There are simply too many variables, and things are happening too quickly. Even with all of our resources, computational and cognitive power, we simply cannot seem to anticipate an enemy that has clearly learned our weaknesses and formulated new tactics."

"Yeah," he said weakly. "It's almost like they know what we're going to do and then plan their attacks to expose our weaknesses. I know we suspected that there could be a mole inside Command, but I can't imagine that anyone would willingly betray their own species like this. It's like we're missing a key piece of a puzzle and just can't see the entire picture. Like there's someone or something else out there, giving the Insectoids the advantage," he said bitterly as he thought for a moment, knowing there weren't any other players that could pull this off.

The Canids had taken advantage of the GCH's attention being elsewhere, claiming a few disputed systems along the frontier and growing bolder as the GCH shifted more attention to the Holt Line, but their ambitions were small. By all accounts, the Reptilian Empire was still in chaos, undergoing what appeared to be a species-based civil war after the ruse that Jackson and his team had pulled off to light a match on an already explosive situation. The Ularans kept to themselves and their core systems, enigmatic as usual. And the Oceanic Union was assisting the GCH with the war effort where they could, helping to protect the several key systems, while still keeping their guard up against the Reptilians.

There simply weren't any other players on the board that had the power or the ability to undermine the GCH this way.

"What's our ETA to FoxBlind?" Jackson asked, frustrated as he struggled to unravel the mystery.

"Eleven hours, twenty-two minutes," Bits replied.

"All right, I'm going to get some rack time. Wake me if anything interesting happens."

"Of course, William. Have a good sleep," Bits said as Jackson headed for his quarters, while he maintained his link with the *Phoenix*'s command-and-control systems. Despite being physically bound to Jackson, within the hull of the *Phoenix*, he essentially *was* the ship.

Jackson fell asleep quickly, exhausted from his mission and the thoughts of war. He hoped he'd dream of something to make him feel better. Like the way he had felt when he woke up in this new life, nearly eight years ago now, but it was not to be. Instead, he dreamed of spiders, centipedes, and other horrors that he hoped he'd never see again.

CHAPTER 2
FOXBLIND

The *Phoenix* exited hyperspace in the Terahdan System, cloaking as soon as it was back in normal space. Jackson signaled the traffic control outpost for permission to proceed, then plotted a course for FoxBlind, the hidden covert operations base and his home for the past year and a half.

FoxBlind was a GCH black site, serving as the base of operations for Admiral Scott's Covert Operations Task Force, an elite group of forty operatives whose mission was to disrupt the enemy war machine via sabotage, espionage, and occasionally outright force. At first, Jackson had been excited, but as the war wore on, and twenty-three of his colleagues never returned, the excitement that he had first felt faded into cold, detached professionalism.

The galaxy was the most hostile and dangerous place imaginable. There was no justice. The good guys didn't always win. And more often than not, people didn't come home.

As the months passed, he had poured himself into his work, mapping out each mission with obsessive precision. He and Bits worked late into the nights to prep for each op, creating backup plans and backup plans for backup plans. Occasionally, in the limited downtime he had, he watched old Earth movies, such as *Die Hard* or *The Wrath of Kahn*, trying to think outside of the box and find new ways to adapt and survive in a no-win scenario. Aside from those brief moments of normality, he was all work, all the time.

Thirty-five times out, and thirty-five times he returned, but he knew that one day, no matter how well he prepared, no matter how careful he was, no matter how clever his "Hollywood escape plan" was this time, that one day, he wouldn't.

Shortly after he arrived, Admiral Scott and his senior staff debriefed him regarding his mission in the XV-151 System, while Bits uploaded the massive amount of data that they had stolen from the Arachnid command outpost. It would be decrypted and analyzed by the base's staff of one hundred and fifty android data-processing specialists. The androids were a key part of the team, tasked with spending every nanosecond cracking enemy codes and encryption, along with sifting through colossal amounts of data. They took that information, using it to create new access codes, back doors, override commands, and scanning for new vulnerabilities in the Imperium's systems, as well as creating decryption algorithms and other tools for operatives to use in the field to gather valuable intelligence or compromise enemy systems. Admiral Scott's goal was simple: to deliver all the data they could to GCH Intelligence while trying to expose any weaknesses in the Imperium war machine and cripple their efforts where possible.

After being debriefed, the admiral gave Jackson several days of downtime while the androids worked tirelessly, sifting through the data and monitoring the hijacked transmissions from the XV-151 outpost, reporting to the admiral anything of interest. Jackson slept, exercised, and had a few good meals, catching up with Ensign Jones, his logistical supply officer and his only real friend at FoxBlind.

He sent a short comm message back to Daria, letting her know how he was, telling her about the new species of Insectoid that got the drop on him, and thanking her for letting him know about Kelara and Verris. After that, he sent a quick message to Johansen to say hi and wish him well. As he made his recording, he asked each of them to give Kelara his best and to take good care of her. He thought about sending her a vid-message as well, but decided against it, unable to find the words. In the end, he sent her a text message, to let her know that he'd heard what had happened and encouraging her to take Daria up on her offer, hoping it would help to sway her to take a break and see some friendly faces.

As he went to sleep that night, he dreamed of Verris for the first time in a long time, remembering their days together at Kishara Station, waking from the dream feeling empty inside as he lay alone in his bed, wishing that he could go back to those days for even just a moment. He longed to hold her hand. To smell her hair. To see her smile. For the simple comfort of her being there with him.

He sat in the mess the next morning, watching on a holo-display while the Fleet news stream played, showing various updates on the war, along with maps, highlighting systems all along the Holt Line where several small-scale actions had recently taken place. Another operative, Kirkland, came in, he and Jackson exchanging respectful nods as they each went about their business.

In the earlier days of the war, the operatives had spent more time together, discussing missions, strategies, and sharing drinks when off duty. But lately, they kept more to themselves, none of them wanting to make new connections only to lose them on the next op gone bad. Jackson felt as though there was a ceremony almost once a month for a lost operative or support staff member who went out and didn't come back.

Everything seemed darker, as though the constant specter of death loomed over FoxBlind, waiting to collect its next victim.

Jackson spent some of his off time with Ensign Jones, the young woman keeping him grounded in human interactions. She always offered a kind word and did her best to anticipate his needs while he prepped tirelessly for each new mission. Jones had a keen mind for covert operations, and he'd originally planned to recommend her for Captain Delgado's program when the war was over. As he got to know her more, however, he slowly changed his mind, unable to bear the thought of losing her as well. In the end, he had decided he would make it her decision, discussing it with her and giving her the option before making the recommendation, wondering if the toll she'd seen it take on him and the other operatives would dissuade her. He took comfort in the thought that she was safely back at FoxBlind and would always be there when he returned. Despite only being eight years his junior, he felt protective of her, like a little sister, unable to imagine her bright smile diminished by the harsh realities of a life filled with death and the losses of war.

The next morning, Admiral Scott summoned him to a briefing. As he entered the conference room, seven other senior officers, along with another covert operative, Frederickton – a cocky but competent officer he'd worked with before – and an android, sat waiting for him. The android's designation was A135-T0H214-S, but as it was the liaison for the base's Data Division, it had adopted the name "Alpha135" to make interactions with humanoids easier.

Androids were common throughout the GCH, administering many of the government ministries and streamlining the bureaucracy of the massive interstellar Confederation, bridging the gap between humanoids and the unimaginable amounts of data that they collected and created each day. Dedicated purely to data processing and analysis, they advised their humanoid masters on how best to use these vast amounts of information. Androids had conscious intelligence and were self-aware but had no desires or ambitions beyond what they were designed and programmed to do. Most citizens never encountered them, as they typically worked behind the scenes. At FoxBlind, however, they were more involved, occasionally participating in briefings and providing back-end processing for military AI units, such as Bits, to run simulations and conduct operations in the field.

The briefing began as Jackson took his seat, the admiral gesturing to Alpha135 to take the floor.

"Operation Gralon," Alpha135 began, its nearly human voice out of place as it came from the tall, gray, generic android form, devoid of any unique features. "Named after the historical figure from Archon who successfully burned down the Batetan fleet while it was docked in Lyrinish during the First Entrarus War of 2421, pre-GCH calendar. This mission will involve both Commander Jackson and Captain Frederickton. The mission profile is as follows: Commander Jackson will take the *Phoenix* to the Imperium System RE-13, while Captain Frederickton will take the *Sulavar* to the Imperium System MK-291. Based on the analysis of the Imperium data provided by Commander Jackson, we believe these systems contain the highly classified Insectoid shipyards where they are building their advanced warships. As you know, the Imperium has been using some kind of cloaking or disruption technology, obscuring GCH sensor scans of their systems, and as such, we have had no reliable intelligence regarding the location of these shipyards, until now."

Alpha135 paused for a moment, allowing the information to sink in, each of the officers present realizing the massive significance of the find. "The mission objective is to use stealth to infiltrate the shipyards, the operatives each approaching, then boarding a single battleship. Your AIs and support officers have received mission packages outlining the specific operational details. Once on board, you will need to locate and disable several fail-safes. From there, you will implant a virus in the main data core. Next, you will find the communications control center in the main engineering section. We've discovered a weakness in the standard Imperium comms protocols we can exploit, which will allow the ship to open a backdoor and establish a one-way connection with the shipyard. Once open, the virus will self-replicate and spread throughout the shipyard, activating shortly thereafter. Once activated, it will perform several actions. First, it will initiate a quantum core overload on the battleship you're on while triggering a dampening field to mask the effect while the power levels build. Second, it will alter a key subroutine in the shipyard's code, creating a temporary loop in the system. Once the loop is active, the virus will trigger a shipyard-wide diagnostic of the sensor arrays, taking them offline while the loop continues to show them as active, limiting their ability to detect the core overload until it is too late. There is a risk, however, in that there is an advanced sensor array in each system which may detect the buildup earlier, but with the dampening field and shipyard sensory arrays offline, it will make it harder for them to pinpoint it until it's too late. The subsequent detonation will create a massive shockwave, which will destroy much of the shipyard, crippling their production capabilities and destroying as many ships as possible in the process. The virus has been designed to activate thirty seconds after uploading to the shipyard, starting a four-minute countdown."

"Why only four minutes?" Frederickton asked.

"Good question, Captain. Once the virus spreads, the risk of detection increases exponentially, as do the chances that the Imperium will be able to stop it," Alpha135 replied. "Four minutes is also the optimal time for the battleship's quantum core to reach critical levels and overload."

"Can we plant the virus, then remote trigger it?" Jackson asked.

"Negative. We cannot risk triggering it remotely. We've run tens of thousands of simulations, and the margin for error is too high. It must be triggered while you're on board the battleship to ensure it activates successfully. There are many things that we know about the Imperium's systems and their new battleships. However, there is also a great deal that we do not know, and as such, we need each of you and your AIs there to adapt if the initial activation does not go as planned."

Jackson and Frederickton shared a look while Alpha135 continued. "Based on the information available, we believe that these are the only two shipyards in the Imperium which are capable of producing the advanced classes of warships. By destroying these sites, and the ships that are currently in production, it should stem the flow of these vessels, helping to tip the balance of power back in the GCH's favor. Questions?"

"Just one," Captain Frederickton said. "Are you *fucking* serious? This is a suicide mission!"

Alpha135 stood impassively, while Frederickton glared at him.

"If we have to trigger this from the main engineering section at the heart of the ship, how the hell are we supposed to get out of there after initiating the quantum core overload in only four minutes without getting blown to hell along with the bugs?"

Jackson had been wondering the same thing, but knew Frederickton well enough to leave it to him to voice their concerns.

"We do not have a viable extraction plan at this time," Alpha135 responded, his tone cold and analytical.

"You don't have a—" Frederickton was about to stand up and tear a strip off of the android, when Admiral Scott interjected.

"We have a window of four days, gentlemen, before this operation has to launch. We'll use this time and all the resources we have available to work on this problem and find a solution."

"Four days, just wonderful," Frederickton griped.

"Could we not just approach under cloak and launch a few dozen high-yield quantum warheads instead?" Jackson asked.

"Unfortunately, no, we cannot," Alpha135 responded. "The Insectoids have extremely sophisticated sensor arrays in both systems, as I mentioned, and any quantum signatures would be detected. In fact, both vessels will need to have some of their armaments removed and their hyperdrives and quantum cores shut down for this mission to ensure that there is nothing that the array will detect while you make your approach."

"Oh, this just keeps getting better and better," Frederickton chimed in. "So, not only are we going on a suicide mission, but we need to be almost completely unarmed going in? Why don't we just park a few dozen dreadnoughts at the edge of the system and bombard the hell out of the shipyards from afar?"

"Both systems are deep within Insectoid territory. The RE-13 system is thirteen thousand light-years from here, and the MK-291 system is six thousand, four hundred light-years from the GCH border. We would have to commit multiple fleets to push that far into enemy territory and would sustain heavy losses in the process. Likewise, it is simply too great of a distance to launch an assault from afar," Alpha135 responded.

"There's also the issue with the mysterious dampening field the Imperium's been using," Admiral Scott interjected. "We have to get up close and personal for this mission to succeed."

"Thirteen thousand light-years, that will take, what, just over thirty days at maximum speed in hyperspace to reach?" Jackson asked. "That's a long time to be traveling in Imperium territory and deeper than anyone has ever gone before, by a longshot. Plus, we'll need to stop and take new astrometric readings every few hundred light-years."

"That's correct; however, this is one area where I do have some good news," Admiral Scott said. "Alpha135."

"We will be retrofitting both the *Phoenix* and the *Sulavar* with an experimental dimensional-shift slipstream drive over the next two days and conducting a shakedown test on the third. These drives will get you there in one-eighth the time by opening a portal to a sub-dimension with different physical properties than our own and traveling through it until you reach the corresponding egress point. The drives have been in development for the past seven years at the GCH Experimental Propulsion Lab on Delconia and have been successfully field-tested for the past three months."

"Better and better," Frederickton mumbled, shaking his head.

"Why is there such a short timeline, sir?" Jackson asked. "Shouldn't we take more time for an op this important?"

"I wish there was more time, Jackson. Unfortunately, based on the intel you provided, there is a large number of the new advanced warships nearing completion, and their fleet operations data shows that they'll be departing in just over nine days. With only four days to prep and your journey of three and a half days to get there in slipstream, we risk arriving after most of the new ships have already left. We have to strike now for this plan to work and to keep those ships from joining the rest of the Imperium forces. Our intel suggests there are fifty ships in various stages of completion in each system. Those ships are simply too powerful, and if we allow them to get away and join the rest of the Imperium forces, they will significantly shift the balance of power. We have to act before they launch."

"Yes, sir," Jackson said, knowing the admiral was right. The new advanced warships were formidable, and many coming off the line all at once would be a significant influx of military hardware.

"All right, everyone, we only have four days to get this all together. The team from the EPL will be here at 1100 hours to install the new drives, so we need to get to work on our part. Jackson, you're with Ensign Jones, Lieutenant Gaspari, and Commander Kennedy. Frederickton, you're with Lieutenant Henderson and Commander Salmon. They'll brief you on the details of your individual mission packages so that you can memorize them and work with your AIs on logistics. We'll meet back here at 0800 tomorrow to work on the extraction plan. Dismissed," the admiral said.

Jackson and Ensign Jones, along with Lieutenant Gaspari and Commander Kennedy, fell in together, heading down the hallway towards another, smaller conference room, where they began looking over his mission package. A feeling of tension began building in Jackson's neck and shoulders as the weight of the task ahead settled on him, focusing his mind and blocking out all other thoughts of his friends that had been floating around his head for the past few days.

This could be a pivotal turning point in the war and a chance to make a real difference.

It was time to buckle down and get the job done.

CHAPTER 3
LAST BREATH

HELSINKI, FINLAND
EARTH 2023

Gray clouds swept in from the west across the city early that morning, their growing darkness a forewarning of the storm to come.

Jackson rolled over, smiling as he looked at Amy, his wife, sleeping peacefully next to him. She breathed slow and steady breaths, her eyelids fluttering softly, a small murmur escaping her lips while she dreamed, stirring slightly. Jackson studied the contours of her face, a smile creeping across his lips as his eyes drifted, taking in every detail. The way a few strands of her hair fell across her cheek. The gentle rise of her cheekbones. The soft curves of her lips.

He was happy to let her sleep in, cherishing that she was finally getting some rest, knowing that she'd need her strength for the trials that lay ahead.

Amy's cancer had been extremely aggressive, and even though they had caught it relatively early, the doctors held little hope. Despite their pessimism, she had battled valiantly for over a year, taking part in experimental clinical trials, trying various naturopathic treatments, and undergoing several rounds of chemo.

Undeterred, the cancer continued to grow and spread, seemingly unstoppable.

Late one sleepless night, while scouring the internet in desperation, Jackson had come across a medical blog featuring a doctor from Finland who had developed a highly experimental procedure. After several tense days of email exchanges, and sharing her medical records, the doctor confirmed that Amy was indeed a suitable candidate and agreed to operate if she consented.

Less than a week later, they flew to Finland, arriving three days before the surgery's scheduled date. The late August weather in Helsinki was perfect for exploring, and despite being constantly tired, Amy was hell-bent on doing as much as possible. They filled their first two days walking the streets, taking in the sights, sipping coffee in outdoor cafés, and exploring the city's museums. At night, they lay in bed, cradled in each other's arms, talking of all of the things that they wanted to do once she was better. Of how they would live their lives differently once this was over. Travel. Downsize. Start a family.

The morning of the third day, Jackson sat at the desk in their hotel room, scouring the room service menu for something special, knowing Amy wouldn't be able to eat again until after the surgery just over twenty-four hours later.

The thought weighed heavily on him that this could be her last meal, and he wanted to make it just right.

"To hell with it!" she announced exuberantly as she headed to the shower. "I'm having bacon…two orders of bacon, in fact. All for me!" She smiled, mischievous. "Oh, and sausage too. And pancakes with blueberries *and* chocolate chips!"

Jackson smiled as he picked up the phone. "Consider it done!"

The day flew by as they walked the city streets and parks, heading back to the hotel for an afternoon nap, Amy's exhaustion catching up with her. After she awoke, Jackson surprised her with an evening cruise around the harbor taking in the sights and attempting to keep themselves occupied, neither wanting to think about the next day or the growing hunger they both felt as he joined her in fasting.

That night, they made love as the light from the full moon crept into their room, taking it slow, exploring and enjoying each other as though they had all the time in the world.

They awoke early the next morning, lying in silence, their bodies entwined, neither one wanting to speak, to break the spell that they were the only two people in the world, to make the day real.

An hour later, they left the hotel in somber silence. Amy pulled on Jackson's arm, directing him across the street, leading him on a short walk in the city's central park, reveling in the crisp coolness of the early morning air. They sat on a bench holding hands and taking in the sights and sounds around them. He glanced at his phone, knowing they needed to head to the clinic soon, while trying not to rush her and ruin the moment.

Time seemed to stop while they sat, Jackson putting his arm around her, the breeze blowing gently through the trees while small birds sang softly, flitting about, looking for seeds. The dark clouds above parted for a moment, Amy closing her eyes and basking in the warmth of the sun, gently squeezing his hand and hoping that the moment wouldn't end.

The gap in the clouds closed once more, the chill in the air now suddenly unwelcome, breaking the spell. Amy stood abruptly a moment later, catching him off guard. "All right," she said, resigned to what needed to be done. "Let's go."

Jackson held the door as they entered the tinted-glass building, stepping into the small lobby of the clinic. He signed them in at the reception desk, while Amy took off her jacket and stood staring at a print of Van Gogh's *Starry Night over the Rhône*, which hung on the wall.

He wrapped his arms around her, their hands inseparable as they waited, her head tipped back on his shoulder, and the smell of her hair filling his senses.

A nurse arrived a few moments later, leading them into a patient intake room where she instructed Amy to sit before she pointed Jackson down the hall.

He turned, hugging her tightly, then kissing her forehead, pulling her in once more, not wanting to let go.

"It's going to be okay," she said, pulling back as she gave him a weak smile.

"That's what I'm supposed to say," he replied, his sad smile mirroring hers. "I'll be right there with you the entire time. The doctor said I can hold your hand," he added, a lump forming in his throat as he said the words, knowing they could be the last he ever said to her. "I love you, Amy." He leaned in, giving her a tender kiss on the lips. "Forever and for always."

"I love you too. Forever and for always," she replied, a tear streaking down her cheek as a nurse came over, ushering him away. Another nurse met him a moment later and instructed him to scrub his hands thoroughly, then helped him to gown up, while several other staff worked to prepare Amy.

Minutes passed while Jackson waited outside the operating room, the grumbling in his stomach replaced by a growing feeling of dread. The surgical team arrived a few moments later, entering the room and beginning the last of the preparations. Finally, after what felt like an eternity, they wheeled Amy in on a rolling bed, his heart dropping in his chest as he saw her.

As he looked at her, it was as though he was seeing her for the first time. His beloved wife, the love of his life, suddenly so frail and weak. How had he not noticed? How had she diminished so, right in front of him?

An IV line extended from her wrist to a drip bag that one of the nurses carried, hanging it up on a stand. Wires extended from her arms and chest connected to a rolling stand of monitors beeping steadily as they tracked her vitals. A wave of fear and clarity, like a shot of adrenaline, suddenly hit him, grounding him. Telling him that this was a defining moment in his life. One that he would remember forever.

He watched and waited while the team worked, moving her to the operating table while they finished their preparations, the doctors entering a few moments later, quickly reviewing to confirm that everything was in order. Jackson held his breath, waiting until the lead surgeon then waved to him to enter the room.

Jackson's eyes met Amy's as time stopped for the briefest of moments, each of them longing to say everything left unsaid between them. Knowing that the time had passed. That what they'd each said in the days and hours leading up to this moment would have to be enough.

A nurse put a hand on Jackson's shoulder, guiding him to a seat next to Amy, near the foot of the operating table, out of the way while the doctors worked on her head where the largest and most critical tumor was located. He leaned forward, taking her hand and squeezing it gently, assuring her that he was with her and that it would be okay, as she gave him a squeeze back. The sedatives took hold a moment later, putting her under, and her grip slackened, his hand remaining as he refused to let go. Wanting her to know that he was with her always.

Jackson sat silently, terrified to make even the slightest sound while the doctors and the rest of the surgical team worked, speaking mostly in Finnish as they began the procedure. An hour passed in agony as he watched on the monitor. Amy's vital signs dropped slightly while they worked, the team approaching the most critical point in the surgery, where time would be a key factor.

He gave her hand the gentlest of squeezes, assuring her of his presence once more while he lowered his head, mouthing a silent prayer. An unexpected alert from the metronome-like monitors pulled him back into the moment, and he looked up, Amy's blood pressure and heart rate dropping rapidly.

The mood in the room shifted instantly. The doctors and their team worked frantically, calling out in Finnish as they darted around the room, injecting her with drugs and adjusting several of the machines. Jackson held on to her hand, feeling her pulse slowing while the beeping from the machines became more and more erratic.

The spiked lines representing her heartbeat grew smaller and farther between while her blood pressure dropped off.

A single palpitation passed under her soft skin, beneath his finger, and he stretched it out to touch the inside of her wrist to feel it more clearly.

The last beating of her heart pulsed, another failing to follow, as the noise from the monitors became a single, pronounced, and ominous tone.

All the pain and fear, the pure hell she'd fought valiantly through for the past year, it all came crashing down as everything ended…as she slipped away while he held her hand.

The last beat of her heart for him alone.

A nurse came rushing over, instructing him to leave the room while they worked. He moved numbly, standing on the other side of the door a moment later, staring through the window in disbelief while they tried for several minutes to resuscitate her.

Time lost all meaning as the precious seconds ticked by and his hope faded. Tears streamed down his face, as the dam he'd been desperately holding back finally shattered.

He looked down at the ring on his finger, adrift in the current of his emotions and memories flooding his mind, his heart breaking as his world crumbled around him.

After a while – how long it had been, he had no idea – a nurse came by, taking him to a room with a comfortable couch and handing him a glass of cold water while he sat numbly staring at the wall. The lead doctor entered the room a short time later, offering his deepest condolences while he explained what had happened. The words sounded hollow, as though he were listening to people speaking in a distant room. When he finished, Jackson shook the doctor's hand, thanking him for trying and doing his best.

After the doctor left, another nurse arrived, carrying forms for him to sign as she explained that they had taken care of everything. Arrangements had been made in advance, in case the worst had happened. Amy's body would be certified by a medical examiner later that afternoon, receiving special permission to fly her home.

Jackson went back to the hotel and slept, the emotional drain and sheer exhaustion overwhelming him. He awoke hours later, his face tilted towards Amy's pillow, the smell of her hair still lingering ever so slightly as he replayed the image of her from earlier that morning, his mind grappling with the impossible; that she was now gone.

The next morning, he boarded a flight to Montreal, where he stayed with Amy's family for a few days while the final funeral arrangements were made. Her parents lived nearby in the Outremont part of Montreal, and she wanted to be buried in their family plot at the Notre-Dame-des-Neiges cemetery, not far from where she grew up. When they used to visit for holidays, they would often walk through the cemetery, the beautiful, peaceful space filled with trees, fields of grass, walking paths and gently rolling hills. Ornate statues and obelisks adorned the cemetery, while a long laneway, lined with family crypts, gave it a unique old-world feeling.

It pained Jackson to think that she would be so far away, but their life, his life, was back in Toronto, just over five hundred kilometers away, and he knew he couldn't stay long after the funeral. He debated quitting his job and moving to Montreal to be closer to her, but knew deep down that it wasn't rational. His family was there, his friends. He had a good career. A good life. The thought of leaving their home filled him with a terrible emptiness as he struggled with what to do next, adrift without her there to anchor him.

The funeral came swiftly as the days leading up to it bled into one another. Friends and family offered their condolences and support. Her parents and sister praised him for everything he'd done for her and how he'd supported her through her terrible illness. As they spoke, he felt a numbness growing inside, going through the motions, but nothing feeling real.

He returned to Toronto the day after the funeral, then after a few more days, went back to work. As the next few weeks passed, he blocked out the rest of the world, working long hours as he tried to keep busy. He left everything of hers exactly as it had been at home, unable to bear the thought of getting rid of any of it. As he lay in bed at night, the faintest traces of her shampoo still lingering in her pillow, he cradled it as he wept softly for a time; his heart shattered as he fell asleep.

As the days wore on, he found himself staring off into the distance more and more, lost in thought. A sound snapped him out of it as his world came crashing back down, the harsh reality hitting him once more, remembering that she was gone.

He made the trip back to Montreal each weekend to visit her grave, longing to be with her. The first time, he stayed at Amy's parents' house, and they were happy to have him, but by the time he left on Sunday, he knew that he couldn't go back. It was still too raw, too painful for all of them, and him being there, alone, only amplified her absence as her parents struggled to cope with the loss of their daughter.

During the next several trips, he stayed in a hotel, keeping a low profile and giving her family space. He spent his time wandering the streets of old Montreal, visiting many of the shops and cafés that they used to frequent together. Each Saturday, he bought her fresh flowers, then sat by her grave for hours telling her about what was happening in his life and how he missed her.

Amy had been gone for nearly a month when Jackson finally took a trip up to his family's cabin, breaking his weekend routine. His despair, pressing down like a weight upon his chest, had grown with each passing day, and he knew that he needed a change of scenery. He'd hoped that the peace and tranquility of getting back to nature could help him heal.

It was a beautiful, late-September afternoon when he arrived at the cabin, the first signs of fall beginning to show on the trees as brilliant reds, oranges, and yellows mixed with the fading greens of summer. The lake was quiet, as was typical for that time of year, and he was grateful for the solitude. He stared out at the lake, the sun shining down on the calm blue water while he stood on the dock, the glittering ripples filling his senses.

After settling in, he spent most of the day doing chores, keeping his body and mind occupied and happy to feel a sense of accomplishment after weeks of feeling useless. A powerful storm had blown through the week before, taking down a number of large branches and one small tree, then blowing over some of the outdoor furniture, scattering it across the lawn. His work complete, he decided to take an afternoon nap, leaving the window open a crack as a soft autumn breeze lulled him to sleep.

He awoke and made dinner, sitting out on the deck with a glass of wine, watching as the sun set over the lake, the breathtaking view never failing to impress. Jackson let out a long breath as the sun slipped below the horizon, feeling at peace for the first time in weeks.

After the sun went down, he poured himself another glass, followed by several more, the bottle emptying in short order. He sat in silence, watching the stars come out, cracking a beer while he listened to the sounds of insects and frogs coming to life in the twilight. Three beers later, he stumbled into the kitchen, looking for something different to drink, unable to decide what he wanted this time around.

Gin and tonic, perhaps? Maybe some scotch?

A bottle rested high on a nearby shelf, catching his eye, the memory of Amy giving it to him earlier that spring for his birthday coming to the surface. She wasn't supposed to drink, but it was her favorite, and she'd indulged in just a wee nip that weekend, something special to savor while they both celebrated being there for his birthday.

The bottle remained exactly where she'd left it, the image of her flashing in his mind, a mischievous smile across her face as she placed the bottle on the shelf, handing him a tumbler.

He walked over, gently pulling the bottle down. Amy's faded fingerprint lingered on the glass as he held it up to the light. He pulled it close, cradling the bottle in his arms, the pain rushing back as tears fell for the first time in nearly a week.

He wiped them away, then he poured two small glasses, raising the first, then clinking it with the second, swallowing it in a single gulp. "Here's to you, Aims," he said, his voice cracking as he spoke her name, holding the second glass up to the light to study its color.

Time slipped past while he savored the next sip, the smoky aftertaste lingering on his tongue while the burn trickled down his throat. He was about to reach for the second glass, when a faint light outside caught his attention. Jackson stumbled over to the kitchen window, looking out as a shimmer rippled on the surface of the water. "Hmph, that's weird."

Carefully, he made his way out to the front deck, overlooking the lake, the faint blue light glowing from beneath the surface, the water above rippling softly. He looked up, the moon nowhere to be seen, nor were there any other lights visible on the lake.

Jackson rubbed his bloodshot eyes, trying to focus through the haze of alcohol. "What the hell?" he muttered, stroking the rough beard he'd let run rampant on his chin for the past week. "It's coming from *under* the water."

He downed the second tumbler of scotch and set the glass down on the railing, then staggered down to the dock, nearly tripping twice, the scotch suddenly hitting him hard.

Jackson climbed into the boat tied to the dock, attempting to start the small outboard, the engine stubbornly not turning over, the effort causing his head to throb.

Undeterred, he walked back up to shore, dragging the canoe down through the damp grass to the water's edge, then retrieved a paddle from the boat.

He stepped into the canoe, careful to keep his balance, then took a seat in the stern, paddling out past the dock, towards the spot where the light had been. The canoe moved farther out, circling while he searched for the mysterious glow, wondering if it had been an optical illusion of some kind.

The dark water swirled with each stroke of his paddle as he looked back at the shore, estimating to the best of his drunken ability the spot where the light had been. He looked back up at the cabin, the flickering glow of dim candlelight illuminating the interior, attempting once more to judge the distance from where his glass still rested on the railing.

This is the right spot, or pretty damn close, he thought, *but where the hell is that weird light?*

He was about to turn around and go back, when he looked up, the stars stretching from horizon to horizon, the universe unfolding before him in all its glory.

"Whoa," he said in awe, his head tilted up at an uncomfortable angle, attempting to take it all in. He slid forward off the seat, lying back on it, carefully putting his feet up on the center yoke while he rested his arms on the gunnel, folding his hands behind his head, the canoe teetering slightly.

The sky looked like something from a movie, the brilliant swath of the Milky Way crisscrossing the heavens, its luminance breathtaking as he stared up, humbled by the immensity of the vast cosmos spread out before him. His mind drifted as satellites passed by on their orbital transits, their dim lights flashing as they made their way across his field of view. Shooting stars streaked across the sky, often several within a few seconds of one another, causing his heart to race with excitement, his alone to behold on the otherwise empty lake.

Several constellations appeared high above, their brightness separating them from the tapestry of pinpricks in the darkness, although Jackson quickly realized that he was far too drunk to properly connect the dots or recall their celestial names aside from the easily recognizable Big Dipper. Time froze as he looked up at the stars, wondering if somewhere up there, Amy was looking back down on him. In that moment, his mind drifted, and he felt a strange connection to her – imagined or something else, he couldn't say.

He closed his eyes, remembering how they'd often stayed out late on the deck at night, lying on a lounger, wrapped up in a blanket and each other, staring up at those same stars together. As the memories came flooding back, Jackson felt a tear stream down his cheek, then another, the stars blurring.

He sat up, wiping his eyes, the motion rocking the canoe sharply as he felt it tipping to his right. His arms flailed, attempting to compensate, but he was too late, his center of gravity too far to one side, his balance impaired by copious amounts of alcohol in his system. In what felt like slow motion, the canoe slowly tipped over, and Jackson fell into the cool late-September water.

He trod water, laughing at his foolishness while he tried to right the canoe, the task proving to be too difficult in his drunken state. "I guess I'm swimming back." He smiled as he looked up, a brilliant shooting star streaking across the heavens above pulling his eyes back to the cosmic light show.

He relaxed, leaning back, his feet rising as he floated, his hands moving in small circles at his sides. He lay there, staring up at the heavens, the cool water sobering him up somewhat.

Slowly, he let the air out of his chest, taking a deep breath to center himself, sinking deeper as he did. He sucked in another breath, rising once more, the sensation of near weightlessness taking hold as he repeated breathing in and back out again, enjoying the simple pleasure of it. In and out. In and out… Slowly, Jackson began to sink deeper, taking only a small breath this time as his legs slipped from the surface of the water, dangling beneath him. Only his face remained above the surface while he swirled his arms gently to keep himself afloat. He took another small breath, then stopped moving his arms, his face sinking beneath the surface.

He gently slipped down, until he was just a few inches below the surface, coming back up and taking another breath before drifting back down again, farther this time, the cool water invigorating. As he descended, the outline of the canoe became clear, illuminated by the light of the Milky Way.

Just as he was about to come up for air, a thought came to him, genuine, pure, and unfiltered, hitting him like a revelation, as suddenly everything became crystal clear. In that moment, he knew what it was he wanted more than anything else… *Amy.*

He longed to be with her. To gaze upon the radiance of her smile. To stare into the deep blue depths of her eyes.

Jackson felt himself slipping away, the urge tugging at him. The thought that, perhaps, he could be with her again if he just let go…

No! Not like this. The thought hit him like a sledgehammer.

He couldn't face her if he died like this. She never gave up, and he sure as hell wasn't about to either.

He kicked his legs as he rose, his body close to the surface, when suddenly, the water rushed around him. The brilliant blue light appeared once again, pulling him down towards it.

Jackson fought against the whirlpool, helpless as he thrashed against the powerful current. He kicked and pulled with all of his might, desperation taking over as his air ran low, his strength fading. He struggled against the overwhelming current, fighting with everything he had as he attempted to escape, the undertow dragging him down, down into the depths.

A hum echoed throughout the water, its intensity growing, the power of the light's pull increasing as Jackson struggled against it in futility.

The last of his breath spent, a thin stream of bubbles rose to the surface as the light in the water engulfed him, his body twitching as he gasped for air one last time. His instincts screamed out, telling him to fight, to survive! The words *Do not go gentle into that good night* flashed in his mind.

But it was over now. The light had him, water flowing freely into his lungs as a feeling of euphoria overtook his senses.

The canoe looked far away now, as far as the stars themselves. His body convulsed as he sucked in water, desperate for air as his consciousness faded, his vision slowly growing darker. His eyes closed, pulling him into the darkness, his mind focused on a single thought as he slipped into oblivion.

Amy.

CHAPTER 4
A BAD IDEA

This is a bad idea.

The thought kept racing through Jackson's mind over and over.

For the past two and a half days, the team at FoxBlind had been working around the clock on an extraction plan to get them off the Insectoid battleships in one piece, but thus far they hadn't come up with anything viable.

Jackson was in the IRC, running another failed simulation, when a thought suddenly hit him. *What if there's simply no way out alive? What if we're going about this all wrong?*

He spent the next six hours in the IRC while he and Bits worked on the idea, contacting Johansen over subspace to get his thoughts, then deciding to take them back to the team. Later that night, Jackson called a meeting with Admiral Scott and his senior staff, along with Frederickton and Alpha135.

"Hi, everyone, thank you all for coming," Jackson began. "So, I'll get right to it. I had a crazy thought this morning about how we could get out of there in one piece. We go with the plan we've created thus far, but we add a cargo matter transporter to each ship and use it to beam ourselves off the battleships after we initiate the quantum core overloads," he said, pausing, anticipating the looks of rejection that quickly appeared on each of their faces.

Before anyone could utter their objections, he pushed forward. "Now I know that CMTs are not designed for transporting a person and that it's never been successfully done, but hear me out. They *can* transport simple organic matter such as fruits and vegetables, right? So, what's the problem with transporting a person?" He paused once more, jumping back in before anyone could respond. "It's that a person isn't just a static object, they're a living organism, with tens of thousands of moving parts from blood cells to bacteria to electrical impulses in the brain. But what's the real problem?" he asked, his eyes scanning the room as he met each of theirs.

"The real problem is ultimately that this complexity can't simply be paused. *Not* the technical ability of the CMT to transport a person from one place to another. But imagine if we *could* pause it… Then we could transport a person from one point to another without any issues.

"Now I know this sounds insane, but I bounced the idea off a friend of mine who works at a classified tech lab at the Institute for Technology on Delconia, and we think we have a working solution. Here's what I'm thinking," he said, continuing to outline his plan to the group and bringing up the details on the holo-display.

He took a seat after he concluded, staring at the faces of disbelief around the table, noting that Frederickton, in particular, clearly didn't like the idea.

"All right, does anyone have anything better?" Admiral Scott asked.

"Couldn't we use a portal instead?" Frederickton asked.

"No good," Jackson replied. "I thought of that too, and my AI ran tens of thousands of simulations. The reality is, a portal is too easy to disrupt and takes about ten seconds to establish a connection, giving the Imperium's automated portal defense systems time to activate. If we could get out before that, we might be okay, but all it takes is the system activating and creating a particle scattering field – standard Imperium portal defense tech – and it's all over. We'll have tipped our hand, and they'll know we're there. Even worse, because it has a fixed point on either end, the Insectoids could use it to lock on to our ships, leaving us stranded on the battleship while they targeted our only means of escape. The cargo matter transporter, on the other hand, can move an object from point A to point B without being tracked."

"What about the energy signature?" Frederickton asked. "If they can track a portal, they can track a CMT."

"Yes and no," Jackson said. "It can track the energy spike from a CMT, but if we park our ships right below a nearby battleship with an active power core, we can hide in the electromagnetic shadow it creates."

"Couldn't you just do the same with a portal though?" Commander Kennedy asked. "Hide under a battleship and use it to mask the egress point?"

"We could try to figure it out, but we ran the sims, and the short answer is no. The same EM field will also disrupt a portal. The bottom line is this: If we lose the element of surprise, we're done for. I feel that CMT, despite the risks, is rock-solid technology and is our best bet to get the job done."

Frederickton shook his head. "I don't like it," he said firmly.

"Believe me, I don't either," Jackson admitted. "But we're on a clock, and it's the best worst idea I've got."

"Very well," Admiral Scott said. "It's nearly 2300 hours, and it's been a long couple of days. Everyone, get some rack time and sleep on it. We'll reconvene at 0800 tomorrow."

The next morning, Admiral Scott stood at the head of the table. "Well, let's cut right to it. Does anyone else have a better idea?"

The room was silent.

"Very well then, we proceed with Commander Jackson's plan. Both ships have had the new slipstream drives installed and are heading out for field testing today. Our operational window is rapidly closing, and we launch tomorrow, so let's get to work."

Jackson and Frederickton spent the next ten hours running simulations in the IRC for their specific mission parameters, taking breaks to monitor the other's progress, and offering advice and feedback. After fifteen solid hours at it, they felt as though they had the best possible plan for a highly imperfect op, deciding to call it a night.

Jackson spent a few hours before going to bed recording messages for each of his friends to be sent in the event that he didn't return within the next ten days, trying to find the words to tell each of them how much they meant to him. He'd recorded messages in the past, just in case, but they'd never felt real before. Not like the looming feeling of this op. The sense of finality hung in the air as he recorded each one.

He recorded messages for Dr. Penfeld, Michaels, McArthur, Morgan, Accari, Beratus, Vorallas, and Captain Delgado, sharing with each of them what they meant to him.

Next, he created messages for Admirals Lighton and Thompson, thanking them for everything they'd done for him. He considered creating a message for Admiral Janus, but decided against it, uncertain what, if anything, he could say.

For Vees and the crew back at Kishara Station, he wished them all well, telling them honestly how serving with them had been the best time of his life.

He then moved on to the crew of the *Phoenix*. To Daria, he told her how her passion for science and unwavering optimism had always inspired him, thanking her again for everything she'd done for Verris. To Johansen, he expressed how much he appreciated having a friend, someone that he could talk to about everything, especially in those first few years when he didn't have anyone else. He left him a list of Earth movies, music, and TV to be sure to check out, smiling as he thought of his friend, pouring a beer for him in his absence.

To Kelara, he told her how much he admired her strength and appreciated all the combat and training tips she'd given him. He added, hesitantly at first, but then emphatically as he got going, that no matter what this war brought, she needed to make sure that she didn't lose herself. That she always remembered how much she meant to her friends and how proud he knew her father would be of the woman she'd become.

To Admiral Valentyen, he thanked him for being a mentor and a surrogate father to him. For the trust and faith that he had placed in him, and for bringing their team together and for his forgiveness after everything that happened when he'd gone rogue.

Finally, he worked up his nerve, recording a message to Verris. "Hey, Ver," he said softly, attempting to hide the nervousness in his voice. "I hope that you never have to see this, but if you do, then it means that things went wrong on an op, and I'm dead. I wanted to tell you how much I've missed you this past year and a half, but despite having access to over forty-five thousand languages, there just doesn't seem to be words to adequately tell you how I feel." He paused, looking down for a moment. "I miss you."

He looked back up, facing the screen. "Not a day goes by that I don't think of you. The time we had together was the best time of my life. You completed me in ways I could never have imagined. You're my best friend, and the love of my life," he said, feeling a sting of guilt as he thought of Amy for a moment, knowing the same had been true about her. He'd loved Amy with all of his heart, but what he had with Verris was different, a new love for a new life. It was impossible to compare the two, but he knew that his love for Verris went right to his core, just as it had with Amy. He dwelled on the pang of guilt in his heart for a moment before snapping out of it, realizing he was still recording. "I'll always be with you. Always." He smiled, blowing her a kiss. "I love you. Goodbye."

The next morning, the team met in the briefing room one last time, reviewing the plan in every detail before the admiral wished them good luck and dismissed them. Jackson and Frederickton walked together towards the hangar bay, stopping briefly before going their separate ways to their respective berths.

"Jackson, you're one crazy son of a bitch," Frederickton said, extending his hand.

Jackson smiled, always finding it funny how some phrases seemed to transcend any one planet, appearing over and over in humanoid cultures.

Frederickton continued, smiling. "But you've got one hell of an imagination, I'll give you that," he said as he shook Jackson's hand.

"Thanks, Cap," Jackson replied. "Be safe out there, okay? Let's both get back from this and have a drink to how utterly stupid this idea was."

"Sounds like a plan to me. Catch you in the next life, Commander."

"Same to you, Captain."

Catch you in the next life. Another common phrase in the GCH, the belief of reincarnation lending itself to a few such colloquialisms. While Jackson had come to believe in the concept, he truly hoped that despite the overwhelming odds, they would live to see each other again in *this* life.

Minutes later, he boarded the *Phoenix*, checking everything one last time, then making his way to the bridge. Alpha135 sat waiting for him, statue-like in the operations chair with his eyes closed, another android waiting on the *Sulavar* for Frederickton.

Alpha135's eyes opened as he detected Jackson's presence. "Are you ready to proceed, Commander?"

"As ready as I'll ever be. Are you all set?"

"All systems are fully functional."

"Good stuff. Let's get this done."

The *Phoenix* powered up, taking off from FoxBlind a moment later. Jackson piloted the ship and set a heading, then, once they reached a safe distance from the planet, initiated the inter-dimensional slipstream drive.

The ship appeared to slowly stretch for a moment, then vanished in an instant, leaving no flash of light, as with hyperspace travel. One second, the *Phoenix* was there, and the next it simply was not.

Slipstream had a strange feel to it, he noted, as if time was somehow distorted, if only for a few seconds after they jumped. The techs who'd installed the drive had prepared him for it, but it was still unnerving.

He moved his hand, holding it in front of his face while he studied it, unable to quantify what was wrong. Curious, he snapped his fingers, the sound delayed slightly before it reached his ears, the distortion effect fading a moment later as time seemed to return to normal.

Jackson activated the external cameras, running multiband sensor sweeps. The cameras showed darkness outside with faint hints of multicolored light which appeared like a shimmer in the distance, both there and not there. The ship's sensors showed they were moving, their velocity increasing as the slipstream drive continued to grow in power. He turned away from the sensors, focusing on the image on the main viewscreen, the faint colors dancing and fading like an aurora.

Jackson took a deep breath, pushing away the thoughts and doubts in his mind as he forged ahead, knowing this mission would test him beyond his limits.

He had to be ready.

Too much was at stake for him to fail.

CHAPTER 5
RE-13

The *Phoenix* exited slipstream just over three and a half days later in the RE-13 System, deep within Imperium space. Jackson engaged the cloak, wasting no time in running a quick passive scan to check for enemy ships while he sat on high alert at the helm.

"Bits, are we where we're supposed to be?"

"Affirmative. We appear to be in the RE-13 System, approximately two-point-three million kilometers from the local star."

The team at FoxBlind had carefully chosen the point of egress: close to the star RE-13 and on the opposite side from the Imperium shipyard and sensor array in order to avoid detection.

Still, there were no guarantees about what would be waiting there for them.

"Good work, buddy. I'll plot a course for the shipyard while you launch the comms probe. Set it to cloak as soon as it's clear, and instruct it to move to an optimal transmission location, then go into hibernation mode and stand by for our signal. After that, power down everything nonessential, including the main power core and flip to auxiliary, then rig the ship for maximum stealth. We need to slip past that sensor array undetected, or this is all for nothing."

"Acknowledged," Bits responded as he launched the probe, then proceeded to power down the various ship systems while Jackson calculated a course to circumnavigate the sun on auxiliary power, putting some distance between it and them to ensure that the star didn't interfere with the cloak.

"How are we doing so far, Alpha?" Jackson asked.

"All systems nominal. I am tied into the ship's sensor and optical arrays, running passive scans and analyzing all relevant data as it becomes available."

"Okay, let me know if anything of interest comes up. I want to know if that sensor array so much as twitches."

"Affirmative, Commander."

"Any signs of the dampening tech the Imperium's been using?"

"Negative. It likely has not been deployed yet this deep inside Imperium space," Alpha responded.

"Makes sense. Tactically, why waste resources this far back from the lines when the war is thousands of light-years from here?"

Hours passed by as the ship rounded the sun. Jackson adjusted their course several times as the *Phoenix* crept through the RE-13 system, keeping the stealth drive to one-quarter speed to minimize its energy signature.

He studied the growing map of the system fed by the passive and optical scans as it filled out the holo-display in real time. The shipyard orbited the sixth planet, out past the rocky inner worlds and icy asteroid belt, the journey there taking eight hours, with help from Alpha135, who optimized their route, allowing them to use gravity assists from two of the inner planets, cutting the time down by several hours.

Jackson sat at the helm the entire time, watching the viewscreen and holo-display while they moved through the system, ready for anything. Insectoid patrols, mostly frigates and destroyers of older classes, crisscrossed the system in squadrons of five, forcing them to avoid anything that could render the ship detectable, even if just for a split second. They slipped through the layers of security patrols and sensor buoys, their own sensor range and data limited, requiring him to make several last-minute course corrections to avoid pockets of radiation, small patches of micrometeorites, and heavier concentrations of interstellar dust that obstructed their path.

As they passed a few million kilometers from the fourth planet, a steady stream of hundreds of small cargo vessels appeared on their sensors. "What are they up to?" he asked.

"The planet is an L4 class, providing a naturally hospitable environment for Insectoid life. I would speculate, based on the high concentrations of oxygen, carbon dioxide, and methane in the atmosphere, that there are a massive number of lifeforms on the surface, likely to provide food for their fleet," Bits replied.

"This conforms to known Imperium supply-management operations," Alpha135 interjected. "The GCH has documented dozens of worlds which have been transformed on a planetwide scale to serve as industrial food-processing facilities."

"That makes sense. I always wondered how they were able to supply so many ships," Jackson said, realizing that his jaw ached from clenching it for the past several hours.

Finally, they approached the sixth planet, a massive ice giant with six icy rings around it, the white-and-purple coloring giving it an ominous appearance. He stood, taking a moment to stretch, finding the rest of his body equally tense as he stared ahead, mindful of the mission clock.

Jackson took a slow, deep breath, attempting to calm his nerves. Despite being a veteran of thirty-five wartime solo covert ops, he found that it never got easier. He closed his eyes, focusing on his training, thinking back to Captain Delgado and the lessons he'd learned all those years ago. The thought of his time on Talzon III and the decades of experience his mentor had shared with him giving him a boost. Despite being a terrible ordeal at the time, thinking back now, it brought him a sense of comfort. It had forced him to learn his craft well, and he carried a quiet confidence that no matter what came his way, he had the tools and skills to figure it out.

He exhaled, opening his eyes and taking two more slow, methodical breaths to relax, then ran through a series of calisthenics to loosen his muscles, all the while keeping a close eye on the sensors.

"Sitrep," he said, breaking the silence for what felt like the first time in hours.

"All systems are functioning at optimal levels," Bits replied.

"The sixth planet is four hundred and sixty thousand kilometers ahead," Alpha135 responded. "The shipyard and sensor array are on the opposite side. I recommend a polar transit."

"Right, the bugs tend to think more in two dimensions."

"Precisely. Their defenses are likely deployed in higher concentrations around the center of the planet as opposed to above or below it."

"Altering course," Jackson said, taking them over the top of the ice giant while gradually reducing their speed. The ship passed over the pole of the planet, the viewscreen displaying an image of the three massive hurricanes raging below, each larger than the Earth itself, spinning at thousands of kilometers per hour.

The *Phoenix* began its downward trajectory, Jackson cutting their engines and allowing them to drift out from the planet to get a better perspective while the shipyard and other structures slowly appeared below, providing them with a bird's-eye view as they spread around the center of the planet and out towards the rings. He adjusted their course, putting them in a high geosynchronous orbit, while they studied the Insectoid structures and defenses, collecting all the data they could.

"Bits, put the shipyard up on the main viewscreen and feed all sensor data to the holo-display. I want to see everything."

The shipyard appeared a moment later, hovering around the massive ice giant. It was an impressive sight, a grayish white and shaped like a crescent moon twenty kilometers long and two hundred and fifty meters high. Construction berths ran along the outer edge, while hundreds of supply bays made up the inner side. Small supply ships came and went, docking with the station, delivering their cargo, then heading back to other points in the system on seemingly endless runs as they fed the Imperium's insatiable war machine.

"The shipyard has one hundred and forty berths in total. All but twenty of them are in the process of building new, advanced Imperium battleships," Bits reported.

"Damn. That's way more than the fifty we expected. A hundred and twenty of those ships would be devastating."

"Agreed. I've also detected new classes of frigates and destroyers being constructed in the other twenty bays. They, along with the battleships, are all in varying stages of construction. The station also appears to manufacture fighters in large hangar bays on either end of the structure."

"This is seriously not good," he said, watching as hundreds of small construction pods scuttled about, welding hulls, installing components, and ratcheting down armor plating. "Alpha, analyze the traffic patterns. Find us a safe route in."

"Acknowledged."

"Bits, zoom out."

The view pulled back, and Jackson took a moment to focus on the other objects in orbit. "Looks like they've spaced out a number of support stations into three rows, one above the shipyard and two below," he said as they came into view on the holo-display, providing a three-dimensional rendering.

"I believe the two larger stations in the top row serve logistical functions to outfit the newly constructed ships," Bits said as he zoomed in on two large stations above the shipyard that sat in a higher geosynchronous orbit. "I've also tracked the ships from the fourth planet, where we detected the food sources, to these stations, along with traffic from several other stations in lower orbit."

"Makes sense. They likely wouldn't supply or arm them until they pushed off the shipyard, just in case something went wrong," Jackson said, studying the stations and the traffic patterns. "What about those smaller ones between them?"

Bits zoomed out, showing the other stations along with multiple ships surrounding them. "The two smaller stations appear to be weapons storage depots. I'm detecting dozens of small craft moving to and from them and the nearby ships with radiological readings consistent with Imperium torpedoes."

"Shit, there's thirty more of the new advanced warships already completed."

"Confirmed. They appear to be in the process of being armed and supplied as they prepare to be deployed," Alpha135 said. "It also appears as though another twenty ships at the shipyard are nearly complete."

"That must be the fifty the intel showed were almost ready, but it's much worse than that. There's a hundred more, and it looks like this entire operation is cranking them out at full capacity."

"Indeed," the android confirmed without a hint of emotion.

"I'm detecting two large battle stations in a parallel orbit to the shipyards, twenty thousand kilometers to either side," Bits said, focusing in on one of the stations, then zooming back out. "There is also a task force of thirty older Imperium ships at a Lagrange point outside the planet's rings, along with hundreds of weapons platforms out there."

Jackson studied the entire scene carefully, noting the deployments of ships and weapons platforms, along with those ships they'd detected patrolling the system earlier. It was a formidable defense, capable of repelling a GCH fleet hundreds of ships strong. "Bits, Alpha, we need to work on an escape plan. Getting out of here is going to be tricky," he said. "At least the majority of their defenses are farther out. If we keep in tight to the shipyard and these facilities, the battle stations and weapons platforms are going to have a hell of a time targeting us with their big guns without risking hitting other critical installations. So, it's really just the hundred or so active warships in the system, along with probably five hundred to a thousand fighters we have to worry about," he said, half laughing at how utterly and completely outgunned they were. "What are the grav specs for the slipstream drive to jump?"

"The slipstream drive has greater tolerances for gravitational forces than hypervelocity drives. We can initiate a jump once we are ten kilometers from the planet's exosphere," Alpha135 replied. "However, we will need to bring the quantum core back online before we do."

"Right," he said, continuing to study the display, putting his experience to work as he looked for any weakness in their defenses. "Any idea what those huge glass-domed stations are below the shipyard?"

"I believe they are Imperium breeding and incubation facilities," Alpha135 responded. "The GCH has documented similar facilities before. They are likely used to produce crews for the ships and troops for ground-based assaults."

"Those stations are massive. There could be millions of Insectoids in each of them," he said, staring at the floating domes in awe, each five kilometers long and three high.

"That is correct. They can likely breed between three hundred to four hundred and fifty thousand new Imperium units per month."

Jackson shook his head, taking in a deep, slow, frustrated breath while he marveled at the efficiency of it all, knowing now why the GCH faced such an uphill battle in trying to win a war against an enemy that could replenish its numbers and ships in such a fashion.

He turned his attention to the ice giant's twenty-three moons, watching them on the holo-display. Many of them appeared heavily scarred, with signs of extensive mining clearly evident. Considerable traffic flowed from several of them to a row of stations in a lower orbit beneath the shipyard and breeding facilities. "Bits, those look like manufacturing and refining stations," he said as he adjusted the view, zooming in closer to study them.

"I concur. Though it is difficult to be certain what they are producing using only passive scans," Bits said, bringing up data on the holo-display. "The two on the left end appear to have significant heat blooms. Based on cargo ship traffic leaving them, I believe they are the sources for the daramite armored hull plating for the ships."

"Makes sense. What about the other ones?"

"Passive scans show radiological signatures on two of them, and the other four appear to be much larger. Two have a higher volume of traffic from the moons, and both appear to flow transport haulers to the neighboring stations. I believe that the first two of the larger stations are used to refine the raw materials and the second two are manufacturing the components for the ships themselves. The radiological signatures could indicate power cores or a weapons manufacturing facility."

Jackson stared at the readouts, agreeing with Bits's assessment. "It looks like they have an entire self-contained supply chain setup in this system." He folded his arms across his chest, pacing while his mind raced. "We need to rethink our plan. I don't just want to take out the station. I want to get it all."

"That is highly unlikely," Alpha135 interjected. "The Imperium stations and defenses are spread out over an area approximately sixty thousand square kilometers. Even if the *Phoenix* was still fully armed, it would be highly improbable to destroy them all."

"What do we have left in the way of weapons?"

"Our current tactical complement consists of two spatial disruption torpedoes, two standard torpedoes, and two gamma torpedoes, along with the ship's plasma cannons, particle beams, and the point defense systems."

"Hmm, not a lot to work with," Jackson admitted. "Bits, any luck finding a primary target at the shipyard?"

"Optimal target located. The battleship in the seventy-seventh berth is nearly complete. Its quantum core is online, as are the cores of several ships on either side of it."

"What's the damage radius if we overload it?"

"Primary detonation will create chain reactions with the vessels on either side, splitting the shipyard in two and destroying dozens of berths in both directions. The subsequent shockwave should destroy or damage two-thirds of the remaining vessels, with the rest losing orbital stability and falling to the planet below, completing our primary objective."

"That still leaves close to forty ships they could recover before the station falls into the ice giant's gravity well, maybe more, depending on the damage they sustain, along with the fighters being produced at either end of the station. And it still doesn't do anything about the thirty other newly completed battleships."

"That is correct," Alpha135 responded. "The logistics stations are too far away, as are most of the other facilities. There may, however, be some fallout from debris from the shipyard that will cause additional collateral damage."

"How large would the explosion have to be to reach the refineries, weapons facilities, and the other stations?"

"The refineries and manufacturing stations are approximately seven thousand kilometers below the shipyard, and the blast radius to reach them would need to be several times more powerful. The weapons and logistics depots where the other new battleships are being supplied are two thousand kilometers above the station."

"What about the sensor array?"

"It is approximately twenty thousand kilometers from the shipyard."

"And the breeding facilities and battle stations?"

"Three thousand kilometers to the breeding facilities and twenty thousand kilometers to each of the battle stations."

"Damn it," Jackson said, frustrated. "We can't just leave all of this here."

"William, I believe it is important not to lose perspective," Bits offered. "If we destroy the shipyard, our mission will be a success. The more we alter the plan, the more we risk jeopardizing that objective."

Jackson paused for a moment, stroking his chin, fresh stubble grating against his fingers as he let out a conciliatory breath. "You're right…but there's got to be a way to have our cake and eat it too. Is there any sign that we've been detected?"

"Negative. The sensor array and enemy traffic patterns are unchanged," Alpha135 replied.

"Hmm, I want to take a bit more time to work on this before we go. What's our window to coincide with Frederickton's op?"

"Captain Frederickton is scheduled to proceed in eleven hours, twenty-one minutes," Alpha confirmed.

The operations had been coordinated to start at approximately the same time, ensuring that if one was unsuccessful or discovered, that the Insectoids would have limited time to react and increase security at the other shipyard. This required them to work in parallel over a compressed period while tens of thousands of light-years apart.

He stared at the holo-display once more, looking over the deployment of the shipyard, ships, and stations, along with the data on each, considering for a moment what Captain Delgado would do in his place. "I know it's stupid to get greedy, but we can't risk them rebuilding. We just can't. And we've come all this way. We have to do this right." He paused, his mind made up, even though he knew the cost would be high, and it meant they might not make it out of there alive.

"*Everything* has a weakness. There *are* holes here, things we can exploit if we plan this just right," he said, focusing in on a few areas and nodding to himself as he saw the operational landscape before him with fresh eyes, looking beyond how formidable their defenses were and finding the gaps. "The shipyard is still the mission. Nothing changes in that regard. But once the countdown starts and we're off the ship, we should still have the element of surprise. And I want to hit them where it hurts! Where they least expect it. They've deployed their defenses to repel an incoming armada, but I don't think they ever anticipated an attacker getting in this close, behind their lines. We have the advantage of stealth, and your slingshot maneuver has bought us some extra time, Alpha. Let's use it to see what we can do to take down this operation for good."

Hours passed while Jackson, Bits, and Alpha worked through various scenarios. Jackson became obsessed with damaging or destroying as many enemy targets as possible, hell-bent not only on taking out the shipyard but also figuring out a way to take out the newly active battleships and crippling the Imperium's ability to rebuild. After going back and forth, they finally agreed on a plan. Alpha135 modified the virus that was created to infiltrate the ship and the shipyard, and added in several secondary objectives to their mission parameters, along with a final sequence that could be triggered remotely if everything else went according to plan, without jeopardizing the primary mission objectives.

"Alpha, status?" Jackson asked, pacing while his mind raced and he considered the audacity of his plan once more, wondering for a final time if he was making the right call or if his own hubris was getting the better of him.

"All systems nominal."

"Bits?"

"Ready, William."

"Very well, initiate the remote back door and start docking procedures with the battleship in slip seventy-seven."

"Back door connection active," Alpha135 said, using an exploit in Imperium comms protocols the androids recently discovered from a salvaged Imperium ship to create a short-range point-to-point tight-band connection, hiding the signal and allowing them access into the ship's systems undetected. "Initiating docking procedure."

"How many life signs are on board?"

"I'm detecting approximately four hundred and sixty Insectoid workers on board the vessel," Bits said. "Most appear to be in the forward section. The engineering section registers only a few dozen bio-signs."

"Any idea what we're dealing with?"

"I cannot be certain based on passive scans. There are multiple species of Insectoids known to perform engineering roles."

"Hmm, we may need a to diversify our armaments to be prepared for anything," Jackson said, leaving the bridge and moving into the next compartment.

He stepped up on the operations platform, the floor and ceiling lights illuminating, and a holo-display appeared before him, showing a representation of his body hovering in midair. Jackson scanned the menu, selecting the covert ops suit along with three supplemental nano-packs to add additional armor and material to create constructs or other objects which could come in handy. He then added a flamethrower, particle beam emitters, electroshock gauntlets, a plasma pistol, and two high-capacity grenade belts.

He taped on the belts, viewing the options menu. "Bits, configure the belts to set all grenades to proximity and remote trigger modes."

"Acknowledged."

Jackson taped the empty slots for the first group of ten grenades, and a menu appeared with options: Amber, Concussive, Cryo, Flash, Foam, Frag, Gas, Plasma, Radiation, Shock, Sonic, Stun, and Vacuum. Scanning the list, he tapped on Foam, and it populated the ten empty slots in the first row. He then repeated the process for the next empty row, selecting Frag, then the next row, selecting five Amber and five Stun. He stared at the menu once more, considering, then pressed eight from the numeric display, selecting Sonic from the list, nodding in approval. Finally, he loaded two Vacuum grenades, just in case.

Once finished, he swiped back to the root menu and selected the mines, choosing a dozen gas mines, adding them to the representation of the nano-pack on his avatar's back. He examined his choices again, still feeling as though something was missing.

He scanned through the rest of the weapons menus until he found what he was looking for: a kyromonite sword, the versatile weapon able to shrink down to just a small blade and hilt, then expand to a meter in length when activated. The kyromonite was an incredibly strong alloy which could be reconfigured into several blade shapes from straight to curved to serrated, and with a powered nano-meter arc-matter edge that could cut through nearly anything. He had limited training with it and was still a bit of a novice, but Kelara had given him some help with his technique during some downtime on their way to Vishnara several years ago, and he was slowly becoming dangerous with it to more than just himself.

He also added a kyromonite shield, attaching it to his forearm just in case. The suit had standard energy shields and could create constructs, but for extreme physical encounters, a solid shield was preferable. When inactive, the shield was the size of a coaster on his wrist, but once activated, it increased in size and could stand up to considerable force.

Finally, he added an advanced med pack to augment the suit's standard triage capabilities, along with the customized med pack the team at FoxBlind had prepared for him before he left.

He was about to step off the platform when he reconsidered, scrolling through the treatment menus, and deciding to add a wasp, scorpion, and ant anti-venom as an extra precaution.

Satisfied with his choices, he tapped the Commit button, and the platform opened several compartments around him. Jackson stood motionless, with his arms slightly out to his sides as the suit flowed up from the floor, coating his body from his feet to neck while several mechanical arms appeared from compartments both above and below, installing the weapons modules he'd selected. Once completed, the suit hardened, and two more mechanical arms lowered from the ceiling, wrapping the grenade belts around his waist. Finally, the sword lowered, attaching to his back with the hilt just over his left shoulder and the shield mounted to his left forearm, the suit flowing around each to conceal them beneath its cloaking tech.

"Systems check," he commanded.

The suit cycled through several modes: sonic suppression, cloaking, shields, basic constructs such as blades on his wrists and spikes on his feet, flight mode and several others, each running a diagnostic.

"Check complete. All systems are optimal," Bits responded. "We're coming up on the battleship now."

"Acknowledged," Jackson said, turning and heading back to the bridge, arriving just as the battleship appeared in full display on the main viewscreen. He watched it intently, the massive ship larger than a GCH Allegiant class battlecruiser and nearly two-thirds the size of a dreadnought. Jackson had never seen one up close before, and very few who had in combat had lived to tell the tale. "Bits, are we recording everything?"

"Affirmative, William. I am collecting considerable data on each of the ship's designs. There are also several sections where armor has not yet been installed, allowing me to pinpoint the locations of several sensitive systems. Once analyzed, it should help to exploit their weaknesses in battle."

Jackson looked across the bridge to where Alpha135 was silently sitting. "Alpha, make analyzing this data your top priority while I'm gone. I want to send a compressed data stream back to FoxBlind through our comms probe before we jump. Just in case we don't make it."

"Understood," Alpha135 responded.

The *Phoenix* continued to approach the Insectoid battleship, silently slipping through the final defense perimeter.

Bits carefully maneuvered the ship into position beside the battleship's rear starboard docking port. "Docking procedure is complete. I've overridden their docking port commands to ensure there is no record of our access and we have a hard seal."

"Great work, buddy."

Jackson walked over to Alpha135. "Are you good to go as planned?" he asked, still slightly uncomfortable around the android. Unlike Data on *Star Trek*, GCH models seemed a little too cold and emotionless for him. Aside from the humanoid android the Omega Team had used, the rest just left him feeling uneasy. Perhaps he was biased, he thought. After all, Data was a pretty tough standard to live up to.

"I have completed my calculations and will await your signal. Once I receive your confirmation, I will initiate the plan," Alpha135 responded.

"Also, William, remember that once Alpha135 powers up the quantum core and the cargo matter transporter, the sensor array will attempt to triangulate our location. It won't be able to lock on through our cloak. However, once we fully power the quantum core, we will only have between thirty and forty-five seconds before they lock on to us, as it is extremely sensitive to energy readings."

"What was it Frederickton kept saying? 'This just keeps getting better and better.'" He smiled. "As much as I hate to agree with the man, this is going to be a rough one," he said, taking a deep breath. "All right, let's get this done."

CHAPTER 6

BEHIND ENEMY LINES

Fifteen minutes passed as Jackson made his way through the bowels of the battleship, its construction and design unlike anything previously on record. The interior was a clean gray and brown metal, a mix of large corridors and small tunnel-like side passages. Instead of crew quarters like on a GCH ship, various perches and outcroppings of metal spread out along the tall, wide corridors for flying insectoids, while hundreds of small alcoves lined the walls providing living quarters for others. Other side corridors appeared as he moved through the ship, leading down into a warren of tunnels resembling an ant hive, and large honeycomb-like structures filled more open spaces, waiting for inhabitants to move in.

Several large rooms sat empty, waiting to be filled with hunting grounds, similar to those on Reptilian ships for the apex Insectoid predators, while smaller feeding and water tubes spread throughout the rest of the ship, delivering nectar and other organic foodstuffs.

The ship itself was dimly lit with a soft purple lighting throughout, and the design appeared far more organized than the normal chaos that filled Imperium ships in all the simulations he'd ever been through.

As he made his way to his first target, it quickly became clear that many of the design elements had been stolen from other races. The overall layout, while similar to that of a Reptilian vessel, with tall, wide corridors and open spaces to accommodate larger creatures, was missing the foliage and nature which comprised the interiors of their vessels. Elements from the GCH, Vehn, Oceanic Union, and Tu'shar Empire, among others, had also clearly been integrated into its systems.

"I know that the Imperium is known for its espionage abilities, but I've never heard of them meshing technology together like this before," he commented. "Is there anything on record like this?"

"Negative," Bits replied. "Insectoid vessel designs haven't changed significantly for the past five hundred years. This is an exponential leap forward for them."

"Keep collecting as much data as you can while we move. How's our timing?"

"We are within mission parameters."

"Okay, let's keep moving."

Jackson continued to navigate through the enormous ship, keeping a close eye on the mission clock, knowing that Frederickton would be doing the same. An hour and forty-three minutes remained until they were due to execute the plan, the coordinated timing one of the hardest parts of the joint operation. If one of them went too early, it put the other in increased danger, reducing the probability of them completing their mission. Still, having to stay on board for an extended period increased the risk for both of them. It was a compromise they each had to make to ensure the success of the other and buy one another as much time as they could in the event that they ran into unexpected obstacles.

Bits had connected to the ship's systems once on board, downloading a schematic, and Jackson had completed his first objectives, disabling several auxiliary control systems and manual overrides. He was on his way to the central computer core eight decks up, the area buried deep within the ship in a heavily shielded section. Fortunately, as the *Phoenix*'s scans had indicated, most of the work crews were in the forward hull, and his route thus far had been mostly clear, allowing him to move swiftly through the main corridors while having to avoid only a few dozen Insectoids along the way.

He entered the core a few minutes later, the entire area deserted as he bypassed the security protocols, accessing the ship's central processing stack. The core itself was dimly lit, consisting of dozens of glowing stacks, many resembling ant hills made from tiny squares of bio-matter mixed with non-ferrous metals, while others reminded him of the inside of a beehive. Several tall pillars pulsed and hummed with energy at seemingly random intervals, while overhead, other constructs hung from the ceiling, stretching down like stalactites, giving the entire space a cave-like feeling. Connecting all of it was a lattice-like web made from techno-organic and various nanomaterials. "Bits, run a scan. I want to capture all of this."

"Scan in progress."

"I've never seen anything like this. Any idea where we can connect in?"

"Sixteen meters to your left, then down between those honeycomb structures, there is what appears to be a standard Imperium data tower."

Jackson moved carefully through the stacks, mindful not to disturb any of the webbing. He reached the data tower, extending his right arm and holding his hand up to the main access port while Bits formed a stream of nanites, flowing them inside. The androids back at FoxBlind had developed the sophisticated virus, which was carefully engineered to infiltrate the power systems, subtly tampering with the safety protocols. The androids were good, and the virus was simple, elegant, and insidious. Once deployed, it would begin spreading, appearing as an automated diagnostic, while jumping from system to system inside the battleship, executing various tasks in sequence. Jackson held his breath as the virus uploaded, knowing that the last-minute changes Alpha135 had made back on the ship increased the risks of something going wrong.

Seconds passed, the hum of the data core filling his ears, the eerie scene around him reminding him how alien and different the Imperium was. The feeling of being watched crept over him, the mission clock in his HUD ticking down while he waited for Bits to update their status.

Jackson's new plan was now in play, and there was no turning back. His mind and will were hell-bent on increasing the fallout and crippling the Imperium's operations.

He waited, counting the seconds until Bits finally reported, "The virus has successfully uploaded and is beginning secondary objectives."

A wicked smile crept across his lips, his desire to hurt the enemy, to cripple their war machine, burning brightly in his mind. "Let's get this done then and make these bastards pay."

Minutes later, he arrived in the engineering section, a large area of the ship consisting of six decks, each responsible for different systems' operations, with several redundant systems between them. The first deck contained a control center for the ship's life support and environmental systems, while the second contained external sensors and ship operations, and the third held the quantum core, which ran horizontally for nearly forty meters along the ship's axis. The fourth and fifth decks contained a series of smaller corridors where power from the core routed through a network of conduits to the rest of the ship, while the sixth held the primary engineering controls where the navigation and tactical systems were located.

Jackson entered the engineering section on the first level, quickly locating the large control room filled with access panels and engineering stations containing readouts of the ship's systems. Bits interfaced with the environmental systems, using an access protocol pulled from the data core, then commenced a low-level internal sensor scan of the ship.

"I'm detecting the Insectoid crew spread out over several decks in this section," he said, bringing up the data in Jackson's HUD.

"Okay, we'll have to take them out one at a time. We can't risk leaving any of them alive," he said, considering a plan of attack. He moved towards the closest three groups, planting mines in proximity to where he found Insectoid engineers working on the first two decks. He breathed a sigh of relief when he discovered they were all small beetle-like creatures, less than a quarter of a meter in length, resembling weevils from Earth. They weren't a species he was familiar with, but he recalled his training, remembering the concept of humanoid bias and not to underestimate them just because they looked like animals. He watched for a moment while they worked, their bodies propped up on dozens of small legs, while others still worked on various consoles, each performing multiple tasks at the same time.

In each case, he followed the same plan: deploying the mines, then making a small noise to get the creatures' attention. Once they were in range of the mine, it showered his prey with a spray of lethal gas while Jackson kept a safe distance, ready to fire if necessary, pistol in hand. So far, the gas had neutralized each of his targets without incident, and he continued to move on, mindful of the time as he knew he was pushing the clock and that Frederickton would be initiating his overload soon.

Once the first two decks were clear, he got to work on the next phase of the plan, accessing the engineering master console, which controlled the ship's primary systems. His heads-up display translated the controls in front of him while Bits walked him through the process to place the system in maintenance mode so that he could interface with it freely. If all went well, the Insectoids wouldn't notice, and even if they did, they would likely think that an engineer was simply running a diagnostic.

That was the hope, at least.

He'd always hated how much of these plans often hinged on an element of hope or luck, not matter how well planned.

Jackson completed entering the command sequence while Bits interfaced with the system, bypassing the remaining protocols using several exploit techniques to gain root access, then implanting a new section of code, a simple command override block that once embedded into the root system was completely immutable unless they fully wiped the entire system.

Once finished, he took the system out of maintenance mode, then proceeded to the third deck, where Bits interfaced with the quantum core control systems, uploading a new diagnostic program that disabled the safety protocols.

Jackson quickly moved up to the fourth deck, accessing the main power relay panel, then used a particle beam to weld the controls in place, ensuring that the relay couldn't trip. Once locked in place, he set a foam grenade on the controls, detonating it with a small popping sound once he was a safe distance away. The foam expanded rapidly, encasing the relay in a rock-hard shell two meters thick within seconds.

He looked at the bottom-left corner of his display. Another item checked off his list as he continued on to the fifth deck. As he made his way down one of the smaller engineering corridors, his heads-up display registered bio-signs ahead. Jackson slowly, carefully peered around the corner, discovering a large orange, gray, and black wasp-like creature standing upright before an access panel. He watched while it worked for a moment, the creature deftly manipulating the controls with small tendrils that emerged from its forelegs. He recalled a lesson from Basic where the instructor explained how many species of Insectoids had evolved different types of appendages over time, allowing them to work with a level of dexterity that made humanoid fingers look clumsy by comparison.

Jackson studied it for a few moments, considering his options, noticing its body was less like a traditional wasp, but rather designed to stand upright on its hind legs and sternum. The creature's eyes focused on its task, its head turning to check a nearby display several times while it worked to verify the readings.

"Tactical analysis," he whispered, moving back out of sight.

Bits ran a quick scan, showing the wasp in detail. "This species is unknown, but closely resembles a similar species documented on several Insectoid worlds. While its appendages appear frail, they are actually quite powerful, and its exoskeleton is four millimeters thick. Its stinger is also barbed, meaning it will detach upon insertion, making it extremely difficult to remove before it deposits a lethal payload. I also suspect, based on an analysis of its movements, that it is highly intelligent. We should not underestimate it."

"I get freaked out when a three-centimeter wasp comes near me, let alone one that's four meters long. Trust me, I'm not underestimating anything." He smiled, knowing from past sims how deadly wasps that were more primitive could be, while considering how one that was highly intelligent might react. "Will a gas mine work against it?"

"Unknown. Its physiology appears to differ slightly from other species on record, but it is likely that the gas will at least slow it down. I would advise extreme caution, however, as wasps are known to be fast, and some have a different temporal perception, allowing them to perceive events faster than a humanoid."

"Right, I remember learning about that. Their reflexes are dialed way up. Can you hit me with a stim to level the playing field?"

"I'm afraid I cannot. It will counteract the other protocols needed to get you off the ship later."

Jackson nodded. "Okay then. All weapons ready," he said, carefully rounding the corner and planting a mine, then moving farther down the corridor to a safe distance. Once in place, he made a small sound by banging on the wall to attract the wasp's attention.

Nothing happened, the creature ignoring the sound and continuing its task.

He tried again, waiting…

It either didn't notice or didn't care.

"What the hell?" he said, banging his foot on the decking to try something different.

Still nothing. The wasp stood fifteen meters away, diligently focused on its work.

"Damn, we need to get it over here. It looks like there's a comms panel a few meters from where it's working. We have to get it away from there so it doesn't sound the alarm. Any ideas?"

"Some species of wasps have an excellent sense of smell and will respond unconsciously to the scent of sugars. This tactic has been successfully used to lure wasps into ambushes before. The suit can replicate a fairly accurate scent; however, it is not perfect."

"Let's give it a try. Hopefully, even smart wasps can't resist a little sugar," Jackson said, raising his right hand out in front of him, then pointing his index finger towards the creature. A second later, the nanites on his fingertip became fluid, releasing a sugary scent into the air while the ones farther up his finger formed three small blades that began to spin, creating a gentle breeze to carry the scent down the hallway.

The wasp continued its work for several seconds, then suddenly stopped.

Bits immediately ceased releasing the sugar scent and reengaged the cloak around Jackson's finger while they waited.

The wasp stood completely motionless for several seconds before turning towards him. A moment later, it stepped forward, approaching slowly. Its antennae moved rapidly while its mandibles twitched, attempting to identify the source of the scent.

As the wasp passed the mine anchored to the side of a bulkhead, a powerful jet of poison gas came rushing out, striking it in the head. The wasp recoiled, twitching wildly, the sound echoing through the corridor. A few seconds later, it rolled onto its side, its movements ceasing.

"Is it dead?" Jackson asked.

"Affirmative."

"Good work. How many bio-signs left?"

"Sensors are detecting four more. Two on this deck and two on the deck above."

"All right, let's get moving."

Minutes later, Jackson cleared two more wasps using the same technique before moving up to the sixth and final deck. As he approached the bio-readings, he discovered two more wasps working together at a large engineering control station. Behind them was the primary power transfer station: the last critical system he needed to compromise before he started the overload.

He crept cautiously, the room similar to that on the first deck, a large open area easily the size of two tennis courts, with several command consoles spread out across it and dozens of monitors and holo-displays showing various schematics and systems status updates. Jackson carefully planted a mine ten meters away, in front of a console where it could spray upward from the deck.

Just as he finished setting it down, one of the creatures stopped its work, turning and moving his way.

Jackson pulled back his arm and froze where he crouched beside the console, holding still while the wasp rapidly approaching his position.

"Oh shit," he said, the mine suddenly activating as it disappeared from sight, realizing what was about to happen.

The wasp's foreleg stepped down a second later, narrowly missing the mine when a powerful blast of poison gas jetted upward. The creature recoiled, twitching for several seconds, before it keeled over, crashing hard to the deck.

Jackson jumped back reflexively to avoid getting hit as its head dropped like a stone towards him, suddenly standing out in the open.

The second wasp turned at the sight of its compatriot falling and detected the visual distortion in Jackson's cloak from the sudden movement, unfurling its wings and launching into the air in seconds.

Jackson turned just in time to see the blur of it bearing down on him and closing fast.

Bits engaged the thrusters on the suit, launching them out of the way at the last second, Jackson's feet sliding along the deck as he came to a stop several meters away. The wasp shot by, its wings narrowly missing him, the force of the wind buffeting him back.

He shook off the momentary shock and raised his arm, tracking the wasp as it circled the large engineering space and coming back around. Jackson let loose with the flamethrower, the powerful stream of fire burning the wasp's wings and setting them ablaze in seconds. The Insectoid fell to the deck but managed to land on its feet, screeching in rage and coming towards him at a charge.

Jackson dodged to the right, evading the worst of the blow as the wasp barreled into him, spinning him around and knocking him onto the deck hard. It reared up, lashing out with the deadly points of its forelegs, Jackson twisting and rolling to evade the thrusts.

"Shield!" he called, raising his left arm, the disk on his forearm expanding to its full size just in time to block the wasp's stinger as it lunged out at him, narrowly deflecting the rapid succession of blows up, away from his body.

The wasp slashed at Jackson with a serrated edge on its foreleg, striking the flamethrower unit and puncturing it. A jet of compressed fuel shot out from his wrist and Bits ejected the unit a second later, the flamethrower launching several meters away before the fuel ignited, creating a burst of flame that radiated searing heat towards them, enough that Jackson could feel it through the suit.

The wasp reared up from the blast, ceasing its assault for an instant and giving Jackson a momentary reprieve. He reached back, pulling the sword from his back, and got to one knee, flicking the hilt of the sword outward. The kyromonite blade reacted, expanding to its full length as it shot out, a thin ribbon of blue light appearing along the edge of the blade. He tightened his grip and swung wildly, attempting to score a hit, content to get the creature to back off while he got to his feet.

The wasp retreated for a moment, then lunged forward again, using its speed to go on the offensive, sensing its prey's desperation. Bits dodged the suit far faster than Jackson's reflexes could, evading several lightning quick attacks from the wasp's razor-sharp forelegs and the deadly stinger as it lashed out.

Jackson ignored the pain while Bits moved him around

like a puppet, focusing his mind on the wasp's attacks and attempting to spot a weakness or pattern, and exploit it.

An instant later, he saw one.

The wasp twisted upward and thrust forward with its stinger, just as Bits spun Jackson to the side, deflecting it with the shield. It came back down with its mandibles and Jackson swiped upward with the sword, anticipating the attack and narrowly missing it, forcing it to rear up on its back legs. Bits parried two more lunges from the deadly serrated forelegs with the shield, and Jackson pushed to regain control, swinging the sword down towards the wasp's leg to his left, forcing it to dodge and shift its balance to the right. He then pushed forward with the shield, leaping off the ground, his thrusters activating, the impact striking the wasp in the thorax with a powerful blow.

Jackson landed and slammed the left foreleg with the shield, the enhanced strength from the suit buckling it, then swung the sword towards an exposed joint, cleaving it off in one strike.

The wasp crumpled to its side, recoiling in pain, its five remaining legs and deadly stinger thrashing wildly, attempting to score a hit.

Jackson moved several steps back and threw a cryo-grenade towards it. The grenade detonated upon impact, coating the wasp in a growing layer of ice, pinning it to the deck, unable to move. Jackson dashed forward, leaping on top of it and driving the sword home, the wasp going still a moment later.

"Well, that could have gone better," he said. "Thanks for the save, buddy. I owe you one!"

"You are most welcome, William. Unfortunately, I have some bad news," Bits said, a klaxon sounding a second later.

"An alarm appears to have been triggered, alerting the workers in the forward section of the ship. We must hurry."

"Can you jam the notification from getting off the ship?"

"The virus has disabled all shipboard comms systems aside from the main one in engineering. They may still be able to get a signal out to the station, however, if they have portable communications devices."

He flicked the sword once more, the blade shrinking in response, then returned it to the sheath on his back. "Not good. Let's move!"

Jackson rushed back to the power transfer station, pressing his hand to the console while Bits interfaced with it and hacked into the system, disabling the safeties. Once their task was complete, Jackson backed off and threw an amber grenade, encasing the controls in a thick layer.

He darted back to the staircase, quickly making his way down to the third deck. Acutely aware that depending on what species of Insectoids were working in the forward hull, that it might not take them long to make their way across the ship.

He hit the third deck at a sprint, quickly reaching the panel that controlled the quantum core. Bits translated the controls on his heads-up display while he keyed in the final sequence to allow the virus to initiate an overload, then smashed the console. Once the process began, only the last auxiliary control panel and the master breakers could stop it.

Jackson fired a particle beam across the room at the auxiliary control panel, destroying it, then encased both control systems in foam, followed by a second grenade each, sealing them in a rapidly growing shell of amber.

The master breakers were one level up in a long rectangular room off the smaller, rounded corridors. He had already cleared the path to them, but for the overload sequence to work, he needed to trip them last.

He ran as quickly as he could, his lungs and legs aching, as sounds of screeching and buzzing echoed from down the main corridor.

A moment later, he reached the room with the main breakers, knowing they needed to be kept open and intact at all costs. He ran through the room to the far door and tossed four sonic grenades down the hallway, pressing a button on the top of each to activate their proximity modes. He then dropped two foam grenades just outside of the door, hustling back into the room while they activated with a pop, the foam filling the outer corridor and sealing the doorway.

Jackson moved towards the master breakers, taking an amber grenade from his belt. He adjusted the settings on it for maximum density, then lobbed it at the breakers. The grenade detonated on impact, coating them in two meters of dense amber that hardened in a matter of seconds.

He sprinted back to the far side of the room, where he had entered, throwing all of his remaining amber grenades back inside the doorway as he left, then ran out of the room. Seconds later, the grenades detonated, becoming a solid barrier of rock-hard amber a dozen meters thick.

As he emerged, the sounds coming from the main corridor grew rapidly closer, reaching a terrifying, visceral fever pitch, filling Jackson with a primal feeling of dread.

A horde of Insectoids was coming, ready to tear him apart.

They were still two levels above him, but the deafening sounds echoing throughout the ship told him that they were close now.

"Status on the virus?" he called, a shiver running down his spine as he caught sight of the mass of creatures rushing towards his location on one of the monitors across the room, a jolt of adrenaline filling his system.

"The shipborne virus has completed all of its tasks. The dampening field is standing by, and all ship's systems are completely locked out. We're ready to initiate the final step."

Jackson made his way to the staircase, throwing all ten of his stun grenades, along with his remaining cryo up and down the staircases, activating their proximity modes.

He made his way back to the corridor outside the master breaker room, placing four more sonic grenades and the rest of his mines at strategic points along the way.

The first wave of Insectoids would be there soon, and time was short. He moved to the communications station, Bits interfacing with the system.

"Bits, trigger comms array to activate the back door to the shipyard and have it start the virus upload sequence."

"Connection established. The virus is uploading… Upload complete. The virus will activate in thirty seconds."

"Okay," Jackson said, trying to control his breathing and waiting to ensure the virus activated successfully, battling every fiber of his being to run, knowing that the horde would be upon him soon.

"The virus is now active," Bits reported. "Dampening field online. Quantum core overload initiated. The loop in shipyards' sensors is now active, and the system has been placed into a locked-down diagnostic mode to keep them from detecting the overload. Starting the four-minute countdown now."

"Good work," he said, letting out a tense breath, then taking several steps back and firing his pistol at the console, destroying it.

The overload was unstoppable now with every possible system to thwart it disabled, blocked off, or destroyed.

Jackson ran, raw fear pushing him that if the Insectoids didn't get him, the impending explosion would. He darted down a corridor, dropping the two vacuum grenades ten meters apart to cover the approach, then stepped inside a small room and sealed himself in with his last foam grenade, taking a ragged breath and knowing that if they got through, he'd be torn apart in seconds.

There was only one more thing to do now.

Jackson's heart pounded in his chest as he steeled his will, thinking of Verris and Amy. Of his friends. That if this was it, at least he'd have died making a difference.

He made his way to the center of the room and stopped, shaking off a chill and letting out a nervous breath before lying down on his back.

"All right, buddy…it's time," he said wearily, the sounds of the grenades in the distant stairwell echoing down the corridors.

"Are you ready, William?"

"No, but I don't think that I want to be here when those fucking things arrive and realize what we've done," he said, taking a deep breath and letting it out once more. "If I don't make it, I just wanted to say that it's been an honor, buddy."

"The honor is all mine, William."

"All right, do it!" he said firmly, closing his eyes for what he hoped wouldn't be the last time.

Bits accessed the medical protocols, disabling them as he took control of all suit functions. He positioned Jackson's right arm across his chest, palm pressed firmly just to the left of center.

Nanoseconds passed while Bits contemplated what he was about to do, the action a violation of his core programming. He accessed the customized med kit that was prepared by the doctors at FoxBlind, injecting Jackson with half a dozen chemical cocktails in quick succession, along with thousands of specialized nanites, then waiting several seconds for them to circulate through his system to ensure maximum distribution.

Bits accessed his explicit orders from Jackson, overriding his core protocols and programming, then activated a carefully calculated charge from the electroshock gauntlet, stopping Jackson's heart instantly as it discharged.

Jackson's body convulsed briefly from the shock, then lay perfectly still.

Bits ran a quick medical scan, confirming that Jackson was deceased, all life signs and neural activity negative. Several seconds passed, a veritable eternity for the AI while he contemplated what he'd done before focusing on the task at hand.

He opened an encrypted channel, signaling Alpha135. "Prepare for transport."

"Copy," Alpha135 responded. "Powering up the quantum core. Initiating transport in thirty-eight seconds."

"Acknowledged," Bits replied, activating the specialized medical nanites flooding Jackson's circulatory system as they rapidly went to work performing carefully designed functions, each intentionally shutting down all remaining bodily functions and organs. Bits monitored the time, waiting until the microscopic soldiers had completed their tasks, then initiated the cryo-unit integrated into the suit, along with specialized cryo-nanites spread throughout Jackson's body.

Jackson's temperature dropped rapidly as the nanites worked to mitigate any cellular damage, the combination of their internal freezing and the cryo spray deployed into the suit putting him into a carefully controlled, if imperfect, state of cryogenic stasis.

In the corridor outside, the mines and grenades detonated in waves, screeches and roars from the Insectoids echoing ominously in response.

If Bits could feel fear, he considered for a microsecond, this would be a moment where it would be acutely present.

Seconds passed while he monitored Jackson's body, ensuring that it was completely devoid of any active life signs. All cellular and electrical activity, aside from Bits himself, had ceased.

A pop went off in the corridor, the telltale sound of a vacuum grenade creating a small, unstable portal into open space, sucking everything around it into the void before it collapsed in upon itself. Only the second one and the last barricade of foam protected them now. Bits knew it wouldn't hold for long against the onslaught once the horde arrived.

He signaled Alpha135 once more, and the android locked on, activating the cargo matter transporter.

Seconds later, Bits and Jackson, entombed in the nano-suit, materialized on the cargo matter transporter platform inside the *Phoenix*. The primary objective was underway and unstoppable.

Now it was time to see if Jackson's secondary plan would work, and if the price he paid would be worth it.

CHAPTER 7

CAKE WALK

Bits quickly reestablished control of the ship, extending his active consciousness from Jackson's lifeless body to the central processing core, increasing his speed and neural net capacity.

"The battleship's core will reach critical in three minutes and eleven seconds," Alpha135 reported.

"Acknowledged, access the data we collected from the station and compile," Bits replied, initiating the stealth drive and plotting a course for the sensor array. He shifted his attention for an instant back to Jackson, knowing that the partial cryogenic freezing had bought them a few extra minutes to work with, but every minute that passed increased the risk. His protocols to protect his host versus the plan Jackson had convinced him was paramount conflicted with one another, forcing Bits to make a decision.

He pushed Jackson's status from his thoughts, focusing on the task at hand.

The sensor array triangulated the *Phoenix*'s position seconds later, the now fully active quantum core's power signature lighting it up like a flare on its ultra-sensitive scanners, and relaying their coordinates to all Imperium ships within seconds.

"We have been detected," Alpha stated.

"Acknowledged. Prepare data transmission to our comms probe," Bits said.

"Data compressed and encrypted, ready for transmission."

"Execute."

Alpha135 transmitted a tight-beam message to the comms probe, outside of the Insectoids' jamming capabilities, ensuring that it would relay their data back to GCH Command. "Transmission complete."

"Target the array's central axis."

"Target locked," Alpha said while Bits bore down on the huge sensor array. Massive butterfly-like panels protruded from both sides, dwarfing the *Phoenix*. Bits calculated their odds, quickly giving up on stealth and switching to standard sublight engines, then pushing them to the red line to get within targeting range as distant fire from one of the battle stations rained down upon them, forcing him to maneuver the ship rapidly.

The two artificial lifeforms worked in tandem, bringing their considerable computing power and nanoseconds' reaction time to bear, acutely aware that with the array locked on to them, every Insectoid in the system was now alerted to their precise position despite their cloak.

The sensor array loomed large directly ahead, Bits dropping the cloak and activating the shields, then initiating a final series of maneuvers as the array's defenses opened fire.

The *Phoenix* rocked from the enemy fire grazing the shields, pressing forward with unflinching conviction and deadly intent. A gamma torpedo launched from the ship at the sensor array as it closed the distance. The projectile shot forward, too close and too fast for the array's point defense systems, detonating a split second later, and releasing a massive burst of gamma radiation, overwhelming sensors and shields momentarily.

Bits opened fire with the plasma cannons, shattering the central column of the crippled array with several direct hits. He pulled up and away as it exploded, scattering the area with debris.

Once clear of the detonation, Bits dropped the shields and cloaked the ship once more, cutting power to the sublight engines and switching back to the stealth drive. He banked the ship up into an inverted loop, all traces of it disappearing from the Insectoid's sensors.

The Imperium ships fired wildly in several directions, attempting to locate them, but Bits was one step ahead, using the cover of the debris from the sensor array to shield their retreat.

In the confusion, he circled back, plotting a course for the row of refineries and manufacturing stations below the shipyard as he noted the time, ever cognizant of how long Jackson had been deceased and the rapidly decreasing countdown of the battleship's core. "Alpha, locate a suitable target."

"Scan completed. Target located. A cargo ship is holding position near one of the manufacturing stations. I'm detecting radiological signatures, likely newly completed weapons. I estimate twenty-seven seconds until we are in optimal firing range."

"Acknowledged," Bits replied, altering course and lining up for an attack run.

The *Phoenix* de-cloaked seconds later, unleashing a devastating volley of plasma fire at the small, unarmed cargo ship, then broke off, re-cloaking.

The cargo ship exploded seconds later, its deadly payload of weapons exponentially increasing the yield of the detonation, catching the manufacturing station in the blast and causing a chain reaction that destroyed the station, along with the ones on either side of it.

Seconds later, powerful shockwaves slammed into the refineries in the row next to the destroyed stations causing significant damage to each of them. The *Phoenix* de-cloaked once more, unleashing a barrage of plasma fire at the closest refinery, the station exploding several seconds later.

The resulting shockwaves spread outward, smashing into two more stations full of volatile compounds, destroying them from the inside out.

Bits pulled up, away from the carnage, re-cloaking, satisfied with six of the eight stations now destroyed and the remaining two both heavily damaged.

The Insectoid fleet scrambled, with ships spreading out in all directions, attempting to locate the attacker within their midst. For all their immense firepower, able to take on an entire enemy fleet, they were unable to destroy the single invisible assassin in their midst as it struck again and again.

Several dozen ships fell back around the shipyard and began flooding the surrounding space with concentrated tachyon beams as they attempted to locate the *Phoenix*, still unaware of the sabotage to the battleship while the core continued to grow critical.

Bits set a course for the closest of the two depot stations between the logistics facilities above the shipyard, noting the thirty new advanced warships were still holding position and that the smaller ships, which had been arming and supplying them, had ceased their operations.

"One minute, twenty seconds remaining until the ship's core goes critical," Alpha informed Bits.

"Bring the slipstream drive online."

"Acknowledged. The drive will be online and fully charged in one minute, seven seconds," Alpha135 said, bypassing several safety protocols and checks to accelerate the process.

"Engaging next target in ten seconds," Bits said as they approached the weapons storage depot. Just as they closed into firing range, the *Phoenix* passed through a focused tachyon stream, lighting them up for a split second.

Half a dozen ships locked on, opening fire along their projected route.

Bits de-cloaked the ship and raised their shields, absorbing some of the damage while he continued on target, firing a spatial disruption torpedo, followed by a standard torpedo several seconds later at the closest of the two weapons depots. He altered course, re-cloaking the ship, the *Phoenix* sustaining several direct hits before disappearing once more.

The spatial disruption torpedo detonated just before hitting the station's shields, its kinetic energy focused into a narrow arc, directing the condensed power of the wave into a single area a few meters wide and punching a small hole in the station's powerful shields. The second torpedo followed close behind, slipping through the hole before the shields reformed, and entering through the huge open cargo bay in the center of the station before slamming into the interior wall.

The station exploded in a blaze of light, a massive shockwave from the munitions store inside rapidly expanding outward, engulfing the nearby advanced warships, the second weapons depot, and the closest logistics station with the deadly force of hundreds of antimatter detonations.

The second logistics station was hit hard, its main power going offline, and the impact throwing it from its orbit, the helpless station drifting downward towards the swirling ice giant below, its fate sealed.

Bits punched the engines and raised their shields as he attempted to outrun the brunt of the shockwave, surprised by the raw power of the explosion. He managed to stay just clear of the worst of it, diving the ship back towards the shipyard, but the wave lit them up momentarily and several Imperium ships locked on. The *Phoenix* took multiple direct hits before the wave dissipated and it vanished once more from the Imperium's sensors, sparks flying and several alarms blaring across the bridge.

"Status?" Bits called out, his full processing power focused on navigation and evasion, their final objective just ahead.

"Lateral armor down to forty-two percent, stealth drive offline, and damage to multiple power conduits. Main power is holding at sixty-four percent capacity. Hull integrity down to fifty-two percent," Alpha reported.

"Status on the slipstream drive?"

"Still charging. However, the reduction in power capacity will require more time to complete the charging cycle. New estimate: one minute, forty-eight seconds to jump capability."

"Insufficient. Cut power to life support and activate auxiliary power."

"Acknowledged. Revised time: one minute, three seconds."

"Dropping cloak and shields," Bits replied, quickly assessing the risk of exposing themselves compared with the countdown remaining on the battleship and the dwindling chances of resuscitating Jackson hanging in the balance.

"Time now thirty-six seconds until slipstream drive activation," Alpha updated his assessment.

"Time to battleship detonation?"

"Thirty seconds."

"Very well. Prepare for jump," Bits said as the *Phoenix* approached the shipyard at full speed.

The Imperium fleet responded in force with over sixty ships, along with hundreds of fighters, converging on their position, closing from multiple vectors and attempting to surround them, cutting off any chance of escape.

Bits sent out a broadband transmission, triggering the final modification to the virus that Jackson had insisted upon.

The code activated inside the shipyard, using the comms exploit to jump to each of the remaining ships docked at the station, powering up the cores on those with them installed to maximize the destructive chain reaction.

Bits recalled Jackson's words: "*This is the final F-you to the Imperium, and no last-minute* Star Trek *techno-babble, Scotty-type shit is going to stop us!*"

If he'd had a body, Bits would have smiled as the code went to work, ship after ship along the line suddenly powering up their quantum cores, leaving the Insectoids only seconds to react as the antimatter reactions became live.

Bits flew in tight above the surface of the shipyard, weaving around several protrusions in the hull and along the inside axis facing the planet, its weapons systems unable to target them in close, while their proximity to the shipyard limited the other ship's ability to fire on them without hitting it.

The fighters were the primary threat now, a wing approaching their six and closing fast.

Bits ejected their remaining spatial disruption torpedo from the rear launcher as he maneuvered close above the station, mere meters from its surface, the end of the crescent-shaped shipyard growing nearer. The torpedo detonated a second later, the carefully controlled shockwave leaving the station mostly untouched, while taking out the fighters in a wave of destructive energy.

He ejected the remaining gamma torpedo seconds later as they passed the midpoint of the station, not far from the seventy-seventh berth. The torpedo detonated, showering the station with intense radiation and obscuring the sensor readings in the area to further mask the imminent core overload, which was rapidly approaching the dampening field's ability to mask it.

As the end of the station loomed ahead, a formation of twenty-three ships spread out, forming a blockade, ready to annihilate the *Phoenix* as soon as it was clear, while dozens of other ships and fighters continued to close from above and on their flanks, waiting until they cleared the station to fire, boxing them in like a pack of wolves stalking a deer.

"Slipstream drive is nearly powered up. Ready for jump in thirteen seconds," Alpha reported.

"Time to primary detonation?" Bits asked, calculating what could be their final maneuver.

Alpha called out the final countdown "Five. Four. Three..."

Bits pulled up and banked hard to port, the Insectoid ships opening fire in response, bombarding the *Phoenix* with a phalanx of heavy fire.

A second later, the sabotaged battleship's core detonated, the damage radiating outward in both directions along the shipyard as the cores of the other ships along the line added to the devastation.

All along the shipyard, the antimatter reactions detonated, adding exponential power to the massive explosion.

The shipyard disappeared in a blinding flash of light seconds later, annihilated by the chain reaction of quantum cores detonating, creating a massive shockwave that swept outward in all directions, devastating everything in its path for thousands of kilometers.

Bits engaged the slipstream drive, opening an interdimensional breach. The *Phoenix* entered the slipstream just as the forward edge of the wave hit them hard and they disappeared while the shockwave continued, radiating outward with immense speed and unbridled destructive power, tearing through dozens of Imperium ships and fighters as they attempted to break off, unable to clear the path of the unstoppable wave.

The remains of the refineries and orbital stations followed, along with the breeding stations and the Imperium ships that had pursued the *Phoenix* towards the station.

Only the battle stations and weapons platforms, too far out from the destruction, were spared. The Imperium's entire advanced shipyard operation in the RE-13 system completely annihilated.

The cost, they would soon find out, was heavy.

CHAPTER 8
DOA

"Alpha, please carry Commander Jackson to the medical bay," Bits said, confirming that they were out of danger, safe in the shimmering slipstream while he initiated a full systems check.

Alpha135 rose from his seat, moving to the CMT platform in the next room and picking up the hardened shell of the suit where Jackson's body lay cryogenically entombed. He laid it on the floor, just outside the medpod, taking a step back while the door opened.

Bits activated the cryo-wake up sequence, the suit warming Jackson slowly over a period of nearly a minute. He then liquefied the suit a moment later, the nano-material flowing into a cube on the floor. The weapons that had been integrated into the suit detached, lying around Jackson's body, a thin layer of frost still coating him.

Alpha carefully picked Jackson up and laid him inside the medpod, the door closing a moment later and as the pod activated.

Bits interfaced with the medpod while automated probes from the sides engaged, running scans and assessing his condition. The words *Subject deceased* appeared on the window of the pod in flashing red letters.

Bits focused on the nanites inside Jackson's body, instructing them to reverse the cryo-protocols. Slowly, over the course of the next minute and a half, the nanites and pod carefully thawed his cells, the air in the pod warming around him and melting the layer of frost on his skin. Next, Bits initiated a carefully designed bio-repair mode, injecting Jackson with fresh nanites from the pod across multiple locations on his body. The tiny devices quickly went to work, addressing the cellular damage caused by the flash freezing and any other potential harm caused by the cargo matter transporter.

Bits allowed the nanites to do their work, ever cognizant of the clock, noting that Jackson had now, technically, been dead for close to six and a half minutes in real time, and close to two minutes as he began thawing out from the cryo-freezing. Still within the parameters for resuscitation, but in uncharted waters after the matter transportation.

He ran a quick scan to check on Jackson's status. Satisfied with the results, he instructed the medpod to begin resuscitation protocols. Two small arms deployed inside the pod, one pressing up against Jackson's chest, and the other, his rib cage under his left arm, followed by an oxygen mask lowering over his face. The monitors on the pod began scanning for life signs while the arms delivered micro shocks, attempting to restart Jackson's heart.

His body twitched as the shocks ran through him, the cardio monitor registering the electrical spikes, then flatlining once more. The words *No independent pulmonary function* appeared on the pod's main panel.

Bits upped the voltage and repeated the process. Again, Jackson convulsed, but still no independent heartbeat followed.

He called for reinforcements, flooding Jackson's system with thousands of new nanites from the medpod's reserves, instructing them to aggressively target Jackson's heart, lungs, and other vital organs, attempting to jumpstart his system, while an unseen force began compressions on his chest, pumping his heart manually to circulate the nanites and initiate a cardiac rhythm.

Minutes passed while Bits allowed the pod and the nanites to work, watching the bio-readings closely and following the various guidelines and protocols the doctors at FoxBlind had added to his medical database. He studied the readings, searching for brain activity while Jackson's organs began to show signs of resuming their normal functions.

Still, his cardiac and neural patterns refused to return.

"His systems are coming online, but I do not believe it is working," Alpha135 said, breaking the silence.

Bits hesitated for a moment, uncertain what to do as the list of treatment options narrowed and the clock continued to tick higher, the chances of irreparable damage growing. "I believe you are correct. Administering adrenaline."

A small device moved into position, injecting Jackson with a dose of adrenaline. The pod reverted back to delivering controlled shocks, Jackson's body convulsing in response before flatlining once more.

Bits noted the time, seven minutes now in real time, approaching an ethical line where he would be forced to decide: follow standard protocols after Jackson reached the nine-minute mark and call his official time of death, or press on and risk resuscitating him, possibly with permanent brain damage.

Jackson's body shook violently as a higher charge shot through him. The cardio monitor displayed the spikes caused by the shocks, but no other activity followed. The team at FoxBlind had prepared for the worst, researching several experimental resuscitation treatments in the event that something went wrong. There were risks and unknowns, Bits knew, but he was losing his best friend and would do anything within his power to save him.

He focused his processing power on the nanites while he interfaced with the pod's three-dimensional imaging and his own internal systems, reconfiguring the nanites to form hundreds of small constructs within Jackson's heart.

The nanite constructs activated, moving in a choreographed pattern, forcing Jackson's muscles to expand and contract as though his heart were beating naturally while administering small internal shocks to stimulate the muscles.

The eight-minute mark passed, Bits running out of options as he accessed the experimental files, scanning for something, anything he could use to bring his friend back.

"What is your status?" Alpha135 asked, his voice conveying the slightest hint of urgency.

"I have been unable to find a treatment that has been successful. There are several options remaining. However, each of them has potentially dangerous side effects."

"I do not know Commander Jackson well, but I believe he would want you to try."

Bits paused at that, considering. "Thank you, Alpha," he said, the android's push breaking the stalemate in his programming as he accepted the potential harm and acted, selecting a serum the doctors had created based on a Canid hormone produced during the apex of the hunt. Bits instructed the pod to inject it directly into Jackson's circulatory system and waited.

Seconds passed as the foreign substance entered Jackson's bloodstream, his body twitching for several seconds, a flash of bio-signs appearing on the monitors as it took hold.

A steady pattern emerged, Bits calling off the nanites artificially pumping Jackson's heart and allowing it to resume normal function.

Several brainwave spikes appeared, the patterns weak but steady.

Suddenly, Jackson's body convulsed violently, his muscles tensing, his body twisting and writhing before falling back in the pod, limp and motionless.

The bio-monitors went flat, a steady droning tone indicating that all vital signs had ceased.

Several seconds passed, a veritable eternity for Bits as he contemplated that this was the end. That his host, his home, his best friend and reason for living, was gone.

Suddenly, Jackson's heart pounded in his chest, his eyes shooting open, bloodshot and full of rage as he frantically clawed and pounded on the glass of the pod, bloodying the clear panel with his fists. A visceral sound came from beneath the oxygen mask over his face as the Canid hormone pulsed through his veins, the rush of it overwhelming all rational thought, activating his fight reflex and dialing it up to eleven.

Bits calmly spoke to him through his auditory implant. "William, it's okay. You're all right. You're back," he said reassuringly, instructing the pod to flow a small amount of sedative gas into the chamber as, slowly, the ultra-adrenaline rush subsided and Jackson's frantic flailing settled.

Bits quickly went to work, restraining Jackson and directing the nanites in his body to collect the Canid hormone molecules, while instructing the pod to attach several tubes to his arms and legs, filtering the cocktail of drugs out of his system.

Seconds passed, Jackson breathing heavily, his vision blurry at first, his hands still clenched shut, knuckles and fingertips bleeding from pounding and clawing on the glass. Slowly, the wave of rage passed, and his mind recovered. "Bits?" he asked, his voice weak.

"Yes, William. You are back on board the *Phoenix* in a medpod. You are alive and are going to be okay."

"Bits…I saw Amy. She was there. They all were there… I—"

"It's okay, I'm here. Please, lie back and rest. Your body has been through a severe trauma, and I need to perform significant maintenance on your system. Please lie still. Everything is going to be all right."

Jackson relaxed, closing his eyes, an intense pain registering throughout his body as he came down from the high: the combination of the cryo-freezing, the aftereffects of the electric shocks, and the side effects of the aggressive foreign hormone in his system. His limbs tingled from the adrenaline, his head feeling light and dizzy while the pod went to work flushing the drugs, excess nanites, and other chemicals from his system, slowly leveling him out.

He folded his hands on his stomach, attempting to focus on his breathing while he pushed away the pain, his mind racing as it tried desperately to hold on to what he had just seen: Amy. His parents. His brother. Friends he hadn't thought of in years. They'd *called* to him. He could see their smiling faces, white light all around them in the distance, their voices echoing in his mind.

He focused on Bits's words: *Everything is going to be all right.*

But nothing could have been further from the truth.

CHAPTER 9
DAMAGE

Jackson awoke to the sound of an alarm blaring across the ship.

"Open," he commanded, the medpod tilting up in response, the tubes from his arms retracting, quickly replaced with small healing patches. The door swung wide, and he leaned forward, carefully stepping out into the near blackness of the medical bay, the only illumination that from the emergency lights flashing in time with the alarm.

Disoriented, he struggled to maintain his balance, moving slowly towards the door on unsteady legs. He stepped out into the corridor. "Bits, report! What the hell's happening?" he shouted, his throat raw, the sound of his own voice sending a wave of pain flashing behind his eyes. "Deactivate alarm!" he roared, leaning back against a wall to steady himself, his eyes closed while his hand rubbed his temples, attempting to quell the throbbing.

The alarm ceased a moment later, Bits responding softly in his auditory implant, "My apologies, William."

"What the hell's going on?" he asked, taking a tentative step, the pulsing from the flashing lights still burned into his vision like sunspots.

"We are in trouble," Bits stated plainly.

"How bad?" he asked, his right arm hugging his chest, cradling his aching ribs while he kept his left out to steady himself, slowly making his way towards the bridge.

"The *Phoenix* has sustained heavy damage from our attack on the Imperium facilities and the leading edge of the shockwave as we entered slipstream. Unfortunately, the slipstream drive has been compromised."

"What does that mean?"

"The drive requires its initial power from our ship's quantum core. Once active, however, the slipstream drive generates a micro-gravitational inversion, allowing it to pierce subspace and opening the conduit for us to travel. As we move through slipstream, the inversion grows, generating its own power as it increases our speed until it reaches optimal levels. The drive has containment protocols to keep the inversion from growing too large, including power regulators to siphon off excess power, thus stabilizing the siz—"

"You can skip the tech briefing, buddy. Just keep it simple," Jackson interjected, the ship rocking, forcing him to steady himself on a bulkhead as he continued towards the bridge.

"Understood. Power levels in the drive have been slowly increasing over the past three and a half hours, as per normal operations, increasing our speed. A problem occurred, however, just over two hours ago, when the inversion suddenly grew beyond specified parameters and created a powerful gravity spike."

"Wait, I know I said to skip the tech briefing, but when you say inversion, do you mean the drive creates a microscopic black hole?"

"Affirmative."

"Oh shit. And it's growing?"

"Correct. The gravity spike caused a surge in energy, and two of the power regulators inside the drive fused in a closed position. Since that time, power levels have begun to exceed the drive's containment capacity, and the quantum inversion has grown considerably, creating a denser, more compressed subspace field that warps space-time around it."

"Well, that doesn't sound good. What can we do?" he asked, finally reaching the bridge and taking a seat in the command chair, his body feeling as though he'd just run a marathon, gone on a three-day drinking binge, then went four rounds in an MMA ring.

"I was able to buy us some time by carefully siphoning power using the remaining regulator, but it is not enough. I have shunted excess power into as many ship's systems as possible, but multiple power conduits have been damaged across the ship, and the drive's internal battery system, where it is designed to go, is offline. Simply put, I am running out of places to route the excess energy, and an overload is imminent."

"Yeah, not to mention we've got a tiny black hole growing inside our ship! Options?"

"With the regulators fused, the only option left is to initiate a hard shutdown. That should collapse the singularity but will still leave us with the problem of hundreds of gigawatts of excess power, which will need to be rerouted elsewhere."

"And I'm guessing that nothing is looking promising to handle that much power, or you'd have done it already."

"That is correct. The only system which can handle that much raw power is the hyperdrive. It was taken offline, however, when the slipstream drive was installed."

"Can you bring it back online?"

"I believe so. Alpha is running simulations now. There are three problems, however: first, the hypervelocity drive is not designed to have that much raw power dumped into it all at once. If we initiate a hard shutdown of the slipstream drive, we will essentially be jump-starting the hyperdrive, rather than powering it up gradually."

"That sounds bad."

"Alpha and I believe it can handle the sudden surge. However, that brings us to the second problem of activating the hyperdrive while still within slipstream. We may fall out of slipstream, or we may remain in the slipstream conduit when the drive deactivates. We don't know for certain. The two technologies alter subspace utilizing significantly different methods to achieve FTL travel. There could be any number of possible outcomes of activating a hypervelocity drive within a slipstream subspace field, most of which are not likely to be favorable."

"Wonderful. What's the third problem?"

"The third problem is that the inversion – the black hole – will create significant gravitational waves before it collapses. We don't know what effects these will have while in slipstream, and, as you know, hyperdrives are more sensitive to gravitational anomalies."

"So, when it collapses and we jumpstart the hyperdrive, we may get a huge gravity spike at the same time."

"Correct. And, when the inversion collapses, it will also release another large surge of energy."

"This is turning into a really bad day. What's our position?" Jackson asked, rubbing his temple.

"We have overshot our egress point for FoxBlind by two minutes, fifteen seconds," Bits stated, as the ship rocked once more.

"What? How's that possible? We should still be deep within Imperium space, shouldn't we? I thought it would take us three and a half days to get back?"

"Normally, that is correct. However, the drive is still experimental. Its potential speed is theoretically much faster than the baseline speed at which it was programed to operate at. As the power in the drive increased beyond normal operational levels, so too has our speed increased exponentially. Our precise position is difficult to calculate. However, I estimate we will reach the far side of GCH space in less than one and a half minutes and will be approaching the outer spiral arm of the galaxy shortly thereafter."

"Shit," Jackson said, realizing that they could end up in the empty space between arms, or worse, the void of open space beyond the galaxy itself. "We don't have a choice. Kill the slipstream drive and shunt power to the hyperdrive," he said decisively. "It's either that or we're dead from the overload, and I think that I've been dead enough already for one lifetime."

"Acknowledged. I strongly recommend that you strap in and activate a stasis field."

"Understood," he replied, activating the command chair's safety harness and a stasis field to protect him from any sudden changes in speed. A soft blue light surrounded him a moment later, creating an artificial gravity field, and he turned to see Alpha135 still in the operations chair, similarly ready, his eyes closed while he sat sitting silently processing. "Alpha, you good?"

The android's eyes opened. "I have completed three hundred million, two hundred twenty-seven thousand calculations and run tens of thousands of scenarios. The results are inconclusive; however, I've calculated our best chance down to the sixteenth decimal place. Precise instructions have been routed to the helm."

"*Right*, so you're good then," Jackson replied. "Great talk."

"Initiating slipstream hard shutdown and hyperdrive emergency startup sequence in ten seconds," Bits stated.

"Do I even want to know the odds?" Jackson asked.

"No," Bits and Alpha answered firmly in unison, another alarm blaring across the ship before Bits deactivated it.

"What was that?" he asked, certain that he didn't want to know.

Alpha responded, "Power levels are reaching critical in the slipstream drive. Overload is imminent. I estimate thirty-nine seconds to core breach," he said in a calm, perfectly detached voice.

"Initiating hard shutdown of the slipstream drive and simultaneously rerouting power to the hyperdrive in three, two, one, execute!" Bits called out as a sound like a switch being thrown echoed throughout the ship as he disengaged the slipstream drive.

Jackson listened as the steady hum of the slipstream drive cut out in an instant, replaced by a trembling *whun, whun, whun* bass as the hyperdrive powered up, the sound echoing throughout the ship. He watched on the viewscreen as the slipstream shimmer faded, blackness filling the screen for several seconds until, suddenly, the *Phoenix* lurched violently back. He gripped the armrests of his chair, a new sound echoing throughout the ship: a tortured, creaking metallic noise, as though the hull was being twisted and squeezed.

"We're rapidly decelerating; however, we have not yet exited the slipstream layer of subspace. I'm detecting high levels of theta radiation. Raising shields," Bits informed them. "The nav computer is attempting to compensate, recalibrating the hyperdrive for slipstream space operations."

Seconds later, the hyperdrive activated, a hyperspace conduit forming ahead of the ship. The *Phoenix* suddenly lurched forward, sucked into the aperture, the stasis fields the only thing keeping Jackson and Alpha from being crushed by the sudden and immense G-forces as the ship jumped a short distance. It reemerged an instant later, still in slipstream space, before initiating another jump, then another, the hyperdrive sputtering like an Indy car attempting to shift from first to fifth gear, then slipping back once more.

"What's happening?" Jackson called over the intense sound of the drive's *whun, whun, whun* thundering.

"The drive has too much power and cannot create a stable hyperspace gateway for more than a few seconds," Bits replied.

"What do we do?" he asked as another hyperspace convergence appeared before them, sucking the ship inside, throwing them hundreds of thousands of kilometers before destabilizing once more.

"Attempting to compensate. Shields are failing and structural integrity is approaching maximum limits," Bits reported.

"Processing," Alpha135 said as he interfaced with the ship's nav computer, his advanced processors attempting to analyze the data from the failed jumps.

"The drive is cycling again. Three of the four capacitors are offline, burned out from the intense power surges," Bits warned.

Seconds passed as the ship groaned around them, the gravitational forces of micro-inversion inside the slipstream drive pulling at them from all directions, twisting the ship and space-time around them.

"Jump solution calculated," Alpha said.

Bits entered the calculations into the helm, recalibrating the hyperdrive while Jackson watched on the screen as a hyperspace conduit formed in front of the ship, the circular opening expanding rapidly. The *Phoenix* launched through the opening with a burst of speed as the micro-black hole collapsed, releasing another surge of energy.

The image on the viewscreen blurred, the lights of hyperspace streaking past like lightning, the flashes leaving echoes in Jackson's vision.

He gripped his armrests, riding out the turbulence for several seconds before the ship slowly decelerated, the familiar colors of the hyperspace conduit surrounding the ship returning to normal. He held his breath, praying that it would hold this time as another wave of turbulence rattled the ship for several seconds before subsiding.

A minute passed, a wave of relief washing over him. "Whew, that was clos—"

An alarm blared out, shattering his respite.

"What now?"

Bits flipped the visual feed to the aft cameras, Jackson watching as the hyperspace conduit destabilized behind them, his mind recoiling in horror as he knew what was about to happen.

The conduit collapsed within seconds, sending the *Phoenix* spiraling out of control, suddenly emerging back into normal space at incredible speeds.

Jackson instantly felt the intense G-forces, despite the stasis field, pinning him to his seat. "*Bits*," he called, struggling to get the word out and another breath in as, all around him, sparks flew and consoles overloaded.

Bits fired the sublight engines and thrusters, attempting to slow them down, the engines sputtering as the ship's main power fluctuated. The *Phoenix* continued to spin out of control at immense speeds, far beyond its structural limits, the hull buckling and twisting from the strain. The sounds of tortured metal echoed throughout the corridors as the cascade of structural integrity failures crushed sections of the hull.

"Report," he called over the sounds of destruction, unable to hear Bits's response while his AI fired the thrusters once more, the spin slowly decreasing.

Nearly a minute passed as Bits focused, the carefully calculated bursts shaving off speed and leveling out the ship.

Jackson felt his body go slack, exhausted from the strain.

"We're back in normal space," Bits reported. "However, the ship has sustained heavy damage in the process."

"How bad is it?" he asked, closing his eyes for a moment while the waves of nausea slowly subsided.

"It will take several moments to assess the damage. Please stand by."

"I'm not going anywhere." Jackson coughed, a thin trail of smoke drifting towards him as he waved it away, turning to survey the still smoldering bridge. Several structural beams had collapsed around him, one narrowly missing the command chair. To his left, the tactical station lay in ruins, as did the helm. He turned to his right. "Alpha, you okay?" he asked, his heart dropping as he saw the android through the smoke, its body partially crushed beneath a beam.

"The damage is *severe*," Bits replied a moment later, pulling Jackson's attention away from their fallen colleague. "Multiple hull breaches detected. I've sealed off several compartments. However, we are venting atmosphere. Life support is at thirty-seven percent and dropping. The hyperdrive, slipstream, and stealth drives are all offline. Communications, shields, weapons, and cloaking systems have been destroyed. Short-range sensors and navigation systems are partially operational. Mid- and long-range are nonresponsive. Sublight engines and thrusters are functioning at twenty-two percent efficiency."

"What's the bad news?" Jackson asked, attempting a weak smile.

"Funny you should ask," Bits responded, attempting to lighten the mood. "The bad news is that the last jolt of energy from when the micro-inversion collapsed somehow supercharged the hypervelocity drive for several moments. It proved to be enough for the hyperdrive to break free from slipstream space. However, it also overloaded over sixty percent of the power conduits on the ship."

"Well, at least we're still alive. Any more bad news?"

"Affirmative. We will run out of oxygen in approximately fifteen hours and twenty-seven minutes, and the temperature inside the ship has begun to drop rapidly."

Jackson let out a breath, noticing the sudden puff of vapor in front of him as he felt the cold creeping in. "Options?"

"Sensors indicate we are close to a planet. The readings

are inconclusive, but based on the limited data, my best guess is an L-class world. The main computer core, including navigational charts, are offline, so we do not know what system we're in. With the ship venting atmosphere, however, we do not appear to have much of a choice but to attempt to land and take our chances."

"Can we estimate our approximate location based on our extended time in slipstream or on stellar cartography?"

"I have been attempting to use short-range sensors and my internal database to determine our location; however, sensors are having difficulty locking on to any recognizable star patterns. I believe that the optical processors are damaged."

"Best guess?"

"My best guess, taking into account the exponential speed we were traveling at in slipstream and the surge of speed in hyperspace, is that we overshot our egress point by approximately two thousand, eight hundred light-years, and are in the outer spiral arm of the galaxy, somewhere in the Celverus region, well beyond GCH space."

"Well…shit. This day just keeps getting worse and worse," Jackson said, realizing that it would take weeks to cover that much space at normal speeds. "Any idea what's out here?"

"Intelligence on this region is limited, with most of the habitable systems controlled by isolated pockets of influence. The Oceanic Union has laid claim to multiple sectors and minor races, such as the Selnirites and Vidarans; each have a small empire in this vicinity. Neither are friendly with the GCH, however, based on our limited encounters."

"The L-class planet you mentioned, any idea if someone staked a claim to it? Any active signals or satellites?"

"No, but it appears to be an oceanic world, as best I can tell, with only several small landmasses visible on optical sensors."

"Sounds like a good candidate for the Oceanic Union, at least. That would be better than nothing. I guess we don't have a choice. Let's land and repair the comms, then try to contact them."

"The ship's comms are severely damaged, but we do have the Guardian armor still on board. It sustained minor damage and is offline; however, its communications components should be salvageable, and are likely sufficient for what we need, as long as there is a ship or station within five light-years."

"Any systems in that range?"

"Unknown due to our limited sensor capacity."

"All right then. Sounds like we don't have much of a choice. Let's get there and hope for the best. How long will it take us to reach the planet?"

"Seventeen hours with our current engine capabilities and attempting to limit the structural strain on the ship. Unfortunately, life support will not last that long. You will need to wear an exo-suit for the duration of the trip. I recommend that you make repairs to get the Guardian back online first. With the ship's systems severely compromised, it will be the safest place to be when we land."

"Okay, set a course, best possible speed without tearing the ship apart. I'll suit up and get something to eat."

"There's one more matter we need to discuss."

"What's that, buddy?"

"You still need another fifteen hours, at minimum, in the medpod to recover. I'm afraid that there are several painful potential side effects from the Canid hormone I used to restart your heart, and you need the pod to continue treatments. I'm going to have to insist that you return to it as soon as the Guardian is repaired to ensure that you don't relapse."

"By *relapse*, you mean die, right?"

"I do. I was attempting to be delicate."

"Thanks for your concern, but I'm okay with it. You don't have to worry about my mental state, buddy. I'm all right. Anyway, it seems like I'm an expert at dying. Apparently, it's what I do best!" Jackson quipped.

"Yes, well, as the one responsible for bringing you back from the dead, I don't recommend trying it again anytime soon, unless you'd like it to become a permanent state."

Jackson smiled. "Yes, Dad."

Jackson suited up and devoured an emergency ration, not realizing how hungry he'd been, taking another portion with him for a snack later. Bits then sealed off the mess, along with the aft section of the ship, leaving him access only to the bridge and the operations room with a breathable atmosphere while attempting to consolidate the remaining heat.

Jackson turned his attention to repairing the Guardian, bringing it partially back online after a few hours of bypassing its damaged systems. Once satisfied with the repairs, Bits closed off the bridge, then opened the bulkhead to the next section of the ship, the remaining air in the operations room rushing out through breaches in the hull as the doors parted and the forcefields designed to keep it in failed to initialize. Jackson's boots magnetized, keeping him in place while the air shot out and the vacuum filled the operations compartment. Once the flow of air had ceased, he moved carefully, passing by a large breach in the hull where he could see clear out into space.

He arrived in the med bay a few minutes later, Bits sealing the door behind him, then recompressing the room, which had its own life support system used for medical quarantine procedures. Jackson returned to the medpod, the suit flowing into a belt around his waist as he lay back. The pod went to work while he slept fitfully for the next nine and a half hours, awakening as the cold began to creep in.

"Bits?" he asked, shaking off a chill.

"Yes, William."

"What time is it?"

"Time seems rather irrelevant at this point. However, it is nine hours and thirty-eight minutes since we last spoke. I was going to wake you soon. The temperature in the medical bay has dropped to negative seventeen degrees Celsius. I recommend that you suit up again before it reaches negative thirty as the med pod can only maintain a fifteen degree delta."

Jackson sighed. Growing up in Canada, he'd had more than his fair share of freezing winters. The one good thing that came from it, though, was that he had a decent tolerance for cold.

"Okay," he said, leaning forward while Bits flowed the suit around him. "Can you power up the ops platform?"

"Affirmative."

The suit crept across his skin as he waited, his body still aching, knowing that he was a long way from being back to a hundred percent after his experience. Within seconds, the suit covered him completely, his HUD showing a hard seal before Bits opened the pod, and he stepped out into the icy chill of the medical bay.

"You said I only got about nine and a half hours, right?"

"That is correct."

"But you'd said earlier that I needed a minimum of fifteen hours."

"Also correct. We will need to add several advanced med-kits to the suit to continue to treat you. The hormone I used to resuscitate you is barely compatible with human physiology and has thrown your body chemistry out of balance. Without treatment, your body will crash, causing severe headaches, nausea, vomiting, difficulty breathi—"

"Really bad stuff, got it," he interrupted, already feeling as though he had the flu, his entire body aching from head to toe. The thought of it getting worse not something he wished to consider at the moment.

Slowly and carefully, he made his way back to the operations room, the vacuum of space filling most of the ship as he noticed half a dozen other breaches and dimly lit corridors where the hull had twisted or was crushed several areas.

He entered the operations room a moment later, Bits sealing the doors and allowing air back in from the bridge, while attempting to reroute heat into the room, the temperature still well below minus one hundred and eighty degrees Celsius.

Jackson stepped up onto the ops platform, a panel appearing before him, flickering slightly. "Bits, can you engage a forcefield around the platform?" he asked, a quick flash of light appearing around him, then flickering several times before finally stabilizing.

"Pressurizing," Bits said, the hiss of air filling the platform a moment later. "Stand by. Atmosphere is stable; however, power is still fluctuating. I suggest that you hurry. The forcefield will likely only hold for a few minutes at most. Cycling heat now. Stand by," he said as he quickly flowed heat from one of the few operational life support units into the space inside the forcefield.

Jackson cycled through the ops platform display while the surrounding air grew warmer, examining his options. After a moment, he selected three extra nano-packs, then added the thermal and aquatic packages, grateful that the current Mark I suit was able to integrate more than one enhancement at a time, recalling the winter training exercise on Talzon III all those years ago where he had been forced to choose.

He switched to the next screen, opting for his favorite weapons configurations: plasma cannons, particle beams, cryo spray, micro-missiles, and a few grenades for good measure. He then added two advanced medical kits, along with another kyromonite sword, having come to trust the weapon and his skills with it far more after the battleship.

The suit retracted, the air still frigid around him, while the platform quickly installed the components, his suit reforming seconds later as he shook off a chill. Finally, he added two advanced med-kits and hit the Commit button.

Once completed, Bits decompressed the air around the platform, then deactivated the forcefield. Jackson moved to the far side of the room, opening a sealed locker and retrieving a handful of rations and water packs, then climbed into the Guardian.

Hours passed while he tried to sleep in the uncomfortable space, his body still sore from head to toe, while the battered *Phoenix* slowly limped towards the oceanic world, uncertain as to what awaited him.

CHAPTER 10
DESCENT

The *Phoenix* plummeted through the upper atmosphere of the oceanic world, surrounded by flames, a bird of fire falling from the heavens.

Jackson held on tight inside the Guardian, the turbulence and G-forces pinning him back while Bits attempted to control their descent.

"Systems fluctuating," Bits reported. "Shields holding at eleven percent. Engines are offline. Attempting to restart."

Seconds passed before the engines finally came back online, Bits pulling the ship up and leveling them out, the rough entry straining the already battered hull. Finally, after what felt like minutes, they were through the upper layers of the atmosphere, Jackson's body relaxing as the Gs subsided, breathing a sigh of relief. "Sitrep."

"We are approximately sixteen hundred kilometers from our target at an altitude of thirty-five kilometers. The ship sustained further damage upon atmospheric entry. Power to vertical landing thrusters is offline, and the port engine is failing."

"Options?"

"There is only one. We will need to make a water landing, which, based on current structural integrity, will be risky at best. I've plotted a series of maneuvers to reduce our speed as much as possible, but the hull may not hold together from the strain. The Guardian is likely to survive a crash landing due to its armor and sturdy design, and the operations center is well fortified. You will need to be prepared to exit the ship as it sinks, however, and I recommend you retrieve an emergency supply pack once we touch down, then leave as quickly as possible."

"Understood. Do what you can, buddy. I'll make a list of supplies to grab. Time to impact?"

"Three minutes, fourteen seconds. Assuming we don't break up in midair."

"Well, that's a cheery thought," Jackson said, focusing on their impending touchdown while pushing the fear from his thoughts. He knew from his search and rescue work that water landings were extremely dangerous, and a lot of things could go wrong. The thought of drowning again filled him with anxiety as he looked around the enclosed space of the Guardian, trying to push it out of his mind.

It was not a death he'd hoped to experience again.

He made a quick inventory in his mind of what he had to work with on board, remembering his training for survival in remote environments. Food, shelter, and weapons were the priorities, all of which the *Phoenix* had in the cargo bay, ready for emergency evac.

"Bits, any idea what types of lifeforms we're dealing with down there?" he asked, bracing his body, the ship banking hard to port as Bits attempted to reduce their speed.

"Negative. Sensors are down to seven percent efficiency," Bits replied curtly, his processors focused on the complex series of maneuvers as he simultaneously monitored the ship's systems, ensuring he didn't push it too far, splintering the fragile hull to pieces.

Finally, the *Phoenix* settled into a glide as they approached the seemingly endless blue waters below. The ship suddenly dropped, a final jolt from the reverse thrusters slowing their descent at the last second.

"Prepare for impact!" Bits called, Jackson activating a stasis field inside the Guardian, his muscles tensing as he awaited the inevitable.

The *Phoenix* touched down on its belly seconds later, the nose up as it skipped across the water, fragments of hull plating shearing off from the force of the impact. Jackson held on tight, his eyes closed, arms out, pressed against the insides of the Guardian should the stasis field fail. The armor jolted hard in the bay as the sounds of the ship being torn apart echoed all around them, Jackson praying it would hold together long enough to come to a stop.

A heavy thud impacted the Guardian from above, causing him to jump, and the ship finally slowed, coming to a stop seconds later, leaving a trail of smoke and debris in its wake.

For a brief second, the *Phoenix* floated on the surface before tipping backwards, the heavily damaged rear of the ship allowing water to flow in freely as it sank rapidly.

"Status?" he said, disengaging the stasis field and powering up the Guardian's systems.

"The *Phoenix* has suffered critical hull damage and is taking on water. Systems across the ship are failing."

"What do we have left?"

"The power core is still operational. However, power is only flowing to a few parts of the ship in the forward and mid sections. I need to cut power to some areas, or the exposed power conduits will electrify the water."

Jackson thought for a moment, quickly running priorities through his head. "What parts of the ship are already flooded?"

"The cargo bay and mess are both nearly submerged, and water is slowly filling the rest of the ship."

"Can you activate forcefields around the med bay and my quarters?"

"Affirmative, engaging."

"Good work. Let's at least keep those areas dry if possible. Can you try to seal the food stores in the mess?"

"Food stores automatically seal in the event of a water landing."

"Is there anything we can do for Alpha?" Jackson asked, a feeling of guilt washing over him that he hadn't thought of the fallen android sooner.

"I'm afraid not. However, his backup data core may still be intact and is waterproof. I recommend that we protect him with a forcefield as well. There is significant technical data that he gathered on the advanced Insectoid ships in his database, and we cannot confirm that our transmission made it out. It may prove invaluable when we return to the Fleet."

"Good call. If the power starts to fail, make the forcefield around Alpha a priority. We owe him that much, at least, for the sacrifice he made."

"Agreed. Activating forcefields."

"Any idea what's out there?" Jackson asked, the ship moaning around him, water filling more and more compartments and stressing the broken hull.

"We are just offshore of a large island, just south of the planet's equator. I had intended to land us farther up the coast, but the engines failed, and I was barely able to get the ship here as it was."

"We nearly landed in the open ocean?"

"Indeed. Fortunately, we appear to be in a good spot. As best as I can ascertain from the limited sensor readings, this area appears to be a stable tidal zone between a large coral reef and the island, near the southern tip. The ship should remain where it is, although there is a strong current running around the tip of the island and up around the outside of the reef."

"Any bio-signs nearby?"

"Negative."

"All right then, time to get moving. We'll figure the rest out as we go," he said, climbing out of the armor. His boots magnetized as he stepped onto the deck, the ship listing heavily to the aft, the air still trapped in the bridge and operations center, keeping it partially afloat. He adjusted his balance, knowing he didn't have long, listening as the sounds of rushing water reverberated throughout the corridors. "Bits, eject the Guardian and remote pilot it to shore."

"I'm afraid I cannot. The portal on the underside of the ship has been badly damaged, and a broken support beam has pinned the Guardian in its bay."

"Damn it. We need that comms array. How do I get it out?"

"It will take time to clear the broken support beam. I recommend that you focus on collecting supplies and return for it later. The armor is watertight, and I can protect access to it with a forcefield."

"That works," Jackson said, realizing he needed to get his supplies out, lest the ship settle in a position where he couldn't access key parts of it. He quickly made his way across the room to the arms locker, pulling out a rifle and slinging it over his shoulder, along with a sonic pistol, integrating them into his suit.

Water flowed into the room as he waded towards the bulkhead, activating his helmet. "Open the doors," he said, bracing himself off to the side, ready to fight the current.

The doors opened, and a rush of water filled the operations room just as Bits activated a forcefield, protecting the Guardian and allowing a space for Jackson to access the armor when he returned. Jackson waited until the room was full and the current stopped flowing, then made his way back through the ship towards the cargo bay.

Debris blocked his path in several places as he navigated the dark corridors, forcing him to reroute several times. The lights from his suit painted the ship in an eerie glow, giving it a foreign and unfamiliar feel.

He approached the cargo bay, the doors bent back out into the corridor, blocking his way. He braced himself with one foot on the wall, using the enhanced strength of his suit to force one of the doors open enough to fit through. Jackson slipped inside, the damage to the cargo bay severe, the ramp twisted and crushed, pieces of the hull above having collapsed, filling parts of the room. He reached the left wall, pressing his hand to a panel. A series of drawers slid open beside him and he reached inside the closest one, pulling out a watertight duffel bag containing emergency supplies, then pulled out two sentry cylinders from the next drawer, along with a flat octagonal disk about the size of a pizza box from the third.

He walked towards the rear of the bay, the drag from various items hanging from his arms making the going slow and arduous. A moment later, he reached the back wall, pressing the button to open the ramp. The gears strained, the metal creaking and groaning before it finally opened.

Jackson stepped out onto the ramp, the ship listing suddenly to the side. The bottom of the seabed rapidly grew closer as the ship glided down backwards towards the bottom, unable to maintain its tenuous floatation any longer.

Jackson dropped the equipment he was carrying, activating his suit's thrusters and rocketing back, deeper into the ship as the ocean floor raced closer. He stopped at the back wall of the cargo bay, grabbing hold of the doorframe just as the ship hit the bottom, the force of the impact throwing him forward through the water.

Two more structural beams, along with half a dozen heavy metal panels from the ceiling of the cargo bay, collapsed around him, one nearly crushing his arm as he managed to pull it aside at the last second, twisting in the dark water to evade the debris. A cloud of sand rushed in, filling the cargo bay, obscuring his vision and leaving him disoriented, uncertain which way was up.

The front of the ship settled on the bottom a moment later with a hard thud, causing two more metal panels to come crashing down from the ceiling, the impact reverberating throughout the ship. Jackson waved his arms to right himself, then magnetized his boots once more to the deck to hold himself upright, waiting for several moments for the sand to settle and the water to clear.

Satisfied, he cleared a path back through the cargo bay, pushing aside debris and heavy metal beams while making his way back towards the exit. The ramp was still partially open, though significantly worse for wear, along with the rest of the aft of the ship, after slamming into the ocean floor.

The current outside the swept away the last of the disturbed sand, the seabed coming into focus ahead of him. After a minute, he spotted the duffel bag on the ocean floor a few meters away. He took a moment to retrieve the rest of his equipment from inside the ship, buried under panels and sand, then stepped forward, venturing outside. Jackson set the cylinders and disk down next to the duffel bag, then swam out from under the ship to the side to check out the damage.

"Bits, any lifeforms around to worry about?" he asked as he cleared the underside of the hull, turning to scan the water around him.

"There is a variety of life around the reef, but nothing within sensor range at this time that poses a threat."

"Good stuff," he said, swimming farther out to get a better view.

He stopped just over ten meters from the ship, turning around and taking in the damage, his heart sinking in his chest at the sight.

The back of the ship and the engines had taken the brunt of the impact when the *Phoenix* hit the bottom, crushing that part of the hull. The forward section, near where the portal for the Guardian was, rested atop a rocky rise in the seabed, the hull buckled and twisted atop it.

"Looks like her back is broken," he said with a heavy heart, the ship bent where it had hit the rocks, the normally straight hull now curved as the front of the ship bent down at a slight angle, shredded metal from enemy fire visible in half a dozen places.

“Indeed. The structural damage is severe,” Bits said, sensing the emotion in Jackson’s voice.

Jackson let out a strained breath, feeling the weight of the mission take hold.

He’d barely made it.

Alpha was offline, perhaps permanently.

And the now *Phoenix* lay broken on the bottom of an alien ocean.

He looked over his shoulder, taking in the vast reef behind him, stretching up along the island to his left as far as the eye could see. Vibrant schools of tropical fish swam around the brightly colored coral and plants, while creatures resembling sea turtles, only longer and with leathery shells on both their backs and bottoms, glided effortlessly, picking at the vegetation as they went. Other fish reminded him of manta rays, but with bioluminescent waves of color flickering along the edges of their wings. Dozens of other creatures he didn’t recognize flowed around the reef, a flourishing mosaic of life, indifferent to trivialities such as galactic conflicts as they went about a routine as old as time, unaware, thus far, of the stranger in their midst.

After a moment, he looked back, past the ship to where the sea floor gently rose, stretching out of the water to where it became a long, sandy beach. He turned to his right, the water growing darker. In the distance, he could see where the beach curved and transitioned into a rocky shoreline that formed the tip of the island. His HUD showed a stream of current sweeping past the edge of the rocks, curving around the outside of the reef and running up along the island. “Probably bringing lots of nutrients with it,” he said, recalling various nature documentaries he'd seen back on Earth. "That's likely why the reef is flourishing."

"Indeed, the current appears to be moving steadily, and I'm detecting rich biological matter, along with smaller life-forms resembling plankton and krill."

"Well, a healthy aquatic ecosystem is another good sign that the OU may have a presence here. I guess we'd better get to work and contact them."

"Agreed."

"Morph the suit to create flippers, would you?"

Bits transformed the suit, forming flippers on Jackson's feet. He reached the bottom of the ship a moment later, collecting his gear, then moving away, closer to the beach. He pressed a button on the octagonal disk, carabiners appearing around the edges that he clipped to the duffel bag and sentries. Satisfied, he pressed a button in the center of the disk, activating it, and the disk rapidly inflated, rising to the surface a moment later as a raft with its cargo in tow.

Jackson followed, stopping for a moment and looking back at the broken ship once more, a feeling of overwhelming loss tugging at his heart as he thought of all they'd been through together. It had been his home as much as anywhere since the war began, and it pained him to see it lying broken on the bottom of the sea, the stark realization hitting him that the *Phoenix* would never fly again.

"Goodbye, old friend," he whispered, turning slowly, then made his way to the surface.

CHAPTER 11
SHIPWRECKED

The raft bobbed on the waves, surrounded by glittering water as the light of the yellow sun shone high in the sky.

He reached the surface a moment later, grabbing hold of the side of the raft and staring at the beach, his HUD showing it nearly forty meters away as he bobbed up and down in the gentle swells. The bay where the *Phoenix* now lay was relatively calm compared to the gigantic ocean waves that crashed and roared in the distance as far as the eye could see past the tip of the island, and he shuddered once more at the thought of how close they'd come to landing in the open ocean.

"Bits, activate aquatic thrusters."

Two cylinder-shaped projections formed on his back, powering up with a hum. He tightened his grip on the raft, moving his right thumb as though he were squeezing an intangible throttle, the thrusters activating and driving him forward, pushing the raft ahead of him.

He reached the beach moments later, releasing his thumb to stop the thrusters, then stood up, walking out of the water, dragging the raft behind him into the shallows.

"All right," he said, unclasping the duffel bag and cylinders, then carried each of them up the beach to ensure they were high enough if the tides changed, before retrieving the raft and pulling it further ashore. "Bits, initiate sensor scan of the area and launch drones in survey mode."

"Acknowledged," Bits responded, a layer of the suit becoming fluid on each of Jackson's shoulders, forming four small drones which rose quickly up into the sky.

Jackson watched in his HUD as the drones relayed information, staring at the overhead view of himself standing on the sandy beach in real time, growing smaller as they gained altitude and more of this new world became fleshed out around him.

"Initial scan of the immediate area complete," Bits reported. "I've detected twenty-one species of fauna within a two-hundred-and-fifty-meter radius. None appear to pose a threat. The drones are approaching mapping altitude now."

"Sounds good," Jackson said, taking a seat on the edge of the raft, breathing heavily while taking a moment to gather his strength. "Wow, I'm really tired all of a sudden."

"That is likely due to the gravity on this world. It is one-point-three times Archonian standard," Bits informed him.

"Yeah, that would do it."

"It is well within tolerances. Your body will adjust in time."

"How's the air?"

"Breathable, but with slightly more oxygen and trace gases than you're used to. You may feel a little lightheaded until your body acclimates."

"Good to know," Jackson said, retracting his helmet, breathing in the warm, salty sea air as he leaned back, feeling the sun and wind on his face while the stunning blue sky, rolling sea, and untouched, pristine beach stretched out before him.

He rose, turning slowly, taking in a 360-degree view of his surroundings, then pulled up the holo-display on his wrist, checking the drones' images from above once more. He stood at the southern tip of the island where the land tapered into a point, forming a crescent shape with the beach tucked in on the west side and the rocky shoreline stretching out to the east. The rocks rose from the seabed, coming out from the water and appearing volcanic in origin. As they rounded the tip of the island, they quickly grew higher, with dark-gray-and-black, granite-looking outcroppings running steadily upward, rising into towering cliffs stretching out as far as he could see in the distance all along the eastern shoreline.

The golden sandy beach continued along the west side of the island, the waters appearing much calmer than on its eastern counterpart. The *Phoenix* lay in its watery grave offshore, at the bottom of the bay, between the protective reef about thirty meters from the tip of the island. A few sparse palm-like trees dotted the beach, leading back towards the thick green, blue, and purple jungle, which dominated the rest of the island.

He placed his hands together, then pulled them apart, the map moving from the display above his wrist into a wider view, that spread out between his hands as the drones continued their survey.

The beach stretched for hundreds of kilometers, a few rocky coves and small inland bays the only things breaking its northward sweep as it dominated the western shoreline. The drone to the east showed a wide valley leading up to grassy highlands before they rose into towering cliffs, dropping off hundreds of meters into the sea below. "Looks like a natural barrier," he said. "That side of the island appears to be where the dominant wind is coming from."

"The prevailing weather patterns so far appear to validate your hypothesis, William; however, they may shift from time to time."

"How far away is the next closest landmass?"

"The *Phoenix*'s optical and primary sensors were functioning at under ten percent efficiency as we came in, so it is difficult to say for certain, but there appeared to be several dozen smaller small islands nearby. There are no other land masses of significant size to the south, east, or west of the island for at least a thousand kilometers that I could detect. Sensors detected more land to the north. However, we came in from a southern trajectory, and it was too far away to get any clear readings."

"It's kinda like we're in Hawaii, then. Out in the middle of the ocean with not a whole lot around."

"That would appear to be an accurate comparison. However, this island appears to be much larger than any of the Hawaiian islands. We won't know the full size until the drones complete their mapping, but I would estimate that it's at least several hundred kilometers long and a hundred kilometers wide, based on the limited reconnaissance I was able to perform on our way here."

"Interesting," he said, continuing to watch the display, the drones showing valleys and rivers, fed from waterfalls in the highlands, crisscrossing the dense tropical jungle covering most of the interior of the island. The massive coral reef continued along the western side of the island, running in parallel and forming a barrier, protecting it from the larger swells dominating the open ocean.

"Have the drones found anything of interest yet?"

"The drones have detected one hundred and sixty-three additional species of wildlife so far, including what appear to be a species of pig, along with freshwater fish in the rivers, and a variety of birds and insects."

Jackson flipped the holo-projection to display the list of fauna, cycling through them to get a sense of what he was dealing with, two species quickly catching his attention. "Analysis," he said, examining the scans of a large predatory cat about the size of a jaguar or leopard. The scans appeared in the display, showing a detailed analysis of the fierce-looking creature: a lithe and agile predator, with powerful legs, razor-sharp claws, and formidable teeth. Tan fur with black spots covered its body, giving it good camouflage in the dark jungle, and a short mane of black fur ran along its humped spine, reminding him of a wild boar. "Let's keep a close eye out for these things. I don't want to run into a pack of them," he said, knowing that they could easily overpower him if he was caught unprepared.

The second species that caught his attention was another matter entirely – a spykeraet. Jackson had never seen one before, but Daria had told him about them once. They were native to many worlds and known to be highly territorial, aggressive, and deadly. He pulled up the scans, watching a recorded feed of the creature, reminding him of a wolverine or badger but with longer fur and sharper-looking features.

He thought back, recalling Daria's description of the creature. "*The spykeraet doesn't appear threatening, which is the mistake most people make. It's a small mammal, covered in soft fur, which mostly hunts rodents and insects. When hunting, protecting its territory, or threatened by a predator, however, its hairs become solid, acting as both a layer of armor and as deadly spikes. The spikes are similar to the quills of a porcupine. However, they secrete a deadly neurotoxin, which immobilizes then kills anything that comes in contact with them in a matter of seconds. The spykeraet also has sharp teeth and claws, which it can use to attack, and can be aggressive at times during mating season. Although they are generally weary of humanoids, they are curious and will attack if they feel threatened."*

"Let's keep away from these things as well," he said, Bits making a note to alert him if any spykeraet bio-signs were detected nearby.

"Fortunately, the drones have only detected half a dozen of them so far, scattered throughout the island," Bits said. "They appear to have large ranges, and so it shouldn't be too difficult to give them a wide berth."

Jackson nodded, watching as the drones continued their survey, switching back to the map view once more and asking Bits to reroute one of them to its maximum height, attempting to get a better view of the entire island, while the others focused closer to ground level on mapping the topology and fauna.

The drone quickly climbed higher, gaining altitude and revealing more of the landmass. As it reached its maximum height, he quickly realized that the island was massive. It would take days to map all of it. Possibly weeks if he needed it in a high level of detail. The island appeared to be over thirteen hundred kilometers long and just over two hundred and forty-eight kilometers across at the widest point. The highlands on the eastern side reached elevations of three hundred meters, and several of the valleys dipped well below sea level. A small archipelago of islands was visible on the western side, farther up near the northern end of the island, each island containing a similar jungle environment.

"What do you think, buddy?"

"The eastern side of the island appears to face the dominant oceanic wind and waves, while the western side is more protected. The majority of the native lifeforms appear to reside in the jungle. However, there is evidence that some of them venture to the shoreline to hunt. I recommend staying on the western side. There are several small coves which should provide shelter and a defensible position."

"Agreed. We'll make camp here tonight, then see about setting up in one of the coves if we're stuck here for a while. Hopefully, we're not here too long."

Jackson worked for the next few hours and, by nightfall, had set up camp near a small cluster of trees which were isolated from the main jungle, giving him good lines of sight in all directions, along with shelter from the wind. He'd found a small tent in the emergency duffel bag and used a cluster of trees to protect one side, while deploying the two sentries to cover the surrounding area. The sentries deployed as small tripods, each with a sensor array and weapons package on top consisting of a particle beam emitter and stunner to keep unwanted guests away.

As the sun set, the night grew significantly cooler. Jackson ventured out, finding some driftwood he'd passed earlier on the beach, and made a small fire in the space a few meters from his tent, sitting out and eating a pack of rations while basking in its heat.

As the distant orange-and-purple light on the horizon faded, the jungle came to life. A cacophony of sounds emanated from the thick foliage, keeping him on edge, his rifle close at hand.

As he finished his meal, he continued unpacking the duffel bag, discovering an emergency comms unit. "What do you think?"

"It is a Mark V emergency transmitter and beacon. Its capabilities are more limited than the unit on the Guardian. However, it has a range of two light-years."

Jackson activated the comm. "This is Commander William Jackson of the GCH. Does anyone read?" he asked excitedly, waiting with bated breath for a response. Static crackled as he rocked on the balls of his feet, his hand gripping the unit tightly. "Are we getting a signal out?"

"One moment," Bits replied, interfacing with the comms unit while he ran a diagnostic. "The signal is transmitting. However, the diagnostics indicate that the electromagnetic field on this planet is extremely powerful and may be interfering."

"Can you compensate?"

"Adjusting frequencies now. Try again."

"Hello, this is Commander William Jackson. Is anyone out there?" he asked, the desperation in his voice growing as he rocked more rapidly.

Silence filled the air as they waited.

Bits shifted the frequencies again, attempting to compensate for the strong electromagnetic field. Finally, after several minutes, he powered the transmitter down. "I'm sorry, William, but I do not believe that this unit has sufficient power to overcome the interference. The transmitter in the Guardian is more powerful and will likely prove more successful. I will, however, continue to send out a recorded message every ten minutes, rotating frequencies while you sleep."

"I guess it was too much to hope for us getting rescued right away," Jackson said, slightly deflated.

"We will find a way," Bits assured him. "I suggest you get some rest. Your body is still recovering and needs time to heal. I will activate one of the advanced med-kits and do what I can. However, your condition will get worse if you don't get proper medical attention soon."

"Well, that doesn't sound like fun. I'll get some rack time then. Keep your sensors peeled and wake me if there're any signs of trouble."

"Acknowledged. Sleep well."

Jackson climbed into the tent, drifting off to sleep moments later, exhausted from his ordeal and the strain of the stronger gravity.

He slept fitfully for the next several hours, tossing and turning as he dreamed of the Imperium battleship. In his nightmare, things had gone horribly wrong, the CMT unable to get him out and leaving him trapped in a small room. His mind raced, playing out the likely outcome, knowing there was nowhere to run while the terrifying sound of the Insectoid horde approached, their screeches and roars deafening as he waited helplessly for them to fall upon him and tear him to shreds.

He awoke, sweating and disoriented in the darkness, frantically feeling the inside of the tent, attempting to look for a way out, the sensation of being trapped in a small space overwhelming him.

"William," Bits said calmly, his voice slow and measured. "It's okay. You are safe."

A moment later, he snapped out of it, his world coming into focus as the dream faded, remembering where he was and relaxing somewhat.

"Right. Sorry, buddy," he said, breathing heavily and lying back down, falling asleep almost instantly.

He awoke hours later, covered in sweat once more, sitting up abruptly in the tent, jarred by the unfamiliar surroundings.

"William, are you all right?" Bits asked gently.

"Yeah…yeah," he stuttered, attempting to convince himself it was the truth. "I'm fine. Just another bad dream… I'll be okay," he said, lying back down, his eyes still open.

"Sleep well."

"Actually, no. I think I've slept enough," he said, noticing the faintest hint of light outside the tent. "Is it almost morning?"

"It is. I was going to allow you to sleep a while longer. Your body needs as much rest as possible."

"Thanks, but I'm not eager to return to *that* particular nightmare anytime soon. What's our sitrep?"

"The night was uneventful. Several small creatures ventured close to our camp, though none posed a threat. A large serpent resembling a python passed several dozen meters away just under an hour ago. I suspect the remaining heat of the fire drew it in, but I believe that once it sensed your presence, it moved on."

Jackson shuddered, his hatred of snakes a primal instinct. "Where's it now?" he asked, suddenly less keen to venture outside the tent, despite his bladder's insistence.

"It has moved off beyond the scanning range of the sentries. I believe that you are quite safe."

"All right, but kick the suit's scanners up to eleven once I'm outside. If horror movies have taught me anything, it's that predators love to attack when you're takin' a leak."

"I'll be sure to remember that wise and learned advice," Bits replied deadpan.

"Hey, don't go knocking horror movies, pal. You remember the museum? There's actually some pretty excellent wisdom in some of them about what *not* to do. Think of it like a training sim full of bad decisions."

"I will endeavor to give the genre another chance with this new analytical lens. And I concur, if our mission in the museum taught me anything, it's that horror movie protocols hold some truths."

Jackson stepped outside the tent, sweeping the area with his rifle, an icy chill shaking his body, partly from the cool morning air but also from the rampant stream of horror movies running through his head as he peered into the eerie darkness of the jungle. "Probably not the best thoughts to start the day," he said as his imagination pictured a set of glowing eyes watching him from the dense canopy, ready to strike.

He quickly relieved himself, then returned to the firepit, lighting the rest of the wood with a concentrated beam from his rifle, sending up a flash of light as it ignited. Jackson sat by the fire shaking off the chill and pulling up the map of the island once more.

The drones were still working, continuing to push farther north, exploring new territory while he slept. They'd now mapped nearly forty percent of the island in a good level of detail, providing him with a wealth of information and options to consider.

First things first, he thought, knowing that he needed a better place to set up camp if he was to be stuck there for a while. The small cluster of trees, while providing some comfort in being separated from the rest of the jungle, wouldn't do much in a tropical storm and provided only the barest of protection from a tactical perspective. He sat, studying several possibilities with interest, when a twig snapped in the distance.

He shot to his feet, the map disappearing as he gripped his rifle, sweeping his surroundings while Bits cycled through sensor modes. "Got anything?" he whispered.

"Negative. I'm not detecting any life signs within a thirty-meter range."

Jackson began to relax when a thump hit the sand just meters away. He turned, firing on instinct as his HUD locked on to the source of the motion.

Flames erupted from where the plasma bolt struck the sand, the view of the perpetrator becoming clear through the smoke. A small object resembling a coconut lay shattered and burning on the beach at the foot of a tree as a wave of relief washed over him, his body relaxing. "Attack of the killer coconuts, eh?"

"Yes, you certainly showed him who's the sentient life form and who's the now inedible fruit," Bits replied, not missing a beat.

Jackson laughed for the first time in days, a feeling of ease washing over him as his pent-up anxiety evaporated instantly. "Buddy, I think you've finally got it. It only took how many years?"

"Eight years, seventy-three days, fourteen hou—"

"Never mind," Jackson cut him off. "We'll work on rhetorical questions next," he said as another of the fruits hit the ground with a thud in the distance.

He sat back down, pulling up the map again. His mood lightened as he got back to searching for a new place to set up camp. Having spent a chilly night on the island already, he decided to revise his criteria to include shelter from the wind, a good stock of nearby firewood, and a source of clean water.

As he studied the map, he decided it was best to remain within a half day or less of a journey back to the *Phoenix*, knowing that if someone came looking, they would most likely find the ship first and start searching from there.

After spending nearly half an hour looking over his options, he settled on a spot about three kilometers up the beach from his current location: a small rocky cove on the west side of the island, which would provide good shelter and was reasonably defensible. A river ran just under half a kilometer away, which, based on the drone's scans, contained fresh water.

Scans of the jungle nearby had detected a number of small primates, which looked like spider monkeys. He hoped that if they were living there, there would be fruits or other sources of food. His emergency rations would last for a month, maybe two if he cut down on his portions, but he would need to diversify his diet over time to get all the vitamins and minerals that he needed to recover.

He packed up camp, still tired from the poor quality of sleep but determined to get moving. As he started walking up the beach towards the cove, the sun rose over the hills to the east. *At least that's something that's familiar,* he thought. *Maybe this place isn't half bad.*

The air grew hotter as the sun continued to rise. Within an hour, he was sweating profusely, struggling to make his way along the beach under the sweltering sun. He pushed on, approaching the cove a short time later, where the beach turned from soft, pristine sand into a carpet of small, smooth, water-worn pebbles. He reached the rocky outcropping which formed the south side of the cove and worked his way around the side, back in towards the jungle.

The rocks comprising the cove were easily six meters high and stretched out from the shore to just over ten meters into the water. The walls ended about eight meters from the tree line, giving some space between them as the pebbles transitioned into hardpacked dirt, leading deeper into the dark jungle canopy. He stopped in front of the entrance to the cove, taking it in for a moment. The rock formation on the south appeared to be made of dark volcanic rock, which curved slightly, creating a larger pocket of space inside. The wall on the north side was higher and flatter on the outside, providing a good defensive barrier. On the inside, it tapered down before disappearing beneath the sandy beach wedged between walls.

A lagoon filled with crystal-clear water rippled and shimmered in the midday sun, the small waves gently lapping up on the sandy beach. An opening appeared on the far side where the two walls dropped off into the sea, leaving a gateway to the ocean five meters wide, giving it a cozy feeling.

Several palm-like trees and plants clung to the wall along the north side, casting shadows inside the cove as the sun moved northwest across the sky.

"This looks pretty good. What do you think?"

"The entrance on the land side is only four and a half meters wide, which makes it easily defensible, and there is a suitable amount of space for a perimeter before the jungle begins," Bits responded. "The walls are tall, providing excellent defenses against the elements and predators, as well as shade. I'm detecting several small species of fish around the edge of the lagoon, and the river is less than half a kilometer away, providing fresh water. Based on the other options available from the drones' observations, I believe this location best meets our needs if we are to be stuck here for a longer period of time."

"Yeah, pretty much what I'm thinking too, although I'm hoping this is just a short vacation stop and we'll be out of here soon," he said, noticing the sun once more to the north as it beat down upon him. Either his sense of north and south was backwards, or they were below the equator, he realized, quickly deciding upon the latter, having already oriented himself with the former in his thinking and planning thus far.

A gentle wind swept through the openings of the cove, providing further relief from the intense tropical heat, and Jackson stood with his hands on his hips, surveying his new home, a smile creeping across his face.

"It'll do," he said, dropping the duffel bag from his shoulder as he got to work and began setting up camp excitedly.

Hours passed, and by the time the sun set, Jackson had settled nicely into his new home, deploying the sentries at either side of the entrance and setting up his tent on the flat ground inside the cove half a dozen meters back from the opening and on the north side to keep it in the shade during the day. Between the tent and the entrance, he laid out a wide circle of rocks, forming a basic firepit with a stockpile of dried wood stacked neatly on the southern side. He left ample room from his tent to the water's edge, lest something creep out behind him in the night. While he rationally knew it was unlikely, his imagination got the better of him once more. After all, he was on an unknown world, in uncharted space, and not a single living soul had any idea where he was. One couldn't be too careful, he figured.

His supplies lay spread out just outside the tent, atop the now deflated raft, using it as a tarp to cover the ground, keeping his gear off the sand. He spent the last few hours of daylight conducting a more thorough inventory of the duffel bag, getting a good sense of what he had to work with.

As evening fell, he began to sweat once more, despite the dropping temperature. His vision blurred as he stared at the fire, a sudden feeling of nausea taking hold. "Bits," he said, pushing down the urge to expel his dinner as he gagged slightly.

Bits, sensing his distress, quickly initiated a medical scan. "Your body is showing signs of sickness."

"Is it another side effect of the Canid hormone?"

"I do not believe so. While it is still having several adverse effects on your physiology, these symptoms are new, and it's possible that you've contracted a pathogen since we landed here. In your weakened condition, your immune system may not be able to compensate for it, even with your implants and the medical nanites. I'll perform a detailed analysis, but I recommend that you get some sleep and give your body time to rest and recover."

"No argument here," Jackson said, taking a sip of water from his canteen, then walking unsteadily back to lie down inside the tent, the feeling of nausea increasing as he felt like he was spinning as he lay down. "Wake me if anything happens."

"Of course, William. Sleep well."

Jackson fell into a deep sleep, while Bits began his analysis, his body continuing to shiver and sweat into the night.

CHAPTER 12
BRAVE NEW WORLD

The next two days were a living hell as Jackson's fever spiked, his body aching as it alternated between shivering and sweating in a never-ending cycle of misery. Hours passed while he lay curled up inside his tent, dizzy and nauseous, drifting in and out of restless sleep.

He awoke the next day in the midafternoon, delirious with a high fever, his head spinning as he crawled from the tent on all fours, the sounds of water lapping on the soft sand calling him to its cool embrace. He pulled himself to his feet, the glare of the sun on the water blinding, the heat unbearable. A gentle breeze caressed his skin, offering the tiniest sense of relief where he stood clad only in his boxers and a pair of shorts on top made from the exosuit. The rest he'd cast aside, his body needing to sweat out whatever it was he was fighting while he battled the raging fever.

He staggered several steps, his equilibrium betraying him as he stumbled into the water, falling onto his knees. Desperate for relief, he reached down, splashing water over his face, the effect refreshing but short-lived, the stifling heat evaporating it almost instantly. He looked up as the sun came out from behind a cloud a moment later, its full force beating down upon him, the warm, shallow water insufficient against its unrelenting power.

Determined to get the relief he so desperately craved, he crawled out farther until his body was completely submerged, the lagoon growing deeper and cooler the farther out he went. He swam away from the beach underwater, coming up for air, then diving down once more to cool his head near the bottom of the lagoon, the feeling of relief intoxicating. As he reached the edge of the cove where the rocky outcropping met the sea, he stopped on the surface treading water and staring out as the breakers crashed on the reef in the distance, the wind having switched directions from the day he'd arrived. He watched, entranced by their rhythmic pounding, the sounds of the ocean filling his senses as he felt the rush of the current just beyond.

Minutes passed, his body temperature slowly normalizing from the cool seawater, the fog which had enshrouded his mind for days finally dissipating. He breathed deeply, the serenity he felt a stark contrast to the agony he'd endured while his body fought off the virus for the past several days.

Suddenly, the current shifted, sweeping into the opening of the cove and grabbing hold of him with one powerful rush of water, pulling him out beyond the safety of the walls.

The current moved swiftly, becoming more and more powerful as it went, dragging him farther out, the riptide pulling him down. Jackson got a quick breath in before the pull sucked him under, battling frantically against the flow, unable to escape its grasp.

Bits redirected the nanites forming Jackson's shorts, using them to create a rudimentary aquatic thruster around his waist and attempting to break them free from the pull.

Jackson thrashed, his air beginning to run low, his instincts pushing his muscles to battle against the raging current. He breached the surface, gasping for air, swimming with all his might but unable to escape the flow as it pulled him under once more between breaths.

His instincts screamed at him to take a breath and replenish the air in his depleted lungs, and he fought against the urge with all of his will, knowing that if he let the water in, he was as good as dead.

Bits rerouted a stream of nanites towards Jackson's face, creeping them up his chest to form a breather, but stopped as the current pulled them down farther, quickly reconsidering and knowing he needed to break them free or it wouldn't matter.

He redirected as many nanites as possible to the aquatic thruster, cranking it up to maximum. The thruster pushed Jackson upwards, tipping the balance, breaking him free from the deadly current. He reached the surface seconds later, gasping for air, his consciousness hanging on by a mere thread. He breathed rapidly for several moments, the feeling of nearly fainting slowly fading as he bobbed in the gentle ocean swells.

Jackson looked around, still disoriented, the island coming into view then disappearing behind the waves. Several seconds passed while he got his bearings. He was free from the current, but still being dragged along by the eddies generated in its wake, panic setting in as he realized the island was growing farther and farther away.

He swam with all his strength, fighting the riptide once more while it continued to tug at him, attempting to pull him back into the suffocating depths. With the thruster's help, Jackson slowly gained ground back towards shore. The cove was nearly out of sight now, the current having carried him farther down along the island than he'd first realized. He pushed the thought aside, knowing that he needed to get to shore first before worrying about anything else.

He looked down, his feet passing just over the top of the reef, the fish below giving him a wide berth while several other creatures looked up at him, most simply content to go about their own business, while others appeared to be sizing him up.

As he reached forward to take another stroke, he felt something rubbery wrap around his left wrist. Jackson raised his arm out of the water, both shocked and terrified to see a small, bright blue octopus-like creature with six tentacles wrapped around his wrist. The creature suddenly panicked from being out of the water, digging its sharp, tiny beak into his flesh as its tentacles squeezed so hard he thought they might break his arm.

He quickly put his wrist back into the water, the creature relaxing slightly but still holding on as its tiny beak remained embedded in his forearm. Several agonizing minutes passed while Jackson continued to swim for shore. The current finally subsided, and the gentle swells pushed him towards the beach while he tried his best to keep his left arm immobilized and submerged, hoping that the creature would let go once he reached the water's edge, while stubbornly continuing to hold on tight.

"Ahh! What the fuck? Let go, you little bastard!" he cursed, resting on his hands and knees, attempting to gather his strength after desperate minutes of intense swimming. Finally, he caught his breath and looked down, gently touching the octopus's skin to the sand, hoping that the texture would trigger a flight response, but to no avail. He raised his hand up, careful to keep the creature's head submerged as he exposed its tentacles to the air, the creature squeezing tighter as a wave of pain shot through his entire arm like an electric shock. Jackson stood, the pain making him desperate as he darted for the nearest rock, his hand going numb, his skin turning purple. Once there, he smashed the creature against the rock repeatedly. "Let go!" he shouted, hitting it again and again until it finally died, and its grip loosened.

He fell to his knees, cradling his arm, his hand blue and his fingers completely numb from a lack of blood as he peeled away the last of the tentacles, trying to make a fist and finding himself unable, the damage to his tendons having sapped the strength from his hand. He reached down with his right hand, delicately pulling the remains of the beak out of his wrist with his nails, gritting his teeth.

"Hold your arm still, William," Bits said, flowing the suit around his wound and beginning medical protocols while Jackson rested, closing his eyes, the realization setting in at how close he'd come to death once more. After a few minutes, the feeling finally returned to his hand. His strength was still negligible, but at least he could make a proper fist again, and the damage didn't appear to be too severe.

He opened his eyes, suddenly becoming aware of his surroundings.

"Oh crap. Where the hell are we?"

"We are just over a kilometer from the cove. The current took you a considerable distance."

"Wonderful," he said, staring into the jungle, quickly realizing he was unarmed and defenseless. "Well, at least my head feels clearer now. And I think my fever finally broke."

"I believe that you still have a considerable way to go, but I'm happy to hear that you're feeling better. I've had your medical implants working on an antibody to combat the virus in your system. The nanites have done a good job thus far keeping it contained, but it is aggressive and replicates quickly. I hope to have the treatment perfected in the next few hours, and then you should notice a considerable improvement over the next few days if it works."

"That's good to hear. Thanks for taking care of me. I know that trying to combat an unknown virus in the field with just my implants and a med-kit is far from ideal."

"I'm hopeful that this will work, and we'll get you feeling better soon. Your immune system still needs time to recover, and I confess, I was very concerned about you these past few days."

"I honestly don't know what I ever did without you, buddy," he said, getting to his feet, the feeling of adrenaline fading as he slowly began walking back towards the cove, sticking to the open beach and keeping back a few meters from the water's edge.

After several minutes, he noticed that the texture of the beach had changed from a soft white sand to a coarse, rougher texture. A short time later, it changed once more, the beach dotted with smooth colorful rocks, spreading from the tree line out into the water.

"Weird, I wonder what created this?" he said as he quickly crossed the rocks, which, while smooth, were hot on his bare feet, relieved to find that another stretch of soft, cooler sand lay ahead.

He kept walking while he stared out at the sea, the trail of rocks continuing out all the way to the reef, an abundance of sea life visible just below the surface through his ocular implants.

This must be where the octopus latched on, he thought,

realizing that he'd been lucky that only one had gotten him as he drifted by, still amazed at how far the current had dragged him in such a short time, making a quick mental note to stay well back from the opening in the cove in the future.

He walked through a large area of soft, sugar-like sand, looking up at the jungle when a motion at the corner of his eye caught his attention. He looked over and saw something moving in the sand a few meters ahead, freezing in his tracks.

Jackson held his breath while standing perfectly still, watching and waiting, uncertain if the heat was getting to him once more or if it had been real.

He turned his head slowly, checking the surrounding area, his sharp eyes detecting several subtle movements all around him beneath the sand. He reached down slowly, finding a small seashell by his feet, then threw it several meters towards one of the spots where he'd seen movement.

The shell hit the ground, a snake shooting out from beneath the sand, striking with incredible speed. Its long, sharp fangs impaled the shell, shattering it to pieces in its powerful jaws.

Jackson felt a wave of fear as he watched the snake examine its catch, cleaning the sand from its fangs with a long, forked tongue. *Fangs equal venom*, he thought, knowing that if he was bitten in his current state, he was as good as dead.

The snake moved again, revealing its full length, just under two meters long, with three small horns on the top of its head and a thin band of red along the line of its mouth, a sharp contrast to its otherwise beige body. Black eyes, with a dull gray at the center, stared ahead, seemingly unable to see Jackson as it moved its head slightly from side to side, probing the air with its tongue. Finding nothing edible, it slowly retreated beneath the sand once more, ready to ambush the next prey that came within striking range.

"Bits," Jackson whispered. As he spoke, he could see multiple signs of motion all around him, moving through the sand towards him while he held perfectly still, not daring to speak again.

Jackson cleared his mind, focusing his thoughts, using their neural link to allow Bits to see what he envisioned in his mind's eye.

Bits reconfigured part of the suit, transforming some of the material that made up his shorts into its liquid form, creeping it up Jackson's body and onto his head. Bits then formed a thin headband with a small window of nanomaterial over his right eye, creating a small heads-up display.

Jackson stared down at the sand while Bits cycled through scanning modes, and he focused his mind on his next objective.

He pressed his hand to his waist and the remaining shorts he wore liquified, routing the material to his right hand, where Bits formed a thin but strong spear, nearly the length of Jackson's body, with a sharp, two-pronged fork on the end.

A second later, the snake came into view, the display over his eye locking on. Jackson turned his head, taking in his surroundings, confirming his fears that a pack of the predators was stalking him.

His heart raced in his chest as he realized he'd walked into what appeared to be a large hunting area where over thirty of the creatures had congregated, waiting for unsuspecting prey.

He carefully twisted his body to look behind him, terrified to see that several snakes had already honed in on the vibrations from his previous steps, cutting off his escape. The thought hit him that if he'd gone much farther, several of them would have closed in from behind, and he likely never would have known what hit him.

As his heart beat faster, the snakes continued to move towards him, sensing the minute vibrations through the sand. He breathed in slowly, attempting to calm himself as the one closest to him slithered silently, drawn in by his pulse.

As the snake came nearer, he realized that pinning it might not be enough. He closed his eyes and focused, Bits responding, transforming the end of the spear into a single, razor-sharp harpoon with a barbed end.

The snake continued to inch closer and closer, its head moving from side to side, trying to locate its elusive prey. Jackson tensed as it reached striking range, remembering its speed as it struck the shell, suddenly uncertain if he'd be fast enough. If he missed and wounded it, its movements would undoubtedly alert the rest of its pack.

He had to kill it with one shot.

He raised his arm, gripping the spear. His hand was steady as he aimed for the wide spot of the snake's head and struck, his harpoon striking the snake in the back of the head, slightly to one side, severely injuring it but not killing it.

The creature thrashed wildly, its body breaching the sand, whipping its tail and striking the ground all around it. The impacts sprayed sand in all directions while Jackson held on tightly to the spear, afraid that it would shake itself loose. He snapped his head to the side, frantically searching for the other snakes, certain that they would be drawn to the thrashing of injured prey. Instead, something unexpected happened; they all backed away.

Jackson whispered to Bits to wrap the end of the spear around the snake so that it couldn't shake itself free, then slowly took a small step forward. Then another. He lifted the spear, bringing the snake's head up with it as he did, its dark black-and-gray eyes staring directly at him, its fangs dripping with fresh venom as it tried to open its mouth, desperate to strike him.

He swung it around, using its still-thrashing tail to sweep the ground ahead of him, clearing a wide path as he moved forward, carefully checking each step. Finally, he reached the end of what appeared to be their hunting area, whispering to Bits, who altered the end of the spear, severing the snake's spine and killing it instantly.

Jackson turned, staring back at the wide stretch of sand, watching as the snakes resumed their hunt, spreading out and lying in wait for the next unsuspecting prey to wander through. A shiver went down his spine as he stared at the two-meter-long predator hanging from the spear, blood dripping from its head. For a moment, he thought about bringing it back to eat, but the thought quickly turned his stomach. He hated snakes and couldn't get rid of it fast enough. He shook the spear, Bits sensing his intentions and releasing it, the snake's body falling to the ground, still twitching ever so slightly.

He continued back to the cove, carefully picking his way along the coastline, keeping close to the water's edge, ever watchful for any other predators. His hand gripped the spear tightly; ready should he need it.

The rest of the walk back was mercifully uneventful, and Jackson breathed a sigh of relief as the cove grew closer. His neck and upper back ached from the late-afternoon sun beating down upon him, burning his skin.

Finally, he made it back to camp. Dehydrated and utterly exhausted, he drank from his canteen, then fell into a deep sleep for hours, the snake haunting his dreams, the image of its eyes and deadly fangs burned into his memory.

CHAPTER 13
INTERLOPER

Several more days passed by while Jackson spent most of his time resting and recovering. The treatment Bits had devised worked, the combination of the new synthetic antibodies and nanites beating back the virus that had plagued him. Finally, he felt as though he was bouncing back both from it and getting over the toll on his body from the mission to the Imperium shipyard.

He'd kept close to his camp for several more days, focusing on small jobs to occupy his mind, while getting his strength back. Slowly, he had ventured out into the nearby jungle, exploring his surroundings and foraging. His hunger had returned with a vengeance as his health improved, and although he still felt somewhat weak from his ordeal, Jackson finally felt as though he was making progress.

The emergency canteen had been a lifesaver, able to siphon water from the moisture in the air and allowing him time to recover and stay near his camp without the need to risk venturing too far into the dense jungle to the freshwater river.

His thirst, however, had been unquenchable, as he sweated constantly in the intense heat and needed fluids to recover. Normally, the canteen would have met his needs, but he was slowly discovering that the planet's unusually strong electromagnetic field was beginning to take a toll on some of his technology. The canteen was only working at about sixty percent efficiency, according to the small display on the side, and simply wasn't producing enough to satisfy his insatiable thirst each day.

Some of the technology, such as his suit, weapons, the sentries, and the transmitter, appeared thus far unaffected. The military grade electronic components hardened against electromagnetic pulses. However, the smaller power cells and batteries within the other tech showed signs of degradation, appearing to be more susceptible. Fortunately, most GCH technology had multiple power generation modes for emergencies such as this, and Jackson was able to supplement their power drain by using solar charging during the daylight hours or recharging some of it from the suit.

"Well, I think today's the day. I need to get out and stretch my legs. How far to the nearest fresh water again?" he asked.

"Approximately four hundred and eighty meters to the northeast," Bits replied, bringing the route up on Jackson's ocular implants.

"Anything to be worried about between here and there?"

"I've detected numerous lifeforms in the area, some of which are dangerous, but none of them pose a significant threat. There are, however, the other lifeforms on the island, such as the cats we discovered when we first arrived, along with around two dozen other species, which are considered hazard-level five or higher."

Jackson let out a breath, relieved that there didn't seem to be any predators in the immediate area, but recalling from his encounters with the octopus and snakes that danger could lie where he least expected it. Although he was back on his feet from the illness, he still had a long way to go to get back to normal, having lost several pounds over the past week. The toll of his death and resurrection lingered, his left side still tender in places, and the stronger gravity, along with the higher oxygen, strained his body and lungs, but as the days passed, he began feeling stronger and breathed a bit easier. Bits had recommended finding a source of natural protein to help his body heal and adapt faster, along with some fruit for additional vitamins and nutrients.

"Status on the transmitter?"

"I have still been unable to penetrate the planet's electromagnetic interference."

"Damn. Well, at least we can still go back for the one in the Guardian. Now that I'm back on my feet, we'll need to get our camp properly squared away, then make a trip back to the *Phoenix*."

"Agreed."

"All right, suit me up. Let's get some water and see if we can find some food along the way," Jackson said, the suit expanding from the belt around his waist and covering his body. He reached down, grabbing the rifle and sword, then picked up his canteen and pressed it to his waist. He fumbled through the duffle bag for a moment, pulling out the plasma cannon and pressing it to his wrist, integrating it with the suit, then stood, waiting while a diagnostic cycle completed in his HUD.

He brushed a large palm leaf from his path, stepping into the jungle, rifle at the ready, sweeping the area, his senses on edge, ready for anything. The foliage looked a lot like that of the tropics on Earth, aside from the odd blue or purple plant, the mostly green jungle providing a sense of familiarity that put him somewhat at ease, even if he'd never been to one before in person.

His mind flashed back to his basic training, reminding him to never take anything for granted, especially on an unknown alien world, and he firmed his resolve to stay vigilant and alert.

Carefully, he made his way through the thick foliage, using the sword to clear a path and keeping his sensors dialed up for any signs of movement or life. Bits kept two drones overhead, monitoring the area around him as he ventured deeper into the jungle. A minute later, he came across a path appearing to be a game trail, heavily worn and recently used. He followed it, using his sword to widen the path where he could, making his journey easier. Not long after, he could hear the river babbling in the distance.

Jackson stepped into a clearing where half a dozen towering trees stretched overhead, thin columns of light streaming down between the branches, limiting the undergrowth. He crossed the open space, taken in by the beauty of the river and the backdrop of the jungle on the far side, the rays of light giving it an almost supernatural feeling.

As he approached the river, Bits ran a quick scan, confirming that the water was fresh, and the area was clear of any threats.

Jackson moved to the edge of the riverbank, the jungle dropping off into a twisted tangle of roots resembling mangroves that continued down into the water, weaving in and out of the jungle floor. The river flowed steadily, close to eight meters wide on average, twisting and turning through the dense jungle. Beams of sunlight cut through the canopy, the water sparkling in its glow.

To his left, the river stretched out for as far as he could see, turning here and there before disappearing into the jungle in the distance. To his right, it banked more sharply, concealing what lay further upstream as it twisted out of sight. Not far from where he stood, a rocky section of the riverbank extended into the water, forming a spit of land.

Jackson made his way down, stopping at the edge and peering into the clear water, then bent down and filled his canteen. The device hummed softly in his hand as it went to work, filtering and purifying the water, then removing any bacteria and parasites. Once the cycle was complete, he retracted his helmet, tipping the canteen back, and taking a long swig as he rose, standing in silence while he explored his surroundings in more detail.

The sounds of the water babbling calmed his mind, taking the edge off, while birds and other creatures chirped and squeaked, the jungle around him full of life. He breathed deeply, the clean air still feeling heavy as it entered his lungs, causing him to wheeze slightly. He relaxed, letting the sounds around him and the smells fill his senses, a feeling of tranquility washing over him as he closed his eyes.

After a minute, he felt better than he had in over a week, reinvigorated by the peacefulness surrounding him. He looked up as an enormous bird resembling a falcon flew past, diving towards the river. Its claws splashed through the surface and latched onto a fish, pulling it up while its powerful wings lifted it back high into the air.

"Looks like I might have to start fishing for some protein," he said, bending down to fill up his canteen once more.

A blur appeared in his peripheral vision a second later, Bits reacting instantly, reforming the helmet and hardening the suit as a large predatory cat leapt from the underbrush down on top of him, bowling him over.

Its razor-sharp claws dug in, gaining purchase as they slowly cut through the outer layer of the suit, Jackson knowing it could only hold out for so long while he struggled to fight it off.

He tried to roll to his side, but it had him pinned on his back, his rifle just over half a meter away. "Bits, activate defenses!" he called, just as the cat's claws penetrated the suit, the tips sinking into his flesh along his ribs, causing him to cry out in pain.

Bits activated the suit's electrical defenses, shocking the cat. It let out a furious roar, but it still held on, determined not to let go of its prey. Jackson's hands held tight, gripping its lower jaw, using all of his enhanced strength to keep it away from his face and neck.

"Blades!" he called through the pain, and the suit morphed, two broad, flat blades forming on his wrists as he let go with one hand and swung wildly, cutting the creature along its neck and midsection, then swiping with the other, forcing it to back off.

He scrambled back across the rocks, putting a few meters between them, his right hand clutching his abdomen where the claws had dug deep, blood flowing freely from the wound. The cat, though injured, refused to retreat. The top predator was unaccustomed to giving up a meal as it circled, prepared to lunge at him again.

Jackson eyed it, anticipating the attack, waiting for the right moment, his left arm extended towards it. The predator crouched down, ready to strike, and Jackson spotted his opening and fired. A plasma bolt ripped through the cat as it fell to the ground, smoke drifting up in a slow curl from the burned flesh and hair.

Breathing heavily and shaking from the adrenaline, he lowered his arm, examining his wounds. The cat had gotten him under his left arm and along his side, an area still tender from the medpod's resuscitation efforts, and he was still shaken up from the initial impact, but Bits's quick thinking had spared him the worst of it.

Slowly, he got his breathing under control, keeping pressure on the wound while Bits initiated medical protocols. "Ahh," he groaned, the antiseptic stinging, compounding his torment with each breath full of pain. "How bad is it?"

"The wounds are mostly superficial. However, you have a broken rib from the initial impact and possibly have a slight concussion."

"Wonderful," Jackson said, blinking as the world drifted slightly in and out of focus. "What's the bad news?"

Before Bits could answer, a deafening roar erupted from the jungle. Jackson jumped back, both arms raised, weapons ready as several low, distinct growls followed, and he staggered back several steps, the suit's sensors attempting to lock on to the sources of the sounds.

"Damn it. The cat was part of a pack!" he said, slowing taking another step back, then reaching down and picking up the rifle. "Why can't I see them on sensors?"

"I do not know, William. They appear to have a natural cloaking ability of some kind. Cycling through scanning modes."

"There," he said as the creatures came into view, seven more of them hidden in the bushes in what appeared to be an attack formation. "Bits, scan the dead one and analyze."

Bits finished his scan a second later. "The one you killed is a female. Smaller than the rest, likely a beta in the pack structure. They appear to be able to mask their bio-signs and alter their coloring to blend in with their environment. These characteristics are rare in mammals and usually confined to reptilians and oceanic species," he said, continuing his analysis as several of the cats stepped forward as one, out into the open. "There appear to be three males and four females."

"That's fascinating, Bits, but can you find me an exit strategy that doesn't involve me being eaten alive?"

"I could activate the suit's flight systems, but I believe they may interpret that as a sign of fear and become emboldened."

"Yeah, well, they wouldn't be wrong. Let's keep that as a last resort. What do you suggest?"

"Back away slowly and to your left. My scans indicate that there is a path that is clear."

"Understood. All weapons ready. If one of these bastards tries anything, I want to be ready this time," he said, slowly backing away from the dead female, making his way along the riverbank back towards the edge of the jungle where it rose back up.

The rest of the pack continued moving towards their fallen comrade, all eyes locked on him. One of the males stepped forward, a low growl directed towards him, its body tensing, legs coiled.

Jackson read its intentions, firing at the ground a meter ahead. The plasma bolt struck a river rock, shattering it, sending scalding hot shrapnel into the air. The cat jumped back, evading the worst of it, the fur on its head slightly singed as it let out a louder, more aggressive roar.

He kept the rifle leveled at the pack as he continued to back away, reaching up with his left arm, despite the pain, and pulling himself up from the bank to the jungle floor, never breaking eye contact. He stood his ground for a moment, then slipped into the brush, the cats still watching but giving no signs of pursuit as he vanished into the dense foliage.

Once he was a dozen or so meters away, he ran, quickly making his way back to camp, the drones overhead keeping watch on his six.

He emerged from the jungle at a full sprint, running back past the sentries until he felt safe within the walls of the cove once more, a feeling of terror mixed with euphoria from his narrow escape washing over him.

"Holy shit," he said, lowering his helmet and catching his breath. "That was way too close."

"Indeed. I apologize for not seeing the initial attack coming sooner. The lifeforms on this planet appear to have unique abilities to mask their bio-signs. I will endeavor to find a solution and continue running multispectral scans going forward."

"Thanks, buddy. And no need to apologize. You saved my ass. Again. If you hadn't reacted, that thing would have probably ripped out my jugular before I even knew what hit me. We're gonna have to figure out a strategy to deal with them. They likely see me as an interloper in their territory. Hopefully, we won't be here much longer and that encounter will make them think twice about messing with us, and they'll leave us alone."

"Agreed. I will continue to analyze the sensor results."

"Sounds good," Jackson said as he sat on the raft, lying back while Bits tended to his wounds. "Damn. I just realized; I left the canteen behind at the river. We'll have to go back and get it."

"I have already instructed the drones to go back and retrieve it once the cats have left the area."

"Did I ever tell you that you're the best?"

"I live to serve," Bits replied cheerily.

"Well, I certainly keep screwing up enough to make sure you're never bored."

"Indeed, you've had more near-death and full-death experiences in the past two weeks than in the past year combined. It is certainly mentally stimulating attempting to keep you alive."

"I'll try not to make such a habit out of it. I seem to be pushing my luck a lot lately," he said, letting out a sigh of relief as the pain meds kicked in and the throbbing in his side subsided.

"Can you deploy a few drones to watch the surrounding jungle? It probably won't take long for scavengers to show up once that dead cat starts to smell, and I don't want another fight on my hands if something comes sniffing my trail."

"Acknowledged."

CHAPTER 14
RETRIBUTION

Jackson rested while Bits and the suit patched him up. His broken rib would heal in a day or two, as long as he took it easy, and the pain had almost completely subsided. Bits cleared him for some light activity and he spent the next few hours puttering around his camp, stockpiling more firewood and waiting until the cats had moved off.

Once the coast was clear, he went back to the river before the sun set. This time, he was prepared, heavily armed and with a dozen drones overhead, all running full multispectral scans to watch for any signs of trouble.

He arrived at the river and grabbed the dead cat by the tail, dragging it to water's edge, then sending it adrift downriver. Its bloated corpse kept it afloat, and he hoped the current would take it far away, keeping it and scavengers from his watering hole.

Jackson returned to camp with a full canteen and a ravenous appetite, eating a pack of rations before settling in for the night. He crept into his tent, too tired to stay up and have a fire, desperate for sleep's sweet embrace.

Jackson awoke hours later to the sound of weapons fire.

"Report!" he shouted over the noise.

"Sentries have engaged multiple targets. The cats you encountered earlier appear to have tracked us back to our camp."

"Oh shit! Suit me up!" he said, getting to his feet as Bits flowed the suit around him, hardening it for battle. "How come we didn't see them coming?"

"They only appeared in the surrounding jungle seconds ago and came in fast."

Jackson stepped out of the tent, rifle in hand. He reached back, pressing the sword to his back, then reached down, grabbing the cryo spray unit and particle beam from the floor of the tent, pressing one to each wrist.

"Sitrep!"

"The sentries have killed three of the creatures, but I'm detecting eleven more active bio-signs. They appear to be learning quickly, evading the sentries' weapons ranges and firing arcs."

"Okay, let's show these things who the new top of the food chain is around here," he said defiantly, gripping the rifle and moving to a firing position just behind the firepit.

"Be careful, William. One cat nearly killed you. You cannot afford to engage multiple animals at close range. They *will* overpower you!"

"Acknowledged. Coordinate with the sentries. Let's keep them at a distance and pick them off one by one."

Jackson flipped the rifle to sniper mode, bending down on one knee and taking his time, the drones overhead and the sentries' scanners locking onto several attackers and relaying their position in his HUD as he fired, picking off his first target easily.

The pack had initially been bold, three of the cats charging directly for the opening, but now that four of them were down, they grew warier of engaging in a direct frontal assault, pulling back and keeping to the trees, out of range of the sentries.

He lined up on another one, watching in his HUD as the creatures turned and growled at one another. "*Great*, they can communicate! This just keeps getting better and better," he said, firing as he picked off another one. "Bits, launch two more drones. I don't want any of them sneaking around behind me."

"Launching."

The drones took off from Jackson's shoulders, hovering over the cove, providing him with a bird's-eye view of the area while four others hovered above the jungle marking the predator's positions.

"Eight o'clock high, on the rocks. A large female is attempting to flank our position," Bits called out.

"On it!" Jackson said, spinning to his left as he spotted the agile female leaping gracefully across the top of the rock wall. He fired, but she was on the move and difficult to hit, bounding effortlessly over the ridge of the cove on the north side.

He watched in his HUD while she circled behind him, closing in on his position, waiting until she had a line on him, letting her believe she had the advantage. Suddenly, he spun and fired, grazing her flank, the cat dodging at the last second, attempting to evade the blast.

The cat roared, increasing her speed and bounding down the rocks towards him while he fired several more times, taking her out with multiple direct hits as she tumbled lifelessly to the ground.

"Two more have broken off and are scaling the rocks on the south side," Bits warned. "And another one of the cats just made a run for the sentries. It's wounded, but both sentries are down and inoperable."

"Watch the opening. I'll deal with these two first," he said, checking his HUD and quickly locating the two cats, switching the rifle to a rapid-fire setting and unleashing several volleys as they came into view. The closest of the two cats narrowly evaded the fire, retreating back up the rocks and out of sight. The second took several direct hits, falling onto the sandy beach and rolling, attempting to put out the flames as Jackson leveled the rifle, wasting no time in putting it out of its misery.

"There's still seven of them out there, but one of them is wounded," he said, turning and sweeping the area with his rifle.

"With the sentries down, they may come at you in force and try to overwhelm you," Bits cautioned.

"Right. We need to slow them down," he said, turning to the firepit, firing a particle beam from his wrist and igniting the dry logs, sweeping the beam across the pit several times to accelerate the growth of the fire. He ran over, picking up several burning branches and throwing them around him, forming a wide, loose circle of flames. Jackson recalled the strategy from several old Earth movies and hoped that these cats feared fire as most creatures did, keeping them at bay long enough for him to pick a few more of them off.

He took up a firing stance and switched the rifle back to sniper mode, lining up another distance shot, and taking down two more in a matter of seconds. A third cat darted from the group, using the trees for cover while he waited, anticipating its path. He fired a split second later, the animal going down.

The pack roared savagely in response. "I guess that was someone important," he said.

"I believe that was the alpha female," Bits replied. "She has been growling at several of the others, possibly giving them orders."

"If we can take out the alpha male, that might break them. Any sign of him?" Just as he finished asking, an ear-shattering roar echoed from the jungle. Jackson's heart skipped a beat as a huge male came barreling out of the darkness towards him, galloping at full speed. The cat closed on him, intent on vengeance.

He raised the rifle and fired, narrowly missing as the beast kept coming. A second later it leapt, soaring through the air and landing inside the circle of flames and lunging at him. Jackson instinctively held the rifle out in front of him with both hands, using it to fend off the cat's powerful jaws, his feet sliding backwards through the sand, unable to hold back the raw power of hundreds of kilos of pure muscle and bloodlust. It released its grip on the rifle, swiping with a paw and knocking it from Jackson's hands, then barreled into him and knocked him to the ground. The alpha male circled Jackson's prone form as he got back to one knee, a low, vicious growl coming from deep within it as it eyed him, the firelight flickering in its eyes.

The cat came at him once more, swiping with a huge paw, the razor-sharp claws scraping across his thigh, the speed and ferocity of the attack overwhelming him in the close quarters as he attempted to scramble back, the cat landing another blow to his shoulder and tearing through the suit.

Jackson pushed through the pain, knowing he had just seconds to live if he didn't fight back, reaching for the sword and spinning just in time to evade another powerful swipe.

Before he could get the sword up into a defensive stance, the cat leapt forward with its full force, barreling him over and slamming him into the ground, the wind nearly knocked out of him as the cat's weight fell upon him. The alpha's front claws dug into Jackson's shoulders as he bashed the side of its head with the hilt of the sword, while keeping the other hand under the cat's chin, fighting to keep its jaws away from his face.

He flicked the sword out to his side, activating it, the kyromonite blade growing instantly. He swung it around, cutting the cat along its side leaving a long gouge along its flank. The alpha male roared, knocking the sword from his hand onto the beach, the sound full of rage and pain deafening him inside his helmet.

The predator pressed down on Jackson's shoulders twisting its head towards his neck and going for the kill.

Bits hardened the suit to maximum, while Jackson got his left arm up, blocking the jaws with his arm at the last second. The cat clamped down, the power of its bite and its knife-like teeth piercing through the armor of the suit, blood flowing from Jackson's arm as his strength faded.

The cat pushed past his limp, injured arm, its mouth lunging for his face. He dodged his head to the side, avoiding the worst of it, but not enough as one of its huge canines caught purchase, cutting through the suit and into his cheek, its dagger-like tooth scraping against his orbital bone and leaving a trail of blood trickling into his eye.

Its breath filled his helmet, the vile smell of it nearly making him wretch as he struck the cat repeatedly with his free hand.

The cat raked its claws down Jackson's chest in response, leaving four deep wounds in its wake as he realized he had just seconds to live.

Bits took control of the suit around Jackson's left arm, using its enhanced strength to strike the cat hard in the ear while creating a construct of razor-sharp spikes on his fist. Jackson cried out in agony as Bits attacked with his badly injured arm, pushing through the pain, knowing that his AI had given him an opening and he might not get another.

He reached out for the sword, the cat rearing momentarily to escape the assault on its sensitive ears. Jackson fumbled for the handle as the creature recovered, shaking its head.

Finally, his hand found purchase on the hilt, his fingers wrapping around it, and he pulled the blade upward, its powered edge slicing through the cat's flesh, rending bone and flesh effortlessly in its path. The cat came down an instant later, its jaws open as it lunged for Jackson's head.

He pushed with all of his might, the sword driving deeper, reaching the cat's heart seconds later, killing it just as its opened jaws locked around Jackson's head.

The cat's full weight settled upon him, crushing him. He let go of the sword, struggling to get his right arm free. Finally, he got it clear, using the suit's strength to roll the cat off of him and slide out from under it, his body covered in blood and gore from head to toe.

Time seemed to slow as Jackson rose to his feet on unsteady legs, the circle of fire still burning around him while he stood over the corpse of the huge cat. He lowered his helmet, allowing the blood to drain from his eye, leaving his vision blurred on the left side.

He reached over, tearing the gore-covered sword from the corpse next to him, turning and facing down the three cats that remained, the group hovering just outside of the edge of the fire, their postures taut and ready to strike.

If they came at him, he was as good as dead. It was as simple as that, he knew.

Jackson raised the sword over his head with his right arm, preparing for the assault which was about to take his life, his left arm hanging uselessly at his side while he stood, towering over the alpha's broken body. He held the bloody sword high. "Ahh!" he screamed, daring them. "You want some more, you fuckers? Come on!"

The firelight reflected in the predators' eyes, each staring at him with cold, calculating malice. He glared back at them, his gaze equally vicious, determined that he'd take at least one of them before they overpowered him, his adrenaline spiking and pushing him to take a step forward.

Seconds passed, the stalemate hanging in the air as each side stared the other down.

Jackson took another an uneasy step forward, blood loss catching up with him, sapping his strength and beginning to make him feel as though he was going to pass out.

He stared into the eyes of the closest of the three, locking his gaze, daring it to come at him as he narrowed his eyes.

It stepped forward, seeing the stagger in Jackson's step and accepting the challenge. Just as the cat was about to strike, Bits redirected the drones overhead, forming them into a single large knife-like construct. The blade dropped rapidly from above, the precise strike driving deep into the back of the cat's head, the creature never knowing what hit it as it fell lifelessly to the ground.

Seconds passed in what felt like an eternity. Jackson's life hovering on a razor's edge. He was out of tricks. Out of options. He glared at the cats, arm raised, blood dripping from the sword in the firelight, ready to meet his fate.

Then it happened.

The two remaining cats slowly lowered their heads in submission.

Their alphas were dead. Their pack decimated. Their will to fight broken.

Each turned, slinking back into the jungle, both going their separate ways.

Jackson let the sword down slowly, letting out a breath he hadn't realized he'd been holding as he watched them fade into the blackness of the jungle.

He had done it. He had broken the pack.

Jackson collapsed to his knees, a vicious smile forming on his blood-covered face as he lay back, resting on the body of the alpha male, losing consciousness seconds later, while a thought filled his mind.

He was the alpha now. The top undisputed predator. And this…was his island!

CHAPTER 15
THE ISLAND

Jackson awoke hours later, the sword still clutched firmly in his grasp as the first rays of the rising sun peeked out from behind the eastern highlands, casting their soft morning glow across the land. He opened his eyes, startled to see a dead cat along the far side of the cove, his heart racing as the memories of what happened the night before rushed through his mind like a freight train.

He looked to the right, scrambling back as the alpha male's head came into view less than an arm's length away, its cold, dead eye staring back at him.

A rush of pain flooded his senses, nearly causing him to pass out as he fell to the sand, reeling. He took a deep breath to steady himself, regretting it instantly, the inhalation causing another wave of pain to wash over him from the rise and fall of his chest.

"Ahh," he said, taking a shallow breath, attempting to minimize the movement from his breathing. "Bits, you there, buddy?" he asked, his voice hoarse.

"I am. How are you feeling, William?"

"Like I'm pretty sure I won…but I'm kinda wishing I'd lost at the moment."

"Yes, you're pretty banged up," Bits replied, attempting to keep the mood light.

"Yeah, ugh," Jackson said as he tried to sit up. "I'd say that's the understatement of the year. I feel like a truck hit me. Twice. What's the sitrep?"

"Eight hours, twenty-three minutes have passed since the remaining members of the pack withdrew. Both headed north on their own, and I monitored them until they moved out of sensor range. It is likely that they will be assimilated into other packs or killed for trespassing in their territory. Based on the typical pack behavior of most large predatory cats, I believe that you now own this territory and will need to mark and possibly defend it."

"Well, that sounds lovely. What do I need to do, go piss on a tree or something?"

"Precisely."

"Really? I was just kidding… Seriously?"

"Yes, the most effective way to mark your territory is with urine, and to leave claw marks on trees. I've had the drones mapping a range for you beginning a kilometer north of here, then running down along this side of the river and towards the southern tip of the island where the *Phoenix* now rests."

"I don't think I've got that much pee in me, buddy." He smiled. "Besides, isn't that a bit much?"

"If we remain stranded on this island for a long time, you will need to have unfettered access to the river for water and fish, as well as to the *Phoenix*. I reviewed the data provided by the mapping drones, and estimate that this is a modest-size territory, and using the river as a border means you'll be less likely to encroach on other packs and face direct challenges.

Marking your presence on the northern border and at strategic points along the river and to the south should suffice. If the surviving cats are assimilated into other packs, they'll likely recognize your scent, warning their new group that you are a threat and should be avoided."

Jackson was silent for a moment, considering the logic in Bits's plan. "Wow, you've really thought this through."

"I have."

"Well, ahh," he said, getting to his feet. "I suppose I'd better go stake my claim, seeing as I have to pee anyway."

"I would not recommend that at this time."

"Why's that?"

"Your wounds are significant, and your urine will undoubtedly have traces of blood in it. I'd suggest that you urinate into the sea for the time being. I'd also suggest that you may want to wade into the lagoon to wash the blood from you. Your suit is covered with bodily fluids from the alpha male, along with blood from your own wounds."

Jackson looked down at the suit, noticing the bloodstains, then focused on his left arm, realizing it was completely without feeling and pinned to his chest, encased in the suit like a cast. "Good call. I see you've been busy," he said, trying not to breathe in the scent of bio-matter on his suit. "What's my prognosis?"

"Uncertain at this time," Bits said, bringing up a holographic image of Jackson's body projected from his wrist. "You have multiple lacerations and contusions from your close encounter with the alpha male. The cuts to your chest are deep in some places, and your left arm is in very bad condition."

"How bad?" he asked, not sure he wanted to know the answer.

"It received extensive damage from the mauling, including two broken bones, along with severed muscles and tendons. I estimate that it will take several months to heal, and even then, we should get you to the ship and use the medpod there to continue the treatments."

"That doesn't sound good. It feels completely numb. Did you drug me up?"

"Yes, I've given you several medications for the pain and set the bones using the suit to put them back in place while you slept. I'm currently focusing on treatment and monitoring for signs of infection."

"Should we go back to the ship now?"

"I considered that course of action. However, you lost a good deal of blood, and I don't believe you're strong enough to make the trip back. The suit is also the only thing holding your arm together at this point, and I don't recommend removing it until you've had some time to heal. Last night's combat and medical efforts drained the suit's power reserves, and it is down to thirty-two percent capacity. For now, I suggest we use the advanced medical kit to enhance the suit's capabilities and allow it to recharge. We can return to the ship for future treatments at a later time."

"Sounds like a plan."

An hour later, after washing himself and the suit, then getting some breakfast, he started to feel as though he was regaining some of his strength. By the late afternoon, he'd managed to drag the dead cats around to the side of the cove using his good arm, his body aching and the nano-stitches holding his wounds together, tearing several times when he exerted himself too much. It took several hours, but he finally collected the bodies and left them where the tide and current would come in and take them.

Hours later, they were gone.

He took a break, checking his supplies, knowing that he needed more water and, ideally, some fresh food if he was going to heal quickly. After a weapons check, he limped into the jungle to replenish his water and forage for food.

He struggled for several minutes as he moved through the dense foliage, every step a test of his will to continue, until he finally reached the game trail, and the journey became less arduous. He gripped the sonic pistol in his right hand while the left still rested immobile and useless across his chest.

Bits kept watch overhead, two drones on constant alert, with one scouting ahead while the other watched his immediate surroundings, both actively scanning with multispectral sweeps. Finally, he reached the river, quickly filling his canteen, the effort to bend down excruciating but worth it as he drained the water in one go once the decontamination cycle complete. He topped it up once more before making the trip back to camp, all the while Bits and the drones keeping a constant vigil.

Jackson scanned the trees on his way back, searching for fruits and taking his time, meandering off-trail to look for food here and there. He was halfway back to camp when he heard something moving in the brush and stopped instantly, weapon raised.

"Bits?" he whispered.

"I'm detecting movement, three meters ahead and to your right."

Jackson took several steps back, putting some distance between himself and the source of the sound, gripping the pistol tightly. Bits cycled through scanning modes, the noise growing closer. Several leaves shook as something small pushed slowly through the underbrush. He adjusted his stance, ready to fire, when to his surprise a small kitten emerged, walking on unsteady legs as it stumbled out onto the path. The creature was tiny compared to the full-grown cats, only about the size of a football, and likely just a few days old.

The kitten wandered blindly, whimpering softly as it sniffed around, searching for its mother.

Jackson's heart sank in his chest, and he lowered the pistol, retracting his helmet. "Damn it," he said, deflated. "Maybe that's why the pack was so aggressive."

His voice startled the kitten, causing it to freeze at the unfamiliar and alien sound. It turned its head from side to side, its body quivering in fear, while its tiny ears rotated and twitched, searching for the sounds of danger. He kept silent for a moment, watching as it began moving once more, slowly approaching him like a drunken sailor trying to walk a straight line.

"The rest of the pack must have abandoned it when they fled. It's helpless and alone," he said softly, pressing the pistol back to his hip, then reaching down, gently picking it up. The kitten squirmed at first, then, after a moment, relaxed and nestled into the crook of his arm, letting out a slow yawn, seemingly sensing that it was safe.

"William," Bits spoke in his ear, "I know what you're thinking, and this is not a good idea."

"But, Bits, he's all alone. And I…I killed his family," Jackson said, suddenly overcome by emotion as he looked down at the precious little ball of life in his arms, rocking it back and forth. "Hey there, little guy," he said softly, gently scratching between its ears. The kitten stretched out, yawning once more and mewing contently while he stroked its head. "I can't just let it die," he said, his voice cracking as he stared down at the tiny, innocent face, unaware of the surrounding dangers of the world it had been born into.

Bits was silent for a moment before responding, "Fine, but you have to take care of it."

"Okay," Jackson replied, half laughing, half sniffling, a smile crossing his lips.

"And you have to feed it."

"Uh-huh."

"And walk it."

"I'm not sure you walk a cat, Bit—"

"And keep it from *eating* you when it grows up," he added sarcastically.

Jackson laughed. "Yes, Dad."

"Okay then, I suppose you can keep it. Although I still have my doubts."

"There, there, little guy, it's going to be okay," he said, patting its head as he rocked the exhausted infant to sleep. "Uh…Bits," Jackson whispered, "what *are* we going to feed it?"

"I think it's time you learned how to fish."

Over the months that followed, the kitten grew rapidly, soon becoming as big as a medium-sized dog. After debating a few options, Jackson named him Razor, for the razorback stripe of hair along his back, calling him Raz for short.

Razor, it turned out, was actually much more like a dog than a cat in temperament. He was eager to please and highly trainable, unlike most cats Jackson had ever met. He was also highly intelligent, so much so, that Jackson had nearly run out of things to teach him after only a few short weeks, during which time Razor had quickly learned to respond to over a dozen commands.

As he grew and his hunting senses sharpened, Razor became incredibly useful. Within a few months, he was helping to hunt for food and keeping Jackson safe from predators, his keen senses able to detect them from afar.

Still, even with his new companion at his side, Jackson had amassed several fresh scars from wildlife encounters, learning many new, sometimes painful, but precious lessons on how to survive in his new home.

As the weeks turned to months, the two of them carved out their territory, marking it by walking the perimeter every few days and urinating on several carefully selected and marked trees where the rain would have difficulty washing the scent away.

Slowly, Jackson learned more and more about his new home, embracing its bounties while respecting its dangers. He quickly learned the sources of food that the small primates ate, discovering that they were quite edible for both himself and Razor.

As his skills and comfort increased and his body healed, he began hunting some of the smaller animals in the area, supplementing his dwindling emergency rations and providing food for himself and his new companion. Razor took to the hunt naturally, following Jackson's lead and heeding his commands, the two of them working in unison and quickly becoming both deadly and proficient.

Bits's suggestion of fishing had proved to be an excellent one, and Jackson quickly discovered that the fish in the river were both delicious and plentiful. Razor had grown strong and powerful from their meat, along with the milk of another fruit which wasn't edible for humans but was rich in protein. It turned out to be a passable supplement for real milk to feed Razor with when he had first adopted him, and the kitten suckled it greedily.

As Jackson fished in the river each day, Razor watched attentively, drool dripping from his jaws, waiting patiently for his master to return with their daily catch. He stuck to spear fishing in the shallows after learning, nearly fatally, that species of crocodiles lived in the river, their bio-signs difficult to detect when they lay motionless on the bottom waiting for prey. Fortunately, the crocs were almost entirely aquatic, their legs comically undersized and weak on land, allowing him to easily retreat if they approached.

Jackson had chosen a spot where the fish were plentiful, with good lines of sight and quick access back to the safety of the shore as he waded in the shallows, just off a small mudflat. While the crocs still posed a threat, they were mostly an annoyance, and there were plenty of fish to go around. After several weeks of daily fishing expeditions, they seemed to tolerate his presence, only becoming territorial if their young were nearby.

He'd tried fishing in the ocean as well but found that most of the fish that were worth catching were farther out on the reef, and he was wary of going that far from shore unless he had to.

The planet's cycle around its sun took some getting used to with the one-hundred-and-twenty-eight-day year affecting the daylight significantly as the tilt of the planet created two extremes. These included a span of nearly a week where the sun was out twenty-nine hours a day, followed sixty-three days later by complete darkness for three days as the temperature dropped to below freezing. This caused Jackson some issues in maintaining his routine and trying to get things accomplished, with the jungle becoming a much more dangerous place at night, limiting him on the shorter days where he decided to play it safe and stay closer to camp.

Many of the island's creatures slept or were inactive during the longer days due to the extreme heat and humid temperatures. However, at night, the jungle was a flurry of activity and, even with the suit's sensors, Jackson was at a significant disadvantage from the creatures who had evolved there for millennia, honing their senses to their environment.

He focused on hunting more during the longer daylight periods, stocking up on foods he could store or meats he could dry in the sun or smoke over his fire. During the darker weeks, he stayed closer to home, working on the camp, doing maintenance, or making improvements and only going for food and water during the peak hours of the day.

By the third week after he'd adopted Razor, he'd cleared the brush back several more meters from the cove, giving the now repaired sentries a greater line of sight, and Bits updated their scanning parameters to better detect the native lifeforms. He also tagged Razor with a tracker, programing the defenses to identify him as a non-threat, ensuring that he could come and go as he pleased.

As the first few weeks passed, hunger had helped Jackson quickly get over his initial qualms about skinning and processing animals, even the odd snake. In a short time, he had become quite adept at separating the good parts, selecting those to eat himself and which to give to Razor.

While they hadn't been attacked again, Jackson feared

that a neighboring pack of cats might eventually figure out that this territory was open, despite his and Razor's urinary warnings and tree markings, and challenge him for control of it. Each morning and evening, he checked on the sentries, ensuring that they were functioning properly, becoming slightly obsessive after waking up several nights dreaming of being surrounded in his tent. Most of the time, they remained in a lower power mode, their operating efficiency dropping slowly due to the constant drain of the strong electromagnetic field.

The other issue that they had run into during the shorter days was a lack of power. Most GCH equipment was capable of solar charging, with solar cells built in that were incredibly efficient. However, the amount of power required to operate things such as plasma cannons and particle beams was significant, forcing him to use them sparingly. On the days when the sun was out constantly, most of his tech was able to fully recharge, but during the shorter days, he had to use it carefully, conserving power in the event of an attack at night.

"Is there anything we can do about the EM drain?" he asked as they sat around the fire one night, Razor asleep with his head on Jackson's lap as he stroked him absentmindedly with one hand.

"This planet's EM field is somewhat unique. I've been trying to adapt our technology, but it continues to elude me. I will continue my efforts, but I fear that over time, all of our technology will become inoperative."

"Yeah, that's what I'm worried about too. The canteen only works when in direct sunlight now, and the sonic pistol has been slowly dropping in power. The rifle seems to be holding up a bit better, at least."

"The M1 has superior EM hardening and charging capabilities. However, it will degrade over time as well."

"How long till we can go back to the ship?"

"Based on your decision to wait for the summer solstice, it will be another fourteen days before we go back."

Jackson sighed, nodding his head. "Let's push it up a few days. We're back to pretty good sunlight now, and I don't want to wait much longer. It's been too long as it is already. I can't believe how the months just flew by."

"I know it's been frustrating for you, William, but your wounds needed significant time to heal, and your left arm has still not completely recovered."

"Yeah, I know," he said, flexing it, the muscle and bone having mostly healed, but a lingering ache remained, and his strength was still a fraction of what it used to be. "It still sucks though. Thank God we had the advanced med-kits or that infection would have killed me."

"Yes, it was pretty severe. I was worried you may lose your arm for a time there."

"Me too. I'm so glad we had Raz to take care of. Those were some pretty tough days and having him really helped to keep my mind focused. I don't know what I would have done without you both."

Jackson closed his eyes for a moment, thinking back to when Razor was around a month old and had become sick. As his condition worsened, Bits became concerned that the lack of milk from his mother, and the natural antibodies it provided, may have weakened his immune system. Jackson had stayed awake all night, cradling the tiny kitten in his arms as he whimpered softly, Razor's fever spiking. The next day, he had convinced Bits to inject Razor with the last of their medical nanites, unable to bear the thought of losing his new companion. Bits directed the nanites, boosting Razor's immune system while they attacked the virus, and within a few days, he had fully recovered and was stronger than ever.

As Jackson bonded with their new pet, Bits's reservations about Razor had subsided, and he convinced Jackson to agree to installing a small implant in the cat's ear which allowed both Jackson and Bits to give him commands from afar, tying him into their comms system.

Razor had been startled at first by Bits's voice but soon became comfortable with the ethereal presence in his ear, accepting him as a second master and listening to his commands obediently. In turn, Bits studied Razor's behavior, body language, vital signs, and vocal expressions, eventually creating a translation matrix which allowed both Bits and Jackson to better understand what he was trying to communicate.

Slowly, the three of them became a family.

Each night the little cub crawled into Jackson's lap as they sat by the fire, Jackson feeding him scraps while talking to him gently, telling him stories of his life on Earth and amongst the stars. During the first few weeks, Jackson had often found himself singing while his little kitten fell asleep and he petted his head. He sang the songs his parents had sung to him around campfires as a child, including his own interstellar version of Johnny Cash's "I've Been Everywhere," along with Raz's favorite, "Puff the Magic Dragon."

As he grew larger, his loyal companion had begun sleeping outside of the tent, always on guard and ready to protect his master. Razor seemed to realize that he was growing, eventually migrating from Jackson's lap to lying beside him and putting his head there instead.

Jackson had never had pets growing up, aside from the occasional goldfish, and was amazed at how the kitten filled a hole in his heart that he had never known was there.

Razor grew rapidly as the weeks progressed, partly, Jackson and Bits theorized, due to a steady high-protein diet and the nanites maintaining his system. By the time he was three months old, he was already nearly fully grown and began to venture out on his own more and more. One minute he would be there by Jackson's side, and the next, he'd be gone, sometimes for hours at a time. He would often come home with pigs or even birds in his mouth, dropping them proudly at Jackson's feet and waiting patiently for an approving look and pat on the head.

As much as Jackson wanted to get home, there were times when he realized that he'd found a peace which had eluded him for most of his life. Those were good days, and despite being stranded, a part of him never wanted them to end.

CHAPTER 16
BROKEN HOME

Finally, ninety-three days after the attack on the cove, Jackson's wounds had nearly healed, and with the summer solstice approaching, he decided to make a trip back to the ship, having allowed his suit and weapons to fully charge over the past few days in preparation.

He'd long since given up on the transmitter in the emergency duffel bag, the device still unable to penetrate the electromagnetic interference, despite Bits's best efforts. The transmitter in the Guardian, however, was significantly more powerful, and Jackson remained hopeful that it would be the key to his salvation.

The morning of his trip, he awoke early, loading up his gear for the walk back down to the southern tip of the island. He'd spent the week prior planning, training, rebuilding his stamina, and rehabbing his left arm as much as possible, regaining some of his former strength and flexibility. As the sun rose, he got walking, keeping an easy pace as he made his way down the beach, careful to keep an eye out for sand snakes while relying on Bits and Razor to watch his back.

After an hour, he reached the southern tip of the island, excitedly deploying two drones to scan the area from above.

"What have you got, buddy?" he asked, pulling up the holo-display on his wrist while he waited for the readings to come in, tapping his foot impatiently.

"Unfortunately, I have some bad news. There appears to be a species of jellyfish surrounding the ship," Bits reported. "The hull of the *Phoenix* may be attracting them, perhaps due to the electrical currents still within the ship itself."

"Can the suit withstand their stingers?"

"Unknown, but I do not recommend taking the chance. They may also be attracted to the current in the suit as well, making you a potential target."

"Well, that sucks. All right, let's set up camp and try to wait them out. Hopefully, they'll migrate away soon."

He headed up the beach to the cluster of trees where he had spent the night after he first arrived, thinking back on how much time had passed since then. By the time dusk fell, he had his camp set up and was well stocked with firewood. Despite having the trees at his back, he felt naked and exposed away from the safety of the cove, sleeping uneasily.

The next morning, he took Razor for a walk, establishing a modest perimeter, including a small stream which ran down from the foothills to the east, marking their territory and keeping an eye out for prey.

During the months while he'd healed, the drones had detected another pack of cats frequenting the southern tip of the island, seemingly claiming the area as their own. Bits had tasked a drone to keep tabs on them, timing their trip to when the pack moved off to the far side of their domain, nearly a hundred kilometers away. He estimated that they had four to five more days before they would return to the area, based on their previous hunting and migration patterns.

Finally, on the morning of the third day, the jellyfish moved on, and Jackson entered the water, eager to get back to the ship after having nothing to do for days on end. Razor stood on the beach, pacing back and forth rapidly, whining mournfully as Jackson walked into the open water. "It's okay, Raz. I won't be gone long. Don't worry, Bits will keep you company."

"Sit," Bits said firmly, the big cat doing as he was told. "Good boy, Razor," he added, monitoring him dutifully while Jackson disappeared beneath the waves.

Razor whined once more, wanting desperately to pull his master out of the sea, fearful for his safety. Despite that, he followed Bits's commands loyally, if impatiently, while he waited alone on shore.

Jackson activated the suit's aquatic systems, diving deeper and quickly making his way back to the ship. The thrusters and flippers made getting around easy, and with the drones high above keeping watch for any aquatic predators, he felt exhilarated to finally return to the ship.

As he approached the *Phoenix*, his heart sank in his chest once more at the sight of her lying on the bottom of the sea. In his memory, she hadn't looked as badly broken, but now, in full view, the sunlight rippling off the hull, it pained him to look at her. Jackson moved closer, noticing half a dozen points where the armor plating had ruptured, along with severe scoring from enemy weapon impacts, realizing once more how lucky they were to have made it out alive after his risky plan to try to destroy as many objectives as possible.

He entered the ramp into the cargo bay, activating the suit's external lights, startling dozens of small fish that darted out from the darkness, rushing by. He carefully made his way through the ship to the operations room where the Guardian armor sat pinned in its bay.

As he approached, Bits activated his suit's shields and modulated the frequency, allowing Jackson to slip seamlessly through the forcefield. He stood in a small pocket of air with the Guardian before him, the back of the armor opening as he approached.

"Is there any way we can get it out?" he asked, considering how useful it would be to have the hulking armor guarding the cove rather than the two small sentries.

A scan appeared in his HUD as Bits analyzed the structure surrounding the Guardian. "I do not believe so. The portal on the bottom of the ship has been crushed, and with the ship lying on the bottom of the sea, you would not be able to exit that way, even if we could get it open. A structural girder has collapsed on top of the suit, pinning it in place and causing minor damage. We could attempt to cut it out with a particle beam, but it would take several hours, and the power necessary would require at least two recharge cycles. Even then, we would need to cut a hole in the top of the ship to get it out. It could take close to a week to accomplish."

"Damn. Well, at least we can still get the comms array. That's the most important part, anyway."

"Agreed. Are you ready to proceed?"

"Let's do it," he said, activating the holo-display on his wrist while Bits instructed him on how to remove the comms module along with a few other key components.

An hour later, he had what he needed, securing the parts in the watertight bag the emergency supplies had come in and coating it in a thin film of nanomaterial from the suit. Once satisfied, he pulled a second rifle from the weapons locker across the room, then pried open one of the access ports in the base of the operations platform, retrieving another nano-pack, which he quickly integrated into his suit. He left the operations room, making his way back to the cargo bay, where he collected a toolkit, along with a new emergency duffel bag loaded with supplies. He took his time, checking over every compartment in the cargo bay, locating an additional sentry and a zero point generator to keep his equipment charged.

"William," Bits spoke into Jackson's helmet.

"Hey, buddy, what's up?"

"Razor has become quite agitated. I suggest that you return with the supplies you've already gathered and give him some attention. I've reassured him that you're all right, but he hasn't moved at all for the past hour, and I'm growing concerned for his mental and physical well-being."

Jackson smiled. "I'm on my way topside."

A few minutes later, his head broke through the waves, Razor bounding excitedly and mewing at the sight of him. As he reached the shallows, Razor darted towards him, jumping up and licking his helmet.

"Okay, okay," he said, lowering the helmet, allowing his companion to see that he was unharmed. "I missed you too, buddy." He laughed, reminding himself that Razor was still less than a year old and more kitten than full-grown cat, despite his appearance. He reached up and settled him down by scratching behind his ears, Razor dropping to all fours and stretching out while Jackson treated him to a thorough round of attention and scratches.

Finally, they headed up the beach together, Jackson depositing the duffel bag, the sentry, the transmitter, and a toolkit in a neat pile on the beach. He turned and pointed towards the ocean once more. "I've got to go back for a few more things," he said, looking back. "Raz, I need you to watch all this stuff, okay?"

Razor nodded, a gesture he'd picked up early on from Jackson, then ran a circle around the pile, stopping and standing in a perfect guard dog/cat pose, ready to protect it with his life.

"Good boy," he said, scratching behind his ears once more. "I've got to go back for a bit more. You stay here, okay?"

Razor let out a short yip, which Jackson had learned meant he understood, then turned back and headed down the beach. This time, Razor appeared much calmer as Jackson disappeared beneath the waves, the reassurance that he'd return, along with the task of guarding his master's precious supplies, keeping him occupied for the time being.

Jackson arrived back at the ship, entering on the far side through one of the larger hull breaches, then moving through several different sections and gathering what he could salvage. In the mess, he loaded up on food, which had remained perfectly preserved in two compartments that pulled out, containing vacuum-sealed rations. He also added some utensils, a luxury he'd not had in some time, wondering, not for the first time, while he pulled several sets from a drawer, why the emergency kit had only come with a spoon and whose genius idea that was.

He continued through the ship, finding several of the corridors impassable, forcing him to exit the *Phoenix* and reenter it through other breaches in the hull. Next, he raided the medical bay, collecting two more emergency med-kits loaded with supplies, including three full doses of medical nanites. Bits had informed him weeks before that his body's nanites were strained to their limits from healing his injuries, and the planet's EM field had begun to take a toll, diminishing their effectiveness.

"Good thing the hull of the *Phoenix* has multiple layers of shielding to protect these," he said, clutching his prize in his hand before placing it back in the med-kit.

"The technology we've recovered thus far is showing some signs of degradation, but you're correct, the *Phoenix* has done well in preserving most of it."

"This will at least give us a fresh start. Is there anything we can use back at the cove to protect them from the EM field?"

"The duffel bag has some EM shielding built into it to protect the emergency kit inside, but it will only make a few weeks' impact at most before there is a drop in efficiency."

"Well, it's better than nothing," he said, turning his head. "How's the medpod?"

"It's still offline. Power systems in this part of the ship are heavily damaged. The forcefield around the bay is still holding, but all other systems inside are offline. The zero point generator should suffice to get the pod back online to run a regeneration cycle."

"Sounds like a plan."

Jackson returned to shore, dropping off the food and medical supplies, then grabbed the ZPG and returned to the ship. After a few moments of following Bits's directions, Jackson had the zero point generator integrated with the medical pod's auxiliary power system and stood waiting while it hummed to life. The door to the pod opened, and he stepped inside, noticing the bloody handprints on the glass from when he'd awoken in a state of hyper-adrenaline. "I'd forgotten about that. Seems like a year ago now."

"Indeed. We certainly seem to have no shortage of close calls. As Captain Saijar put it, 'You seem to have a knack for attracting trouble,'" Bits observed while Jackson stepped into the pod, deactivating the suit into a belt around Jackson's waist.

"Yeah, the captain was certainly right about that," he said, thinking back to the captain and the crew of the *Dark Syre* and how horribly wrong things had gone there. "How long will this take?"

"I'm going to run a short diagnostic cycle on you first," Bits said, closing the door to the pod, the inside pressurizing with a hiss.

Jackson lay back while lights and sensors from the pod swept over him. After a moment, Bits brought up a holographic image. "The pod estimates that you need eight to ten hours to fully repair the damage to your system. However, we cannot leave Razor for that long. As such, I've instructed it to focus on your left arm to being with. The procedure will require microsurgery and take approximately an hour and eighteen minutes, plus some time for subdermal and dermal regeneration. The pod will sedate you during that time."

"All right. Will you keep an eye on Raz while I'm out?"

"Of course, William. Would you like to talk to him for a moment?"

"Sure."

"Go ahead."

"Hey, Raz," Jackson said.

Razor perked up instantly at the sound of Jackson's voice, ignoring the crab he was following as it scuttled sideways across the beach near the surf. He turned to check the area for him, then looked back at the sea while the holo-display in front of Jackson showed an image of him from one of the drones above.

"I'm still on the ship. Stay and guard our stuff, okay?"

Razor yipped a gleeful response, happy to hear Jackson's voice, and resumed his vigilant guard duty.

"All right, I'm good to go," he said, closing his eyes, a hiss filling the pod a moment later as he fell into a deep, anesthetic-induced sleep.

He awoke a few hours later, the world coming back into focus as the door to the pod opened and cool air from the ship rushed inside.

"Mmm, hey, buddy. How'd it go?" he asked sleepily.

"The procedure was successful in repairing some of the deep tissue and nerve damage in your arm. It is still not completely healed, but it should have more feeling, and your strength and dexterity should improve. The pod also healed several other small wounds once your arm was repaired and flushed your system of all the inactive nanites, then ran a maintenance cycle on your implants."

"Wow, that's great," he said, holding his left arm up in front of him and flexing his fingers, noticing an immediate difference. "I feel much better. I think I'd just gotten used to how run down I'd been."

"I'm glad that this trip has been worthwhile, then."

"Yeah, I wish we could have come sooner, but better late than never. How's Raz doing?"

"He appears to be keeping himself entertained and has not strayed far."

"Good stuff. Let's get the rest of what we need, then get back to the beach. Things are finally starting to look up."

Jackson spent the next half hour gathering more supplies and making several trips to shore to drop off his hauls. Each time, he spent a few minutes with Razor, playing and telling him what a good boy he was for keeping guard over their camp, then headed back into the surf.

He returned to the ship one last time, entering his still-sealed quarters, the room virtually untouched, taking him aback for a moment at how normal it looked compared to the rest of the ship, as though nothing had happened at all. He lay down on his bed for a few minutes, enjoying the comfort of his mattress for the first time in months while he looked around the room. For a few moments, he considered taking a nap, but knew that Razor would worry if he was gone too long and that the other pack of cats was overdue to return to the area soon.

Razor was growing into a powerful predator in his own right, but he still wouldn't stand a chance against a full-grown adult, let alone an entire pack, and he didn't want to leave his friend alone for too long. He collected a few of his possessions, including the photo of the crew from before the war and another of Amy, along with the one of Verris. He stuffed some clothing into an empty duffel bag, something that he'd overlooked in his haste when leaving the ship the first time, excited to wear fresh fabrics again after being limited to only a few pairs of emergency clothing and the nano-suit.

With the duffel slung over his shoulder, he made his way back to the cargo bay, about to leave the *Phoenix* for the last time when Bits received an alert from one of the drones keeping watch overhead. "William, a large aquatic creature is approaching."

Jackson froze, staring out into the clear blue water on either side of the ship. In his HUD, he could see a large shape in the distance swimming towards the ship. Seconds later, it came fully into view, Jackson taking in its massive size while it swam by close to the ship on the beach side, then watching in the top-down view while it circled.

"Oh crap, that's not good." He swallowed, a primal fear building as the predator moved with a natural grace and speed as it cruised by once more, a single black eye staring coldly at him.

"Agreed," Bits replied, displaying an analysis in Jackson's HUD. "It appears to be a type of shark, approximately eleven meters in length with bioluminescent stripes along its nose, likely to lure unsuspecting prey in the darkness. Scans are detecting organs similar to the Ampullae of Lorenzini on its snout, but much more advanced, along with a lateral line running across its body that appears to be highly sensitive to vibrations and electrical fields."

Jackson moved deeper into the cargo bay, staring out with a mix of awe and terror as the impressive predator swam past once more, its dorsal fin half a meter taller than he was and its muscular gray-blue body as wide as a pickup truck. The shark turned, revealing its white underside and several subtle yellow stripes along its flanks as it circled once more. He watched the deadly predator glide past, growing closer to the ship with each pass, its jet-black eyes scanning for any signs of movement while its oversized jaws revealed rows of serrated teeth, each easily as big as Jackson's hand.

The shark slowly circled the *Phoenix* several more times, examining the strange object while Jackson stayed deep within the cargo bay, hoping that it would lose interest. "What do you think, buddy?"

"I believe this creature is sensing the electrical current in the ship and possibly your suit."

"That's not good. Options?"

"We cannot outrun it. I estimate that it can move between fifty to sixty kilometers per hour, based on its size, musculature, and the hydrodynamics of its body. We could attempt to distract it, or we could wait it out to see if it leaves. Our only other option is to attack and attempt to frighten it away. But I do not recommend the latter, as power levels are down to thirty-nine percent and each blast would drain them by an additional five percent with the current accelerated drain rate from the EM field."

"What do you suggest?"

"I could launch an aquatic probe using the excess material on the suit, setting it to emit a higher electrical frequency in order to draw the shark away."

"Well, it's better than waiting here. It's going to be dark in less than an hour, and we need every advantage we can get. Let's give the decoy a try."

"Acknowledged."

Bits carefully reinforced the suit to withstand the pressure, then used the pack on Jackson's back to form a small V-shaped construct with an aquatic thruster. The decoy exited the *Phoenix* a moment later, setting a course farther out to sea while Jackson waited, watching as it made its way out into open water, slowly ramping up its electrical signal and moving away from the beach.

The shark took the bait and, on the next pass, and broke off, heading directly for the decoy. Jackson quickly exited the ship, engaging his thrusters and making a beeline towards the beach.

He was a quarter of the way back when the shark approached the decoy. Bits initiated evasive actions, but it was fast and agile, easily matching the maneuvers. A moment later, it struck with an incredible burst of speed, crushing the decoy in its jaws.

The shark let go, immediately realizing that what it was biting was not prey, then circled back towards the ship, its advanced senses detecting Jackson's presence seconds later.

The shark rocketed forward with another burst of speed, quickly closing the distance.

"William," Bits said into Jackson's ear, urgency clear in his voice.

"I see it! How long until we reach the beach?"

"Forty-three seconds."

"How long until it catches us?"

"At its present speed, twenty-six seconds."

"Crap! Keep us moving. I'll attempt to change its mind."

"Be aware that once power drops to below fifteen percent, particle emitters will not function, and we need the remaining power to maintain propulsion and life support."

"Understood. You drive. I'll shoot."

Jackson twisted his body, the suit responding, rolling him so that he could see more clearly behind him as he raised his arm, attempting to get a bead on his target. He waited, the suit's targeting sensors attempting to lock on while the pressure from the water moving past shook his arm slightly. He aimed as best he could, twitching his thumb to fire.

A short-burst particle beam shot out from his wrist, streaking past the predator as it dodged to the side. He fired again, closer this time, but the shark evaded the attack once again. "Bits, how the hell is it doing that?"

"Unknown. It may sense the electrical build up in the particle generation chamber before you fire and is intelligent enough to take evasive action."

"Wonderful. I'm going to wait until it gets a bit closer and try again."

"Power is down to twenty-six percent. You only have two shots remaining," Bits cautioned.

Jackson aimed as the shark continued to close in, its jaws twitching in anticipation of the kill, the predator now just under thirty meters away and quickly continuing to close the gap. He fired, narrowly missing, the sudden blast of heat just enough to make the shark veer off slightly, buying him a few precious seconds. The shark, however, was far from giving up, its speed increasing as it closed to just under fifteen meters. Then ten.

Jackson reached for his belt, pulling out a grenade in each hand and holding down the buttons to activate proximity mode, then let go of the first grenade.

The frag grenade detonated seconds later, sending a shockwave which threw the shark off course, injuring its left pectoral fin and flank. He released the second, a foam grenade, quickly grabbing two more.

The grenade went off, coating the shark's skin, but was diluted from the water, limiting its effectiveness. Jackson dropped the next two grenades, sensing his chance as the creature was temporarily blinded. The second frag grenade detonated, shredding the shark's underside while the small shockwave stunned it. The last frag grenade found its target, slipping inside the predator's gaping mouth, the subsequent explosion blowing off its lower jaw entirely and leaving a hole along the right flank where its gills had been seconds before.

The shark's trajectory changed instantly, arching downward towards the sea floor.

The huge predator hit the sandy bottom at full speed, its velocity terminal, the impact finishing the job the grenade had started, as thousands of pounds of weight and speed snapped its spine from the blunt-force impact.

A wave of blood drifted up from the shark's body, its tail twitching slightly while it lay otherwise unmoving.

Jackson scrambled up the beach seconds later, not stopping until he was ten meters from the waterline. "Holy shit, that was close!" he called.

Razor bounded over once more, tilting his head and looking at his master curiously, sensing that something was wrong.

"I've always been fascinated by sharks," he said, his heart pounding in his chest as he paced back and forth, breathing heavily and trying to get the adrenaline out of his system. "But I think that's as close as I ever want to get to one ever again."

Bits retracted the helmet, allowing him to breathe more freely, and he stood bent over, with his hands on his knees, Razor moving closer to lick his face.

"Good boy," he said, greeting his loyal companion. "It's funny how the human mind works, eh? I can face off against an entire pack of vicious cats and not lose my cool, but sharks and snakes. Ugh," he said with a shiver. "Some things just set a person off, you know?"

"Indeed. That is perfectly normal. Perhaps in a previous life you were eaten by a shark, carrying that fear into the next life."

"Well, that's a morbid thought, but it certainly would explain things. Maybe I've had some bad run-ins with snakes in other lives too."

"Or perhaps sharks and snakes are just scarier to you than cats are."

"Yeah, you've got me there," he said, looking down at his feet and realizing that he'd dropped the bag of clothes. "Damn it. Can you locate the duffel bag of clothes?"

"One moment. The bag has floated up and is drifting along with the current. I'll task a few drones to retrieve it."

"Thanks, buddy. I don't quite fancy another swim anytime soon."

Darkness fell less than an hour later, the sunset seeming to last forever as the longest day of the year ended, and he sat on the beach sipping on a bottle of whiskey he'd kept aboard the ship for special occasions. He'd changed into a set of clothes from his quarters, the feeling of wearing fabrics again like silk on his skin after months of only having his boxers and the thin layer of beat-up, skin-tight material he'd worn beneath the exo-suit.

Despite his newfound comfort, he slept fitfully that night, images of the shark still lingering in his mind, its jaws mere inches from his feet in the exaggerated memory and the fear that another pack of cats could return at any time keeping him on edge.

The next morning, he packed up his camp, making several trips to the cove and back, carrying with him everything he'd been able to salvage. He carefully tucked the comms array from the Guardian in an empty rations case and ate a good meal, then, after a quick trip to the river for water and fish, settled in for the night once more, exhausted but happy to be back home after a productive trip.

He slept better that night than he had in months, his mind at ease for the first time since he'd arrived while he allowed himself to ponder what it might be like to go home again.

Home.

The word seemed strange. Where was home exactly?

The cove, the *Phoenix*, FoxBlind, the Hideaway, Kishara Station, Talzon III, Earth?

Jackson smiled as he drifted off. *I guess home is wherever it needs to be,* he thought. He hoped that when he finally got out of there, that his home would be back with Verris.

CHAPTER 17
LOST

Two hundred and twenty-seven days later, Jackson emerged from the jungle with a small wild pig slung over his shoulder.

Razor trailed not far behind, having fully grown into adulthood and now standing nearly a meter and a half tall and easily the size of a Great Dane, and a good third of a meter taller than any other cat they'd seen on the island.

Jackson wore only the shorts he'd pulled from his quarters on the *Phoenix*, along with ankle-high shoes made from the exo-suit, and a hat and visor covering his eyes to protect them from the sun's harsh rays as it fed him sensor information. A rifle rested slung over his other shoulder, while the sword hung from his waist by a thin belt made from the suit. A long wooden spear tapped the ground in time with his feet, clutched in his free hand and sharpened into a deadly point, hardened in the raging inferno of a bonfire. Traces of fresh blood glinted in the sunshine on the tip of the spear, still fresh from the kill.

As he reached his camp at the cove, he dropped the pig by the firepit, stabbing his spear into the ground while barely breaking his stride and walking down towards the water.

He reached up, flipping his shaggy hair from his beard as the wind caught it, his right arm still carrying a jagged scar from a recent encounter, while his ribs poked out beneath his scarred and tanned flesh.

Razor stopped to sniff their kill, knowing better than to eat without his master's permission, then finding his usual spot in the shade of the trees on the north side of the cove and stretching out while playfully raking his claws and creating wavy patterns in the sand.

Jackson strode to the water's edge while Bits completed a quick scan. Satisfied with the results, he waded into the clear blue water, slipping beneath its glassy surface. He dove to the bottom of the pool, always aware of his surroundings, the rifle and sword ready should they be called upon.

As the months passed, he'd discovered that the ocean was full of hidden dangers. After several close calls with creatures such as predatory eels and a species of small fish that hunted in packs like piranhas, along with highly aggressive and territorial crabs, he'd decided to stick to the fresh water river for fishing.

Now when he swam, it was only to bathe or cool off, and he never stayed in the water for longer than a few minutes. Any more and a predatory species always seemed to sense his presence, trying for a taste. He sported several new and wonderful scars, along with enough nightmares to last a lifetime from the sea alone.

After a quick swim, he emerged from the water, stopping to stand in the heat of the sun for a moment while the moisture evaporated from his skin. Then, moving back to his firepit, he sat, preparing the pig for dinner, cutting off an ear and throwing it to his loyal companion while he went about his work.

He dressed the pig expertly, feeling as though he'd done it for the thousandth time.

While he and Razor had become excellent hunters, he soon learned that there were many dangerous predators lurking in the darkness of the jungle, ready to pounce on unsuspecting prey. Several poisonous snakes, along with a large species of constrictor, kept him on edge each time he ventured for his daily trips to the river and to mark his territory boundaries. He quickly realized how blissfully ignorant and lucky he'd been in his first few months, and he shuddered to think how careless he'd been in those early days compared to what he knew now.

As the days turned to weeks and the weeks to endless months, he began to lose track. The ever-changing seasons became his only concept of time, as the daylight ranged from nonexistent for several days to unrelenting at the opposite end of the spectrum.

The day after he had returned to the cove from the *Phoenix*, still rattled from his close call with the shark, he'd attempted to get the Guardian's comms module working. A critical component, however, was damaged from the crash, and despite his and Bits's best efforts, they lacked the resources to repair it. After exhausting every option, he'd finally decided to wait for a cycle for the long summer days to return, when his suit and weapons would be fully charged again, before making another trip back to the *Phoenix* to see if he could salvage the parts to repair it.

As he prepared to return to the southern tip of the island, he sent the drones to scout the ship ahead of time. His heart sank when he discovered that a reef had grown over the ship, nearly consuming it. There were still a few access points visible, but the *Phoenix* was now teeming with life.

The drones ran comprehensive scans of the lifeforms, while Bits conducted a detailed analysis, quickly determining that there were several species now living in or on the ship which were either highly toxic or predatory, posing too significant a danger for him to return.

Disheartened but not defeated, he had Bits construct an aquatic drone, sending it down under remote control, to see if it could retrieve some circuit boards or other materials that he could use to repair the comms array. The drone entered the ship while Jackson watched on his holo-display. Less than a minute in, it was attacked by something before going permanently offline, costing both his chance at the parts he needed and more of his suit.

Jackson watched in despair, collapsing to his knees on the beach, his hope crumbling.

Help wasn't coming.

This was his home now, and he had to accept that.

Razor and Bits were his family. His world.

Jackson got to his feet, standing tall as he composed himself. Razor came to his side, and he petted him absentmindedly, a plan forming in his mind.

If this is really my home now, then it's high time I go Swiss Family Robinson *on its ass and tame this fucking island!*

Jackson awoke and started his morning routine.

He had been industrious in the weeks since he'd given up hope of ever leaving the island, building a new shelter made from trees and driftwood that was a decent compromise between practical, defensible, and comfortable. The cove was his, and he had made it his kingdom.

Once his new and improved shelter was ready, he'd begun

in earnest, clearing a wide path through the jungle to the river. As the days passed, he'd marked trees with his sword, the slices resembling claw marks, and he and Razor walked the route now without fear, leaving their scents all along the path to ward off anything that dared to pass through his domain. Next, he went to work setting traps, further carving out his territory, and deploying parts of the exo-suit to act as sensors on the game trails he found, ready to alert him should anything larger than a pig or a small marsupial breach his borders. Finally, he and Razor had aggressively hunted the snakes and any other predators they found, to the point where few dared to venture into their realm.

As a full Earth year of time finally passed, he had to admit, despite all the hardships, life was finally good, and despite being stuck there, he was happy.

Every night he sat by the campfire under the stars with Raz's head his lap, while embracing the simple joys of living.

He only wished that Verris could have been there to enjoy this new, simple life with him.

He still thought of her nearly every day, providing him with an anchor, that helped to keep him going and wondering if they'd finally created a treatment. The last message he'd received from Daria indicated that the doctors were close to a possible solution and were hopeful for the first time in a long time that they could bring her back from the abyss of temporal stasis where she'd been for so long now.

Perhaps she's out there, somewhere, he mused, *looking up at the stars and thinking of me.*

He held the thought close to his heart, keeping him strong on his darkest days, knowing that she had people there to support her as she, hopefully, had fully recovered by now and resumed her life back on Kishara Station.

He also thought about Amy, recalling how vividly he'd thought he'd seen her when he first arrived in the future, and again how it had felt like she'd been there with him when he'd died on the Insectoid battleship. Jackson focused on the calm he'd felt, like her calling him home, as he let himself go towards the light.

She was tied to him. A part of him. Just like Verris was.

One night, as he stared up into the heavens, he had the strangest feeling that Amy was still out there somehow. That maybe she'd been reincarnated and was living another life.

He held the thought in his mind like a cloud of mist, the slightest breeze ready to dissipate it into nothing while he prayed that somehow it was true.

As the year mark passed, he thought back on some of the dark days he'd had since crash landing on the island. Days where his heart ached, and his spirit was ready to give in. But now, sitting with his loyal pet, his trusty AI, and enjoying the warmth of his fire and the light of the stars, he couldn't imagine a more perfect place in the galaxy to be.

Little did he know that his serenity was about to be shaken to its core.

CHAPTER 18
THE LONG WALK

"Are you sure?" Jackson asked, the urgency in his voice surprising even himself.

"I am ninety-eight-point-seven percent certain," Bits replied.

"Holy. Shit."

"Indeed."

"I-I need a minute to think..." he said, pacing back and forth across the cove, Razor lifting his head from a lazy mid-afternoon nap to watch him curiously.

Bits had found it. The one thing that could get them off of this planet.

It was a dream he'd given up on. A fantasy he'd made his peace with. But now, there it was, the scans hovering in front of him, taunting him with the promise of salvation.

He knew it was a last-ditch Hail Mary in a series of failed last shots. But it was a chance to take his life back. A chance to leave this place.

Yet, strangely, he found himself questioning if he even wanted it anymore.

Life was finally good here. The war was far away. He had a home, food, companionship, and peace. If he succeeded, all of that would be gone.

After over a year on the planet, however, most of his technology had degraded significantly from the EM field, and a dark shadow loomed in his thoughts as he imagined what life there would be like once his technology failed entirely. The island was a dangerous place, and without it…he shuddered at the thought.

His rifle was at less than half power, and the sonic pistol, which he'd never even used, was little more than a paperweight now. His suit was still functional, but its battery capacity was degenerating, and he relied on the ZPG to keep it going during the shorter days of the year.

Even Bits was starting to notice the effects. While his power levels were stable, due to his ability to harness energy from the heat Jackson's body generated, his cognitive interface and control over Jackson's implants had begun operating at a reduced capacity.

Bits estimated that the suit and his weapons were declining faster now due to the prolonged exposure and that it was just a matter of time before they became barely functional and went offline for good.

He feared that if he didn't get off this world soon, he might lose Bits too.

The thought of having to choose Bits over Razor tore his heart in two.

If he were, somehow, able to get off this world, what would happen to Razor?

A pang of guilt tugged at Jackson's heart at the thought. He couldn't bear to leave him there, but he knew that there was no way he'd be able to bring him home. Wherever the hell "home" really was these days.

He knew that he only had one shot at this. That if he didn't succeed, his technology would be useless in a matter of weeks, maybe months, at most. He had to try, now, while he still had the opportunity. If not for himself, then he at least owed Bits that much.

His decision loomed for several days while he tried to push it from his mind, going about his daily routine with the focus of a Buddhist monk. Finally, on the third day, he knew he had to try. He'd been miserable since he'd found out that there was even a chance, and he knew he needed to have the matter settled once and for all.

Jackson buckled down, preparing for the next three days, gathering and stockpiling food and meticulously ensuring his equipment was ready.

His preparations made, he settled into bed early for a final good night's sleep, then awoke just before sunrise, well rested and with a sense of purpose he'd not felt in a long time.

Today is the day, he thought. He was finally ready.

Over the past year, he and Bits had attempted to repair the comms array from the Guardian several times. However, the parts that they had salvaged were not enough to get it fully operational. They were missing one critical component: isilium.

While Jackson had never seen it, he was very familiar with its importance from his time on the *Algeron* and what happened with Verris, knowing that the precious metal was used in many advanced computers and electronic circuits.

Isilium was nothing short of miraculous, along with being very rare. It was also relatively soft and malleable, like gold, making it easy to work with. It was only toxic in its liquid form when smelted and purified, Bits assured him, and they needed only to harvest and melt small amounts at a time, then manipulate it and allow it to return to its solid form in order to suit their purposes.

"Isilium is highly conductive," Bits explained, "and can handle a heavy electrical load. We'll melt it down, then form several strands by creating basic molds out of wood and use it to connect the zero point generator to the comms module from the Guardian, then connect that in tandem with the comms modules from the emergency duffel bags to boost the signal strength. With the three combined, we can significantly boost the signal output. We'll also need to make basic heat sinks from the metal to place over the CPUs in order to cool them from the extreme power they'll need to get a signal out."

"Make sense. How much do we need?"

"Approximately five hundred grams of raw isilium should suffice. This should be enough to prevent the modules from overheating and allow us to boost the signal well beyond the transmitter's normal operational parameters to send a subspace communication powerful enough to punch through the interference."

"Sounds simple enough. What's the catch?"

"The catch is that we'll likely only get one shot at this, as the transmitter will almost certainly short out from the overload due to the amount of power we'll need to route through it and the strain of pushing it well past its design specs. But it should be enough to get a multiband subspace distress signal several light-years out, if all goes well."

"Okay, let's run through the plan one more time," Jackson said, the map of the southern half of the island hovering before him.

"Very well. We must proceed across the island on an easterly vector for approximately ninety-six kilometers, crossing several rivers along the way and navigating through the dense jungle. Next, we must cross a small valley leading up to the highlands. Once there, we will have to climb the cliffs until we reach this area," Bits said, highlighting the location where the drones detected the deposits. "Then locate and mine the isilium."

"Seems simple enough. What could go wrong? Just a hundred kilometers or so of deadly jungle, crossing through other cats' territories, watching out for poisonous snakes and half a dozen other dangers with tech that's slowly failing. Then making sure we have enough power left to get up the cliffs and do some mining, hoping there's enough isilium actually there and that it's accessible with the limited tools we have. Oh, and while not running out of food and starving to death. No problem."

"Just another day at the office," Bits quipped.

"Yeah, seems about right. Well, the sun will be up soon. We'd better get moving."

Jackson eagerly packed up the rest of his supplies, a spring in his step as he went about his preparations, along with a nervous excitement and a sense of hope he'd not felt in as long as he could remember.

In the days leading up to his departure, he'd spent considerable time catching fish and hunting pigs, drying their meat in the sun and over a fire to preserve it for his journey. He left his tent and sentries behind, as they were too bulky to bring with him, knowing he'd have to sleep up in a tree each night, cocooned in the suit and suspended from a branch to avoid predators. He wasn't crazy about the idea, even though he'd done it many times before in sims and back on Brestin III, but he simply couldn't carry all of his gear that far and knew that it was still safer than sleeping out in the open on the ground.

Jackson wore the exo-suit, which was down to just its base configuration, having spent all of the extra nanites on drones and lost aquatic constructs over the past year. It was still fully functional and had some excess material to spare for drones or constructs, but needed constant charging as the overall power efficiency had degraded significantly. He decided to leave the zero point generator behind, after giving the suit and rifle a full charge, knowing that if it got damaged, all of his efforts would be for nothing. He secured it, along with the comms modules and toolkit, in a duffel bag, then buried it in the sand and piled several small rocks on top of it to keep it safe. The island had been plagued by tropical storms in recent weeks, and he didn't want to take a chance that they could be lost or damaged somehow.

As he stood to go, he took a final inventory. "All right, cryo spay, check. Particle beam, check. Grenades, rifle, and sword, ready to go. Canteens are full, and I've got enough food to make it there, plus a couple of days extra. I've also got three emergency rations left if I need them," he said, his stomach rumbling just at the thought of them. "And if need be, I can always stop to hunt, but we'll try to avoid that, especially once we're in the territories of other cats. Ideally, we'll keep moving and, hopefully, remain undetected."

As he packed the last of his dried meat, the thought hit him: *After over a year on the island, I might never eat fish or bacon again!*

He shook his head and laughed out loud at the thought while his mind wandered for a moment.

What I wouldn't give for a burger. With cheese...and, all right, maybe bacon.

Or a steak.

Or pizza. Oh my God, pizza!

Mmm, and beer.

God, what I'd do for an ice-cold beer...and a beautiful woman to drink it with.

Jackson smiled to himself, shaking his head at the flight of fancy while standing at the edge of his camp, holding his arm out in front of him with his fist closed, a juicy morsel of fish inside.

Razor sat patiently, salivating, waiting for his master's command, knowing his favorite treat was just a "good boy" away.

"Stay here, Raz, and guard our camp. You can hunt for yourself, but you can't come with me. You won't be able to make the climb, and I don't plan on coming back the same way that I came. So, you need to *stay*. Understand?"

Razor tilted his head to the side in a very doglike manner, something which still threw Jackson since he was clearly a feline. From the database of responses Bits created, he knew that this meant that Razor was questioning what he was saying and not fully understanding.

Still, he sat obediently, licking his chops at the smell of the treat and waiting for another command.

"Stay."

Razor bobbed his head quickly three times, indicating that he understood. Jackson then opened his hand and threw the treat into the air. Razor snapped it up, then sat once more, showing that he was indeed doing a good job of staying.

Jackson turned and started walking. As he approached the tree line, he turned back and saw Razor still sitting obediently guarding the camp. "Good boy," he called, reaching into his pack and throwing another treat his way, then reiterated the command.

Satisfied, he turned into the jungle, making his way along the path they'd carved to his usual spot along the river where he fished.

Bits had used the information from the drones to plot the best route, one with the least natural barriers and thick jungle to navigate, while also providing places where he could stop to refill his canteens along the way. The first canteen was nothing more than a shell now, all of its electronics having long since ceased to function. The second, the one he'd recovered from the *Phoenix* on his last trip, was still working to purify water but could no longer harvest it from the air. It wasn't great, but it was enough.

Jackson arrived at the river and stood atop the bank, staring at the other side, realizing that this was the farthest inland he'd ever been. He took several strides back, then ran towards the edge, leaping into the air, his suit's thrusters activating, giving him a quick boost across.

He landed on the other side, looking back, checking once more that Razor hadn't followed him. "All right, here we go," he said, staring at the jungle ahead. He was now in uncharted territory for the first time in a long time, a feeling of adventure and excitement beginning to take hold as he pressed forward into the untamed jungle.

The drones had been busy for the past few days as Bits monitored the movements of several packs of cats which inhabited the interior and eastern side of the island, mapping their territories along his route. Bits had recalled the drones the day before they left, reintegrating them into the suit to shore up its failing resources and preserve as much nano-material as possible.

Jackson had studied the map and all the data available in the days before he left, choosing a circuitous route to avoid the primary areas where the packs of cats appeared to hunt, and feeling fairly confident that he could avoid them if he was careful. Bits deployed two small drones to scout out the path ahead, ensuring that there were no surprises waiting for them. He also kept one drone overhead to watch their back, knowing that many of the creatures on the island were expert ambush predators, and Jackson checked his three-sixty-degree view in his HUD frequently as he waded through the thick jungle.

It was mid-fall on the island, as Jackson had decided to call it, which meant that he had approximately thirteen hours of sunlight each day. The suit could generate some kinetic power from his movements, but solar was his best way to keep the levels up. This forced him to be careful with his power usage within the jungle canopy and the more limited sunlight meant that his power would depreciate each day, even with minimal usage due to the EM drain. The tradeoff, however, was that it was cooler during the day, a more manageable twenty-five degrees Celsius, making the physical exertion of the task ahead considerably more bearable than in the unrelenting heat of the summer and forty-degree plus days.

As he made his way deeper into the jungle, he admired the beauty that surrounded him, something he hadn't appreciated since his first month on the island. Tropical plants of all shapes, sizes, and colors, along with lush green, blue, and purple foliage, spread out all around him. If it wasn't for something trying to kill him every other day, the island would have been a paradise.

Several hours passed before he stopped to rest, making a minor course change along the way after the drones detected what appeared to be a nest of constrictor snakes ahead. Jackson studied the readings on his wrist holo-display: a large female guarding a clutch of eggs. He gave it a wide berth, putting a few hundred meters between them as he circled around, trying to stay as quiet as possible.

Hours later, he reached the bank of another river, much wider than the one near his camp, the water flowing significantly faster. "What do you think, buddy?"

"I recommend we make camp here for the night," Bits replied. "There are several large trees which will provide safe locations to sleep in, and the sun will be setting soon."

"Sounds good. Best not to push it too much on the first day. That was more tiring than I expected."

As the sun set, he ate his dinner of dried fish strips, washing it down with some water, the days slowly growing shorter as dusk settled upon the jungle. He brought up his route in the holo-display once more, noting that he'd covered nearly twenty kilometers of thick jungle that day.

Not too bad for the first day, he figured, noting that he was around a fifth of the way to his destination. He'd hoped to cover twenty-five klicks or more each day, but the jungle had other ideas, and he soon found that it was slower going than he expected. He knew all too well that he had to be careful and cautious above all else, especially now that he was in new territory.

As he finished his meal, his immediate concern turned to finding a safe tree to sleep in.

"What do you think?" he asked, looking up at the huge trees along the river's edge, many of them easily thirty meters tall.

"I've located a suitable tree nearby. It has several long, sturdy branches which extend out well over the river."

"Good thinking."

"The tree is to your left," Bits said, highlighting it in Jackson's HUD.

Jackson approached the base of the tree, stopping while Bits reconfigured the suit to take him up, forming four strong spider-like legs, each gripping into the trunk and carrying him up smoothly. Once they were high enough, Bits maneuvered the suit out on to a branch.

"Hey, buddy, hang on a sec," Jackson said, reaching back while he pulled a foam grenade from his belt and placed it in a knot in the tree. "Activate proximity mode and enable remote deactivation."

"Proximity mode and remote deactivation enabled."

"Okay, let's keep going."

Bits used the suit, taking them away from the trunk until they were well out over the river. "Are you ready, William?" he asked, knowing Jackson didn't care for this part of the plan.

"Do I have a choice?" he replied.

"You can always sleep below and wait to see which predator finds you first. My money is on the snakes."

"Wow, Bits, nice one! Yeah, I believe I'll be sleeping in the tree. Thank you very much."

"Is there anything else that you need?"

"Just make sure that you've got the sensors set to maximum, and let's hope for the best."

"Of course. Good night, William. Sleep well," Bits said, pulling the suit in close to the branch and connecting the four legs around it, while expanding the suit into a pod-like shape, the outside hardening, providing him support to lie back and enough room inside that he could pull his arms in and move them freely in the small space.

"Good night," he said, rolling onto his side as he tried to forget he was over ten meters off the ground, in the middle of a dangerous jungle, with a river running beneath him.

CHAPTER 19
HOMECOMING

Jackson awoke the next morning stiff and a little sore, but generally refreshed. "Good morning, Bits." He yawned. "How was the night?"

"Good morning, William. The night was uneventful for us, but there were numerous creatures investigating our trail, including a group of cats and a whitehead snake. Fortunately, they were not able to detect your scent through the suit and moved on to hunt elsewhere."

"Well, that's good, if not somewhat terrifying. How are the drones?"

"Resting at the top of this tree. Their solar collectors are angled towards the sunrise and have been charging since dawn. They will be fully operational in the next ten minutes."

"Good stuff. Let's get a bite to eat and get on the road. Is it all clear down there?"

"Affirmative."

"Okay, then take me down, and let's get this day started."

Jackson ate as he stared out at the far side of the riverbank, eager to get some ground under his feet. "How are we looking for a place to cross?"

"The river is quite wide for several kilometers in either direction. I recommend a running start and using the suit's thrusters."

"Makes sense. How's our power?"

"The suit is at seventy-three percent."

"We can spare a bit then. Let's go," he said, getting to his feet and walking back half a dozen meters. He stopped for a moment, stretching, then moved to a ready stance and darted forward, using the enhanced power of the suit to get a good head of steam.

As he approached the edge, he leapt into the air, the thrusters firing as he flew across the river. Suddenly, the thrusters stuttered, Jackson losing altitude, then crashing down hard on the other side of the riverbank.

"Bits…" he said, struggling to speak from the wind being nearly knocked out of him. "What the hell happened?" He got to his feet, gingerly clutching his ribs on his right side.

"I'm very sorry, William. The burst drained power from the nanites in the suit around the thrusters, and normal energy routing operations failed momentarily. My control over the suit or my 'reflexes,' as you could call them, appear to be decreasing as the suit's overall functionality degrades. I'm so sorry."

"It's okay. We made it across, at least. Is there anything you can do about the suit?"

"One moment. Let's take care of you first. Initiating medical scan. Scan complete. You have bruised one rib and fractured another. Rerouting nanites and administering an analgesic. The nanites should be able to repair the fracture fairly quickly, but you will be tender for several days."

"Thanks," Jackson said weakly.

"I'm running a diagnostic now. The outer layer of the suit is showing decreased response times. I believe the EM field is affecting it more due to the strenuous use. The good news is that the inner layers are slightly more shielded. One moment, I will reroute the outer layer into a pack on your back and keep it in reserve."

The suit became liquid on the surface, rippling as the outer layer of nanites moved across the surface, flowing to his back. "I believe that will remedy any further issues for the time being," Bits said confidently. "However, the overall degradation will continue."

"Another reason to get this done, I guess. Let's not waste any more daylight."

Jackson kept walking for the next five hours straight, using the sword to cut through the densest parts of the jungle and finding several game trails that, while taking him somewhat out of his way, sped up his overall progress considerably. After a short break, he pushed on for four more hours, finally deciding to make camp early to rest and recover.

"Our campsite is still two-point-nine kilometers away," Bits informed him.

"I know, buddy, but I honestly don't think I can make it. My ribs are killing me, and I'm exhausted."

"Very well. There's a tree thirty-eight meters ahead where you can sleep. However, the nearest source of water is over a kilometer and a half away, and we are still deep within the territory of a large pack of cats."

"Noted," Jackson said as he rested on a rock, his ribs still hurting like hell from the constant movement and the need to clear a path. He drank what water he had left, then ate some of the pig jerky before Bits carried him up into the tree to sleep, upping the dosage of the analgesic to help numb the pain.

Jackson awoke early the next morning, his ribs still sore after a fitful night's sleep, but the fracture caused him considerably less discomfort than the night before, especially when taking a deep breath.

Bits lowered him to the ground, and he decided to get moving early with a nagging thirst and eagerness to make up for lost time pushing him forward.

The early morning light cut through the canopy, streaking sideways as he moved cautiously through the jungle, finding another game trail to make his passage easier. Bits had left the drones behind, waiting for the sun to recharge them, forcing them to use the map and leaving them without the protection of their normal overwatch.

The jungle was alive in the early morning twilight as he crept carefully, a cacophony of sounds all around him. Jackson used his sword to clear a path, widening the trail and purposely making some noise to warn anything ahead of his approach, and hopefully scare it off.

Minutes passed as the distant sky turned orange and purple, more streaks of light cutting through the canopy at sharp angles as the sun breached the horizon. The highlands to the east still blocked most of the light, but the jungle began to pacify itself, most of the nocturnal creatures retreating to their daytime dens as the surrounding sounds diminished steadily with each passing minute.

Jackson moved faster, emboldened by the steadily increasing light, the voices of the jungle dropping off one species at a time. Morning birdsong filled the void, and he lowered his helmet, the cool morning air welcome against his skin after having been cocooned inside the suit all night. He kept a visor over his eyes while Bits continued to cycle through scanning modes, watching for trouble.

Thirty minutes later, the sound of rushing water filled the air, his pace increasing while his thirst pushed him on. The jungle cleared ahead, a wide glen appearing as sunlight poured through the openings in the canopy. Soft green moss carpeted the ground, draped over smooth rocks while the river rumbled farther ahead, just out of sight in the distance. All around the clearing stood colorful tropical flowers opening their petals to take in the early morning sunshine now beaming down from above. Jackson walked carefully, the moss slippery underfoot as he crossed the expanse of open space, taken in by its beauty.

He made his way to the far side of the glen, the river coming into view in the distance through the leaves. He turned back to look once more, burning the beautiful, peaceful scene into his memory when a feral roar shattered the serenity. Jackson spun to his left, losing his footing. He hit the ground on one knee, scrambling for a moment to get the rifle up as eight cats emerged from the dense jungle all around the clearing, surrounding him on three sides.

"Shit," he whispered, watching as a single male stepped out into full view, the hairs on its back raised as it stepped closer.

"Helmet up and harden the suit. Full power to weapons," he said, reaching back and pulling the sword from his shoulder, gripping it tightly in one hand while he kept the rifle leveled at the male in the other, his mind quickly assessing the tactical situation.

The rest of the pack emerged from the shadows, a dozen strong now, their eyes fixated on him.

"To hell with it. Prepare to engage flight mode," he said, realizing that a strategic retreat was his only option.

Growls echoed around the circle, the predators communicating, each competing for the privilege of the kill.

"Yeah, screw this. Bits, get us outta here!" Jackson called.

Just as Bits activated the suit's thrusters, a blur suddenly appeared in his 360-degree view, hitting him from behind while he rose up in the air, knocking him down hard.

He hit the ground, rolling on the rocks, the suit hardening and adapting as he tumbled, providing what protection it could. He was up in an instant, slipping on the moss while he attempted to get into a combat stance. Fresh streaks of blood ran from his shoulder, left by the cat that hit him as it circled, then bent on all fours, ready to strike again.

"Battle stim!" he called, a rush of strength and adrenaline flooding his system a moment later as he closed his eyes for a second, a wave of lightheadedness washing over him, then quickly fading. He opened them once more. His senses enhanced, time seeming to slow somewhat as the chemical cocktail took hold, altering his reaction time and perception.

He held up both arms towards the cat that had hit him, ready to unleash the cryo spray and particle beams, while he risked a glance at his three-sixty-degree view in his HUD to locate his lost weapons. The rifle lay several meters away, the sword closer, but still not close enough as he looked up, the huge male coming closer and glaring at him with murderous intent.

Jackson stared it down, studying its body language, knowing how Razor moved and attempting to predict when it would pounce. The cat lunged an instant later, its rear foot losing traction as the smooth moss slid out from under it, the predator fumbling for a second before regaining its balance. Jackson unleashed a quick blast of the cryo spray, causing the cat to recoil while he reached out with his right arm, the suit forming a tendril that shot out, grabbing the sword and quickly pulling it back into his hand.

"Come on!" he called, the sword held high, ready to cut it down as the cat shook off the blast of intense cold, a ice crystals covering its fur in places.

The cat accepted the challenge, lunging forward, this time surefooted. Jackson twisted his body, moving with unnatural speed as he swung, slicing the cat along its flank in midair, while narrowly sidestepping the attack. The predator hit the ground beside him, its left legs limp and useless as it crashed into the rocks, sliding to a stop, twitching and yelping.

Jackson walked closer, stabbing down with the sword, silencing its cries. He pulled the sword out, holding it high, and turned back to look at the pack, the blood of their brother dripping from his blade. "You want some more!" he yelled defiantly.

The alpha male growled and three of the cats dashed towards him from different directions, ready to avenge their fallen kin.

He dropped to one knee, spinning on the smooth moss, his sword leading the way as he slashed a wide circle around him, driving them back momentarily, then raising his left arm, cryo spray catching two of the cats on their flanks and driving them back. The third, however, had matched Jackson's maneuver, attacking him from behind as it leapt upon him, its razor sharp claws penetrating the suit and raking into his flesh.

Bits reinforced the suit as they fell forward, the weight of the cat nearly knocking the wind out of him on the rocks. Jackson struggled to move, attempting to slash with the sword but lacking the leverage to do any real damage as the weight of the predator pressed down upon him.

"Bits, spikes!" he called, struggling to get out the words.

Bits morphed the suit, creating a cluster of spikes beneath the cat's paws, piercing the leathery flesh and forcing it to rear up on its hind legs. It slammed its forepaws back down upon him, smashing him into the rocks once more.

"Suit controls failing," Bits said. "Attempting to recalibrate."

The cat raised its head and roared, ready to finish Jackson off with its powerful jaws.

It looked back down at its helpless prey, taking in the scent of Jackson's blood and fear as it salivated, ready to strike.

Suddenly, a blur emerged from the jungle, barreling into the cat with incredible speed, bowling it over as it rolled on the rocks and sending it tumbling for several meters.

The cat came to an abrupt stop as it slammed into one of the larger rocks, its body battered by the impact. Its cries filled the air for several seconds before a set of jaws wrapped around its throat, lifting it high, then snapping its neck before the eyes of the pack as it let out a final, feeble squeal.

Jackson rolled over, struggling to breathe, but forcing himself up to one knee, his arms out, ready for the next assault. He looked up to see his savior, another cat, much larger than the rest, standing over his attacker. "Razor!" he called out hoarsely, lowering his helmet.

Razor turned, the two locking eyes in a look they'd

shared a thousand times before during the hunt, yet somehow different this time.

The alpha male entered the fray, moving towards Razor from across the rocks with a low growl. Razor met the pack leader head on, standing tall as he let out a fierce roar in response. Jackson held his breath, quickly realizing that while Razor was larger, he didn't have any experience fighting with other cats, having only his hunting skills to rely upon.

The two engaged each other, snapping with their jaws and swiping aggressively with their claws, while working to get body position on one another in order to strike for the neck. The alpha male lunged forward, biting Razor's ear, tearing away a tiny piece of flesh and leaving a small V-shaped gash in its place.

Razor pulled back, learning quickly and going on the attack, using his superior size, strength, and speed to his advantage. A second later, he darted forward, smashing the bony top of his head into the side of the other cat's ear and jaw, stunning it momentarily, then using the opening to pounce on it, swiping his claws across its flank and leaving a row of deep gashes.

The cat scampered away, a low growl echoing its anger as it recovered.

Razor barred towards it, batting it across the head with his claws, the impact knocking it to the ground. He followed with a deafening roar as he stood above the prone alpha, asserting his dominance while he raised his head high, placing a huge paw upon its neck and pinning it to the ground.

The alpha whined and squirmed, feebly attempting to snap at him. Razor bent down, sinking his teeth into its neck and finishing it off.

Several seconds passed, the pack staring at the sight of their fallen leader. The alpha female called to the others, and two cats approached Jackson from the opposite side of the glen. Razor ran back, putting himself between them, growling aggressively. The two cats crept forward, undeterred, ready to pounce, confident that they could overpower him together.

Razor didn't hesitate, charging at them instead, taking them both by surprise, moving with lightning speed as he raked his claws across one's face while he sank his jaws into the other's neck, snapping it in one fluid motion with a sound that made Jackson want to retch, then throwing it several meters in a display of power and dominance.

The first cat recoiled in pain, whimpering as it moved back, quickly bowing its head. The alpha female moved forward, sensing an opening as her jaws latched onto Razor's haunches from behind.

Jackson watched in horror as his friend let out a yelp of pain, the image of Razor as a kitten curled up in his arms rushing through his mind, pushing him past the fear and pain as he got to his feet. He lunged forward, swiping at the female with his sword, narrowly missing as she released her grip at the last second, evading the blow, and turning to face him, teeth bared.

It was all the time Razor needed.

He barreled into her from the side with blinding speed, knocking her to the ground, then pouncing on her exposed flank and slamming her hard into the rocks with his two front paws as she attempted to get up, pinning her helplessly.

He stood over her, growling, his teeth bared, blood from his previous kills dripping down.

Jackson stood ready, watching their backs while the rest of the pack looked on.

The female's demeanor suddenly shifted, and she turned her head, exposing her neck.

Razor, sensing the change, released her, and she rolled onto her back, exposing her vulnerable underside in a full and surprising show of submission.

One by one, the pack followed suit, bowing their heads and mewing softly, a sound Jackson hadn't heard since Razor was a kitten.

Razor raised his head high, the fur on his back standing on end as he stood tall in the center of the pack, now the undisputed alpha male.

The alpha female mewed once more, rolling over, and Razor leaned down, licking her face.

Jackson lowered his sword, staring in awe at the sight before him. He'd always suspected that Razor was bigger than the other cats he'd seen on the island, but now he could see that he was nearly one and a half times their size, the pinnacle of their species.

The alpha female got to her feet, standing before Razor, the two rubbing the sides of their heads together in what Jackson could only assume was a bonding ritual. After a moment, she fell in beside him, turning to face Jackson.

A low growl came from her throat, and she attempted to move past Razor towards Jackson.

Razor let out a sharp growl in response, and the female submitted instantly, falling several steps back, her head lowered.

Jackson stood stunned, staring at his friend. "I thought I told you to stay," he said, smiling. "But I guess I'm not your master anymore, am I? You're the alpha now. The leader of your own pack."

Razor moved towards Jackson, nuzzling him affectionately while Jackson returned the embrace, knowing he was saying goodbye for the last time, like a parent sending his child out into the world. "I'm gonna miss you, buddy," he said, tears streaming from his eyes. "But I'm happy for you. This is where you belong. Where you were always meant to be."

Razor lowered his head, nestling it into Jackson's chest. Jackson hugged his friend for the last time, kissing the top of his head, then petting him gently, not wanting the moment to end while scratching the spot behind his ears that he knew he loved. "I'll miss you," he said, his voice cracking as he looked his former pet in the eyes. "Take care of yourself and teach them to be better."

"Goodbye, Razor," Bits added. "We will miss you."

Razor pulled back from Jackson's embrace, a look of sadness on his face that Jackson had never seen before as he turned, walking back to where the rest of the pack had assembled, each of them falling in line behind him, leaving Jackson unmolested.

Razor reached the edge of the clearing, then turned back, giving his master one last look.

In that moment, Jackson swore he actually saw him smile.

A tear fell from his eyes as he watched Razor slip into the wild with his new family.

"Goodbye, my friend. I love you," he whispered, the glen suddenly feeling darker, his life emptier without his trusted companion.

CHAPTER 20

THE ASCENT

Jackson sat and ate his breakfast in silence near the river, still struggling to believe that Razor was gone.

He'd been lucky in that Bits had hardened the suit just in time before the attack, the cat's claws having only penetrated a few centimeters into his flesh and the impact not causing any major injuries aside from some tenderness and bruising.

He sucked it up, pushing past the pain, and got to his feet, knowing that the longest part of the journey was still ahead.

Hours passed in what was a mostly uneventful day as he made his way across the island. He'd managed to find several other game trails, following them where possible, making the trek through the jungle much easier, the kilometers passing by in a blur while his thoughts drifted back to Razor, wondering how he was doing. That night he slept in another tree, his dreams filled with memories of the kitten he'd raised into the powerful young adult he'd become.

He awoke the next morning, emotionally drained but determined to press on. His suit was running low on power, and he knew he needed to make the final push to the valley and the highlands beyond before it reached critical levels.

Jackson pressed straight ahead through the deep jungle. Despite the path being more difficult, he tried to take the most direct route, eager to get to his destination.

He'd gained a better sense of the creatures which inhabited the interior of the island over the past few days, and where they liked to be, allowing him to stay clear of any nests or sleeping nocturnal predators. Bits kept their sensors dialed up to maximum, and with the drones overhead, Jackson moved confidently, avoiding any areas which posed a danger.

He reached the edge of the valley just as evening fell. The stunning vista spread out before him as the setting sun bathed the lush landscape in its orange light, the valley running north-south along the eastern side of the island for hundreds of kilometers.

Jackson stood on the western side, staring across at the foothills leading up to the highlands and scouting out possible paths. A river ran at the base of the valley, with dozens of smaller streams running down from the hills above, several of them converging to form spectacular waterfalls that rained down, rainbows cast in the mist as they crashed down into the river below. The scene reminded him of a helicopter ride on Kauai that he and Amy had taken for their honeymoon through Waimea Canyon in Hawaii, with stunning waterfalls running down from both sides.

Jackson retracted his helmet and stood for a moment, admiring the view, the warm sun on his face as he breathed in the clear, fresh air. "Hey, Bits, can we see the caves from here?" he asked, raising his left arm to engage the holo-display.

Bits brought up the three-dimensional map, indicating their destination. "Affirmative, they are approximately here," Bits said, marking their location high up in the rocky hills. "We will need to cross the river, then make our way up the far side. It will be a difficult climb once we reach the highlands, and several of the rock faces are a sheer ninety-degree vertical."

"How are our power levels?"

"The suit is down to eighteen percent, and the rifle is almost completely drained from the effects of the EM field and only small amounts of light to recharge it for the past several days. We should be able to charge both during our ascent tomorrow, as the sun will be on our backs for several hours. I have sent the drones up into the treetops. Once they are fully charged, we can use them in a worst-case scenario, reconstituting them with the suit to provide a six percent boost in power."

"Okay, let's make camp and get some rest. Tomorrow is going to be a big day."

Jackson awoke early the next morning, quickly breaking camp, his excitement growing at the thought that he was almost there, and eager to get the next part over with.

He moved to the edge of the valley, finding a rocky ledge that provided an excellent vantage point. He stood, sipping the last of his water, listening to the sounds of the jungle while looking up at the momentous task that lay ahead of him.

His will fortified, he wasted no time in making his way down to the bottom of the valley, careful to keep a watchful eye for predators with the drones still in the tree high above where he'd slept, topping up their power while the sun rose over a cloudy sky.

He followed the river north, the roiling whitewater growing louder as he made his way downstream to a location the drones had scouted as the best option to cross, lowering his helmet to enjoy the cool spray of mist on his face.

A tree rested tenuously, half uprooted and tipped over the river at a forty-five-degree angle. Bits morphed the boots of the suit to form spikes, and Jackson raised his arm, Bits launching a long, thin tendril of nano-material up towards one of the higher branches, latching on and wrapping around it. Jackson began to scale the tree, carefully pulling himself up, stomping with each step to ensure he had a firm purchase, the raging whitewater flowing beneath him.

After several minutes, he reached the top, the tree extending nearly halfway across the river. "Okay, here we go," he said, taking another step, then leaping forward, the suit's thrusters activating and pushing him as he reached up, Bits launching another tendril out ahead of him and connecting with a nearby branch, allowing him to swing across the remaining distance.

He hit the ground seconds later, his feet skidding in the soft dirt as he came to a stop. "That was awesome!" he said excitedly, an alert chiming in his ear a moment later. "Report."

"The suit's power level is down to ten percent," Bits replied.

"Figures. Well, let's keep moving. We need to reach the highlands and get out from under the canopy so we can recoup a little power."

"Agreed. There is a path to your left which slopes more gently and should provide an easier climb," Bits suggested.

Jackson worked his way up the far side of the valley, pressing on for the next several hours. Finally, he reached the edge of the jungle, the foothills stretching out before him, the open space seemingly out of place after days spent in the thick, tropical tangle of vegetation. The hills sloped upward, covered in knee-high yellow grass with several rocky formations jutting out in places, reminding him of islands in a sea of swaying yellow.

His eyes followed the curvature of the land as the foothills rose, spanning the gap from the jungle to the highlands, where massive vertical formations of rock rose to dizzying heights, forming cliffs and breathtaking peaks.

Jackson filled up his canteens from one of the small waterfalls, then continued on for several more hours. The climb was arduous, but a refreshing change from the confines of the inner island. The hike was uneventful, and by the time the sun was setting, he'd reached the top of the foothills where they met the rocky highlands and cliffs.

He set up camp atop a large, relatively flat boulder and sat facing the setting sun, the clouds having finally cleared, allowing him to recharge his gear while he ate the last of his fresh food.

"What do you think? Looks like we're almost there. Should I just try to climb it now?"

"I don't think that's wise. The climb is going to take a considerable amount of time and energy. It is also higher than it looks, and it will be technically challenging in places."

"What about the charge we're getting now? Could we just fly up?"

"I would not recommend that. The power drain on the suit is accelerating as the levels get lower, and I'm increasingly concerned about the reliability of certain functions, such as the thrusters. I believe your best course of action is to climb by hand, with the suit providing assistance."

"All right. I might as well get some rest then and attack this thing first thing in the morning."

"We may have another problem," Bits said, bringing up a series of readings in Jackson's HUD. "Based on my analysis of meteorological data from the last year, I believe that another large tropical storm will be inbound soon."

"Of course. It can never be easy, can it?"

"I'll keep monitoring it. It's possible it will miss the island, but I recommend we get up early and get started as soon as there is sufficient daylight."

"Sounds good. Let's hope we get some luck on our side for a change."

Jackson awoke early and ate the first of the final three GCH rations he'd been saving, the meal high in both protein and carbs, the perfect food for what lay ahead. He filled his canteens again from a small waterfall tumbling down from high above, stretching as he got ready to move out.

"Well, buddy, this is it."

"How are you feeling, William?"

"Not bad. I'm excited, actually. How's the storm looking?"

"I sent a drone up to its maximum altitude and confirmed that a storm is rapidly approaching from the east. It may still turn and miss the island, but it is currently on a course directly for it. I estimate that we'll start to feel the effects in approximately four hours."

"All right, then. There's no time to waste. Let's do this."

I've marked the optimal path," Bits said, the route appearing in Jackson's HUD as he stood facing the wall before him. "There are several challenging spots. However, the climb is mostly a test of endurance, rather than skill. And despite the formidable appearance, I don't believe it will prove too difficult to climb. There are only half a dozen spots which will require more technical climbing skills."

"Well, that's good news, at least. How long do you figure it will it take?"

"Approximately three hours."

"And then we're at the caves, right?"

"Affirmative. Once there, we can make camp and get to work extracting the isilium. Unfortunately, I have some bad news."

"Let me guess, there's no room service?"

"Sadly, no. In addition to the shocking lack of amenities, the approaching tropical storm has strengthened and is picking up speed."

Jackson shuddered at the thought, recalling the last several storms that hit the island. "Always something, isn't there? How bad?"

"In Earth terms, I estimate that it is comparable to a category three hurricane."

"Shit," Jackson said, deflated. "What are our options?"

"We could wait out the storm here. There are a number of overhangs nearby that will provide adequate protection, or we could climb up now and hope to beat the storm, riding it out in a cave."

Jackson thought for a moment, running the scenarios through his head. "Is there anywhere I can get food in either location?"

"Negative, and the foothills appear to only be sparsely populated with wildlife. The highlands, however, appear to be barren, aside from small avian lifeforms."

"So, I'd have to head back down to the jungle or the lower highlands to hunt, then?"

"Correct."

Jackson looked back at the valley below. It was a long way down, and there wasn't much cover from the storm down there. "How long will it take to harvest the isilium?"

"I cannot say for certain. The drones located several deposits. However, we won't know until we arrive precisely how difficult it will be to extract."

"Best guess?"

"Six to ten hours, accounting for time to recharge the rifle in between."

"Hmm. What do you think we should do?"

"I believe that your best course of action is to wait out the storm here and return to the jungle for food once it's over. It may add several days, but I believe it's the safest course of action."

Jackson thought for a moment, attempting to weigh the logic of his options against his emotional need for this journey to be over. "To hell with it. We've wasted enough time already. We're climbing."

"Are you certain—"

"I can't go back. I just can't. Let's just get this done."

Bits hesitated for a moment. "Very well, William."

Two and a half hours later, Jackson was three-quarters of the way up the rock face of the highlands, his legs and arms burning from the constant exertion. Determined, he struggled forward, pushing through the physical discomfort while keeping his eyes fixed on his goal. Finally, he stopped on a wide ledge, taking a break and eating the second of his three rations, while taking several long pulls from his canteen.

After resting for fifteen minutes, he was on the move again, the wind picking up. The sun disappeared minutes later, swallowed by a wave of dark, ominous clouds sweeping over the peaks above like an avalanche plummeting down a mountain slope.

The wind gusted, then increased to a steady stream within minutes, the force pressing against him as thunder rumbled in the distance. Bits brought the drones back, their power failing, and merged them back into the suit.

Jackson stopped on the next small ledge for a quick break to catch his breath, staring at his last obstacle, a near vertical climb for just over twenty-five meters to reach the top. He retracted his helmet, taking a drink, finding the air thinner than he was used to. "Okay, buddy. We've got this."

"I've mapped out an optimal route with a variety of hand and foot holds. It looks daunting, I know, but it isn't any more difficult than an average climbing wall. As you reach each hold, I'll morph the suit to fill the contours around your fingers, providing you with a better grip. You will still have full control, but this will allow you to save some of your strength. The sensation may feel odd, however, so I wanted to prepare you, as you might feel as though your grip is slipping at first."

"Good to know. I don't know what I'd do without you, Bits. After Raz—" He paused, his exhaustion having left him more emotionally drained than he'd realized. "After everything that's happened in the past year, I…I just wanted you to know that no matter what happens, you've been the one thing that has kept me from falling apart on this godforsaken island."

Thunder rumbled, closer than before.

"Of course, William. I will always be here for you."

"All right, let's finish this," Jackson said, standing and taking a moment to stretch.

He reached for the closest handhold, leaning out from the ledge, his fingers gripping the rock, the suit flowing and gripping the surface, the sensation, as Bits had prepared him for, feeling somewhat like slipping. He focused his mind, ignoring his instincts, trusting in his AI, then moved his leg into a foot hold Bits identified, stepping off the ledge.

Several minutes passed while he climbed quickly, the sheer vertical face spread out before him while he resisted the urge to look down. He reached up when a powerful gust of wind slammed into him, twisting his body, his right arm and leg left flailing in midair as he fought against it.

The gust subsided, and Jackson swung himself back towards the rock face, grabbing hold, then pulling himself back in until his chest was pressed up flat against the rock, minimizing his profile just as another powerful current whipped past. "It's getting worse!"

"Indeed. Wind speeds have increased significantly. The center of the storm, however, has turned and is moving north. It will miss the island, but we'll still be well within the affected area."

"That's a bit of good news, at least."

"The winds will still remain powerful for the next eight to ten hours before it moves off."

"How much farther?"

"Eleven meters to go."

Jackson checked the top-right window of his HUD, watching the active feed from the remaining drone, which had set down on the top of the nearest peak to monitor the hurricane. The feed looked east out over the ocean, showing the black clouds with bands of dark gray swirling rapidly. Lightning flashed, streaking through the clouds, illuminating the storm's terrifying size and the speed at which it moved, Jackson thankful that it wouldn't hit with its full force.

The sky continued to darken, the only light that of the occasional flash of lightning followed by a deafening rumble of thunder as he continued to press on. Jackson reached up, grabbing a handhold, when suddenly the top of his hand erupted in a torrent of excruciating pain.

He pulled his hand back in agony, nearly losing his footing as the wind kicked up, attempting to separate him from the rock face once more. "Ahh," he yelled, shaking his hand, a feeling of fire rushing through his veins. "What the hell was that?" he asked, feeling his hand swell rapidly.

Bits morphed part of the suit into a small spider-like drone, carefully scaling it up the cliff to determine the source. "It appears to be a scorpion of some kind. Its camouflage is highly advanced. The drones didn't detect it on their earlier passes."

"Bitzzz, ma arm is swellin…huuuuulp," Jackson mumbled, his swollen hand reaching reflexively for his throat.

"You appear to be having a severe reaction to the scorpion's venom."

"Bitz..." he said, trying get more words out, his throat closing rapidly, his body convulsing as his airway swelled shut. Suddenly, his body went limp, slowly tipping back from the cliff.

Bits activated the thrusters, ascending rapidly while battling the wind and attempting to land near the cave. Jackson came down hard, the thrusters failing, the suit's power reaching critical levels. The drone studying the scorpion lashed out with a tendril of nano-material, killing it instantly, then dragged its corpse up to the ledge near the cave to conduct a venom analysis.

Bits initiated a scan, running simulations to map and counteract the poison.

Jackson's heartbeat slowed, his body shaking as he lay on the ledge, precariously close to the edge.

"Hold on, William," Bits said, administering epinephrine and diphenhydramine to counteract the reaction.

Jackson let out a last breath, his throat closing completely shut seconds later. His hands clawed at the suit, fighting for air, his face turning blue.

Bits interfaced with the suit's medical systems, the nanites around his throat forming into a large cluster, then hardening the material near his skin into a small, razor-sharp blade. Bits directed the scalpel, slicing into Jackson's throat, just below his Adam's apple, breaching his trachea, then morphing the nanites and flowing them into the incision. The nanites expanded to form a round tube, moving down into Jackson's windpipe until it reached his lungs, splintering off to feed each side with oxygen.

Jackson gasped as the air rushed back into his lungs, his body twisting in pain from the venom coursing through his veins while he forced himself not to touch the tender skin surrounding the site of the emergency tracheotomy. Inch by inch, he dragged his body into the dark cave ahead, the force of the storm hammering the island.

The wind gusted outside, reaching speeds over one hundred and seventy kph while lightning streaked through the skies, illuminating the night. Thunder rumbled inside the cave, forcing Jackson to shield his ears while he lay curled up, his body twitching involuntarily.

Bits injected him with the last dose of medical nanites, directing them to aggressively attack and break down the poison.

Hours passed while Jackson lay in agony, his shoulder badly bruised from the rough landing and his hand and arm throbbing. Bits worked tirelessly, adjusting dosages of medication and analyzing the venom while the nanites attempted to break down what they could.

Finally, Bits completed a full analysis of the venom from the scorpion corpse, using it to engineer an antivenin based on templates from thousands of recorded compositions. Once the reaction was under control, he administered several anti-inflammatories to reduce the swelling, attempting to restore the normal flow of blood before any permanent damage set in.

Heavy rain blew into the cave, flowing down into the darkness where it pooled, causing more scorpions to emerge, driven from their shadowy hiding places. They came at Jackson, aggressively attacking the intruder in their midst, forcing Bits to react quickly, hardening the suit to protect him from their stingers while they crawled over his prone form, searching for any weak points.

Jackson fell into an exhausted, feverish sleep, delirious from the combination of the poison and the drugs. His heartbeat fluctuated as traces of venom made their way to his organs, the nanites in his system working to intercept the deadly toxin and eradicate it.

Outside, the hurricane raged while inside the cave, the battle within Jackson's body had just begun.

CHAPTER 21
HOPE

Bits worked throughout the night to counteract the venom from the scorpion sting, then set to work hunting down the rest of the ones in the cave. Once he felt reasonably sure that Jackson was safe, he formed the majority of the nano-material making up the suit into a single large drone, taking a risk with the power levels at critical as he battled through the raging winds to take it up.

Finally, the drone broke through the cloud cover of the fading storm, hovering high above for hours while recharging, reaching thirty percent capacity by midday.

Bits brought the drone back down, reforming it into the suit, then amping up the suit's medical treatments and using the additional power to boost the efficiency of Jackson's failing medical implants. He repeated the process several hours later, reconfiguring the drone, then taking the rifle up along with it for several hours to charge in the sunlight.

By sunset, the suit and rifle both had good power levels and were ready for the task ahead. Bits kept Jackson sedated to minimize the pain while the swelling slowly reduced. On the morning of the next day, he finally awoke, his entire body aching, his mouth and throat parched while his stomach growled greedily.

"Good morning, William," Bits said. "Please don't try to talk. I only recently removed the tracheotomy while you slept. The nanites and suit's medical systems are still repairing the incision site, and your body will need time to heal once they complete their work. I've successfully removed the scorpion's neurotoxin from your system. You will still have some pain and discomfort while the swelling reduces over the next few days, but I believe you are past the worst of it now. I suggest that you try drinking a small amount of water."

Jackson nodded, sitting up and opening his canteen. He gingerly sipped some water, his throat aching as the cool liquid flowed down. Finally, after a few hours of taking it slow, he was able to eat half a pack of rations and drink a full canteen.

He fell back to sleep, sheer exhaustion taking hold once more, waking several hours later feeling much better, though still barely able to stand. After eating the second half of his ration pack and gulping down the last of his water, he got to his feet with great effort, taking a few tentative steps forward.

"How are you feeling, William?"

"I've been better, buddy," he replied, his voice hoarse. Slowly, stiffly, he moved to the cave entrance and stopped, staring out at the late-afternoon sun blanketing the island, the sky a brilliant blue stretching as far as the eye could see.

"I know you are still very weak, but with only a small portion of rations remaining, I believe it is critical that we mine the isilium now, before your strength fades once more," Bits said.

"Yeah, you're right. Where is the nearest deposit we can harvest?"

"Fortunately, we are not that far. There is another cave farther up the rock face."

"My hand…" he said, trying to flex it, his fingers unable to move.

"I've immobilized it, hardening the suit around it, keeping it numbed with a local analgesic."

"I won't be able to climb without it."

"The suit has enough power that I can initiate flight mode to take you there. Then you will need to make your way inside and use the rifle to mine the isilium."

"I can do that. How'd you get the suit and the rifle both charged?"

"I took them both up above the clouds to solar charge."

"That was risky."

"Agreed. However, I didn't see any alternative."

"You did great, buddy. Thanks for taking care of me and saving my life."

"You are most welcome, William."

"All right, let's get this done."

The next few hours passed quickly, Bits taking them up to the cave with the largest deposit of isilium. Jackson took out several more scorpions on his way inside before reaching the wall where the scans showed the precious metal was buried. He quickly got to work, following Bits's instructions carefully, and used the rifle in a wide-beam, low-power mode to shave off several layers of rock until he reached the desired depth. Next, he carved out a line around the deposit, the rifle running out of power halfway along the cut.

"Damn it!" he spat. "How long to charge it again?"

"It is currently night outside. The sun will rise in six hours, twenty-two minutes. I can then take the rifle up with a drone to an optimal position and should achieve a sufficient charge within a few hours."

"I guess I might as well rest then," he said, laying down the rifle and leaning back against the wall of the cave. "Do you really think this is going to work? That all of this wasn't for nothing?"

"I do, William. I have hope."

"Hope..." Jackson repeated, the word trailing off as he slid down the wall, moving to find a comfortable position, then rapidly drifting off to sleep, the word sounding alien to him, like something out of a dream.

"Good morning, Bits," Jackson said, waking up and feeling better than he had in days. "How long did I sleep for?"

"Nine hours, twenty-three minutes. I let you sleep longer in order to regain more of your strength and to maximize the charges on the suit and rifle."

He sat up, suddenly more awake at the idea that he was almost there. That his quest, as he'd come to think of it, was nearly at an end. "All right then, let's get to it!" he said, standing up slowly, his stiff body struggling to match his enthusiasm.

Minutes later, he was back at work, continuing to trace around the deposit with the rifle, then carefully carving angled cuts from both sides to separate it from the wall, the chunk of rock, the size of a football, falling to the cave floor as he finished.

"We're lucky that it wasn't too deep," he commented, shouldering the rifle, then hitting the deposit with a blast of cryo spray to cool it rapidly. He bent down, picking up the rock with his left hand and cradling it to his chest where Bits flowed a thin layer of the suit around it, firmly attaching it.

"How much to do you think we got?"

"Scans show just over nine hundred and eighty grams, nearly double what we need."

"Finally, some good news," he said as he made his way out of the cave and into the midday sun, the warmth washing over him. He stood with his helmet down, basking in the light, soaking up the heat. His prize secured, he took a moment to enjoy the view from his towering vantage over the island.

Lush greens and blues, with the faintest hints of purple, stretched north as far as his eyes could see, with several rivers crossing the landscape. He turned towards the southern tip, where the *Phoenix* lay in its watery grave, a wave of sorrow washing over him as he thought about the ship, and Alpha, still on board. After a moment, he turned to the west, locating the cove, a mere speck of rock from this far away. "Any sign of Raz?"

"Scanning. One moment. I've located his communicator, one hundred and sixty-seven kilometers northwest of our current position. The nanites in his system are slowly shutting down, as they are in yours. However, their last report indicated that he was still in excellent health."

Jackson smiled, happy for his friend despite the feeling in the pit of his stomach that he knew he'd never see him again. He gave himself a moment to miss him, allowing the bittersweet memories to flow, wishing he could run his hands through his soft fur once more as he nestled his head into Jackson's lap, staring up at him with his brilliant golden eyes.

After a moment, Bits spoke softly in his ear. "Are you ready to go home, William?"

"I am *beyond* ready, buddy! Let's get the hell out of here!" he said, stepping closer to the edge of a sheer drop, moving his arms down along his sides, then pausing for a moment as he felt the suit flow before bringing them up again. Wings expanded out from his arms, growing to nearly a meter in length on each side, while small fins appeared on his legs for stabilization and maneuverability.

"Flight systems ready," Bits informed him.

Jackson took a deep breath, jumping out as far as he could, the wings hardening as he glided out, away from the cliffs, Bits activating the thrusters and picking up speed.

The trip across the island was stunning, like something out of a dream. Jackson pondered how a place so beautiful and full of wonder could be so deadly and unforgiving. The calm winds carried them effortlessly as he retraced some of his path back home. He looked north, spotting several tropical lagoons and small archipelagos near the western shore. The center of the island stretched as far as the eye could see, dominated by the never-ending jungle.

In just under an hour, they were back at the western shore approaching the cove. Jackson circled slowly, noticing a number of items scattered along the beach to the south. He reduced their speed and altitude, lining up for a landing. Bits assisted with the thrusters, and they came in gracefully, his feet touching the ground in a half run as they gently landed on the sandy beach, the wings morphing back into the suit.

As he walked back into his camp, his stomach dropped on discovering the area had been ravaged by the storm. The sentries were on their sides, one of them smashed against the rocks of the cove while the other lay half buried in sand. He returned to the spot where he'd buried the duffel bag, finding the rocks still atop it and the contents undamaged.

"Well, I guess I've got some work to do," he said, looking around at his battered home, items scattered everywhere, but otherwise appearing intact.

Five hours later, Jackson had his camp back into some semblance of order while Bits began to work on the deposit of isilium.

Jackson gathered up most of his possessions, taking a quick inventory of what he'd salvaged and noting a few things that were missing, then headed for the river. After a quick scan, he waded into the water, spotting a shiny fish just beneath the surface. Raising his arm, he thrust his spear down, impaling the fish dead center. He pulled it from the spear, his right hand still lacking dexterity but slowly becoming useful again as the swelling reduced. He threw the fish on shore, spearing a second, much larger fish a moment later. Satisfied, he filled his canteens and walked back to shore, placing the first fish back on the spear.

As he made his way back to camp, his stomach rumbled at the thought of fresh fish, and he felt relaxed for the first time in almost a week, happy to be back in his own territory. Halfway there, he stopped suddenly, a low growl in the bushes ahead freezing him in place.

Jackson reached back for his rifle, remembering that it was nearly spent after completing the mining. He had his spear, along with the partially charged weapons still in the suit, but knew he was ill-prepared for a confrontation.

Slowly, he took several steps back, holding the rifle in front of him, the readings in his HUD showing it was good for one, maybe two shots at best.

The brush ahead shook as he steadied himself, waiting for a clean shot, his spear clutched tightly, the fish still impaled on it throwing off the balance.

The palm leaves parted a moment later as a fully grown spykeraet emerged, its spikes up and teeth bared.

"Scans indicate that the creature's adrenaline levels have spiked. I'm detecting fatal levels of neurotoxin in the quills," Bits warned.

Jackson backed away slowly, avoiding eye contact with the creature, hoping that like most small mammals, it wouldn't attack unless threatened. The spykeraet took several quick steps forward, then stopped abruptly, its large claws digging into the hard ground, leaving long deep marks as a threat display.

Jackson kept his arm level, the rifle locked on target, the creature letting out a low growl more befitting a bear than the small badger-like creature it was.

"Easy there, fella. Easy." Jackson spoke softly, lowering the rifle, then slowly tucking the shaft of his spear under his right arm and reaching for the tip with his left hand. The spykeraet tensed, ready to pounce, while its eyes followed Jackson's hand as it moved slowly towards the fish, staring at it intently.

He slowly pulled the smaller fish off of the spear, holding it out. "Here you go, little buddy. This is for you," he said, gently tossing the offering towards it, the fish sliding across the ground, stopping just in front of the spykeraet's paw. The creature looked up at him, distrust in its eyes. After a few seconds, it bent its head down, careful not to look away from

Jackson as it sniffed the fish, pawing at it uncertainly before snapping it up a second later in its powerful jaws, cartilage snapping, making Jackson's blood run cold as the creature devoured the fish in seconds.

He stood perfectly still, and the spykeraet eyed him a final time before letting out a short grunt. It turned, the spiky hair on its back lowering as it waddled back into the jungle, disappearing into the underbrush.

"I need a vacation from this shit," Jackson said, barely getting the words out as he felt a tightness in his chest. "Bits, would you mind initiating a scan of the area and launching a drone to check our path back to camp?"

"Scan initiated. Drone launching."

"Oh, and one more thing. If I ever, *ever*, run off blindly into the jungle like that again, please feel free to give me a swift kick in the ass with my own foot!"

"I've added your request to my command subroutines, William."

The rest of the walk back to camp was uneventful, something Jackson was grateful for after his close call. He quickly lit a fire, cooking the fish and salivating at the smell as it roasted slowly. Before going to sleep, he took another dose of medical nanites from the advanced med-kit he'd left behind, Bits putting them to work to repair the damage to Jackson's hand and heal the other injuries from his journey across the island.

He awoke the next morning, feeling rested and with his arm and hand feeling much better, though still not completely back to normal. Excited to be home, he hunted a pig that afternoon, laying out strips from his kill to dry in the sun, then got to work on making molds for the isilium, his dexterity not quite back to a hundred percent, but enough to follow Bits's instructions and carve several shapes into the pieces of wood he'd scavenged.

Since their return to the camp, Bits had worked diligently, using nanites from the suit to eat away at the rock surrounding the isilium, isolating the deposit. Once the metal was free, Jackson built a roaring bonfire, heating the deposit in the coals, then chipping off small slivers with the kyromonite sword and using the tools he'd salvaged from the *Phoenix* to press and shape the malleable metal into the molds he'd carved.

He worked late into the night, and by the next morning, he had rudimentary covers to absorb heat from the CPUs and transmitter modules on the three comms units, along with six thin strands of wire, each the length of a ruler.

Jackson got some rest for a few hours, then got back to work, carefully following Bits's step-by-step instructions as he connected the zero point generator to the comms module from the Guardian before connecting it in sequence with the other two emergency comms modules.

Once ready, he hunted and went for water, then went back to sleep, tossing and turning for several hours in anticipation before waking in the early hours of the morning when Bits calculated, as best he could extrapolate, that their side of the planet would be facing towards the closest nearby stars within range, ready for their last-ditch effort to reach out for help.

Jackson sat silently, the sun's rays still well below the horizon with just the faint light from the stars and twin moons overhead illuminating his breath in the cool morning air.

"William," Bits finally said, breaking the silence. "It's time."

Jackson let out a deep breath. "Okay, here goes nothing," he said, trying to relax while he watched helplessly, waiting to see if this worked.

It was a pivotal moment. Possibly *the* moment that would define the rest of his life.

If it worked, and they could get a signal out or, better yet, make direct contact with someone, they could get off this accursed rock and back home. But if it didn't…then he'd likely spend the rest of his life on the island.

The thought filled him with dread, knowing that his implants and the nanites in his body were failing, and he'd already begun to feel the effects of aging taking hold once again, no longer feeling like he was twenty-five and in his prime. It wouldn't be long until he began to feel his actual age, a spry forty-three. Still not bad, but without the technological intervention, he'd be lucky to reach fifty with all the dangers the island held. A simple scratch could turn into an infection, and there were certainly viruses and other dangers that, without his enhanced immune system, could easily prove fatal.

The thought of dying there, alone, terrified him.

He'd always held a belief that he'd get off this planet. A hope, buried deep inside that after everything he'd been through, this was just going to be another trial for him to overcome.

Now, the moment of truth had finally arrived.

The implications of his last Hail Mary possibly failing loomed large in his mind.

"Beginning activation sequence," Bits said as Jackson leaned forward, waiting with bated breath. "Suit communications systems have successfully interfaced with the comms arrays. Power from the ZPG is flowing into the units. Running diagnostics now. Stand by."

Jackson sat silently, the seconds passing while he waited, the sounds of gentle waves lapping at the shore and noises from the jungle growing distant as his heart beat faster in his chest, the sound thrumming in his ears.

"Diagnostics complete. Our repairs have been successful in bypassing the damaged sections of the Guardian module's main board, and all three units are connected in parallel and synching up. Power is steady from the zero point generator. Isilium heat sinks are operating nominally. All systems are ready."

Jackson let out another breath. "Here we go. Fingers crossed."

Bits activated the holo-display, appearing from the suit lying on the sand in front of him, showing the comms modules at seventy-five percent power, along with two boxes: one with the outgoing signal displayed and another to detect any incoming transmissions.

"We'll start at a lower level and ramp up from there. We will only have one shot at this. Once we begin, we cannot abort," Bits cautioned, running several more quick diagnostics on the transmitting functions, then adjusting the array's primary and secondary transmitters to different frequency modulations in an attempt to cut through the powerful EM field. "We're ready to proceed."

"Do it," Jackson said.

"Initiating distress call."

A signal wave pattern appeared on the display. Jackson watched intently as the waves rose and fell.

The signal was simple this time, a lesson learned from their earlier attempts. Bits theorized that voice transmission likely wouldn't make it through, so instead they sent a short binary message containing their coordinates (as best as Bits could calculate them), the locations of several nearby astronomical objects for reference and triangulation, along with Jackson's military ID and their request for urgent assistance.

Jackson sat cross-legged, waiting as the transmission cycle ended, watching for any sign of a response. "Is it working?" he whispered, not wanting to risk talking over any response, despite knowing that was unnecessary as Bits was connected directly into the comms array.

"It is transmitting and receiving within normal operating parameters. The CPU, however, is beginning to heat up, an anticipated side effect from our bypasses on the circuit board. I am attempting to boost the signal to ninety percent power."

The comms speaker remained silent while Jackson waited, watching the wave patterns repeat. Suddenly, a blip appeared on the incoming screen, followed by a short burst of static. "Hello!" Jackson blurted out desperately as he rose to his knees, rocking steadily back and forth while he awaited a reply.

"I do not believe that a voice response will be possible with the interference," Bits reminded him, tempering his excitement.

"Right," Jackson recalled, having acted purely on instinct and adrenaline.

The array was silent again as Bits ran another series of diagnostics.

"Bits?"

"Checking. No response. Boosting the signal to one hundred percent."

Jackson held his breath. Still nothing.

A minute passed while he watched for the slightest sign of a response.

"I am attempting to boost the signal to one hundred and ten percent, altering the frequencies and modulation through several bands," Bits said, the bar at the top of the small window reflecting his efforts.

A burst of static erupted from the speaker a moment later, followed by low screeching sounds, the incoming transmission screen showing spikes of activity.

"What is that?" Jackson called over the noise.

"I believe that I have found the problem. Our signal is being bounced back off the atmosphere," Bits said, the noise subsiding as he turned down the volume. "The subspace phase modulator is slightly out of alignment and is defaulting to short-range communications. Overriding the modulator now at the firmware level to force it into long-range mode."

The activity on the incoming feed ceased, and Jackson waited, the seconds continuing to pass.

Still nothing.

"Diagnostic confirms that we are now transmitting on a long-range band. Frequency modulation adjusted and confirmed. CPU temperature continues to increase. I recommend we increase power one more time before it reaches critical."

"Do it."

"Acknowledged. Boosting the power to one hundred and twenty percent."

Seconds passed with no response.

A cold sweat ran down Jackson's back as the thought crept into his mind that someone could be receiving but *choosing* not to respond. Unfortunately, they had no way of actually knowing if they were even reaching anyone.

"The temperature on the transmitter is approaching critical. I am going to boost the power one final time to maximize the signal strength in the alpha and theta subspace bands. Based on diagnostic data, I believe they stand the best chance at breaking through the interference. Increasing signal power to one hundred and fifty percent of design capacity."

"To hell with it," Jackson said, rising to his feet. "Bits, record a voice message. It probably won't go through, but we have to at least try." There was a small beep as Bits engaged voice mode. "Hello? Is anyone receiving? If anyone is there, please acknowledge!" Jackson said, pausing as a slight blip appeared for an instant on the incoming band, then disappeared once more. "I am a GCH officer in need of assistance!" he yelled, panic flooding his voice as his emotions poured out. "I'm stranded here and need help!"

The transmitter began to smoke. "William, I need to—"

"Is anyone out there?" he pleaded, tears streaming from his eyes as his hope began to burn, the smoke from the transmitter drifting higher. "Please! Please… Help me!" he said, his voice trailing off as he collapsed to his knees.

Bits cut the power to the comms array a second later, the smoke turning dark, the isilium melting from the intense heat as it hit the board, smoking as it landed.

"Rrrrrraaahhhh!" he screamed, smashing his fists into the sand, then rising to his feet in a fit of rage and stomping down on the comms arrays with his boot, his emotions boiling over.

Jackson stood, breathing heavily for a moment, his fists clenching and unclenching as the waves of anger, frustration, and despair washed over him.

All of his suffering, all of his efforts were for nothing.

Finally, he fell to his knees once more, his energy spent as he bent forward, his forehead pressed to the sand, overwhelming despair taking hold.

After several moments, he sat upright, closing his eyes and taking several deep breaths to regain his composure. "Fuck it," he said, his voice bitter and defiant as he abruptly got up, walking over and lighting a fire to warm up, leaving the discarded remains of the comms units smoking in the nearby sand.

The rest of the day passed swiftly, Jackson barely speaking as he went about his normal routine.

Bits remained silent, responding only when asked, knowing that Jackson's mental state was fragile after everything he'd been through.

A sullen, bitter fog settled around Jackson as he stomped through the jungle that evening, daring any of the creatures there to oppose him.

That night, he didn't dream at all. He had no more dreams to live for.

CHAPTER 22

ALONE

Six days later, Jackson's implants began to go offline. Failing one by one. The decline of his suit and weapons also continued, able to charge now directly from the zero point generator only, and even then only maintaining a charge for a few hours at most.

He awoke one morning a few days later, tired and sore from a restless sleep.

"Bits, what's our status?" he asked, getting up slowly, exiting his tent, his spear in hand as he checked the cove in the early morning light. "Bits? You there, buddy?"

No response.

"Bits, this isn't funny. Joke's over. You...you can't go... please. I-I can't do this without you."

Jackson stood in silence, the cool morning breeze blowing through the cove as he realized now that he was truly alone.

Razor was gone. Bits was gone. He had no technology left, save for one or two items which barely functioned.

He stared into the jungle, shadows looming as a sense of foreboding and dread took hold.

After his failed attempt to call for help, he thought he'd

reached rock bottom, but he now realized that he'd had farther still to fall.

He was going to die there.

Utterly alone.

Eight days later, Jackson emerged from the jungle, thinner than he had been since he was a teenager. With Bits gone, his forays into the jungle had become less and less frequent. The path, once his kingdom, was now a dark, dangerous road, filled with sounds and predators potentially lurking behind every bush. His paranoia had grown as the days wore on, the realization hitting him that he hadn't walked and marked his perimeter in weeks, knowing it was only a matter of time before another pack of cats moved into the area.

As the days wore on and the jungle became less and less hospitable, he kept mostly to the beach and several nearby trees where he could collect fruit, eating a few small meals each day, but just enough to get by on. Jackson ventured into the jungle once every two days for water and fish, and then only risking wading into the water when he was certain that the crocs weren't lurking nearby.

He spent most of his time focusing on making small improvements to his camp and doing simple projects that kept him busy, raising his spirits in tiny increments.

Still, it wasn't nearly enough.

His heart ached as he sat by the fire each night, lamenting his lost friends, a deep depression taking root. He slept less and less each night, even the slightest sound waking him, his spear and the sword never leaving his side.

His routine was the only thing that kept him sane.

Wake up, eat, stretch, check the camp, get water every second day, collect firewood, nap, prepare the firepit, eat, sleep, repeat.

He mixed in small projects for variety: so far, he had made a new, better rack out of wood for drying strips of fish or pig; a small fenced-in area, where he was contemplating keeping a few small pigs he was planning to capture; and a hat out of palm leaves and vines. A few more ideas percolated, but his lack of ambition and energy had quickly beaten them down.

Jackson awoke early the next morning and crept back through the jungle to the river. He returned with three large fish stowed in the duffel bag that was slung over his shoulder and both canteens full, his senses on high alert as he gripped his spear, moving slowly and cautiously along the trail. The sword hung on his hip at the ready, but the powered edge had long since stopped working and his rifle was down to just three shots on a full charge, its battery capacity down to almost nothing.

Two days earlier, he'd spotted the tracks of a large cat near the river. That morning, there were three more.

He'd caught two more fish, throwing them to the far bank in an attempt to lure the predators away from his side, but in his heart, he knew it was a vain attempt to buy some time, nothing more. His thoughts became focused while he struggled to come up with any type of scenario where he could square off against a pack and come out alive. If they came to his camp or ambushed him on the trail, he knew he was as good as dead.

So far, stealth and caution seemed the only two things that held any hope of avoiding a confrontation.

Fearing that the scent of the fish might attract them, or other unwanted predators, he'd begun tucking them in the duffel, hoping it would help to mask the odor, and keeping his fire high each night to ward off any animals curious enough to venture near his camp.

He moved slowly now along the overgrowing trail; the duffel sealed tight, stopping frequently to listen for the slightest sounds of activity.

He was nearly back to the cove when a twig snapped nearby, freezing him in his tracks.

Jackson crouched into a defensive stance, surveying the area slowly, knowing only too well how many predators could camouflage themselves and ambush their prey. He stepped carefully forward, keeping his spear ahead of him and gripping it tightly. He listened intently, his heart pounding in his chest, his eyes narrowing to focus on anything that seemed out of place.

Seconds passed as he crept slowly forward, stopping every few steps to listen, the only sounds those of the breeze through the treetops, the hum of insects, and the birds singing their cheerful songs.

He looked around carefully, checking his six, recalling how the cats had gotten the jump on him twice before by attacking from behind.

As he turned forward staring down the path, he noticed a slight distortion ahead, turning his head to the side as he studied it. Suddenly, a blast of energy shot out of nowhere, striking him dead center in the chest.

Jackson dropped to his knees, his consciousness slipping away as he fell to the side.

He looked up; the distortion growing bigger as the assassin approached, uncloaking and standing above him, a weapon trained at his head, a blue scaly hand coming down towards him, the world going dark around him as he blacked out.

CHAPTER 23

CRIMES AGAINST NATURE

Jackson awoke with a start, twitching instinctively, the memory of his attacker rushing back. He opened his eyes, a stinging sensation hitting them an instant later as saltwater rushed in. Panic quickly followed as he realized he was underwater.

He gasped for air, his senses recoiling, uncertain which way was up, his hands reaching out, pressing up against the inside of an opaque glass cylinder, his breathing frantic as air somehow flowed into his lungs.

Jackson reached a hand up to his face, confused, his fingers running over a soft, bumpy surface covering his nose and mouth. As he felt around the strange object, it reacted slightly to his touch, muscles twitching just below the surface, pulling his hand back as he realized that whatever it was, it was alive!

He looked down at his naked body, quickly discovering more parasites attached to him, each a different shape, color, and texture. Some resembled starfish, while others appeared gelatinous, like jellyfish as they clung to his body.

His mind raced, struggling to comprehend where he was, when suddenly the glass around him became clear and a tall, thin, fish-like humanoid hovered before him, suspended in water, staring back with its deep-blue alien eyes.

The creature blinked, two eyelids coming together from either side and meeting in the center as it stared at him, studying him like an animal in a zoo exhibit. It examined Jackson with its impassive eyes, moving its hands to manipulate the water around it as one would a computer console.

Jackson watched, studying the creature in return, its body thin and streamlined. Wide, webbed feet spread out from its muscular legs, leading up to its torso. The creature's chest and back appeared to be covered in ridges of cartilage running up from its waist in a hexagonal pattern. It had powerful shoulders and lithe arms with small fins on its wrists. Its hands moved gracefully through the water, wide and flat, with long, bony fingers separated by thin, nearly transparent webbing. Its rounded head tapered into a pointed fin on the back, while its face appeared somewhat humanoid, but with much larger eyes, a subdued nose covered in tiny pits, and a small mouth with thin lips and sharp teeth.

He breathed deeply, focusing his mind while remembering his training.

An Opherik, he recalled, one of the three core species that made up the military arm of the Oceanic Union. He closed his eyes, attempting to remember Captain Delgado's talk on them, his concentration broken a moment later when an ethereal and alien voice spoke in his ear. "Name and rank," it said, Jackson stunned as the creature spoke in perfect Archonian.

"Commander William Jackson," he said, the creature over his mouth stretching effortlessly while he spoke into it. "GCH serial number—"

"State your purpose on our world."

Jackson calmed his mind, pushing aside all of his questions as he focused on his answers. "I was stranded there. I—"

"You are a spy, sent to infiltrate our space!"

"A spy? No, I'm just a test pilot. I was conducting a field test with an experimental propulsion system when suddenly it malfunctioned," he explained, certain that they would have already scanned the *Phoenix* and discovered the presence of the slipstream drive for themselves. "The drive overloaded, causing catastrophic damage to my ship, forcing me to put down on your planet."

"Lies. You will tell me what I want to know, or you will suffer."

A jolt of pain shot through Jackson's left arm, the creature on his wrist stinging him. "Ahh. What the hell?"

"You will tell me what I want to know, or you will suffer," his interrogator repeated firmly, its gaze unwavering.

"I'm telling you the truth," he said through gritted teeth. "I'm a GCH officer. We're allies. I'm not your enemy!"

"That remains to be seen."

The interrogation continued for the next hour as Jackson was repeatedly shocked and stung for information. He kept to his cover story, knowing that if the OU checked with the GCH, they would back it up. Finally, he passed out from the pain and exhaustion, falling into a dreamless sleep.

He awoke sometime later, another creature floating before him, watching him intently. Jackson racked his brain, unable to recall the name of the species. It was similar to the Opherik, but with green skin and longer legs. Short black barbs protruded from its wrists and feet, possibly the delivery system for a poison or neurotoxin. An Iverian, he recalled, the barbs giving it away.

"How are you feeling, Commander?" it asked, its tone cordial.

Jackson looked down, noting the creatures still latched on to his body. "I've been better."

"I apologize for your earlier treatment. I'm afraid that Shrawl Kavath is very…*thorough* in his work. Can I get you some food?"

"Food?" he repeated, realizing it had likely been days since he'd last eaten. He nodded, and the officer manipulated the water, its eyes remaining firmly fixed on him as his tube began to drain, a hiss of air filling the chamber. The lifeforms attached to him released one by one as the water drained, each swimming off into small tubes at the bottom of the tank that closed behind them. His feet settled on the floor a moment later as the last of the water retreated, forcing him to brace himself against the sides to remain upright in his weakened state.

Another hiss of air followed, and a small platform lowered from above. He looked up to see a bowl filled with small, circular objects. Reaching up, his hand shaky, he picked one up between his thumb and index finger, rolling it gently between them. The texture was rough as he studied the sphere, uncertain what to make of it. The creature outside gestured, moving its hand to its mouth, and Jackson slowly mimicked the action, his eyes watching his captor intently for any sign of malice, before placing the sphere between his teeth.

A grain-like taste hit his tongue as he bit down, the crunchy shell revealing a soft, chewy center with a slightly salty aftertaste. It took some getting used to, but he quickly got over it, inhaling the contents of the bowl in less than a minute, his hunger all that mattered in the moment. As he reached up to replace the bowl, he noticed a tall glass of water which hadn't been there a moment before, and drank it greedily.

The creature outside the tank smiled, its sharp teeth giving it a sinister look as Jackson finished the last of his meal. He set the glass back on the platform, which retracted into the ceiling a moment later, leaving the two of them staring at one another once more.

"Thank you," he said.

"You are most welcome, Commander. Please let me introduce myself. My name is Sar'kaj Nevmoth, second-in-command of the Oceanic Union destroyer *Pensar*."

Jackson nodded, uncertain what to say.

"What is the last thing you remember?"

"I was walking through the jungle when I was ambushed. And then I woke up here and was being tortured!"

"That was…unfortunate. I apologize on behalf of my people. There is a lot of distrust of outsiders these days."

Jackson nodded. "Where are we now?"

"As I mentioned, we're aboard one of our ships in orbit around Alath-argha, the planet where we found you."

"So, now what? Will you take me back to the GCH?"

"I'm afraid not. We must prepare."

"Prepare for what?"

"For your trial."

"My trial? For what? I've already told you, I'm not a spy!"

"Yes, we've contacted your people, and they've verified your story. However, you misunderstand. You are on trial for crimes against nature."

"I'm sorry, what?"

"Our rescue team discovered the remains of a large aquatic predator that you killed during your time on Al-ath-argha. A very serious crime indeed."

"The shark, you mean?"

"Precisely."

"But it was trying to eat me! I was only defending myself."

"I suggest that you save it for your trial, Commander. Anything you say to me *can* be used against you. I'll ignore what I've heard thus far, as I'm your advocate in this case, and you're still under mild sedation, but I'd advise you to say nothing further."

Jackson stood in stunned silence, a feeling of helplessness mixed with panic taking hold. "If you're my advocate, aren't you supposed to listen to my side of things?"

"How would that change anything?"

"What do you mean, 'How would that change anything'? Aren't you supposed to defend me?"

"No. And if you confess to me, I am required to admit it into evidence. There is no confidentiality between us like in your system. You are accused of crimes, and I am an Oceanic Union officer. I serve my people in all things."

Jackson paused for a moment, considering his predicament, pushing his emotions aside and focusing on the problem at hand. "What do I do now?"

"I'll bring you something to wear. Your trial will begin in less than an hour."

"What?"

"Yes, the tribunal is assembling now. They will be ready for you soon. I suggest you use this time to prepare your defense. I'll conduct the formalities, as your advocate, and interject where appropriate, but you will be responsible for explaining your actions."

"But I don't even understand what I've done wrong, or what your laws are, or what my rights are!"

"I'm afraid that ignorance of our laws is not a viable defense, Commander. I'll return shortly before the trial begins."

And with that, Nevmoth turned, swimming gracefully out of the room, leaving Jackson to contemplate his fate.

"Bits, are you there, buddy?" he asked, hoping against hope that he would be back online now that they were free of the EM field.

Silence followed.

What if he's gone for good?

Jackson quickly pushed the thought aside, knowing that he needed to focus on his upcoming trial. He was in uncharted waters with no idea what to expect.

He tried to remember what he knew about the Oceanic Union. They were enigmatic, preferring to stay out of most galactic conflicts and were at one time an adversary of the Confederation. They lived mostly on aquatic worlds, were highly territorial, and from what he recalled from Basic and his co-ops training, very black and white in their views.

Over the centuries, the two empires had found common ground against the Reptilian Empire, and in protecting the environment and preserving the natural order of nature, several of the founding principles of the OU which, much like the GCH, had brought many aquatic species together in a common cause. While their fleet was considerably smaller than the GCH, their ships were fast and powerful, focused on protecting a vast swath of the galactic arm of the galaxy where their empire resided.

The Oceanic Union and the Reptilian Empire had fought several long and bloody wars over the centuries, and the GCH had eventually become involved, backing the Oceanic

Union, turning the tide of the war, pushing the Reptilians back. The two had become closer allies in the centuries that passed, leading to a formal treaty hundreds of years ago, which ensured that if one was attacked, the other would come to their aid.

Jackson had successfully prevented a war with the Empire years before, and the OU had honored their obligations under the treaty, if grudgingly so, in the aftermath. While they had not engaged the Insectoid Imperium in open conflict, their ships shored up nearly a dozen sectors along the Confederation's borders with the Empire, the Vehn, and several other areas of contested space. This allowed the GCH to focus on the war effort with the Insectoids while the OU looked out for their interests and watched their backs.

How does this help me? he thought as he prepared himself, trying to recall what he could about their laws and society but coming up blank.

Nevmoth returned several minutes later, providing him with a set of clothing resembling a skintight wetsuit, along with earpieces to protect him from the pressure of the ship and to translate for him. Once dressed, the tank began to refill, and the creature which had allowed him to breathe returned, attaching itself once more to his face as he tried to remain still, holding his breath until he felt it seal around his nose and mouth like a mask.

The tube opened and Jackson swam out, treading water as he hovered before Nevmoth.

"You will speak only when asked a direct question. Is that clear?" Nevmoth asked firmly.

"Understood," he replied, the feeling of speaking through the small creature affixed to his face still just as strange as it had been before.

"I'll begin the formalities. You are to do what I do. Bow when I bow. Nod when I nod. When I speak, you will keep your head low. You will only look at the tribunal when you are allowed to speak. Is that clear?"

Jackson's mind raced, trying to process the rules and protocols, not wanting to make things worse by breaching them. "I understand. I'll try my best."

Nevmoth smiled. "Watch my hands. If I move two fingers in a small circle, it means be prepared to bow. You may have difficulty in the water, so take a moment to practice."

"Thanks," he said, taking his advocate's advice and attempting several clumsy bows before finding the right motion to make it look at least somewhat respectful and civilized.

"If there's a pause and I tilt my hand towards you, it means you are permitted to speak. When I straighten my hand, it means your time is up. You'll have less than one of your minutes each time, so be sure to be concise and factual."

Jackson nodded.

"And remember, no matter what happens, you need to refrain from *any* emotional outbursts. This will only make things worse."

Jackson thought for a moment, sensing there was something his advocate wasn't telling him. "Is there anything I should know?"

Nevmoth floated silently for a moment, looking back over his shoulder before leaning in close. "No matter what happens, you *will* be found guilty," he whispered. "So be prepared. I can't say any more, but know that one of your ambassadors has arrived and will be in attendance," he added, nodding slightly and giving Jackson a knowing look.

Just as Jackson was about to ask another question, two OU officers, both Opheriks, entered the room, quickly swimming towards Jackson and fixing him with restraints while Nevmoth supervised. He complied, allowing them to take him by the arms and pull him swiftly through the ship to a large room where the tribunal awaited.

Nevmoth floated beside him as the proceedings began, while Jackson kept his head respectfully low, avoiding eye contact and watching for hand signals. He understood little of what transpired at first, the formalities of the trial quickly covered, and terms he didn't recognize dictated and agreed upon.

After the first few minutes of preamble, his crimes and trespasses were listed. After hearing them translated in his earpieces, he quickly realized that the trial was little more than a farce, designed to frame him for the so-called "crimes against nature" that he'd committed on Alath-argha to provide leverage against the GCH in negotiating his return.

A holographic display appeared, showing evidence of the shark that Jackson had "brutally and unjustly murdered," along with the fish he had in his duffel bag when he was captured. The evidence mounted as the trial continued, compounded by Jackson's recorded admissions from his interrogation that he'd killed several cats, snakes, pigs, and other creatures during his time there, further building an ironclad case against him.

Scans of the *Phoenix* appeared, presenting it as a deadly stealth warship on a mission to infiltrate their core systems. A first-strike weapon that could wipe them out before they even knew what hit them.

Finally, the image of the smashed body of Alpha135 was presented as evidence that Jackson was conducting covert information-gathering against the Union using a sophisticated intelligence-gathering automaton.

For every false claim and wild accusation, he was given a brief opportunity to speak. He tried his best to be concise and justify his actions, while still maintaining his cover story that he was merely a test pilot on a failed mission. After nearly thirty minutes of intense scrutiny and accusations, the prosecutor finished presenting his case. Jackson was then allowed two minutes to state his final defense before he was summarily found guilty on all charges and sentenced to twenty years in an OU correctional facility.

As he was led from the tribunal chamber in dismay, he kept his composure, as Nevmoth had advised, noticing a humanoid near the back of the room for the first time. The bars on the shoulder of her aquatic suit identified her as a GCH ambassador. Just before he was escorted out of the room under armed guard, she met his gaze, giving him the slightest hint of a nod.

Hours passed while he waited, confined to his tube and kept in isolation with only minimal rations. Finally, Nevmoth entered the room with the ambassador in tow, and he was released from his incarceration and taken to what appeared to be crew quarters. Once alone, the ambassador explained that after nearly six hours of tense negotiations between herself and the Upper Dectent of the OU Justice Tribunal, an agreement had been reached.

"This is how the Oceanic Union often operates," she explained. "They seem to relish in taking offense and hosting these sham trials in order to extract concessions both from other political factions within the OU and with their allies. You obviously didn't do anything wrong, but they wanted some leverage to negotiate with and used your guilty verdict to extract some concessions from the GCH."

"I'm sorry for causing such a problem, ma'am."

The ambassador smiled. "It's not a problem at all, and it's the least we can do after all of the sacrifices you've made."

"What happens now?"

"Get some rest. A ship is on the way to pick us up, and we'll be leaving in the morning."

The following day, an unarmed GCH salvage vessel, along with a small corvette, arrived, coming into orbit alongside a group of six Oceanic Union warships above Alath-ar-gha. Jackson was transferred on board the corvette *Cierion*, and they jumped into hyperspace shortly after, while the salvage ship worked under the careful supervision of the OU to tractor the *Phoenix* from the sea floor, loading it into its massive cargo bay.

Once on board the *Cierion*, Jackson reported to the medical bay for a physical, the doctors running a battery of tests and injecting him with medical nanites, along with a cocktail of other drugs, to flush his system. The doctors then took a long look at his left arm, administering several injections and using a dermal regenerator to heal it completely.

"You've got a number of maladies, Commander," the lead physician said. "You're lucky to be alive. You're malnourished, must have broken one of your ribs at least twice, have about twenty scars that we've healed up, and had several nasty ailments that could have become serious over time. It's a good thing you were rescued when you were."

Jackson nodded numbly as the doctor listed off the litany of items, having been more worried about predators than his failing health. Finally, after fourteen hours sedated in a medpod, the medical staff completed their work, giving him a clean bill of health, and a tech from engineering arrived, working to reactivate his implants and bring Bits back online.

"There you are, Commander. You should be good to go now. Your AI will be back online in a few seconds," the tech said.

"Is he all right?" Jackson asked, concerned that Bits had been damaged from being offline for so long.

"Based on these diagnostics, he's fine. His consciousness never went offline. He was merely cut off from your cognitive, auditory, and visual implants as they ceased to function. His matrix appears to be fully operational. It will just take a minute for him to reestablish control over your body's systems while they run through a series of diagnostic and security checks."

"Thanks," he said, tapping his foot while he waited anxiously.

"No problem. If there's anything you need, just let me know. The name's Ensign Cooper," he said, shaking Jackson's hand, then turning to leave the medical bay.

Jackson sat silently while his implants came back online one at a time, his visual display appearing in his ocular implants, showing details about the world around him. A slight blip in his ears followed as his auditory implants activated, followed by Bits's voice, a sound he'd not heard in weeks.

"Hello, William."

Jackson held back his tears at the sound of his friend's voice, the loneliness he'd felt since Bits went offline overwhelming him. "Hey, buddy," he said softly, a single tear breaking through his shattered defenses and streaming down his cheek. "I've missed you."

"And I you, William. I'm sorry I couldn't be there for you, but I was always with you."

"I'm just happy you're okay. I was so worried," he replied, his voice cracking slightly as he took a breath, shaking off the sadness that had overcome him, the joy of having his best friend back washing over him.

"I will not leave you again," Bits stated solemnly. "I promise."

The next hour passed quickly as they caught up, Jackson relaying everything that had happened since he went offline, while Bits listened attentively. That night, he slept in a bed in the quarters they assigned him, sleeping better than he had in well over a year.

Jackson arrived in the Archon system eight days later and was taken directly to the Admiralty tower in the GCH Command complex for debriefing. Admiral Valentyen was talking with Admiral Scott as he entered the room. Each of the men gave him a nod as he walked to the front, taking a seat before two of the fleet admirals, Holup and Dash'ari, who sat behind a long, ornate table. Fleet Admiral Lighton appeared a moment later as a holo-image, overseeing the debriefing via a remote link while Jackson relayed what happened during his mission in the RE-13 system and how he had successfully destroyed the Imperium shipyard.

Bits continued the debriefing, relaying the series of events that occurred after Jackson's death, while he and Alpha135 completed the mission, displaying the visual and sensor records showing the carnage they'd unleashed in wiping out the Imperium shipyard, orbital facilities, and enemy ships.

"You've been through quite an ordeal, Commander," Admiral Lighton said. "And accomplished an incredible and unprecedented feat, significantly impacting the war effort. We thank you for your service to the Confederation. In recognition of your achievements and sacrifices, I hereby award you with the Silver Star for unparalleled bravery, selflessness, and dedication. I also hereby promote you to the rank of Captain, with all of the rights and privileges thereof. Congratulations, Captain Jackson," she said, a hint of a smile appearing through her otherwise impenetrable mask of authority.

Jackson beamed brightly, standing at attention while Fleet Admiral Holup rose, stepping forward and presenting him with the Silver Star award and a Platinum Star to denote his new rank, the insignia of the GCH engraved on the surface.

"Thank you, Admirals," Jackson replied, saluting crisply.

The room cleared out a moment later as several other high-ranking officers, who'd been at the back of the room, stopped to thank him for his service. He spoke with Admiral Scott for a few moments afterwards, who explained how they'd mounted a search, as best they could, with long-range reconnaissance probes. After nearly two weeks of searching, they eventually gave up, believing that he and the *Phoenix* had been lost during the destruction of the shipyard and that he'd officially been listed as Killed in Action.

The admiral also brought him up to speed on Frederickton's half of the mission. "I'm afraid that Captain Frederickton didn't make it," he said solemnly. "He was successful in destroying nearly a third of the Insectoid shipyard in MK-291 System, but was confirmed KIA and his ship was destroyed before it could escape."

Jackson nodded, thinking about Frederickton, hoping he was at peace.

"I want you to know that what Fleet Admiral Lighton said was true; your missions significantly impacted the Imperium war machine. After you destroyed the shipyard, and Frederickton crippled the other one, the Insectoids were far more guarded with their remaining advanced ships, using them only when they had superior numbers," Admiral Scott explained. "The GCH Fleet went on the offensive shortly afterwards, the 8th Fleet setting out on a bold strike, pushing deep into the heart of Imperium space and, at great cost, finishing the job that Frederickton had started. With both advanced shipyards destroyed, the Insectoids pulled back and only mounted limited offensive strikes for nearly six months. It's been a long, bloody struggle, but we've slowly regained some ground and are now holding them at bay in most sectors."

Jackson nodded, gratified to hear that he'd made a difference while saddened to hear of Frederickton's loss.

"I want you to take a month of leave, Captain, before reporting back to FoxBlind for duty. I wish I could give you more time, but we've still got a war to fight, and we've lost a lot of good people. You're one of the best operatives we have, and I need you back in action."

"Thank you, sir," Jackson replied. "I'll be there."

"Enjoy some rest, Captain. You've certainly earned it."

Admiral Scott moved off, and Admiral Valentyen approached, the two men exchanging a respectful nod as they passed.

"Congratulations, Captain," Admiral Valentyen said.

"Thank you, sir," Jackson replied, happy to see his former CO for the first time in years.

"Why don't we take a walk, if you've got some time?"

"I seem to have an abundance of it suddenly." He smiled, falling in beside the admiral as they took a lift down to the ground floor, then walked around the grounds of the Command complex for the next few minutes, the admiral filling Jackson in on the latest galactic events and updating him on the status of his former crew mates.

"Daria is still on Delconia working in her lab, and Henrik is on Cetarus II at the moment, assigned to a top-secret project. They were both overjoyed when they learned that you were still alive and are planning a little get-together for you a few days from now. They would have come sooner but wanted to give you a bit of space to acclimate and knew you'd have to be debriefed once you got back. Kelara's unit has been in blackout for the past eleven days, running a series of black ops along the Holt Line. I contacted her CO, informing her that I wanted to speak with Leutienant Quentarus as soon as she returned, but it could be another seven to ten days until they're back on the grid."

"I'm just happy she's still alive. Daria had told me what happened on the Outlier colony just before I left and that it had really impacted her. I was worried about her."

"From what I understand, she had a rough few months, but it seems like she's recovered and has been doing excellent work based on the reports that I've seen over the past year.

Daria and Henrik took her out on Delconia for a couple of days when she was on leave, and I think that helped. I tried to make the trip myself but couldn't get away."

"It's just good to know that everyone's okay and that, hopefully, if what Admiral Scott tells me is true, the war could reach a turning point soon."

"Actually, that's partly what I wanted to talk to you about. Let's take a seat," he said, finding a bench in a grassy area just off the main paths. "You recall the Imperium's newfound ability to hide their fleet movements?"

"Of course," Jackson replied. It had been a significant tactical advantage for the Imperium and one the GCH had struggled to overcome, allowing their fleets to move freely on their side of the border without being tracked.

"It's continued to grow as the war progressed. At first, we called it 'Shadow Tech,' as they were able to mask the presence of several of their fleets using what we discovered was a specialized ship which blocked our sensors. As time passed, entire systems and in recent months, entire sectors of their space have become hidden from our sensors. At first we believed that they had developed some type of localized cloaking or jamming tech, but as sectors expanded to encompass entire regions, it became clearer to me what it possibly was."

"It sounds like what Alura described," Jackson said.

"Precisely my thoughts: the Phague Shroud of Darkness."

Jackson shook his head. "But how is that possible?"

"I'm honestly not sure, and it's just a theory at this point, but there's enough similarities and it's such a big technological leap for them that I can't ignore the possibility that they've somehow recovered Phague tech and adapted it. I contacted Captain Delgado several months ago and commissioned a covert mission into one of the regions of Imperium space where our sensors had just become blind. He sent a stealth ship with a team of his best officers a few days later on a reconnaissance mission."

"What happened?"

"They crossed the border under cloak and entered the nearest known enemy system. After several hours of searching with their scans finding nothing, they discovered a series of cloaked, uncrewed stations scattered throughout the system. They couldn't even detect the stations until they were almost right on top of them. Their analysis showed that each one created a dampening field of some kind which blacked out the area to our sensors."

"How did they find them?" Jackson asked.

"Mostly by luck," the admiral admitted. "They had an android aboard to assist in processing the sensor readings and to look for even the slightest anomalies. The android discovered a tiny gravitational and magnetic signature, one that even the best AI would likely have missed, and that led them to one of the stations."

"That's a huge discovery."

"Indeed. And once they knew what to look for, they were able to detect over a dozen of them in the system. The lead operative, Commander Beratus, attempted to capture one to bring back for study. His team knocked out its comms and were in the process of tractoring it in when a destroyer jumped in, almost right on top of them. They didn't stand a chance and were just able to get a message out with all of their data before they were destroyed," he said sadly, pausing for a moment. "Our engineers think they must have a monitoring system setup, so that if one station goes offline, the others alert all nearby Insectoid forces."

Jackson paused for a moment, recalling his time in covert ops training with Beleclas Beratus, and how he'd become part of his little group with Sherenah, saddened by his loss. "Do you think it's a coincidence that they could have developed this tech? Could it really be Phague technology?"

"I'm still not certain, but let's look at what we know. First, the Imperium has built new, advanced warships unlike anything they've ever had up to this point, and based on your report, it appears that they've likely stolen many of the design elements from other species in order to create them. Second, this sensor-jamming tech is unlike anything we've ever seen before, able to obscure star systems, and now entire regions of space, from our scans. The only other reference for this we have is the Phague. Third, the scans that came back of the station indicated that the design was unlike anything the Imperium is known to have. So, it begs the question, where did they get it from?"

Jackson was silent for a moment as he processed the logic of the admiral's conclusion. "Yeah, it makes a lot of sense. Especially since we know that many of the Ancients' home systems were once within Imperium space. It's possible that they could have recovered a surviving piece of Phague technology and reverse engineered it."

"My thoughts exactly."

"So, what do we do?"

"Just before we lost you, I began planning an op, one to infiltrate the Imperium network to see if we could recover any data on this new technology. I was hoping that we could plan it together, but then when you never returned…"

"I'm sorry, sir," Jackson said, truly saddened by the pain he'd caused the admiral.

"It's not your fault. You did a marvelous job, Will. I'm just sorry for the price you had to pay. In any case, I later tried coordinating with Admirals Scott and Webb, both of whom were operating in regions where the Shroud wasn't yet active. They each sent a covert team to attempt to infiltrate what we believed were key Imperium bases to steal what data we could. Unfortunately, neither team ever returned."

Jackson was silent for a moment, his mind racing, imagining what happened to the two brave crews who lost their lives. "I'm sorry, sir," he said softly.

"As am I," the admiral said, the weight of those lives still clearly on his conscience. "After that, I took a step back, accessing all of the enemy's tactics thus far, and came up with a plan."

Jackson leaned forward, eager to hear what the admiral had devised.

"A week later, with Command's blessing, I diverted just over half of the 19th Fleet, weakening our deployment in the Davatos System, which was protecting a strategic mining operation. Within two days, the Insectoids took the bait, sending in a fleet of their own, over twenty-three hundred ships strong, including sixty of their advanced warships. The hyperspace defense grid was fully active when they arrived, taking out several of their scouts and a small part of their forward strike force, forcing the rest of their fleet to jump in just outside of its protective field, slowing their approach and buying precious time. What remained of the 19th Fleet organized in a defensive formation to protect the mining operation, despite being outnumbered nearly five to one. As the Imperium fleet closed in, we disengaged the defense grid and the 19th, 23rd, 29th, and 44th Fleets arrived, coming out of hiding in a nearby stellar nursery. Suddenly, our forces outnumbered them nearly two to one, crushing them while only losing three ships in the process."

"That's amazing, sir," Jackson admitted, his spirits raised somewhat by the decisive victory dealing a major blow to the enemy.

"We shifted tactics again, knowing that the Imperium would be looking for a win to bolster their morale. I had the Confederation corps of engineers working a few weeks ahead of time reactivating a fleet of old mothballed vessels, mostly just cargo ships with modified transponders and a few decommissioned destroyers. We then deployed them to the Garalin System, not far from a system on the other side of the Holt Line known to be a major Imperium fleet hub. We made it appear that our forces were preparing to mount an offensive, using mechs to pilot the ships as they lined up in formation. It didn't take long for the bugs to take the bait once again." The admiral paused, a smile creeping across his face. "They attacked with a battle fleet of nearly six hundred vessels, devastating our 'fleet' with a surprise attack. Just as they entered the Garalin System, however, we counter-attacked with our own strike force of close to six hundred ships, hitting their fleet hub, which was left with only thirty vessels and a few hundred weapons platforms defending it, most of the ships in the process of being repaired. When the Insectoid fleet returned, they found their bases and infrastructure destroyed, along with their jamming stations. We also left behind some nasty surprises for them in the form of cloaked mine fields and hundreds of powered-down, auto-guided torpedoes, which targeted several of their ships as soon as they exited hyperspace, hitting them before their shields were up and they knew anything was wrong. Intel indicated that we took down another thirty-three ships, while forcing them to abandon the system and retreat farther back to within the protection of the Shroud."

"Sounds like you turned the tide of the war."

"They were good victories. Unfortunately, the Imperium adapted and started engaging in more traditional tactics, which worked for a short time. They began interspersing traditional fleet engagements with surprise attacks to keep us off-balance, and it's been mostly a stalemate ever since. We've hit a few of their systems where the Shroud wasn't active yet, but it's nearly everywhere now. If you jump into an area of space with it active, you're essentially blind. We know how to find the stations operating the Shroud, but can't see any enemy ships coming until it's too late and we're left sitting ducks. It's left us with few options to go on the offensive and we're mostly holding our lines at this point, responding to their movements."

"So, what do we do now?"

The admiral smiled. "I was hoping you'd ask. I have a lot more to tell you, and I'd like your help with something I've been working on, but now's not the time."

"Sir?" Jackson asked, confused.

"Will, Verris is awake."

CHAPTER 24
REUNION

Jackson stepped off the ramp onto the hangar deck of Kishara Search and Rescue Station. It had taken just over five hours to get there by shuttle from Archon, and although he was tired, his excitement and nervousness had him on edge.

"Jax!" came an excited call from across the hangar.

Crap, he thought, *so much for keeping a low profile.*

One of the deck crew quickly made his way over to greet him.

"Hey, Ankers, how's it goin'?" Jackson asked.

"Holy hell, man. We all thought you were dead!" Ankers said excitedly. "Wait till everyone hears. Shit, we're gonna have one hell of a party!"

"Actually, I'd like to keep it quiet for a while, if you don't mind," Jackson said, taking a step closer and keeping his voice low. "I was hoping to talk to the captain. Is Vees around?"

"Right...of course," Ankers said awkwardly, clearly realizing the implications of Jackson being back. "Yeah, Vees is up in the hub, as usual."

"Thanks. I appreciate your discretion. Hopefully, we can grab a drink later. It's good to see you, man."

"Yeah, you too, Jax. Take care."

Jackson quickly exited the hangar bay, noting that all of the rescue ships aside from the *Griffin* were out on assignments. He glanced longingly at his old, trusty ship, a feeling of warmth flowing through him that Vees had kept her around, despite having lots of shiny new options to replace her with.

He ducked into a side corridor, taking the lesser-used parts of the station and back stairs as he made his way up to the command center, passing a few unfamiliar faces along the way and giving them a nod, but not stopping as he pressed forward. A few minutes later, he reached the command center, or the hub, as the crew called it. He entered the room, spotting a few officers he recognized on duty, all of whom were too occupied with their work to notice him.

He quickly made his way over to the captain, clearing his throat as he approached to alert her to his presence. Vees, as often happened, was lost in her work, and with the bustling sounds of the hub, it was easy to startle her. She turned, her eyes lighting up as she saw him.

"Will! Holy shit!" she said, moving towards him and embracing him in a giant hug, a look of disbelief on her face. Jackson returned the embrace, genuinely happy, and moved to see his former commander.

After what felt like a minute, Vees pulled back, her face beaming with joy. Suddenly, she realized why he was there, her expression saddening. "Lieutenant, no…wait," Vees said, eying Jackson's uniform. "Well, I'll be, *Captain* Jackson," she said, her smile brightening for a moment before dimming once more. "It's so good to see you again, Will, and *alive* at that! We were all heartbroken when we heard you were missing in action and presumed lost. I was very touched by the message you left me, and we all took your loss pretty hard around here."

Jackson nodded, thinking back to the message that auto-transmitted after he was declared overdue. Most GCH officers recorded messages to their friends and family in the event of their death. Jackson had recorded several before he left.

"Thanks, Captain," he said, noticing that her expression hardened for a moment at the formality. "I mean, Vees. It's good to be back. I've missed you all. But I guess you know why I'm here."

"Of course," Vees said awkwardly, leading Jackson to the conference room at the back of the hub. "She's out on an op right now, but should be back within the hour. I'd be happy to tell her you're here when she reports in."

"Actually, I'd like to surprise her in person, if that's okay?"

"Will," Vees said, placing her hand on Jackson's shoulder, "I'm not sure what they told you, but she's…she's not the same person you knew. She doesn't have any memories from the past few years. She's still mostly herself, but I'm afraid that she won't know you and…and she might not want to… Verris has been trying to move on. She's shut most of us out, retreating into her work. It's been tough to watch, honestly. She does her shifts… Hell, she takes as much work as she can get, and she rarely ever comes down to the bar or sits with anyone in the mess. And she gives me shit if I try to send anyone along with her on an op, even when she knows she needs the help." Vees took a deep breath. "I'm afraid that you're not going to find what you're looking for, Will." Her eyes went to the floor, unable to look at her friend while she destroyed his hopes and dreams.

"I know," he said softly. "I've heard it from a few people already, but I have to try."

Vees nodded. "Well, you're welcome to stay up in the hub till she returns. You two can talk in here once she reports in. Fewer people will see you that way than if you're wandering around the station."

"Good point. Is there anything I can do to help? I'd prefer not to just sit on my hands and wait."

"Sure there is," she said, brightening. "You know we can always use an extra hand around here. Why don't you take the aft station? It'll keep you out of sight and you can help the operators to coordinate. Today's been a busy day, and I'm sure they'd appreciate another set of hands. Just stay off the outbound comms, and I'll let you know when she gets back."

Just under an hour later, the *Dagathon*, one of the new ships which had been delivered the day that Jackson and Verris were reassigned years ago, arrived in the hangar bay.

Verris exited the ship, making her way up to the hub, where she made her report, unaware that Jackson was watching from the back of the room.

"Good work out there," Vees said.

"Thanks, boss. I'm gonna go hit the mess, then get some rack time. I'll be good to go again in another nine or ten hours at most."

"Actually, there's one more thing," Vees said, gesturing with her head towards where Jackson stood leaning against a console.

Verris turned and saw him, taking a moment before recognizing him. "Shit," she whispered under her breath, turning to look at Vees. "I thought… I thought he was dead…"

"Well, it turns out he's not. So, be *nice*," Vees stressed, putting her hand on Verris's arm and gesturing for the two of them to head into the briefing room.

Jackson entered first while Verris followed, hesitantly. They stood for a moment staring at each other before he finally broke the silence.

"Hey," he said gently, having envisioned this moment a thousand times in his mind over the past few years.

He would see her again, and their eyes would meet. They'd laugh. They'd cry. They'd embrace each other, and everything would be right with the world once more.

But now, here he was. Everything resting on this moment. All of his hopes and dream hovering on a razor's edge, and he knew he had to tread carefully.

Verris stared at him for a moment. "Hey," she replied softly, looking away.

"It's okay. I know you don't know who I am."

"Oh, I know who *you* are," she said, the undercurrent of anger clear in her voice.

"I-I guess the first thing I should say, then, is that I'm sorry. And that I'm just here to talk, okay?"

Verris nodded slightly, her arms folded across her chest.

"So, you know who I am, but I'm guessing you can't remember me…but I remember you. I remember us."

Seconds passed while she glared at him, unflinching.

"After you were injured saving me," he continued, "I spent days by your side. But once they put you in temporal stasis…the doctors, they finally told me to go. That it could be years before they could help you. It pained me more than you'll ever know, but I agreed to leave and went back to work. I kept messaging the hospital, hoping for some news, but they said that a treatment would be incredibly complex and… And then the war started, and I spent the next year and a half fighting, but I never forgot about you. Not even for a minute. I checked in with Daria and the hospital every time I could. Every time I went out on an op, I checked with them as soon as I got back."

He put his hand on top of one of the chairs as he spoke, squeezing the back and fighting a wave of frustration and helplessness, attempting to keep a tight rein on his emotions. He longed to go to her, to hold her, to tell her that everything was going to be okay. But her body language and the look on her face told him that this was not the time. "I never, ever, gave up hope."

He took a breath, letting the conversation lapse for a moment, hoping for something in return. Some crack in her armor to appear. To show that he was getting through to her. That she remembered something, *anything*.

Instead, she still stood rigid with her arms crossed in front of her chest and a cold, detached look on her face.

He quickly read the signs, sensing that she might try to flee at any moment, knowing that he had to press on.

"Then I undertook a mission," he said tentatively, looking away slightly, the mixed emotions from his ordeal on the island difficult to discuss, as he was still coming to terms with everything that had happened to him. "It was a very dangerous op and, unfortunately, it didn't go exactly as planned. I ended up marooned on an uncharted planet for a long time. During that time, the only thing that kept me going was the thought of *you*," he said, his voice cracking on the word, a tear welling up in the corner of his eye.

"I thought about you every day. I even talked to you sometimes. It's stupid, I know, but…but *you* kept me alive on that island. And now…" He swallowed. "Now you're back.

And I know—I know that you don't remember me, and that's okay. We have time. We can start over. We can make it work again. I know, I know it in my heart that we can."

Verris stood in silence for a moment, her arms dropping to her sides, her stance softening. After what felt like an eternity, she finally spoke. "I got your message," she said, looking away once more. "I heard everything that you said in it. I also watched my message to you. I saw how much I loved you. I've…I've never said anything like that to anyone before. Ever. So, I know how hard this must be for you." She straightened her posture, looking Jackson squarely in the eyes. "I wish that I could remember you…and us, I really do, but…but I'm not that person anymore. I don't know you… and… I'm sorry, but I-I don't want to. At least not right now," she said, a tear streaming down her cheek.

Jackson felt dizzy, his mind reeling, lost, as though he was staring down into an abyss.

"I'm still trying to get my life back together. To figure out who I am again," she continued.

"We can do that together," Jackson pleaded. "We ca—"

"No," she said firmly. "No. I'm not *her*. I'm not that person…and I don't know that I ever will be again. I'm really sorry, but she's gone… She's gone," she whispered.

Jackson stood in stunned silence, his heart shattered. "Okay. I…please. Just…let's just talk."

Verris's face changed suddenly, her compassion giving way to something else, something buried down deep coming to the surface, her eyes boring into him. "I have nothing else to say to you. I don't want you in my life."

"Okay, but can we jus—"

"I woke up in a hospital, Will! They'd healed my body, but I'd lost years of my life! I had to learn how to *walk* again!

I lost Altara! They recovered her from a backup, but she's not the same. Not to me. It took me months to fully recover, and then months more before I could even fly again. And I…I *hated* you for that. You, this person I supposedly knew and loved, who took me with him on some highly dangerous mission and nearly got me killed!"

Verris reined herself in a moment later, looking away as she spoke. "I need you to go. And please, don't come to see me again. If you ever truly cared for me, I need you to promise me. Please…just leave me alone."

"Okay," he said numbly, his heart breaking at the pain he'd caused her. Imagining what it must have been like for her, to wake up in the hospital, surrounded by people like Daria, who she had no memory of but who knew her. He thought about how he'd lost Bits on the island, considering how she must have felt with Altara having to be restored from backup, wondering if the "real" version of her AI had died. He let out a breath, struggling for something, anything to say.

Verris turned to leave, stopping just short of the door, standing still for a moment before taking a breath. "I'm so sorry, Will, but the woman you knew is dead. I'm sorry for your loss."

Jackson watched helplessly as the woman he loved walked out the door before he collapsed into one of the chairs, the pain of her words overwhelming him. He felt as though he was going to be sick, his heart aching like nothing he'd ever felt before. Not since Amy's death all those years ago.

He sat alone for some time, how long he wasn't sure, before Vees came quietly into the room.

"Are you all right?" she asked, coming up beside him and placing her hand on his shoulder.

Jackson looked up and shook his head, unable to speak through the lump in his throat. Vees crouched down and gave him a hug. "I'm so sorry. I can't imagine what you're feeling right now. We've all had to deal with this in our own way, but not like this. Why don't you stay a few days? The rest of the crew would love to see you."

"I can't. I've got to go. I have to get back anyway."

"Will, you just got here."

"I promised I'd stay away, Vees! I have to give her space. I…I don't know what else to do."

"Okay," she said sadly after a moment. "Then at least let me walk you back to your shuttle, all right?"

He nodded and she took his hand, helping him up, walking him down to the hangar bay. They hugged once more before he boarded the shuttle, knowing that word would spread amongst the crew that he'd been there and that it would make it awkward for Verris.

From what Vees had told him, she was already antisocial enough, and he didn't want to push her any further away from human contact.

"Please, just make sure everyone knows that I left and that it was *my* choice," Jackson said. "I don't want anyone saying anything to her. She needs you all right now, more than she knows."

"Of course," Vees said, nodding slightly. "Take care of yourself, Will."

"Thanks, you too. And watch out for her, please."

"I will. Always."

Jackson took a final look around his former home, giving Vees a nod, then activating the controls to close the ramp of the shuttle. He departed moments later, looking back at the station, from the outside, thinking once more about what

Verris was going through, putting himself in her shoes and imagining how she had woken up, years of her life missing, badly injured, and no memory of how it happened or even of the person who she'd been in a relationship with. And then the news that he was dead.

Of course she's moved on. What else could she do? All my coming here did was bring up more pain and loss for her, reminding her of everything all over again.

He took a breath, knowing as well as anyone that sometimes it just took time to heal certain wounds.

He hoped that was all it would take for her.

As his shuttle jumped into hyperspace and he settled in for the long trip back to Archon, his thoughts darkened and he tried to push down what just happened and focus on work, on the war, turning his pain into thoughts of vengeance.

Back on the station, Verris sat quietly in her quarters, weeping softly, having just finished replaying the message he'd sent to her upon his death as she looked out, the flash of light from his shuttle as it entered hyperspace like a dagger of guilt stabbing at her heart.

This was the person she'd secretly blamed for what happened to her. For nearly getting her killed, and for losing years of her life. For losing herself.

Yet despite all the anger and sorrow that raged inside her, she felt a connection with him, even though she'd never really met him until just today.

Part of her regretted pushing him away.

Perhaps she should have given him a chance. Tried, even a little, to see if she felt something, anything for him.

Anger at what had happened to her boiled to the surface once more, of how years of her life had been stolen from her. The doctors had warned her that this would happen, that it would take a long time for her to deal with it, but she had convinced herself that she was strong enough to overcome it. Now, sitting in silence as rogue tears escaped the prison of her eyes, she finally began to let herself feel everything again, the emotions flooding her heart and mind, overcoming her. She lay down on the bed, curled up in a ball, willing herself to be strong, to be the person she always had been.

After a few moments, she regained her composure, looking out at the stars and the location where Jackson's shuttle had been just moments ago.

He was gone now. As lost to her as she was to him.

Perhaps it was for the best, she tried to convince herself. She could never be the woman he'd fallen in love with. She'd always be second best, she told herself. It wasn't fair to either of them.

It was better this way.

She wiped away her tears as she picked herself up, walking out of her quarters, a weight lifted from her shoulders.

This was her life now, and she was determined to live it *her* way.

CHAPTER 25

DEADLY HORIZON

Jackson returned to Archon, having barely slept on the way back from Kishara Station, still devastated by Verris's last words to him and struggling to accept that the woman he loved was really gone.

His appetite disappeared, and he found himself staring off into the distance more than once, lost in memories of the time they had shared together, unable to reconcile how to move on without her.

He checked into a hotel in Ty'coa, the city surrounding GCH Command, and fell into an uneasy sleep, dreaming that they'd just escaped from Praxian Prime all over again, only this time there was nothing they could do for Verris, and he was forced to watch helplessly while she faded away.

He awoke exhausted and emotionally drained, messaging Admiral Valentyen to see if he could meet later that day, eager to get back to work and to have something to focus on.

"I'm sorry, Will, I'm tied up in meetings for the next several days," Admiral Valentyen said shortly after receiving his message. "I'm afraid I didn't expect you back for a few more days. Why don't you reach out to Daria and Henrik. I know that they'd love to hear from you. I'll catch up with you in a couple of days."

"Sounds good, thank you, sir," he said, closing the comm and contacting Daria over subspace. A few hours later, she and Henrik were on their way to Archon, the three of them planning to meet up for dinner that evening.

Jackson booked a table at a nearby restaurant, and they arrived shortly after, each embracing him in a long hug, the sight of his friends lifting his spirits somewhat. As they sat around and ate, he told them what he could about his mission to the shipyard, leaving out the classified parts but telling them enough that they understood the immensity of the task and the long odds of pulling it off. He then recounted his time on the island, telling them about Razor and his ordeal to get the isilium, along with the unanswered transmission that finally broke his spirit, despite it ultimately being his salvation. He then detailed how he lost Bits, all hope abandoning him, as he hit absolute rock bottom.

Jackson skipped over his visit to see Verris, and both Daria and Henrik did an admirable job of maneuvering around the subject, but he knew that the admiral would have told them that he'd gone to see her. Finally, he brought up the subject of her, asking how the doctors were able to bring her out of temporal stasis and remove the liquid isilium poisoning her.

"It's actually quite brilliant," Daria began. "There were half a dozen really creative proposals put forth, but the one they went with used a specially designed drone that utilized temporal shields to protect it from the effects of the field. Once inside the chamber, it moved next to Verris to begin the procedure. It deployed custom-designed nanites that were slightly out of phase with our dimension, allowing them to move into Verris's brain without being affected by the temporal stasis field, once outside of the drone's temporal shields."

"The phase shift is actually incredibly, technically complex," Johansen chimed in. "We've used phase shift tech on larger scales, but to do it with nanites is a massive leap technologically. They're so small that the power and circuitry required to put phase shift devices on them just wasn't achievable. So, what they did instead was slightly phase them out of our dimension in a controlled quantum state using a specialized chamber, then extracted them and loaded them into the drone using a containment pod. Again, the engineering was groundbreaking just to get there. Then they created another type of specialized nanite, a bit larger than the other ones, that could emit a tiny reverse quantum field, triggering the others to phase back into our dimension."

"Interesting," Jackson said, the science well above his head, but understanding the essence of what his friends were describing.

The doctor continued. "Once in position, the nanites were injected and moved into Verris's brain tissue, occupying the same space as the liquid isilium and surrounding it entirely. Then, once the team was confident that they had every micromillimeter covered, they sent the command, and the other nanites triggered the quantum field shift, forcing all the nanites out of phase to shift back into our dimension."

"This is where it gets a bit technical," Johansen said.

"You mean it wasn't before?" Jackson teased, flashing a quick smile.

"Fair. This was the biggest gamble, then," Johansen corrected. "You see, isilium in its liquid form looks for something to latch on to. It's drawn to electrical currents. So, the theory was that it would coat the nanites, drawn to them by the tiny amounts of power they produced."

Jackson nodded slowly, considering where this was going. "So, the idea was that they would essentially soak up the isilium?"

"Exactly," Johansen replied.

"As Henrik said," the doctor interjected, "it was risky. If the isilium didn't coat them when the temporal stasis field was turned off, then it would come into contact with the cells in Verris's brain, necrotizing them and killing her."

"We were both there, along with the admiral, when they did the procedure," Johansen said. "We all felt that we should be there for her, no matter what happened."

"Thanks," Jackson said, a feeling of guilt washing over him that he was half a galaxy away, stranded when all of this was happening. "I really appreciate you both being there for her."

"Of course, Will," the doctor said, placing her hand on his. "Anyway, we were there when Dr. Stevenson and his team slowly shut down the stasis field, time restarting inside the chamber, but at a much slower pace, fractions of a second passing in there while seemingly endless minutes passed for us."

"We watched for nearly, what, twenty-five minutes?" Johansen asked.

"Yeah, probably closer to thirty."

Johansen nodded. "It was brutal, standing there helplessly, waiting to see if it worked."

"As time slowly sped up inside the chamber," the doctor continued, "the readings from the drone showed that it was working. It then inserted a long needle into her brain, injecting a specialized techno-organic fluid that created a cell-like structure around the nanites, encasing them in it. Then, after a few minutes, ensuring that the liquid had done its job, the needle sucked it all up, getting the nanites encased in the fluid out before they made contact with her cells."

"Couldn't they just have sucked out the isilium?" Jackson asked.

Johansen shook his head. "Too risky. First, time had to be moving again in order to suck anything up. The needle, once extended, was outside of the drone's temporal shielding. Second, the isilium would have been attracted to the electrical activity in Verris's brain. That's why the nanites occupying the same space were critical. The team needed to be absolutely certain that once time began to flow, the isilium would be attracted to the nanites, not her. Their electrical signals had to be stronger, and the only way to guarantee that was to have them phase back in, literally in the same physical space. Third, injecting the specialized liquid that formed a cell-wall-type structure around the nanites was also really important, or they would have come into contact with her cells and it all would have been for nothing."

"Wow. Yeah, that makes sense. But if the isilium had already leaked out, wouldn't it already have been in contact with some of her cells?"

A shadow crept across the doctor's face. "That's exactly what happened, unfortunately. Only an incredibly tiny amount of it had leaked out before they got her into temporal stasis, but yes, they confirmed once it was all over that there had been some damage. That may be where the memory loss came from. However, it's impossible to say for certain, as her brain suffered a significant amount of trauma, and that wasn't the only injury."

"Once the team was sure they'd gotten all of it, the drone deployed another needle, injecting her with medical nanites, as time continued to speed up, using these to repair the damage. They also used another specially designed type of nanite to coat her AI's modules to ensure that they were sealed tight and could be extracted without risking any more contamination," Johansen explained.

"That's incredible. Wow, they weren't kidding when they said it would take years to figure out a way to do it. It sounds incredibly complex. What happened next?" Jackson asked.

"Within about an hour, the temporal stasis field shut down entirely. The doctors then pulled Verris out and rushed her back to the OR. She flatlined twice, the toxic shock to her system causing her to crash, but they were able to bring her back quickly both times and got her stabilized. From there, it was a long road before she woke up. They pulled out the modules and did extensive regeneration treatments to heal the surrounding brain tissue. Then, once she was stable and strong enough, they began the procedures to regrow her leg and regenerate the major damage to her arm. They decided not to put her AI back in until she was fully recovered months later and she was kept under for about three weeks in a medically induced coma. The doctors then contacted us, and we were there when she woke up."

"But she didn't remember any of you," Jackson said.

Both Daria and Henrik nodded sadly, Jackson quickly seeing the pain written across their faces.

"We stayed for a few days, all of us spending time with her. Your former commander from Kishara Station, Captain

Vance, also came, along with Verris's parents and two of her brothers," the doctor said. "We were grateful that she recognized them all, at least, but she sometimes got agitated when we were there, so we decided to give her some space."

"Daria and I came back about three weeks later, and she was gone. She'd been moved to a facility on Kishara Prime, where she recovered for the next few months," Johansen said. "We reached out a couple of times but never heard from her again."

"Yeah, I'm not surprised," Jackson said. "She blames me for what happened to her and doesn't want to connect with anyone from the period of time she can't remember, which I get."

"That's what we figured too," the doctor offered. "So, we let her be. Captain Vance was kind enough to reach out a few times to let us know when she went back to work and how she was doing, but that was about it."

"Thanks again for being there," Jackson said. "I know that must have been tough, but I really appreciate it." Jackson put on a brave smile, changing the subject. "So, what else have you both been up to?"

The doctor jumped in, telling him about her work, analyzing the hundreds of new species that the Insectoids had been deploying in battle.

"Most of them are just animals, really," she said, the sadness audible in her voice. "But they've been outfitted with these neural control collars and implants, crude devices that the Imperium developed to make what we'd consider non-sentient species controllable, allowing them to be weaponized. Many of them likely wouldn't be a threat if you encountered them in the wild, but once their scientists finished with them, even the most peaceful of them are now put to deadly use."

Jackson listened attentively as Daria explained how she'd reached out to Henrik, bringing their teams together to work on countermeasures that could short out the control interface, hoping to take the poor enslaved creatures out of the fight. So far, they'd made good progress, but needed to run more field tests before they'd know for sure if what they had was a viable defense. "While still potentially dangerous in the wrong circumstances, we think that they'll revert to their natural state if the control interface is broken," she said, her tone optimistic.

As she finished, Henrik began telling them how his team had coordinated with the GCH Armored Research Division, designing and building a new type of heavy armor specifically for battling the Insectoids. It had eight arms, like a spider, each of which could be used to strike or slash, while a phalanx of small, defensive particle beams, like point defense systems on a starship, covered the undersides of the legs, able to pick off smaller crawling threats before they could get close enough to engage, allowing it to focus on larger targets with its heavy turrets and other ordnance. "So far there's only ten of them in production, and Command's been using them sparingly in combat to test their capabilities. But the results are promising and give us an element we've been missing in certain engagements to deal with wave after wave of smaller Insectoids that are harder to pick off."

"That's pretty cool. Have either of you heard anything from Kel—"

An alert suddenly sounded, the sound echoing throughout the city. Holo-displays activated around the restaurant as the room turned quiet, all eyes fixed on the images before them.

"...reporting from the Kuteria System, where a major Imperium incursion is taking place," the Fleet news anchor said, the anxiety in her voice barely contained as she stood in front of a gray military bulkhead. "Just twenty-eight minutes ago, a force of approximately a hundred Imperium vessels jumped into the system, somehow able to get through the hyperspace defense grid. The ships immediately spread out, targeting the grid satellites and taking out several hundred while the 48th Fleet responded. The attacking ships ignored the fleet, sacrificing themselves and taking down as many of the grid units as possible before finally being destroyed minutes later." The anchor paused, her voice grave. "Before the 48th could regroup, however, a massive battle fleet of over eight thousand Imperium warships arrived, jumping in just outside the defensive perimeter of Kuteria Prime."

Jackson, Johansen, and the doctor looked at one another, the horror written across their faces, each knowing in their hearts what happened next while praying that it somehow wouldn't be so.

The anchor moved, a large window appearing in the background, flashes from the distant battle appearing behind her. "All we know for certain at the moment is that the Imperium forces have engaged the starbase and orbital defense stations all around Kuteria Prime and elsewhere in the system. They appear to be suffering heavy losses, but with the Fleet scattered, they are inflicting massive damage at key locations. The...oh my God!" she said, an Imperium battleship suddenly appearing outside in the distance.

Dozens of bursts of light flashed outside the window

behind her, the shields from wherever she was holding off the onslaught from the battleship as it poured on the assault.

The anchor turned and faced the camera once more, time seeming to stop for an instant. Jackson watched helplessly, transfixed by her deep blue eyes, the look of sheer terror and grim acceptance on her face…both knowing what was about to happen.

The sound of an explosion echoed a second later and the anchor, along with the camera, rushed away in a blur of motion. A roar from a torrent of air filled the broadcast before the camera emerged into the blackness of space and silence followed, the anchor drifting nearby surrounded by a growing cloud of debris as she spun slowly in the vacuum.

The feed went dead seconds later.

Jackson rose from his chair, several dozen other officers in the restaurant following suit. "We have to go. Now!" he said, turning to his friends.

They darted for the door, a flood of off-duty officers and personnel following, heading for GCH Command or to their posts.

"Jackson to Admiral Valentyen, come in!" he said, his finger pressed to his ear.

"Valentyen here. I just got to GCH Intelligence a few minutes ago and have been monitoring the situation. We're coordinating a response now."

"What can we do to help?"

"Command is rerouting the 6th, 19th, and 33rd Fleets to respond now. They're keeping the 7th here, to guard the Archonian System, along with the 3rd in Delconia and 63rd in Cicarrus. If they can hit a core system like Kuteria, they could hit anywhere. We can't take any chances. Kuteria is only eight light-years from here."

"We can take a shuttle for all it matters, sir. We just want to be there to help."

"Understood, but I don't want any of you in harm's way. I'll see what I can do."

"Thank you, Admiral," Jackson said, closing the channel. He turned to the doctor and Johansen, both winded but keeping up on his right. "The admiral is going to work on getting us a ride. We need to get to the landing fields."

They arrived minutes later, stopping at the assembly area along with hundreds of other officers, all eager to help in some way while they awaited instructions.

"Jackson, do you copy?" Admiral Valentyen's voice chimed in his ears.

"I'm here, sir."

"Head to landing pad Bravo-niner. The corvette *Axiom* is about to depart, and I've briefed Captain Noga that you're there under my direct orders and what your skills are. She's grateful for the help. The *Axiom* is one of our newest and fastest ships, so you'll likely be there with the first wave of responders. Do what you can to help, but I've ordered the captain to stay clear of any active combat zones. The 19th Fleet should arrive in minutes, and once the 6th and 33rd arrive in about fifteen and forty minutes respectively, we'll outgun the Insectoids and should be able to beat them back, but don't take any chances, understood?"

"Understood, and thank you, sir. We'll do our best to help."

"I know you will. Valentyen out."

"All right, this way. We've got a ride, but we need to hurry!"

Less than an hour later, the *Axiom* arrived in the Kuteria System, exiting hyperspace near the moon around Gaventry, the second planet from the sun, a hundred and fourteen million kilometers from Kuteria Prime.

"Report," Captain Noga said, standing in the center of the bridge, her gaze fixed on the holo-display while her crew worked feverishly at their stations.

"It's chaos, ma'am," the Ops officer said after a moment, shaking her head and turning to face the captain. "I'm detecting thousands of distress calls from military and civilian vessels all over the system. Scans show that the Fleet is still heavily engaged around Vencedes, the largest moon of the gas giant Ulkara, where the shipyards and the Point Echo Fleet base are located. Scans also show a few dozen other small skirmishes still ongoing throughout the system."

"What about Kuteria Prime?"

"Looks like the battle there is over. Half a dozen ships from the 3rd Fleet are still nearby, mostly just frigates and a few corvettes spread out between it and Cala'hue, the fourth planet. My best guess is they're holding a line in case any enemy ships get away and try to make a suicide run for the planet. I'm connected into what's left of the GCH Traffic Control network and detecting at least sixteen hundred GCH Fleet transponder IDs spread out across the system."

Captain Noga stood silently for a moment, watching as the data from the scans continued to appear, the display flooding with information and objects. Huge swaths of debris appeared, showing the sites where the main engagements took place, sporadic power readings appearing in the analysis windows beside them. "Bring up grid 312, mark 18," the captain said, and the main viewscreen zoomed in, focusing on the area, the wrecked hulls of hundreds of ships appearing, floating in the void, both Imperium and GCH alike. She turned to her first officer. "Commander Norwood, tactical analysis."

"I concur with Ops, Captain. We appear to be safe for now, and should be clear to jump in closer," he said, looking up from the tactical console. "All enemy vessels near Kuteria show no active power readings, and the nearest active enemy ships are millions of kilometers from here, engaged with the rest of the Fleet."

"Very well. Helm, plot a course and jump us into an open space near Kuteria Prime. We'll then commence rescue operations. Captain," she said, turning to Jackson, who sat with Johansen and the doctor at the rear of the bridge. "The admiral said that you worked SaR ops for several years. What do you recommend?"

Jackson stood, moving to lean on a railing, facing the center of the bridge, taking in the impossible scope of destruction before them. "They'll be dozens of search and rescue ships here soon, Captain. Along with other Fleet and possibly even civilian ships from neighboring systems. My AI just ran a quick scan on the transponders in-system, and we appear to be the first ship on the scene in a search and rescue capacity. I think the best way we can help is to direct the rescue operations. I've got Admiral Valentyen's operational authority, and SaR ops personnel will be looking for direction in all of this chaos when they arrive. I recommend that we tag every GCH and civilian ship we can find registering bio-signs to make it easier for the rescue ships to find them. The *Axiom* isn't built for towing, so we won't be much help in that regard, but it's quick and maneuverable. I recommend that we set a course to survey the major orbital installations around Kuteria Prime, then its two moons, tagging any ships as we go and documenting as much as possible to direct other search and rescue ships when they arrive. Do you have any shuttles on board?"

"Two."

"Let's use them as well. We can fan out in a search pattern and increase our area of coverage. Once more ships join us, we can instruct them to proceed on different vectors, creating a search grid and triaging the ships and stations with the most bio-signs or those in the worst shape." Jackson paused, studying the display for a moment, considering how Vees would attempt to contend with such vast amounts of destruction and so many lives in peril. "We should also launch every probe you have as well. There's likely a number of ships whose engines are offline and in low orbits and they'll need help soon, or they could crash into the planet below. Most search and rescue ships are smaller and can't tow much more than a destroyer, so we'll need the bigger ships to help move anything larger, like a battlecruiser, explorer class, or dreadnought. Admiral Valentyen messaged me before we departed, informing me that the 47th Fleet is on their way and should be here in the next three hours. It looks like most of the enemy ships that pose a threat are already being mopped up by the rest of our forces, so we'll need to put the larger ships in the 47th to work, tractoring the other damaged warships to safety and boarding them to look for survivors. I checked and the 47th has three Viceroy class dreadnoughts, ten Allegiant class, and twenty-five Olympic class battlecruisers, along with four Stingray carriers. We'll use them as rescue decks, directing the other ships to tow smaller military and civilian craft into their cargo bays and flight decks. We can also have them deploy their fighters. The Fleet registry shows just over sixty-five hundred of them spread across the 47th. They can't do much to help with the rescue operation, but deploying them will significantly help with survey operations to comb through the main engagement zones and search for survivors."

Captain Noga nodded. "Agreed. Helm, set a course into the debris field and get our shuttles airborne. Captain, I'll follow your lead and coordinate the tagging and scanning efforts with our two shuttles while you run the larger search effort and direct ships as they come in. Commander Norwood and I are here at your disposal, as is my entire crew. You call the ball, and we'll defer to your expertise."

"Sounds good, Captain," Jackson said, moving to stand before the holo-display and calling out orders as he manipulated the holographic image, zooming in and signaling Chief Johansen and Dr. Duratis to join him and lend their expertise as they tried to navigate through the tens of thousands of objects littering the system.

Hours later, search and rescue ships from a dozen different systems, including Kishara Station, had arrived and Jackson contacted the lead ship from each, assigning them sections the *Axiom* had surveyed and tagged, and calling out priorities. Vees and the other commanding officers took charge of their teams, while Jackson focused on the task at hand and continued to oversee the larger rescue effort.

The 47th Fleet arrived shortly thereafter, giving him a much-needed distraction after he noticed the transponder for the *Griffin* popping up, knowing in his heart who would be at the controls. He quickly contacted Admiral Jeffries, commander of the 47th Fleet, on board the dreadnought *Elysium*, bringing him up to speed.

"Excellent work, Captain. You've done an exemplary job under these terrible circumstances and seem to have a much better handle on what's happening here than I do. And you've got Admiral Valentyen's confidence, which is more than good enough for me. Proceed with overwatch and coordinating rescue activities. The 47th is here to help in any way we can and are at your disposal. Let us know where to start."

"Thank you, sir," Jackson replied, explaining his plan to use the larger ships as rescue decks and to search the engagement areas with fighters and smaller ships, along with sending other larger ships to help with tractor operations for various warships that were in tenuous orbits and too big for the search and rescue ships to pull out.

The hours passed as he coordinated with the Ops officers on the larger ships and carriers, assigning search grids for their shuttles and fighters to map out. Within an hour, there were thousands of ships, shuttles, and fighters scouring the wreckage of the main battle zones, tractoring ships to safe Lagrange points, and sending teams to the battered battle stations and other smaller orbital facilities that were still intact. It was exhausting work, but the pure adrenaline kept him going.

As more and more ships arrived, he quickly found that, like working Ops, if he delegated and focused on the higher-level tasks, he could manage the overall rescue effort and assign smaller tasks to the thousands of ships there to help, dividing up the work.

Fleet Admiral Lighton arrived several hours later on board the *Waverly*, and Jackson contacted her, briefing her on the ongoing operations and suggesting he pass on operational command to her.

"You have the best handle on the situation here, and I have the utmost confidence in you, Captain," she said, her face ashen at the sight of the destruction and the loss of life before her. "I want you to continue to run all in-system rescue operations. I'll assume overall tactical command and head farther out in the system to regroup the other fleets and assess our losses, along with any remaining enemy threats."

"Yes, Admiral."

"I know you've been at this for hours and must be exhausted, but I need my best people running this to save as many lives as possible."

"Understood," Jackson said, exhausted, but unwavering in his need to help and knowing how many lives hung in the balance.

Dr. Duratis, meanwhile, headed down to Kuteria Prime on the first available shuttle once the 47th Fleet arrived to help with the wounded. The planet had suffered intense orbital bombardments to several cities once the starbase and battle stations went offline. On top of that, a dozen heavily damaged enemy ships crashed on the surface in suicide runs before the Fleet could take them out, causing massive swaths of destruction. She spent days working at a field hospital outside of the heavily damaged capital, Rygalius, performing emergency surgeries and attempting to save as many lives as possible.

Johansen transferred to the heavily damaged starbase, a vast, towering complex with over two hundred and fifty thousand permanent residents, working to restore the main power to keep the station from falling to the planet below. While Johansen worked, Jackson rerouted thirty large warships to tractor the crippled station into a higher orbit, buying the chief time.

Jackson worked tirelessly, coordinating the largest-ever search and rescue operation in Confederation history, instructing admirals, captains, and ensigns alike where to focus their efforts.

Finally, after being awake for just over two and a half days, he handed over operational command to Admiral Easton on the *Vengeance*, a former SaR officer who now commanded the 6th Fleet. Jackson transferred all of their data over, while the crew of the *Axiom* stood down and got some much-needed rest after days spent responding to the devastation.

CHAPTER 26
DARK FRONTIER

SEVEN DAYS LATER.

"What's the current count, sir?" Johansen asked.

"Thirty-one million, three hundred and fifty-six thousand dead, along with millions more injured and thousands still missing," the admiral replied.

"Damn it," he whispered, shaking his head and looking down at the table for a moment.

"Reports are still coming in, and they're miraculously still finding survivors, but the numbers they recover are growing smaller each day. Still, every life we can save is worth it," Admiral Valentyen said, turning from the display showing the latest images of the aftermath of the Imperium attack as the crew sat in a conference room back at GCH Intelligence on Archon.

"With all due respect, sir, we should still be out there helping," Jackson said, thinking about all the people he'd seen in the news feeds and the countless voices he'd heard over the comms calling for help, the images and sounds still haunting him.

"I know how you feel, Will, and I wouldn't have brought you all back here if this wasn't important. But the four of us have some things to talk about that only *we* can discuss," the admiral said. "I wanted to include Lieutenant Quentarus in this discussion as well, but she's still out on assignment with her unit, and I don't think this can wait any longer."

Jackson nodded, a cold rage still simmering inside from the attack and the suffering he'd seen in the past week.

"Do we have any idea how the Imperium got through the grid during the initial assault?" Jackson asked.

"Not yet. Command believes that they may have captured one of our ships and somehow gotten through the encryption to get the current grid vectors. With so many ships still missing or unaccounted for, it's impossible to know for sure."

"I thought that was supposed to be impossible," the doctor said.

"It is. Or it was," Johansen offered. "The encryption on our ships' systems is state of the art. Even a hundred androids couldn't crack it in a week, and the algorithm shifts every twenty-nine hours. It should be impossible…but maybe they found a way."

"Could they…have tortured the crew?" the doctor asked.

"No, there are safeguards to prevent that from happening," Johansen said. "The crew's AIs are required in order to access any classified information, and they won't do it if the crew is under duress. Even though their primary directive is to preserve the life of their host, protecting classified and highly sensitive GCH information trumps that."

"We still don't know what happened for sure," the admiral interjected. "One prevailing theory is that the initial wave of ships was actually much, much larger, possibly thousands of ships in total. There's evidence to suggest, based on sensor log spikes in the grid satellites from just before the attack, that this is exactly what happened. That waves of Imperium ships all came at once towards the system from different approach vectors, playing the numbers, something only the Imperium can do with their incredible number of ships and expendable crews. We think that the grid did exactly what it was supposed to do, taking most of them out when they crossed through it in hyperspace, scattering their atoms over half a light-year. If that is indeed the case, then the grid destroyed possibly thousands of ships, maybe with just skeleton crews on them – though we may never know for sure – and the Imperium rolled the dice to see if one wave could make it through."

"That sounds like something they'd try," Jackson said bitterly. "They don't value life the way we do, and the reports I saw on the ships in the first wave indicated that they were all old, obsolete models. Expendable, like you said. A means to an end."

"Again, it's still just a theory at this point, but there's a growing amount of evidence to support it, and if they can pull it off once, they can do it again. As a result, the GCH has put nearly every system into full lockdown, and all travel and trade has been suspended across the Confederation. The only ships moving anywhere on our side of the border across an eighty-light-year span are Fleet warships, and even then, the grid vectors have them limited to narrow routes between systems and only then for emergency operations."

"So, what do we do now?" Johansen asked.

"That's why I called you all here," the admiral said. "I'm meeting with the fleet admirals in just over three hours, and they want to consider all options. Since the attack a week ago, the Imperium has hit us in half a dozen other border systems with smaller, surgical strikes. These have been kept relatively quiet for now, and with morale already at an all-time low, the Admiralty didn't want news of more attacks to create any more hopelessness than there already is. But… the reality is that things are very grim. With the Fleet mostly locked down, at least for the time being, there's been serious talk of the GCH pulling back. Evacuating and abandoning entire systems along the Holt Line and consolidating our borders to make them more defensible."

"This is the worst-case scenario you warned us about, Verris and I, when you came to Kishara Station years ago and we started to look for Ancient sites," Jackson said. "You said that if we ever did pull back, once we do, we'll likely never be able to go back. And once we start getting boxed in, it may lead to the beginning of the end of the Confederation."

The admiral smiled weakly. "Excellent memory, Will. That's exactly what I feared then and what I'm afraid may happen now."

"So, like Hen said, what do we do, sir?" Jackson asked.

"Well, there's a few options. First – Doctor, Chief – I'm going to bring you in on something that's been highly classified, and this doesn't leave this room, understood?"

"Yes, sir," they responded in unison.

"Since the start of the war, the Imperium has had the element of surprise. At first, we didn't know how, but over time, we learned that they'd developed a new technology that allowed them to cloak their ships from nearly all of our mid- and long-range sensor scans, leaving us only visual and short-range detection options. At first, they used it to attack key systems, allowing them to jump in under this cloak undetected. But over the past few years, it's expanded, covering nearly all of the Imperium. We've sent ships into their space, into systems where we know there's a huge military presence, and detected nothing…until one of our scout ships came across a satellite that put out a sensor disruption field unlike anything we'd ever seen before."

"Like the Shroud of Darkness?" Johansen asked.

"Exactly."

"If they got hold of advanced Phague technology…" The doctor trailed off.

"Think about the attack on the *Viceroy*, the subspace weapon they used. Their new, advanced warships, and now this sensor-masking technology. It all points to a major technological leap for them," Jackson said.

The crew was silent for a few moments, considering.

"You said that there was something that you could only discuss with us," the doctor said hesitantly. "You don't mean—"

"I do, Doctor," the admiral said. "With the GCH already in full crisis mode, and potentially on the cusp of contraction – maybe, eventually, even collapse – we have to consider all possible options…even the unthinkable."

The room was silent for a moment as they all considered the admiral's words.

"There's got to be another way, sir," Jackson said. "There still has to be more we can do, isn't there?"

"There is, and we have teams here at Command along with thousands of androids working around the clock on options. But we need to seriously consider that if we can't find another way… That we may need to use one of the Light warheads to stop the Imperium."

The admiral paused. "I did some research on your home planet, Earth, before we first met, Will, and I know it was a little before your time, but this could very much be a similar choice to what happened in the Second World War, where nuclear weapons were used for the first time in order to show the incredible destructive power that one side held, in order to get the other side to yield."

Jackson thought for a moment, considering the world he had grown up in, the threats of nuclear war, the genie out of the bottle that changed everything. "I…I think we need to do everything in our power to find another way, Admiral. We don't even know what those warheads will do. How much damage they may cause. I-I don't know if I could live with myself if I had that much blood on my hands."

"It wouldn't be your decision, Will. I'd take this to the Admiralty, and they'd ultimately be the ones who decide."

"But I'd still be the one pulling the trigger, not them!"

"Will," Johansen said, turning to face his friend, "millions of people just died. Hell, billions have died already in this war. If we could stop it tomorrow by using one of these warheads, then isn't that something we have to consider?"

"I can't believe we're even discussing this," the doctor said. "Are we really considering a retaliatory strike that could kill…we don't even know how many sentient lifeforms? I know they're Insectoids, but if we start to devalue life the way that they do, then we're no better than them."

"I agree with you, Doctor, I honestly do," the admiral said. "But I think we at least have to consider the possibility. If we don't, and billions more GCH citizens die, then isn't that blood on our hands as well when we had the power to potentially stop it?"

The crew sat in silence for nearly a minute, each wrestling with the moral and ethical decision.

"We have to put an end to this war," the admiral said finally. "But I don't think we're to the point yet, however, where we throw away all of our principles, like the doctor said, to do so. But I think that we have to at least *consider* the possibility and have a plan if it comes to that. I still have some other ideas, including one I've been working on for a few years that I was going to bring Will in on before he disappeared. I'd like to try to find another way first, but if it comes down to it, I'm not willing to let humanity die to save our morals and principles." He looked around the room, meeting each of their eyes. "Are we all in agreement, then? We'll keep this secret for now, but at the end of the day, we'll do whatever we have to do. Whatever it takes to win this war and protect the Confederation?"

Johansen looked around the room at his friends. "Yeah, we have to," he said softly.

The doctor closed her eyes, lowering her head and pinching the bridge of her nose. She looked up, her face anguished. "Agreed."

The admiral turned to Jackson, who sat with his hands folded on the table in front of him, deep in thought.

Jackson took a deep breath, hardening his resolve, then looked around the table at his former crew, his mind made up.

"Whatever it takes."

EPILOGUE

PRAXIAN PRIME

Arkamus rose to his feet, wiping his hands on his pants while staring down at the mess of wires and technology spread out before him on the deck of the *Ranger*. He'd been working steadily for hours, stopping only for short breaks to stretch his legs and check the perimeter. So far, he'd extracted nearly half of the modules and components he needed, but he still had a long way to go.

He looked up through a crack in the hull, noticing the waning daylight while he considered his options. If he made it back now, he might get there in time before they came. If not, he was better off spending the night on the *Ranger*.

They'd find him either way. They always did.

He took a frustrated breath, fortifying his will for what was to come.

Nearly a year had passed since he awoke from his hibernation, forced into cryo-sleep while his body healed after the crash landing on this accursed planet and fending off the surviving Insectoids for months. The *Ranger* had made short work of the first battle cruiser and eventually took down the second, but the Imperium ships outnumbered him and, after a protracted battle, had finally overwhelmed him before he took them down with him. His desperate maneuver to save the second son had paid off, but left him stranded there. Alone.

He cursed himself for his failure, knowing that Lecari and his kin would take advantage of his absence, moving ever closer to completing their goals. His mind raced, considering their next moves and what he needed to do when he eventually escaped from this prison.

A bitterness crept into his thoughts that the second son had never returned to see what had become of his fallen savior, a blackness filling his heart that he had been left here to rot.

A sound like thunder in the distance pulled him from his thoughts. His eyes drifted back to the dim light outside.

Night was falling. They would be coming soon. He had to be ready.

His revenge would have to wait until another day.

He looked down at the parts he'd salvaged, a grim smile crossing his lips. Perhaps that day was not as far away as it had once seemed.

To be continued in *Legacy – The Shroud of Darkness*

BRADLEY ELLIOTT

is a writer based near Toronto, Canada, where he lives with his wife and two children. He's an avid hockey fan, board game fanatic, and lover of the great outdoors. An unabashed geek at heart, he's always up for discussing sci-fi, fantasy, movies, or why Han shot first and Greedo had it coming.

You can find out more by visiting:

WWW.BRADLEYELLIOTT.CA

Printed in Dunstable, United Kingdom

80990317R00214